TWILIGHT IMPERIUM

THUNDER'S EDGE
ECHOES OF MEMORY

Sarah Cawkwell

First published by Aconyte Books in 2025

ISBN 978 1 83908 352 5

Ebook ISBN 978 1 83908 351 8

Cover art by Mauro Dal Bo

Galactic map by Ryan Hong

Printed in the United States of America and elsewhere.

9 8 7 6 5 4 3 2 1

ACONYTE BOOKS

An imprint of Asmodee North America

Mercury House, North Gate,

Nottingham NG7 7FN, UK

aconytebooks.com

TWILIGHT IMPERIUM

Intergalactic empires fall, but one faction will rise from the ashes to conquer the galaxy.

Once the mighty Lazax Empire ruled all the known galaxy from its capital planet of Mecatol Rex, before treachery and war erased the Lazax from history, plunging a thousand star systems into conflict and uncertainty.

Now the Great Civilizations who span the galaxy look upon their former capital hungrily – the power and secrets of the Lazax await a new emperor…

To lay claim to the throne is a destiny sought by many, yet the shadows of the past serve as a grim warning to those who would follow in their footsteps.

For my dad – my first hero.

THE GALAXY

THE GHOST
WORLDS
NEKRO SPACE
OUENWARI CLUSTER
KENARA
SYSTEM.
ARRETZE
HERCANT
KAMDORN
ORDINIAN.
FORMER NAAZ-
ROKHA COLONY.
OVERRUN BY THE
NEKRO VIRUS
CORMUND.
DESOLATE
MINING COLONY
CORE SYSTEMS
ORDINIAN NEBULA
MECATOL
REX.
SEAT OF THE
GALACTIC COUNCIL
THE GREAT HEART
OF THE GALAXY
MAP KEY
HOME SYSTEM
CULTURAL PLANET
STAR SYSTEM
MECATOL REX
INDUSTRIAL PLANET
HAZARDOUS PLANET
WORMHOLES
ANOMALIES

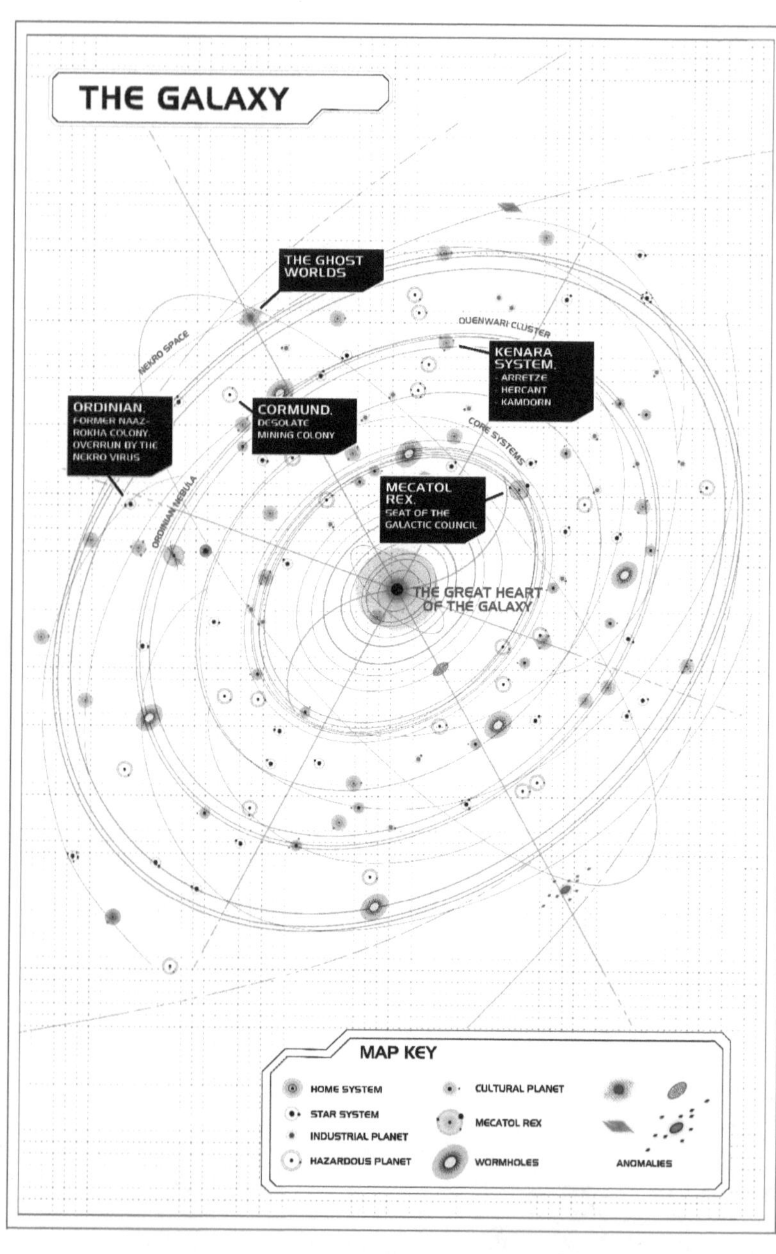

PROLOGUE

THE IVOREST NECROPOLIS
DRUGT, PANALAGAN DUSTLANDS
QUOLOTYL SYSTEM

The night was clear, the galactic vista spread out above like a sable sheet scattered with silvered dust. Stars, distant heavenly gems, twinkled from afar, silent and enigmatic. For millennia, they had captivated countless pre-industrial civilizations and yet, for the Titan recently named Junior, the astral phenomena held few mysteries. His logical mind regarded them for what they were – nuclear crucibles, many of which were already long-dead echoes, the fading pyre lights of far-off planetary systems.

The truth, Junior found, was often far less poetic than many species across the universe chose to believe.

While his visual senses roved across the welkin, his aural receivers soaked in the song of the cosmos. The Titan had quickly learned that his companions tended to regard the void as silent. A nonsense, of course. To him, it was a tapestry of stellar radiation, electromagnetism and fragmented communications of a billion beings. Echoes, like the light of the ancient stars, adrift in the universe.

"…requesting a secure approach vector…"

"…breached the second and fifth decks and are advancing…"

"…cargo transfer authorized, please proceed to…"

"*…breached the atmosphere, fall back! Fall back immediately!…*"

Without context, it was largely gibberish – requests, orders, hope, defiance, victory and defeat. All of it little more than a disconnected morass of *whens, wheres* and *whyfores*.

"Junior!"

A shrill exclamation cut through the susurrating tumble of transmissions. Though Tai didn't even come up to the Titan's knee, he had the kind of voice that could puncture Junior's moments of introspection comprehensively. Once, his feline companion named Dart had stated that Tai, when angry, was capable of shattering glass with his pitch. Now, the huge biomechanoid turned to regard the diminutive figure in front of him. The Naaz stood close by, his upper arms folded and lower hands on his hips.

"The Golden General has resigned his position," the Titan said, solemnly. "The battles on and around Ordinian grow ever more desperate. It will fall within a few of their solar days."

"What?"

"The Golden General has…"

"Junior!"

The voice's pitch sharpened enough that Dart's prior claim might just prove true. The Titan tuned the mess of transmissions and solar noise out, turning his full attention to the present, and the little Naaz before him.

"Yes, friend Tai?"

"You're daydreaming again!"

"But it is not day, friend Tai. It is night. And I am not dreaming. I am studying the skies. I am listening to the sounds of the galaxy."

"My mother called that daydreaming. Not to mention that everything you're talking about has already happened. You must just be picking up old messages or something."

"Indeed. I believe that the cosmic chronology of…"

"Junior!" Tai shrilled. "Snap out of it! We need to get back to the ship before…"

"Before *they* arrive."

The small-statured Naaz was interrupted by a deep, soothing baritone. Where Tai was the peal of a particularly annoying bell, Dart was the rumble of a river falls.

Junior looked past the Naaz-Rokha pair to determine exactly what it was that was about to arrive. At this distance, most individuals could not have hoped to make out what was contained within the approaching cloud without enhancements. But Junior, who was not most individuals, could clearly discern several shapes obscured by the billowing shroud. Several large shapes wielding an alarming array of weaponry.

"Whose wrath have you incurred this time, friend Tai?"

"What do you mean, 'this time'?" The effrontery apparent in Tai's tone would have been comical under other circumstances. Dart stooped, allowing his partner to scamper up his black fur into the harness strapped to his back. The Naaz settled in, declaring his readiness to depart. "We haven't incurred *anybody's* wrath," he affirmed as Dart set off at a loping run, a pace that Junior matched effortlessly. "It's just that when they get here, it will probably be best if we are not. Because they might be a little bit wrathful."

"A little bit wrathful is enough."

"Huh." Tai sniffed with extraordinary indifference. "Have you got the box, Dart?"

"What do you think, Tai?"

The Naaz's face broke out in a cheeky grin and Dart's mouth curled back in a matching smile, revealing his sharp fangs.

"Never doubted you for a second. Well, maybe *half* a second…"

"Do you wish to know what else I have learned from the cosmos this evening?"

Junior, keeping up with the feline Rokha, asked the question to which he knew the answer. He asked anyway, because the Naaz-Rokha had already accused him on more than one occasion of keeping secrets. The concept of trust, he had come to understand, was considered highly important in the interpersonal relationships of many biological species – including Dart and Tai. Since they had pulled him from his mysterious stasis and brought him along on their adventures, he had surmised that maintaining their trust was the optimal approach.

"Maybe later, Junior," said Tai, his voice bouncing up and down with Dart's gait. "When we're back on the ship and safely on our way to a freeport to see what we can get for this thing."

"Maybe later," agreed Junior. But maybe not. With Tai and Dart, you never could tell for sure. "Some of it may be important, after all."

Tai waved the sentiment away in a gesture of vague indifference. "We will see," he said, dismissively. "Later. Assuming there *is* a later. Dart, my dear friend and life companion, I am remarkably fond of you, but I think it goes without saying that I would be even more fond of you if you were to pick up the pace *just* a little."

PART ONE

CHOICES

ONE

Dawn had always been his favorite time of day. The stark, white light of Kenara kissed the golden sands of Hercant, heralding new beginnings and opportunities waiting to be grasped. That simple pleasure had soured since the beginning of his journey, however. Now, he often wished that he could stay shrouded in the comforting folds of night. Even troubled sleep was preferable to the frustration and creeping helplessness that had come to plague his days.

Harrugh Gefhara stretched his long, lithe arms, his claws extending from his paws as he stared up at the cool stone ceiling of the cave in which he had slept. The air was already beginning to warm, despite the early hour, and the first skirls of hot wind scattered sand into the mouth of the hollow. It was a harsh, sometimes brutal environment, but it provided the solitude he had been craving and, or so he had believed, needed to resolve the mystery that tormented him.

It wasn't in Harrugh's nature to feel self-pity, but he knew that was exactly what he was doing. His voyage across the sand plains had begun as a pilgrimage in search of answers; a self-exile from the complications of his former life. Eventually, it had become an escape. He had tasted a freedom he'd long thought forgotten and it was exhilarating. The pang of guilt that came with doing something just for him after what felt like a lifetime of service still nagged at him, of course, but Harrugh was old enough and wise enough to know that such feelings would pass.

In the wake of the chaos following his resignation as Quieron of the Hacan, Harrugh had quickly moved to distance himself – metaphorically and literally – from the politics and intrigue of Harcarun. It was not unheard of for Hacan to make a harvest pilgrimage to the equatorial regions, following in the footsteps of their ancestors. Leaving behind the trappings and technology of modern life – along with the concerns of balancing the clans and the emirates' competitive financial endeavors – and giving honor to the ways of the desert was said to bring clarity of thought and purity of vision to the worthy pilgrim.

He had reached the tumultuous heartlands, or as close as any Hacan could come to the ash blizzards and thermal curtains of the equator. He had entered the red mesa and walked the fertile caverns in phosphorescent twilight and washed his face in the still waters of the aquifer. His existence diminished to the particulars of survival and the day-to-day rituals of shelter and foraging. It was a cleansing of sorts.

But despite it all, even stripped of the concerns of power and position, he could find no answers, no peace. No longer the Quieron, he was now just Harrugh, and that should have been enough. In many ways, it *was* enough. The mantle of leadership had never sat comfortably upon his shoulders and his escape from that life had been an unburdening. But even as one burden was set down another was taken up.

Thus, convinced of their own significance, the ignorant march ever forward.

The aphorism echoed in his mind. He snorted irritably. Sitting up, he rubbed his remaining eye to remove lingering flecks of sleep that crusted there. His other eye was a mechanical implant and needed no such treatment. He mentally catalogued every new ache in his body – a daily ritual that he'd practiced as the years crept up on him. Rolling his shoulders, he winced. Then he got to his feet, shuffling to the mouth of the cavern. The wind tugged at his coat and sand-scarf, ruffling his fur. Closing his eye, he turned his focus within, preparing his body and mind for another day's toil.

Beyond the diminishing shadow of the cliff, the hinterland desert of Hercant stretched out before him. Ochre buttes rose up to meet the clear, azure sky. Pale dots of numerous spaceships and satellites cut through the atmosphere and beyond them were the distant, spidery shapes of huge orbitals. Harrugh sipped from a half-empty flask, lowering his gaze to the horizon where a trio of spehat fungus cultivator towers drifted lazily on their grav-fields, following the thermal currents. Raffir was still some way off.

Setting down the flask, Harrugh turned his attention to the two items sitting in the dust of the cave floor, his expression darkening into a scowl. He'd once again sat awake until late into the night attempting to make some sense of their mystery, but still their purpose and function defied him. *Let them sit awhile longer,* he thought, bitter. He pulled strips of dried meat from his pack, chewing on them moodily. His tail swished beneath his clothing.

If he set off now, he could make good progress toward the city, marking the end of his pilgrimage. *Some ending,* he thought with a grimace. An ending bereft of the answers he had set out to find. He chewed for a little longer and then, with a *harrumph,* reached down, snatching up the first of the two artifacts. At first glance, it appeared to be a simple, gray metal ingot without obvious markings or adornment. Were it not for the small indentations along one edge it would have seemed entirely featureless. Despite its innocuous appearance, Harrugh knew that the object was far from it. In addition, it was sealed with advanced nanotechnology that required the correct cipher to access. A cipher he apparently did not possess.

He had spent many long and fruitless hours attempting to solve the riddle and quelled the urge to hurl the damned thing into the desert. What was he supposed to do with a data vault that he was unable to open? Despite the apparent futility, he keyed a fresh series of ciphers into the holographic display, pushed at its surface and uttered a few archaic epigrams in an effort to elicit a response from the artifact. As ever, nothing happened.

Harrugh mastered his frustration, setting the ingot down before turning his attention to the other item. He took it up, handling it with a reverence he didn't quite understand. It was due to the manner in which the stranger had handed it to him. He had sensed that the sealed vial he held before him contained something precious and so he treated it as carefully as he was able, given his irritation with it.

The vial was everything the data vault was not: ornate to the point of ostentation, but elegant enough to still be attractive. An intricate exterior design was picked out in tiny jewels which Harrugh's ocular implant told him were real, arranged in the shape of a single teardrop. *The Prophet's Tears*, Harrugh had been told, and there had been an odd note of sadness in the synthesized voice of the one that had delivered it to him. *Probably the most important thing you will ever hold in your hands, Harrugh Gefhara.*

"But why?"

He released a snarl that echoed in the empty cave. His grip tightened on the vial, claws emerging with soft clicks as they scraped at its surface. He stood there, teeth bared for a long moment before he sagged to the ground with a soft sigh and uttered the question again.

"Why?"

The inquiry was directed toward more than just the object in his hands. He had charted the course of an intergalactic trade empire from its halls of power and had been reduced to a vagabond in a dusty cave by... a bottle and a puzzle box. He bowed his head, burdened by the weight of memories.

BEFORE

The meeting with the Veiled Skies clan had been long and fractious. At least two members of the emir's advisory entourage had clearly been selected for their capacity to find fault with the minutiae of the shipping contract. Had it not been for the apparently inexhaustible patience of his own councilors he would have grown weary of the negotiations while the sun was still high. Not for the first time, Harrugh Gefhara lamented his election as leader of the Hacan. While he liked to think he possessed enough economic acumen to maintain the complex web of treaties, commitments and commercial interests, the politics of it all frustrated him.

As a general he expected to know who his enemy was, conceive a strategy and overcome them in the most efficient way possible through power or guile. Negotiating the economics and complexities of the emirates' trade networks often felt like trying to fight smoke. In a culture where commercial sense was practically considered the highest art form, Harrugh felt like a fraud.

"Thank you, Councilor Rudragh." Harrugh formally dismissed the last of his retinue from the darkening chambers. "Your advice is, as always, greatly valued. We will reconvene in the morning."

The Hacan gave a short bow from the waist and the door slid shut with a hiss. For the first time in many hours, the Quieron was blissfully alone. He pushed the hood of rich red and gold fabric off his head, exhaling in a long sigh that allowed the stress of maintaining a proper poise to drain out of him.

Turning from the doors, he padded across the chamber. The conference room was large, tiled in polished, sandy stone and dominated by an enormous table of glossy black glass. It was quiescent now but earlier had danced with the holographic projections of a dozen worlds, screeds of commercial data and projected economic margins. Harrugh trailed a hand idly across its inert surface, approaching a gently angled window spanning the chamber wall.

At a growled command, the opacity filter faded, revealing the sprawling vista of Raffir beyond. The flank of the palatial ziggurat sloped away precipitously below, its gilt surface plunging into the morass of towers and domed residences that housed the local emirs and their favored clans. Beyond them the city stretched out like a carpet of jewels as thousands of evening lights winked on, illuminating the expansive trade floors, mercantile halls, cartel complexes and the numerous residence blocks of the Hacan who serviced them.

Harrugh gazed past it all, to the dozens of floodlit platforms of the spaceport where shuttle and freight traffic endlessly ferried to and from the near-space orbitals. Further still, occupying the rear of the vast city-sled, were the bulbed towers of the Veiled Skies clan. While many clans considered proximity to the palace of the Quieron a mark of prestige, the Emirs of the Veiled Skies had long ago recognized the practical value of positioning themselves close to the source of business. With just about complete control of the galaxy's largest cargo hauling concern, the decision had cemented the emirate as one of the preeminent powers within the Hacan.

Past the glittering towers of the Veiled Skies, the darkening desert stretched out as far as the eye could see. The running lights of a few spehat fungus towers drifted in the far distance, haunting the carved furrow of the city-sled as it made its stately way across the northern sands.

"Home is not a place, it is a feeling." The deep voice growled from the gloom, tinny and heavily synthesized. Harrugh froze, his quiet contemplation fleeing, his hackles rising. He had been quite certain the chamber was empty.

He turned to face the speaker, acutely aware that while there had to be dozens of guards nearby and several discreet weapons tucked away in this very room, he was essentially unarmed in the presence of a stranger, in the very heart of the most secure facility in all the Emirates.

"Have no cause for concern, Harrugh Gefhara, I mean you no harm."

Three points of lambent green light hung in the deepening shadows of the hall, the lenses of an advanced respirator mask completely concealing the wearer's features. For a moment, the figure reminded him of a specter appearing in the desert, like the hrrtos from the old tales. The intruder took a single, measured step into the fading light cast by the window and Harrugh noted that they were swaddled in heavy, dark robes with a high collar and neck scarf.

Harrugh smoothed his hood back into place and mastered his apprehension, masking anxiety with propriety. He was not unfamiliar with attempts on his life, but they had been before he became Quieron and under very different circumstances. The idea that someone or something could strike at him in the seat of his power was deeply unsettling. The stranger made no further move toward him and without any immediate threat Harrugh hesitated before responding to their statement.

"An easy claim to make when one has the advantage," he challenged. "Perhaps if you were to identify yourself, I would be more compelled to believe you, but instead you appear like a ghost."

"A hrrtos, then," the stranger rumbled in its modulated voice. "You may call me that, but I am one that means you no ill will. I consider myself a nobody, only a helpful nomad."

The hrrtos circled slowly so that the bulk of the table was between themself and the Quieron, careful not to approach any closer than they already were. *Smart,* Harrugh thought, *put a barrier between us, diffuse tension, build trust.*

"Time," the hrrtos continued, "is a valuable commodity and I have little of it to spare." They gestured with a metallic hand to the opposite side of the table. In the failing light, Harrugh could not determine whether the limb was synthetic or clad in some sort of armored gauntlet. "There is something we need to discuss."

Had the circumstances been less remarkable, Harrugh would not have entertained the idea of dialogue with an intruder for any longer than it would have taken to summon the guards. No sane assassin would introduce themselves in such a manner, though, and that, coupled with their ability to gain access to the highest echelons of the palace undetected, was nothing short of extraordinary. Harrugh knew that seated at the table he would be able to raise the alarm in an instant, as well as discreetly withdraw the concealed beam pistol if required. If the stranger was aware of either of these two facts, they gave no indication.

"Very well, *hrrtos*," Harrugh acceded. "What exactly is it that you would like to discuss?"

It did not take long after leaving the cave to locate the passage of Raffir. Even the wind and endlessly shifting sands of the desert could not quickly erase the broad valley carved by the immense city-sled. After so long out in the wilderness, returning to civilization would be a shock, but with no progress toward solving the enigmatic artifacts tucked away in his pack, perhaps a shock was what he needed right now.

He scrambled and slid his way down the steep flank of the dune canyon, hastening along the hard-packed sand of its floor. Swarms of tiny scavengers drawn to the insects and reptiles unearthed or crushed by the city-sled skittered away here and there at his approach, only to close in again once he had passed.

"The desert feeds the desert," his clan-father had once told him. "Nothing is wasted."

The days when the capital stood motionless were long gone following the conflicts with the imperious L1Z1X. A city in motion made for a more challenging target and by the Quieron's decree, the great city-sled once again traversed the desert by day, resting at night. By the afternoon, Harrugh could clearly see the sun catching on the spires and towers of the Veiled Skies clan compound and feel the low, tectonic rumble of Raffir's motion. To an observer from afar, the city and the herd of titanic Tuuran that pulled it appeared to travel at a stately pace, in much the same way a falling building seemed to move in slow motion as it crashed to the ground. The reality, when confronted in person, was very different and could be equally terrifying if unprepared.

He noticed shoals of sails and numerous motley pennants adorning clan skimmers, grav-speeders, solar-schooners and more traditional Tuuran-drawn sand-sleds as they jockeyed along the valley sides on their approach to the city. Travelers traditionally approached Raffir on foot in daylight hours due to its motion, but Harrugh liked being the exception, and raised a hand, making a signal, to denote him as a pilgrim. It was considered good fortune for a clan to assist a pilgrim or wanderer to complete the final leg of their journey as well. Several sleds passed him by, kicking up high plumes of sand in their wake, until a speeder bearing the colors of the Dawn Star pulled alongside and pulsed its running lights.

"Sun follow your steps, wayfarer!" a gruff voice called from the deck and Harrugh looked up to see a Hacan with pale, sun-bleached fur offering a hand to help him. Harrugh gratefully accepted the offered limb, swinging up onto the open cargo deck of the craft. He looked around. Several dozen crates and casks were secured beneath tension netting while the craft's small crew readied the speeder for the final approach to Raffir.

He returned his gaze to the apparent commander of the vessel. "And yours, shipmaster."

"Korroq, of the Dawn Star," the shipmaster supplied. His thick brows furrowed beneath his billowing hood. "Do I know you, wayfarer? You have the look of one who has walked the harvest way but have the bearing of an emir!"

"You honor me to say so," Harrugh replied, "but I am no emir, simply a walker of the way coming to the end of the long road."

The speeder passed into the shadow beneath Raffir, the huge hull of the sled closing over them like a steel sky suspended between the immense runners. Cavernous hangars yawned wide in the belly of the city, powerful gravity nets drawing in the smaller craft like a feeding sandmaw. Korroq barked several orders, and the crew angled the craft toward one of the waiting bays.

"We don't see many wayfarers these days," the shipmaster continued, once he was satisfied they were on target. "It does me good to see that we haven't completely abandoned the old ways." He absently scratched at his whiskers. "Did you find the clarity you sought?"

"Sadly not." Harrugh shook his head. "Now that I've returned, however, I'm hoping to succeed with the help of a friend where I failed alone."

Korroq clapped him on the shoulder, offering a toothy grin. "It is good to know ourselves, wayfarer." He looked around at his crew. The speeder jolted as it was snared by the gravity net and pulled into one of Raffir's many maws toward the waiting dock. The shipmaster turned back to Harrugh. "But it's a wiser mind that knows we are stronger together. Blood and clan."

"Blood and clan." Harrugh repeated the benediction.

Once the speeder was secured, Harrugh bid Korroq farewell and good fortune. The pair engaged in the traditional offer of coin and refusal to accept it which made Harrugh's heart lighter than it had been that morning. He made his way down the cargo ramp into the controlled chaos of the arrivals hangar. More than a hundred vessels were moored up, variously loading or unloading. Crew, porters, inspectors and more swarmed around them and the air was filled with the hue and cry of the collision between commerce and industry. Machine noise thundered in the hollow space as mechanics and fitters tended to the vessels overlaid by the constant bass tremor of Raffir. Here, in the belly of the city, the sound was impossible to escape. After his sojourn in the desert Harrugh took a moment to breathe it in and then headed to one of the numerous elevators that would take him up to the market floor.

The hubbub of the market washed over him like a particularly tumultuous and disparate tide, at least as deafening as the hangar but wholly different in its tone and energy. Countless conversations and trade deals were occurring around him as he strode from the elevator and into the surging crowds. Clans from across the northern hemisphere and beyond plied their trade in the sprawling plazas, buying and selling everything from gerr root to information. There were innumerable such markets across the city, from the enormity of the Horizon Exchange to street corner boutiques catering to specific and exclusive goods.

Harrugh remembered his first trip to the market plazas when he had been little more than a cub, clinging onto his clan-uncle for dear life. He tasted the memory like a drop of water on his tongue: the sense that he might get lost or swallowed into the throng as though he were a morsel waiting to be devoured. Everything had felt so overwhelming, so *vast*. He had loved it then and he loved it now. It was vibrant and so very, very alive.

He passed by two dozen vendors, one of whom attempted enthusiastically if unsuccessfully to sell him a bottle of exquisite Yssaril sweetwater. While the Hacan had long been familiar with the varied narcotic applications of their native flora, the precious nature of water meant that they had come late to the discovery of alcoholic distillation. Even after their diaspora to the stars they still considered the consumption of liquor, particularly in excess, something of an extravagance. It brought to mind youthful dalliances, laughter, and camaraderie.

How do you feel, Harrugh?

Her voice echoed in his memory so clearly that he turned physically, half-expecting her to be standing behind him. Ashalla

Kar would be waiting for him, he knew, though there was every chance it was simply so that she could berate him at length for leaving without so much as a farewell. Carth would be less forgiving if she ever deigned to speak to Harrugh again. They had both messaged him with increasing urgency prior to his hasty departure from one of the most powerful positions known to Hacan, but haunted by his own paranoia and in the uproar left in the wake of his resignation, he had ignored his two oldest and most valued friends. Harrugh sighed, electing not to investigate the older missives and relive their fury and confusion. Life-long friendships had been torn asunder by his decision and of his many regrets, losing those friendships ate at him the most.

But at the time – and even now – it was still a necessity. He had made a leader's hard choice to depart his position as leader, a convoluted train of thought that bothered him even now, just as much as it consoled him.

"Clan-cousin, please?" The voice was small and reedy, barely more than a whine and could easily have gone unnoticed. Indeed, judging by the number of people ignoring the youthful Hacan, she had to be clanless or at least of low station. "Clan-cousin? Will you spare a moment for my wares?"

Harrugh hunkered down beside the girl. She was barely more than a kit, really: spots of mange and pale scars marred her golden fur. Her bright, amber eyes were tinged with the kind of weariness that one of her age had no right to know. Harrugh's heart went out to her.

"What are you selling, little one? Present your stock and we can talk terms." He kept to the formalities, even as kindness crept into his tone. Initially, she appeared shocked that anybody had stopped but she was, after all, a Hacan and it was no time at all before she began excitedly unfolding the embroidered cloth from her battered basket. It was a saqq, a traditional Hacan headscarf. The fabric was coarse but the stitching admirable, demonstrating both artistic talent and skill.

Harrugh took up the cloth, shaking it out. It would make excellent desert wear. "It is good," he observed. "Did you make it yourself?"

"My aunt helped me to get it started," she admitted and then held her head up. "But mostly, it is my work, and it can be yours for the right price."

"Ah, now the negotiation." Harrugh chuckled. "All right, little one, let's begin, shall we? What do you think is a fair price for this saqq?"

They engaged in haggling: she naming a price that was far, far too low for her to make any sort of living, but he engaging her in the time-honored tradition of claiming that she was asking far too high a price. They settled, eventually, on six tercets, the currency of the tri system, and he pressed ten into her hand.

"For the company," he said, by way of explanation. "I have been troubled of late and you have brightened my day. Let's say the extra will cover that, hmm?" An additional four tercets would feed her for a day or two; perhaps lift some of the child's own woes for a while.

The youngling simply stared up at him and from the evident brightness in her eyes, it was clear to Harrugh that she was only just maintaining proper composure. He pressed his palms together parallel to the ground and inclined his head to her, a gesture of respect, and walked away before she could refuse the gift. She needed the coin far more than he did and besides, it made him feel better to do some tangible good.

"What was it you said to me once, Ashalla?" he mused absently to no one. "That quote about altruism?"

Harrugh weaved through the market, trying and failing to recall Ashalla's words, slipping past ranks of spice traders, produce merchants and transit brokers. "There is no such thing as altruism," he muttered under his breath, but the remainder of the adage remained elusive.

"There is no such thing as altruism, Harrugh Gefhara," came a smooth voice, tinged with amusement. "Because doing good for others makes you feel good about yourself and isn't that a prize in and of itself?"

Ashalla Kar, his childhood friend, leaned against a market stall, her arms folded in front of her. She wore simple clothing worked in white, trimmed with intricate embroidery, and a dignified saqq covered her head, keeping most of her face in shadow. Only her eyes were clear and that was enough to allow Harrugh's heart to catch briefly in his throat. They were the intense deep green of perfect emeralds, humor dancing in them. She was tall and slender, her posture full of the elegant bearing that had always been so appealing. Something in the way she held herself made Harrugh suddenly conscious of his weary slouch.

"A prize well won, I would say, though," he countered, continuing the conversation as though only minutes had passed since their last discussion. "For if you feel good about yourself, you are more inclined toward further charity. Perhaps just to see if it engenders the same sentiment, true, but surely helping those less fortunate is a worthy endeavor."

"Hello, you silly old fool," she said. There were only a handful of months between them in age; he was her elder, but she was – and always had been – the sensible one. She pushed away from the stall and stood before him, looking him up and down, taking in the dust and threadbare clothing.

"You look *terrible*," she asserted cheerfully. "Like you've been dragged through the desert by your tail. When you left without a word, I had half a mind to do exactly that when I found you, Harrugh…"

"I would prefer it if you didn't?"

She ignored that. "You are also decidedly *pungent*." She wafted a hand in front of her face, but he recognized the mockery in her tone. She was taking no real offense from his less than regal appearance. The smile dropped for just a moment. "Are you all right?"

Three simple words carried such weight. She could have been asking if he was all right in terms of his health. She could have been asking something much, much deeper. He knew that his reply to such an open-ended question could be critical at this point. He needed to be honest with her.

"I have … been better, Ashalla, I will not lie to you. I am troubled by things I do not entirely understand." He looked up at her from beneath his hood. "I need a friend."

Again, that devilish sparkle in her eyes.

"Oh, *now* you need a friend?" She closed what was left of the distance between them, and her arms came around him in an easy, unashamed embrace. She pressed her muzzle into the hollow of his shoulder and let out a soft sigh. "I've got you now. You can share your burden."

Endless possibilities of what they might have become together flashed through Harrugh's mind, but he had learned a long time ago not to dwell. "Do you still have your apartment near the embassies?"

"No, they evicted me the moment you left." The look of shock lasted long enough for Ashalla's delight to become obvious. "Of course I do, you abject fool. You can clean yourself up, I will feed you, we can talk. It will be like old times." She slid a hand into his, leading him through the crowd of traders and steering them in the direction of the looming palace.

"This is how it's going to be now, then, is it? Until I am forgiven?" Harrugh's voice was a rumble. He hoped he would be forgiven, but Ashalla had always had a heart deeper than an ocean.

"Just like old times," she repeated in a softer, more affectionate tone.

TWO

Ashalla's lodgings were situated in the lower levels of a tower adjoining the residences reserved for off-world dignitaries. As a councilor of the former Quieron she retained a certain, if tainted, degree of status that had miraculously survived the uproar of his departure, despite the public slander. Compared to the stifling heat of the city, the apartment was cool and comfortable and Harrugh sat down on a set of plump cushions that felt like pure luxury.

"How has it been, Ash'ka?" He used the diminutive form of her name, the syllables tripping off his tongue with ease.

"You mean how has it been in Raffir since you upended centuries of tradition and ran off?" She fetched water from the kitchen, also setting out a platter of cold meats. He identified at least one as an off-world import. "Or do you mean how has it been with me specifically after you left Carth and I to answer the questions of the emirs and the Sword Fleet admiralty while a new Quieron was elected?"

"It's really going to be like this for a while, isn't it?" He gratefully accepted the water which she handed to him in an elegant, wooden goblet. Every sip was as nectar, running down his parched throat and washing away a little more of the travel dust. "It's still good to see you."

"It's good to be seen," she replied pointedly, settling in front of him with her own goblet in hand. "So, what brought you back? The Golden General resigns his position and goes gallivanting off on a harvest pilgrimage of all things, only to return looking like a clanless vagabond with the weight of the three jewels of Kenara even heavier upon his shoulders."

"Please don't call me that, Ash'ka, you know it doesn't sit well with me." While he had been promoted to the rank of general for orchestrating the stunning Janndaq Plains counterattack during the L1Z1X incursion, he hailed from the slums of the Silver Sands, and the moniker had always grated on his nerves. He had no idea who had said it first, but suddenly it was everywhere. He was the Golden General and no amount of protest could make it otherwise.

Whilst he had been Quieron, Harrugh had known what it was to experience adulation and though he wanted his people to thrive and to flourish, he begrudged the attention and public scrutiny associated with the position.

"Very well, my Quieron," she said, good-naturedly.

She sipped her water, lounging back with such languid ease that Harrugh was jealous. He couldn't remember the last time he had felt as relaxed as she looked right now. There was still no trace of gray in her muzzle or dulling of the eyes and her fur was as glossy as it had ever been. Perhaps that insouciant attitude to life would keep her youthful forever, he considered. By contrast, while his mane remained flaxen, the snowy whiskers and white on his chin revealed the toll of leadership, and the reasons leading to the torturous decision to give it up.

But to still call him "my Quieron"… he shook his head helplessly, feeling fond despite the time apart. Both she and Carth had insisted on calling him that at every opportunity for weeks after he'd been elected. In public it was only right and proper, but it had also been their joke in private and, for a while, it had even been funny. *Would you pass those notes? Yes, my Quieron! Would you pass the water jug? Yes, my Quieron!* And he would roll his eyes and ask them please not to, and they would agree not to. Of course, they would do it again next time anyway.

"So, you said you needed a friend. You have one. How about I help you out here?" She tapped a claw thoughtfully against her chin before holding it up as though she'd experienced some sort of epiphany. "Let's pretend we've done all the catching up about your pilgrimage – and the chaos you left in your wake – and we move straight to whatever it is that's got you sitting there as though you've eaten all the sour fruit from the bowl. Does that seem appealing to you?"

"How well you know me," he said, swallowing hard. "I think, as ever, you are absolutely right. Although what I have to say will probably confuse you just as much as it has confused me." He resisted the urge to glance over his shoulder. "It has haunted me, this mystery…"

"A mystery?" She interrupted him mid-flow. Another veil of weariness lifted from Harrugh's soul. Maybe he could save what was left of their relationship. "We used to *love* those, Harrugh. So come now. Tell me *everything*."

"If you would stop talking for more than six heartbeats," he said, but with enough authority that she knew he meant it, "then I might just be able to do that." She put her hand over her mouth in a gesture of contrition. He narrowed his eyes, then flashed a brief smile. He took another gulp of water, gathering his thoughts before reaching for his travelling pack.

"Let me tell you about the specter that haunts me," he said. "Let me tell you about the hrrtos."

BEFORE

The hrrtos had not waited for permission before dropping into one of the chairs at the table and now, in the half-light of the conference room, Harrugh interpreted the newcomer, with their lambent eye-lenses and heavy robes, as more of a wrathful hrrtos than a living being. Something like a wraith that had stepped out of the old desert tales to bargain with the living for promises of power. If it even was a living being at all.

"You are going to need to lead, Harrugh," the hrrtos rumbled, their tinny voice grating in the gloom.

Harrugh snorted, making a point of looking around the chamber before returning his gaze to the intruder. "You're a little late with that assertion, hrrtos. Look around you. What exactly is it that you believe I have been doing here?"

If the hrrtos was affronted by Harrugh's derisive tone it gave no indication. The inscrutable lenses remained fixed on him. "Yes, as Quieron, you lead. But it is a mantle that sits poorly upon your shoulders."

Harrugh bristled. It wasn't that the statement was incorrect – he had said as much in as many ways to Carth and Ashalla more than once – but having someone else state it out loud was discourteous at best. From a *stranger*, it was insulting. He opened his mouth to offer a rebuke, but the hrrtos cut him off with a nonchalant wave of their hand.

"Spare me your indignation. I do not have the time or the inclination to listen to your refutation."

"So why don't you just tell me what you want?"

"Because there are some truths that cannot simply be told, they must be learned."

"That sounds like an excuse."

"Does it, Harrugh? If I were, at this moment, to recount to you an absolute truth that challenged your view of the galaxy, would you accept it without question and act upon it accordingly?"

Harrugh drew breath to reply, checking the sharp response.

"Better, Harrugh, better."

The Quieron settled in his seat, irritated at having been momentarily wrong-footed. "So how would you have me learn this great truth?" The question was loaded with reluctance.

The hrrtos reached into its robes. Harrugh deftly activated the panel hidden in the side of the table. It slid open soundlessly and he closed his hand around the compact beam pistol hidden within. He was confident that he could draw and shoot fast enough to at least incapacitate the intruder and take cover.

The hrrtos produced a small, cloth-wrapped bundle and Harrugh fractionally relaxed his grip on the weapon. They set the object down on the table, peeling back the fabric to reveal a small collection of items. The first looked like an ornate vial and the second an unremarkable ingot of dull metal. The third looked very much like a data-chip, though it lacked any ident-markers or code strings signifying its purpose.

"This–" the hrrtos indicated the vial "–is called the Prophet's Tears. This–" here, it gestured to the ingot "–is a data vault containing everything you will need to know." It turned softly glowing lenses toward the data-chip. "*Almost* everything." With a deft flick of its fingers, it sent the chip sliding across the table toward Harrugh.

The Quieron looked down at the chip, then back at the hrrtos. "You expect me to use this now?" he stated flatly.

"You wanted an answer." A brief shrug hinted at casual nonchalance, something that irritated Harrugh immensely.

"This could be anything."

"Yes, it could be, but if I intended to do you harm, do you not think I would have done so before asking you to sit within easy reach of the alarm and that weapon you are hiding beneath the table?"

Harrugh masked his shock and drew the beam pistol out before setting it on the table in front of him. "How did you know that…"

"It doesn't matter, Harrugh. Everything that *does* matter is now in front of you." The hrrtos gestured again to the artifacts and the data-chip. Harrugh scooped up the chip, inspecting it with care. It shared the same style of connector as any other of its kind, but on closer inspection contained more than double the usual number of micro-fiber couplings. Harrugh supposed that would be needed to transfer a greater volume of data than a standard chip. He looked up at the stranger.

"Something I have learned from fighting the L1Z1X is that technology can be perilous," he said. "Particularly when introduced to the body."

"Don't you want to learn how Ashalla Kar will die? Or Carth?" The words were spoken in the same neutral, synthesized tone but they stung like barbs. "The knowledge is right there."

"Is that a threat?" Harrugh's nostrils flared. The beam pistol snapped up to point directly at the stranger's masked face. There was still no reaction.

"No, Harrugh. It is merely knowledge. Motivation, let's say. Shooting me won't change that. It won't change *anything*."

Harrugh snarled, holding his aim for several heartbeats before exhaling with a hiss. He lowered the weapon to the table but kept one hand resting meaningfully on its grip. For a moment, he considered sweeping the chip from the table and crushing it beneath his boot. Then he shook his head, lifting the damned thing to the socket built into his ocular implant. Ploy or not, any threat to Ashalla and Carth would be taken seriously.

The hrrtos said nothing more, just nodded, approving of his choice. Harrugh sighed and pushed the chip into the slot. It slid into place with a soft *click* and then…

The world turned beneath him, a sandy jewel of umber and ochre and he immediately recognized the geography of Hercant, first planet of the Hacan – the world on which he now stood. The fidelity of the image was incredible, as if he were gazing down on it from a platform in near-space orbit. Hundreds of ships and dozens of orbitals crowded the void like shoals of silvered fish, their bustling, frenetic activity a contrast to the lazily turning globe below.

The change, when it arrived an instant later, was sudden and profound.

The ships and orbitals simply died, running lights blinking out as they tumbled, blind and uncontrolled. Explosions blossomed as vessels collided, filling the vacuum with spinning debris, flash frozen fluid and plunging bodies. It was nothing compared to the effect upon the planet. Vapor and thin ribbons of cloud streamed away from the upper atmosphere of Hercant and glittering clusters of night-side lights vanished into darkness.

The scene hung like that for several long, aching seconds and Harrugh felt his breath catch in his throat, horrified. Whatever had just happened, the world was already dead or at least dying.

The thermal blast wave of silver-white fire that followed completed the execution.

Everything still in orbit vaporized in an instant without a scrap of debris to mark their passing. Hercant burned. It burned with an intensity that scoured the surface down to the crust into a streaming comet tail of gaseous particulate and boiled its remaining atmosphere. In the final moments before the image mercifully blinked off, Harrugh saw the tortured skin of the planet finally crack and spill its molten blood into the void.

Harrugh swallowed his scream, reaching out as if he could push the parts of the planet back together with his paws. His throat went dry, parched by the vision of atrocity. The terror made him want to vomit. He tried to rise but stumbled against the edge of the table. It seemed the impossible pyre of the dying world robbed him of his strength. The spectral chaos of a billion extinguished souls rang in his ears, and he knew that his best friends in the entire system were part of that death. "Hrrtos," he managed to croak in the darkness of the conference room. "Hrrtos, what have you done to me?"

The fur beneath his good eye was damp as he scrambled to remove the data chip from the port. There was a hiss, a spark and a brief scent of sizzling circuits. A drizzle of blackened dust dribbled from the socket.

"Hrrtos!" Harrugh roared into the gloom. There was no reply.

He was alone. And transformed forever by what he had seen.

"Hrrtos!"

They talked until night fell and apart from the occasional request for clarification, Ashalla remained quiet. When he was done, she remained silent for a long time, clearly weighing her response carefully.

"A simulation," she stated simply. "A holographic construct designed to provoke a deep emotional response."

Harrugh shook his head. "Obviously it was a simulation, Ash'ka, but it was unlike anything I have ever experienced before. It felt … it felt *real*." He shuddered at this fresh recollection. "The universe … everyone in it …"

The little cub he'd met in the market. The Hacan who'd given him a helping hand to reach the city. Even they would be burned to cinders if such a horrendous thing came to pass. Everyone he met, touched, spoke with … nothing but ash.

"Do you still have the chip?"

He shook his head. "I wish I did, but removing it triggered some sort of failsafe. There wasn't much left except for carbon and silica dust. The hrrtos clearly didn't want me to be able to prove what I'd seen to anyone." His jaw clenched.

"Tell me that you checked the …"

He held up a finger to forestall the line of questioning, his expression pained. "The security detail arrived right after that, summoned by my shouting. I had them check audio visual feeds, visitor manifests, maintenance records and access logs. The palace was locked down for two days while every route of entry or exit was inspected."

"I guess they found nothing," Ashalla stated. It was a rhetorical question because she suspected she already knew the answer.

"Even the ultrasonic and thermal imaging of the room showed nothing. The palace staff picked over every floor, wall and ceiling." He shook his head again and growled darkly. It was as if he was reliving the panic and fear caused by that nomadic wraith all over again. "When it became clear there was no evidence that there had ever been an intruder, I'm sure they started to believe I had lost my mind. And yet…" Harrugh produced the data vault, turning it over in his hands before handing it across to his friend for her perusal.

"This is an elaborate piece, Harrugh," she observed. "I don't think I've seen anything quite this advanced before. Have you been able to get anything out of it?" Her expertise in extracting information from people was unquestionable, but in her time as a diplomat Ashalla had also become adept at procuring information from more archival sources as well. It paid to know the details of those with whom you were negotiating.

He stood, agitated, beginning to pace the room. He stopped, absently checking the apartment. "Nothing beyond what is shown by the touch activation," Harrugh replied. "I have no idea how, but I suspect it's gene-coded to me." His lips twitched in a smile. "A simple message and numeric string. The same thing, on repeat." Ashalla looked up at him from her spot on the cushions where she was examining the small metallic block.

"If you tell me the start of the string is 1-2-3-4, I won't believe you."

"I won't tell you, then."

She chuckled. "I'm guessing the numbers aren't recognizably sequential." Of course they weren't, and she knew it. "I wonder why…" She trailed off, but he knew what she was going to ask.

"Why I can't decipher it?" Harrugh cut in, harsh.

She studied him with concern.

"Ash'ka," he said, lowering his voice, "I tried. I tried to summon the finest minds of the emirates to assess this riddle." He waved a hand dismissively, counting things off on his fingers. "Off-world. Unavailable. Engaged with projects that couldn't be delayed." He became animated as he paced again. "I tried to use agents to investigate covertly via unofficial channels." He gave a hollow laugh. "I even paid a mercenary outfit to dig into it. Someone from outside the palace." He stopped, glancing at the door again as though someone might burst in there and then. As if the hrrtos might be waiting to appear out of thin air and hand him another piece of the future that would ruin his present.

"And?" she prompted.

"And? Nothing. Nothing, Ash'ka. Databases mysteriously empty, or formerly reliable contacts suddenly absent. It was… it is… exasperating. The mercenary outfit contacted me shortly after heading off-world to tell me that they'd received triple their fee to go do a job for someone in the outer reaches."

Ashalla stood, wordlessly moved to his side and placed a gentle hand on his shoulder. "Harrugh…"

"It felt like some shadowy force was set against me. You and Carth were both off-world, resolving the Tendranah issue and…" He paused. "I started to believe that the palace had to have been infiltrated. How else could someone… or some*thing*, know my mind so profoundly? To so deftly counter all my efforts? Know exactly what I was trying to do? What if I confided in you and Carth and then you both suddenly went missing? Everything was tied to me, maybe this disaster was caused by me, and I couldn't continue chasing my own tail. So…"

"So, you left."

He nodded. Some of the tension that had built during his tirade drained from him. "To get away from whatever it was that watched me from the shadows. To get away from the sourceless, ephemeral weight of expectation pressing down on me." He stopped, rubbing his good eye. "But I can't escape what I saw. Or what it said. It haunts me, every moment."

Harrugh had spent the majority of the pilgrimage trying to fathom out how more of the information within the artifact might be accessed. Constantly testing, using every piece of knowledge from his past to solve the riddle. "I believe that the hrrtos, or whoever they are working for to deliver these things to me, *wants* me to solve whatever this is." He gestured to the vault. "But there is some sort of lesson here." He shuddered. "A truth that needs to be learned, rather than told."

"So, now you have finally come home and brought it to me. How *very* flattering." Ashalla shook her head. "We didn't know, Harrugh. I was… hurt when you left like that. Confused. But Carth? Well, she was very…" Ashalla shrugged. "She was very *Carth* about it."

He grimaced at that. "I didn't want to send any messages. I was afraid they might be intercepted. Or worse."

"Peace, Harrugh. You are here now. I am grateful to have my friend back." She patted his shoulder until some of the anxiety ebbed, then she ran a single claw down the small indentations on the side of the object. She glanced at Harrugh. He pressed his palm to the artifact for a moment before withdrawing. "There's something oddly endearing about the idea that this has been made just for you."

"Endearing," he replied, "or terrifying." In response to Harrugh's touch, a string of digits swam across the surface of the device. A vocal emitter spoke in the synthesized tones of the hrrtos.

"*Your memory will be your guide, Harrugh Gefhara.*"

"Oh," remarked Ashalla. "So *that's* what you mean. You need to crack the riddle or figure out the code to unlock more. What ideas have you tried so far?" She tapped the side of her cheek thoughtfully as she studied it.

"I thought it might be an orbital registry, it has the right format," he replied. Her enthusiasm for the puzzle reignited a little of his own. His frustrations over the past weeks had pushed him to a point where he had stopped caring. He'd buried the thing in the bottom of his pack for days at a time. It wasn't that he was *annoyed* with it…

No, that was incorrect. He *was* annoyed with it. Furious, even.

"But it isn't an orbital," he continued. "I ran a directory search for all active registries, and it came back with nothing. If I could have solved the thing myself, I would have done so." The words came out far harder than intended. His frustration spilled over to encompass Ashalla, and he was immediately contrite. "I'm sorry. It's been difficult, even on the pilgrimage. Difficult and…" He passed the back of his hand across his eyes and sighed. "Frustrating. Two things I do not enjoy, as well you know."

"No need to apologize," she said, staring at the data vault, her eyes intent and focused. "I understand now. I learned to tune out your ill moods years ago. I didn't even hear anything you said past 'orbital registry.'" She looked up, smiling brightly.

His stomach chose that moment to rumble and she laughed loudly, dispelling the pall that had settled over them. "I am an appalling host," she exclaimed. "We've sat here for *hours* with nothing but this meat platter and a cup of water. Let me prepare some food for us and we can work this puzzle out." She reached over to lay her hand over his and held his gaze. "Together."

He did not even bother protesting. When Ashalla decided on a course of action, even if it were only something as straightforward as preparing food, trying to dissuade her was harder than turning aside a dreadnought. While she busied herself in the kitchen, he took the data vault back. At his touch, it obediently repeated its enigmatic message. Perhaps he *would* be able to solve it with Ashalla where alone he had failed.

Food, when it came, was abundant and delicious: fresh, thick-cut steaks drenched in rich sauce, sweet pallup fruit in cream and an ice-cold glass of Arretze gold. Harrugh ate with the voracity of one who had spent long days foraging for survival in the desert. They ate in companionable silence and when they'd both taken their fill, Ashalla tidied things away, returning with more water.

"Let's put the vault aside for now," she said. "What about the other item?"

"This is even more perplexing," said Harrugh, sifting through his pack until he found the bottle, carefully wrapped in a long, winding strip of fabric. He freed it from its trappings and held it for a moment. For an item so very small, it was unexpectedly weighty. "And entirely more esoteric. And fragile. Do treat it with some respect, Ash'ka…" He let out a barking laugh as she pulled a face at him.

"What did you say it was called?"

"The hrrtos said that this was called the Prophet's Tears. I have had it analyzed as best I can without unsealing the vial. It's a biostatic solution containing some sort of microbial culture."

Her nose wrinkled. "Sounds delightful. I can understand why you haven't opened it."

"I have no idea what I'm supposed to do with it. I have it on good authority that the solution has no odor." She examined the bottle while listening. "Also, it has no color. While I generally wouldn't shy away from sampling something new and exotic, Ash'ka, consuming an unknown liquid given to me by a mysterious intruder *generally* gives me pause for thought."

"The Prophet's Tears?" Her brow furrowed. "That seems a little ostentatious, don't you think?" The bottle was a beautiful thing; clear crystal cut glass with ridged facets that caught the dim light of the room's overhead strip lighting and sparkled in her hands. On a planet of desert sands, glass was not exactly a rare or precious commodity. But worked glass, like this, was still considered an artform. She admired the craftsmanship for a while. The liquid contained within the bottle came up to about three quarters full, sloshing a little as she turned it this way and that.

"It might just be a symbolic thing," she suggested. "You know – the traditional giving of water to a stranger in the desert, showing marked respect and all that. But given the circumstances you've outlined, I'm going to guess that isn't the case in this instance. Let me see if I can discover anything." She handed the bottle back to him, getting to her feet and walking to the far end of the room. She picked up a savant, the greenish glow of its surface suffusing her face with its light.

Taking the Prophet's Tears back, Harrugh rewrapped it. Sitting staring at it was something he'd been doing for long enough. Ashalla might think of something he had not or at least have contacts he was not familiar with. Anything that might offer insight had value at this point. She was absorbed in her work and seemed to have apparently forgotten he was even there. Glancing up, she gave him another smile.

"Why don't you rest for a while? You look tired."

"I'm not…" His protest faltered before it even got started. It felt like a long time since he'd slept on something that wasn't the ground, and the prospect of an actual bed was very welcoming. And he *was* weary. "Maybe just a nap," he conceded. She waved dismissively in his direction.

"Dream deep and dream well, old friend," she said, and was quickly immersed in the task she'd given herself, leaving Harrugh to his own devices. He smiled inwardly: *like turning aside a dreadnought once she was under way.* He decided to take her up on her suggestion. Just a nap wouldn't hurt, and so he left the room, clambering onto her bed without saying another word. He was asleep in seconds.

THREE

He awoke the following morning. Ashalla was nowhere to be seen and he rose, guilty, from the bed, embarrassed for having taken advantage of her hospitality in such a way. He scratched at an itch behind his left ear, yawning widely as he investigated the apartment. Seen in the half-light of the previous evening, it had seemed sparse and unadorned. Now that daylight poured through the high windows, pooling on the tiled floor in splashes of warmth, he could see the little touches where she had made it her own.

He'd slept fitfully and could feel the knots in his shoulders and legs, the tender legacy of his long trek again reminding him that he was not as young as he'd once been. He noted the cushions and blankets heaped casually on the floor and his guilt grew more at the realization that she must have slept there after he commandeered her bed.

It was some time before she returned, during which he kept busy, tidying the apartment by way of apology. On discovering her guest was awake, her expression brightened. "You needed that," she said, as her greeting. He shrugged. There was no response other than to confirm she was correct. "I got us breakfast. Here."

She offered up a package containing fried, spiced meat in a light batter, and pastries filled with sweetened hurrluk fruit. "I've been thinking about the data vault," Ashalla said, her mouth filled with pastry. He patiently waited for her to finish before she continued. "I also did some digging to see if there was anything I could discover about anything called the Prophet's Tears. I've been busy while you were snoring the night away."

"And I am grateful for it, Ash'ka. What did you find?"

"I will tell you exactly what I found, Harrugh Gefhara," she said, licking sugary condiment from her finger. "A whole heap of nothing. A few esoteric spiritual links, a fragment of text from a dig on Indar's World and an oblique reference to something called 'Zembasi', but nothing recent. So, there's every chance it's a complete hoax. You've been duped into believing it's something significant and this hrrtos has deceived you into resigning your position to disrupt the stability of the Emirates and permanently reshape the position of Quieron."

Harrugh felt her final words strike him like a physical blow. "I heard that it was bad, that they changed the laws of leadership. Do you really think…" He could feel his hackles rising at her crass accusation, but the moment passed when she pealed with laughter.

"Of course I don't actually believe that," she reassured him. She reached over and patted his shoulder with clear affection. "I'm sorry. I've missed seeing you sputter in indignation. It's been a trying time, one way or the other, despite some truth to my jest. No, I believe everything you've told me about this hrrtos is true, that you've come into possession of something quite unique, but I also need you to understand things *will* be different now. You upended centuries of tradition and walked away from the most powerful position in the Emirates. Many Hacan were angry about that. A lot of them still are. I was among them for a time." She finished off her pastry and set the empty plate aside before continuing.

"I can only guess at what the Prophet's Tears might be. I'd say take an experimental slug of that liquid and find out, but I'm rather fond of you and wouldn't want you to ingest some mutagen, or worse. Perhaps the answers we are looking for are contained within the vault. Solve one, solve the other, sort of thing." She chewed on her lower lip for a few moments before shaking her head. "I thought about what you said. About the code looking like an orbital registry."

"Yes," Harrugh replied, chastened. "But as I said before, I ran a search of all our active registries and found nothing."

Ashalla gave a sly smile. "What if it's no longer active?"

"Then it's for one of our orbitals that's been decommissioned and we're still no further forward. A scrapped platform isn't going to exist any longer. Anything bought by a private interest isn't going to have the registry listed anywhere."

"Anywhere *official*," Ashalla corrected.

"Ashalla, former councilor to the Quieron," Harrugh replied in mock outrage. "It sounds as though you are suggesting that you may have contacts that are less than salubrious!"

"Sometimes you need to get things done properly." She beamed. "Sometimes you need to get things done *efficiently*. Fortunate for you, then, that I know people suited for both instances. So, if you're done sleeping and eating, let's get going."

Harrugh shook his head with a rueful smile. "By all means, lead on."

"Do you want to leave your things here?" She asked the question as they made to leave, since she'd noticed Harrugh picking up his pack and preparing to shoulder it. "I don't think they'll let you back into the Quieron's manse…" She trailed off and shrugged.

"I don't want to go back there," he said immediately, all good humor evaporating instantly. He chanced a quick glance at the door. "I'll leave it here. I put everything else important away with a discreet security cartel before I left. Anonymously, of course. I can get it on the way back if I need it."

The morning sun blazed on the cuneate flank of the palace, stippling the nearby embassies and towers with golden light. While the hour was still relatively early, the sky was already a brilliant blue, and this close to the administrative heart of the city the thoroughfares were shielded by mechanized awnings in a riot of red, yellow and ivory. The motors whined softly as they adjusted to shield the walkways below, the fabric rippling in the light breeze.

"I'm not ashamed to admit," said Harrugh after they were a short distance from the apartment, "that I missed the comfort of the city. While I may not have found the answers I was looking for, I really needed to be away from it all for a while. Remember my roots…" He tailed off and looked up to see her watching him intently. "I may no longer be Quieron," he finished, "but I still think of them as my people."

"Some of them may not think of you with as much affection."

"Perhaps not. And I would understand their misgivings."

It was a telling moment. He loved Ashalla more than most of those who had come and gone in his life. Her thoughts were important to him. She glanced at him solemnly before putting one hand over his.

"You were a good leader, if that helps at all," she said. He felt his response catch in his throat and for a moment was lost for words. Then she snorted in amusement, shaking her head. "Don't get emotional on me now, it would be unseemly out here. Let's just get across the city instead and see what we can figure out. Action now, sentiment later. Or something like that."

"Agreed," he said, regaining his composure. "Perhaps you can tell me how other things have been since I left?"

"Maybe some of it," she replied, mischievously. "But you're still not forgiven for vanishing without a word."

"Fine. I guess I still deserve it," said Harrugh, enjoying the old and comfortable rapport. "I'm sure I have bored you half to death with my miserable tale enough for now."

They left the softly sighing awnings behind and headed into the cover of a noisy trade floor. This close to the palace, the plaza was a prestigious location, bedecked with dozens of trade clan sigils, mercantile banners and consortium insignia. Grav-drones buzzed around the throng, their rapidly cycling screens displaying rolling screeds of prices and exchange values as tercet changed hands at every booth and kiosk. If there was a single, unifying truth of Kenara it was that commerce never slept.

Harrugh eased his way through the patrician clientele of the plaza in Ashalla's wake. A few heads turned his way as he passed, but if anybody recognized him for who he was they chose to maintain decorum. Ashalla had not yet revealed the location of her unorthodox contact, but the further they travelled from the palace, the less likely it was that he would be recognized. Few residents of the outer districts would expect to find the former leader of the Emirates wandering in their midst.

Once the clamor of the trade floor was behind them, he spoke up. "What did you do after I left?" The question was blunt and would have been considered rude among less familiar company. "I'm surprised the new Quieron didn't have the good sense to keep a Hacan of your standing on their staff."

Ashalla made a face that instantly caused Harrugh to regret his choice of words. "I, along with the rest of your staff and councilors, kept the great sled of the emirate moving while the emirs argued over how to handle the unprecedented circumstances," she replied with a hint of bitterness in her tone. "Carth and the clan consuls managed to keep the Sword Fleet in line, not that I believe there would have been a problem. The admiralty are even more tightly bound by tradition than the emirs. I handled the trade groups, freight lines and transport commissions."

"It wasn't my intention to put that on all of you." He sighed. "But I was not thinking clearly by the time I left. All I could see was the world burning every time I closed my eyes. Fear ruled me. It still does." His gaze roved the shadows for a moment as though he sought answers within them. "It felt like something was there in the palace, laughing as it blocked my feeble attempts to solve the puzzle while nobody believed me. I had to get out." He took a breath. "I just had to."

"We would have believed you," she said, softly.

"It was never my concern that you would not believe me, Ash'ka."

"Oh?"

"After what I had seen, I was concerned that you *would*. It was my choice to resign and tarnish my reputation, but there was no reason at all to drag you down with me."

The warm shade of the broad transit avenue was divided into regular sections by shafts of morning light. One shaft illuminated Ashalla's face as she paused and studied him. "I would have liked the opportunity to choose for myself," she said.

Harrugh could see the lingering sadness in her, feeling fresh pangs of his own regret. Then the sly, mischievous smile returned – something he had begun to recognize as her own mask. "And now here you are, drawing me into your nonsense anyway. Imagine the torment you could have spared yourself!"

He laughed at that statement, and they set off again, leaving the transitway via a skywalk passing between the glittering solar arrays of several habitation domes before linking to one of the numerous magrail stations that threaded the city like arteries.

"You should pull up your saqq," Ashalla advised as they padded onto the elevated platform. "I doubt it will matter if you're recognized up here, but we're going to be heading into the sub-level and folk down there are more likely to take an interest in your business, if you understand what I mean. Probably best not to draw attention."

He understood. He reached into his pack and retrieved the saqq he'd purchased from the young kit in the marketplace, tying it behind his head and then lifting it up over the white-streaked sandy fur of his muzzle. There wasn't much he could do about the optical cybernetic, but they were common enough not to give him away. It would, Ashalla asserted, have to be enough.

She slipped into the crowd of waiting passengers with the practiced ease of one who knew exactly where she was going. She wore a silver-trimmed black hood of her own that kept her features in shadow and shielded her from the rising heat of the day. Even here on the platform a few traders called out greetings from recessed booths and she returned them in kind, exchanging occasional pleasantries. The magtrain arrived with a ripple of displaced air and the doors slid open with a hiss, disgorging travelers and artificially cooled air in equal measure.

The pair boarded the vehicle and in moments it was on its way again, winding deeper into the city. Market plazas and habitation domes gave way to vertical agriplexes and industrial production facilities, their conical cooling stacks and cyclopean moisture recyclers casting bulbous shadows over the magrail. Many of the Hacan that flashed past on the skyways wore the heavy goggles and hazard suits of fabricator clans.

The magrail dipped and the train plunged into the twilight beneath a structural lattice supporting a billowing canopy of thermal nets. Autonomous harvesters worked alongside dozens of laborers tending to layered fungus beds with a dozen different medical uses. Condensation momentarily beaded the windows and then the train emerged once more into the dazzling light of day, evaporating it in an instant.

The colossal bulk of the Raffir spaceport towered before them, a trio of expansive towers fringed by scores of landing discs that had been repurposed shortly after the decision to make the city mobile again. An endless procession of shuttles, tugs, skiffs, cargo barques and freight haulers streamed to and from the enormous facility. While the embassies clustering around the palace housed the visiting dignitaries of foreign powers, the port, surrounding tenements and more upmarket lodges were by far the most cosmopolitan region of the city. Harrugh's gaze lingered on the structure and its ceaseless stream of traffic until it vanished from view as the train flashed into a tunnel.

"Harrugh?" He looked up at Ashalla. She studied him with a thoughtful expression. "You're miles away. Where are you?"

"I was just thinking how long it has been since I properly spent time among our people," he replied, then countered. "When was the last time you were off-world, Ash'ka?"

"A couple of weeks before you returned," she replied. "It was only as far as Langstrathe. A dispute resolution between the Restless Spire and the Day Moon. I was there mostly as an accessory to their negotiator, I admit, but there are still diplomats who are smart enough to know that an accessory is the best at listening while people in the room are talking." Her smile was radiant. Harrugh had seen firsthand that Ashalla could engage with anybody, from clanless porters to foreign ambassadors. She had learned the basics of spoken language for several other species without the need for an ambassador translator. She knew well that something as simple as "thank you" in another species' language could leave a lasting impression.

"Have you ever considered our people through the eyes of others?"

"Often." She was every bit as cheery as before. "Our ways must seem strange to them, the significance of clan and the subtle art of commerce. I have yet to encounter another galactic power who places as much value on their trade networks. But their ways seem just as strange to us. Can you imagine living as a human? Their expressions are so limited and direct! I'm fond of the Xxcha, though – their reservations about conflict are delightful."

"Does it bother you? What others think of us?"

"Yes," she replied, "and at the same time, no. I think it's important that we are recognized as a power in the galaxy, but whether they appreciate our culture, our history? That's on them." She tipped her head to the side again, curious as to the reason he'd asked her. "What's gnawing at you, Harrugh? Is it just this hrrtos business? Or is it something else?"

"Just pensive," he replied with a gruff chuckle. "Second-guessing everything and wondering at my purpose after everything I have left behind. Do you remember what you used to ask me when you were feeling particularly sharp? Harrugh Gefhara, you would say. I don't know what you're even *for*, but it's certainly not enough for me to actually *care* about."

Her laughter was cleansing, and he welcomed the sound as it washed over him. For the briefest moment, the blanket of apprehension that had settled across him lifted, leaving him feeling more like the old Harrugh than he had done in months. She was still laughing softly. "I remember. You must be sure to let me know when you find out."

"Not forgiven yet then?"

"Not even close," she said. "So for now you should probably shut up with your introspective brooding while we solve this little conundrum."

He laughed at her determined voice. "I admire your optimism."

The train emerged on the other side of the spaceport and began descending rapidly. The bulk of the passengers had departed along the route, allowing the pair to be comfortably seated for the final stretch of the journey. Harrugh caught a glimpse of the towers of the Veiled Skies silhouetted against the sky. The high-pitched whine of a grav-motor passed overhead and a sleek skimmer trailing the colors of the Cresting Dunes raced away in the direction of the palatial complex, no doubt on some urgent business of their clan.

"You should have taken one of those on your pilgrimage into the desert," observed Ashalla wryly. "I'm sure one of the emirs would have been happy to loan you one."

"That rather defeats the object of a harvest pilgrimage."

"I know, but then you might have got back in time to help clear up the mess you left behind."

Another gentle rebuke. He deserved it, he knew he did. It didn't make it any less uncomfortable.

FOUR

The dazzling sunlight winked out as the magrail descended beneath the surface of the sled-city and into the sub-level. The massive structure was a warren of air circulators, coolant sinks, power relays and bulk cisterns, storage for the water demands of the mobile city as it traversed the sands. It was also home to the communities of less influential clans who tended to the more elementary needs of Raffir, as well as where the clanless gathered. All in all, there was a thriving trade in illicit goods and services.

The train turned a long, gentle corner before sliding to a stop at a platform illuminated by strip lights and the occasional shaft of natural sunlight that found its way in through thrumming ventilator shafts in the ceiling. "Here we are," Ashalla announced, stepping out of the carriage with Harrugh in tow. The air smelled dry and dusty. The low grind of Raffir's motion trembled the steel bones of the city beneath their feet. For a moment, Harrugh was transported back to his childhood in the slums where smells and sounds like this were commonplace.

"Here we are?" Harrugh echoed with a knowing look at his companion. "I would be fascinated to learn where we go from here, who we are going to see and, most of all, how you came to know them – anyone we might know from our youth?"

"I'm sure you would," Ashalla replied, setting off at a brisk pace, down a broad hall of gently soughing ducts. Hacan laborers crawled over and around the dizzying tangle, their clan colors proudly striping their coveralls. "And my answers would be, in this order, this way, a business associate and that it's a long story better told another time in a different place."

Harrugh noted the particular use of "business associate" rather than "friend", an important distinction in Hacan society as it was heavy with nuance. In this context it could mean anything from an individual with whom dealings were infrequent through to a potential rival with whom dealings were mutually beneficial. Based on their surroundings and Ashalla's tone, he suspected it leaned more toward the latter.

"Don't worry," Ashalla added, "we won't be meeting anyone we once knew today."

"I should hope not," Harrugh said. "We wouldn't want anyone to recognize me."

They turned from the hall of ducts, passing down several avenues of sub-level habitats, each bearing the sigil of the Crying Wind. Outside, a pair of clan-mothers dutifully watched over an obedient mob of fidgeting kits as they were instructed by a mentor on the particulars of hierarchy.

One of the youngsters turned their way and Harrugh gave him a sly wink before wiggling his eyebrows beneath the saqq. The child giggled before being called out for inattention. They turned another corner, and the ubiquitous rumble was joined by the rolling hubbub of a busy plaza. The place was designated as Shallow Market, according to an illuminated sign suspended between a pair of thick stanchions.

"Everything is different," Harrugh stated as he looked over the bustling space.

"And yet everything is the same," Ashalla replied. "It's just easier to pick up things that are a little more…"

"Illegal?" Harrugh interrupted.

"I was going to say exotic. Words *matter*, Harrugh."

"We're simply going back to our roots." Harrugh smiled softly.

"Can you imagine what we might have become had we stayed in places like this?"

"Well, our past experiences certainly make navigating *places like this* easier."

"Words *matter*, Ashalla," Harrugh said, his smile widening to a grin.

"Finally, you understand."

They pushed into the throng and Harrugh observed quickly that everything from the utilitarian to the frivolous appeared to be available. Vendors with stacks of respirators, filters and photo-goggles bartered their wares alongside merchants offering sable-glass beads, Rost silk and salt sculptures. The majority of the population were native Hacan, but a few humans, scaly hunched Xxcha and even a Hylar in a gurgling environment suit mingled among the shifting crowd. The entire market was illuminated from below by the cool blue-green glow of covered algae beds irrigated by water flushed from the habitation recycling. It suffused the vaulted space like a cave and Harrugh was reminded of subterranean galleries he had explored during his pilgrimage.

They passed a group of clanless mercenaries playing Triora with a worn pack of cards, then left the Shallow Market behind. The open hall narrowed into a series of rattling walkways and stairwells. Two floors down they turned into what appeared to be a service tunnel lined with mesh doors, some of which were daubed with names. Ashalla headed toward one of the doors that had the words Bhagrra's Place boldly displayed in uneven lettering on a panel above the entry.

She paused outside, peering at Harrugh from beneath her saqq. "Hopefully Bhagrra will be able to help with our little mystery."

"Without cost?" Harrugh gave her a skeptical look.

"Of course not, but you don't need to worry yourself about that."

"I shall endeavor not to."

"And keep that scarf up. Try to be less… Harrugh."

"This was your idea."

"I know." She sighed, pushing the door open. Harrugh followed her in.

The space inside felt like a repurposed maintenance cavity, not even large enough to house a modest clan group. Part of it had been sectioned off with surprisingly ostentatious shutters painted in red and gold. Most of the room was given over to a motley array of workbenches, cabinets and what looked like the stacked remains of auto processors and savants. A stretch of wall paneling had been stripped away, and a tangle of wires and conduits were spliced into the systems beyond.

A figure in heavy overalls turned from the workbench as they entered to reveal narrow, feline features beneath a hood of faded blue. The amber fur on one side of the face was creased with pale scars pulling the mouth up into a toothy, perpetual half-smile. Bhagrra looked his guests up and down before grinning.

"Ashalla Kar," he purred. He set down what looked like a heavily modified data drill and wiped his hands on a nearby rag, which largely served to make him even grubbier. "And this is?"

"A friend," Ashalla replied smoothly, her posture betraying nothing.

"Bhagrra is always interested in making new friends, particularly friends with influence. Come, come, no need to be shy, be at your ease and tell Bhagrra of your need."

The scarred Hacan spread his arms in a gesture of welcome, his gaze lingering briefly on Harrugh before he returned his attention to Ashalla. "Always a pleasure to be of service to prestigious clientele. Good for Bhagrra's reputation. Good for business."

"We need to look up an orbital registry," Ashalla stated. "One that would no longer be listed in the active records. For all we know it might have been scrapped, but if it hasn't…" She paused and gave a sly smile. "I'm sure you have a way of identifying it for us, Bhagrra."

"A lost orbital!" His delight was evident. "How *intriguing*!"

Bhagrra sifted through several partially disassembled savants before selecting one. Cables trailed from its open back, snaking into the exposed wall systems. He tapped at the screen with one claw a few times and then looked back at his guests.

"Bhagrra can help you find your lost orbital." The scarred Hacan beamed. "You know my stock, now we must talk terms."

Ashalla forestalled his pitch with a raised finger. "You can't be sure we will be able to find anything. As I said, it may have been stripped for parts, so there will be nothing there to find. I'm not going to pay for information on nothing."

"Ashalla Kar wounds Bhagrra," the Hacan replied with a mask of indignation. "Bhagrra will have given Ashalla Kar his valuable time and is not absence still an answer itself, hmmm?"

"If we find the information we are looking for," Ashalla countered, "then I will consider your debt paid in full." Bhagrra's eyes widened fractionally but he otherwise kept his expression carefully neutral. "If we do not, then for your time and the knowledge that the orbital has likely been scrapped…"

"Bhagrra would like to learn more of your friend," he interrupted. "Yes. If your orbital is gone, that is Bhagrra's price for his time. No more. No less."

She hesitated for a few moments, clearly cautious of risking Harrugh's identity – but hopeful that she would not have to. "Deal."

Bhagrra grinned again and he and Ashalla briefly touched hands, his turned toward the floor, hers toward the ceiling, to seal the agreement. Harrugh had accrued a small library of questions over the last few moments but decided that it was wiser to hold his tongue for now. The information broker had clearly taken an interest in his identity, that much was clear. What was more troubling was what value that knowledge might have.

Bhagrra, who now seemed entirely too pleased with his own cleverness, tapped away on the screen of the savant for a few seconds before fishing around in his coveralls for a data crystal, snapping it into a port that looked far from standard. Lines of text and numerals scrolled across the display before pausing at an open query. The cursor blinked invitingly.

"What is the registry of the orbital that you are seeking, Ashalla Kar?"

She glanced at Harrugh, who pulled the bundle containing the data vault from his pack, removing it from its wrappings. At his touch the numbers obligingly streamed across its surface again and Bhagrra watched in obvious fascination.

A synthesized voice began to speak from the vault. *"Your memory will be your guide…"*

"Bhagrra!" Ashalla spoke sharply over the top of the voice. The information broker's gaze snapped to her with irritation. "What do you think of the data vault?"

"Bhagrra thinks he would very much like to be able to study it. Looks like nanotech. Very advanced. Very expensive. Bhagrra would like to know where Ashalla Kar and her friend found such a thing."

"It was a gift." Her reply was nonchalant.

Bhagrra gave her a skeptical look. "Then Bhagrra would like to meet this giver of mighty gifts. Very much."

"That wasn't part of our deal, Bhagrra."

The information broker's expression soured and he returned his attention to the savant, diligently tapping in the registry details listed on the data vault held tightly in Harrugh's grasp. More figures streamed past on the display, fading eventually to be replaced by a single, flashing entry.

"It would seem your orbital has not been scrapped, Ashalla Kar," Bhagrra said, gesturing to the screen. "Belongs to Kamdorn waystation five-nine-four. Early platform. Used for near-space cargo relay, mass freight conveyance, off-world storage. That sort of thing. Not many still around."

"So, what are they used for now?"

Bhagrra shrugged. "Whatever the owner wants to use them for. Kenara is the busiest trade hub in the galaxy. Lots of orbitals, lots of stations. Hard to keep track. Some emirs use them as neutral space for contracts, talking terms or off-world trading they want to keep out of sight of other clans. The emirates won't tolerate pirates in-system, and the clever trader knows that chaos is bad for business, so they're not lawless. But not exactly lawful either." He chuckled.

"Who bought that waystation?" Ashalla asked.

He shrugged again. "Don't know. People with aurei to buy stations either want others to know that it's theirs or they don't. Both have aurei to make sure that happens. Purchase was recent though, not so long before the *departure* of our infamous Quieron."

"Five-nine-four," Ashalla muttered, maintaining her neutral expression. She scratched her nose thoughtfully. "Five-nine-four." She was quiet for a few moments, the silence of the room disturbed only by the soft chattering of the machines and the ubiquitous rumble of Raffir. Harrugh saw the light of recognition dawn in her eyes.

"The Gloaming!" she exclaimed.

The orbital register of waystation five-nine-four vanished from the display on the data vault to be replaced by several much longer strings of numbers.

"*That's correct, Ashalla Kar, the Gloaming. You are going to need…*" The grating, synthesized voice of the hrrtos was abruptly muted to a muffled buzz as Harrugh hastily stuffed the vault into the depths of his pack.

Bhagrra's gaze followed the artifact into the bag and then returned to Ashalla. "You have always brought Bhagrra the most *interesting* things, Ashalla Kar, but I believe that might be the most interesting thing you have ever brought. That and your friend. A pity that Bhagrra will not also have the chance to become his friend."

"Our business is done, Bhagrra, as agreed." She paused, studying the broker carefully. "And as promised, I consider your debt repaid in full." She glanced at Harrugh, her fierce gaze indicating they needed to leave as soon as possible. "Sun follow your steps, Bhagrra."

"And yours also, Ashalla Kar."

They retreated from Bhagrra's Place, closing the door behind them. The information broker watched them go, resuming the task of tidying the small workshop even as he listened to their footfalls retreat down the rattling steel walkway of the corridor outside.

It was true that Ashalla Kar had always brought him the most interesting puzzles and requests, but for her to surrender the debt she held over him meant that the information he had retrieved had to have some value. If not to her, then certainly to her interesting friend. While he had remained silent and concealed throughout the exchange and had done his best to slouch nonchalantly, it was virtually impossible to conceal the stance and bearing of one used to authority.

Bhagrra snapped the data crystal from the savant, tucking it away in his coveralls before tapping the comm-bead in his ear. "It's Bhagrra." A pause. "Bhagrra would not be speaking to you if it was not." Another, longer pause. "Of course. Something of interest will soon be on its way to the Gloaming. And someone. Bhagrra knows you have an interest in both." A slow smile spread across his face.

"Of course I haven't spoken to anybody else."

FIVE

It was late by the time they returned to Ashalla's apartment, the magtrain sliding through Raffir as dusk closed in and the city came alive once again with evening light. They took a brief detour so that Harrugh could reclaim his effects. He had surprisingly little to his name for one who had risen to the highest echelons of the Emirates. A savant, ambassador translator and comm-bead, a small box of accolades awarded throughout the years, favored articles of clothing, a pouch of galactic aurei and local tercet, a richly embroidered saqq and a long dune spear with a notched blade. This last item was retrieved with the greatest reverence.

The archaic weapon was somewhat incongruous in the confines of the train and drew more than one curious look, but Harrugh would never have left it behind with an uncertain journey ahead. He ran a claw through the gouge in the spearhead, glancing over at Ashalla. They had spent the bulk of the trip in silence, keen to discuss their findings, but reluctant to do so in public.

"Do you trust him?" Harrugh finally asked as they approached the embassies.

"Before today I would have said yes." Harrugh frowned at her response, and she continued, "Oh, don't misunderstand me. Bhagrra is as mercenary as they come and would sell you out in an instant unless the agreed terms very clearly stated otherwise. You live and die by your reputation in his line of business. Now that his debt is cleared, anything we said and anything he saw is a commodity and he will turn it into profit if he can find an interested buyer."

"There's no reason why anybody would be looking for us." It seemed to be a half-question and Harrugh glanced around the train.

Ashalla shrugged. "Perhaps not specifically, but like it or not, you *are* a person of interest and even with your face covered…"

"There's opportunity everywhere." They spoke the aphorism in unison.

They re-entered the apartment, Harrugh immediately checking the door was locked behind them. He retrieved the presently silent data vault, setting it down on the low table. Ashalla fetched fresh goblets of water, and they spent a long moment in companionable silence sipping the cool liquid. When they were done, he once again unwrapped the artifact, placing a hand on its cool surface. The long number strings danced across the display once again as the audio crackled into life.

"That's correct, Ashalla Kar, the Gloaming. You are going to need a ship and a crew if you are to take the steps necessary to prevent the coming disaster and you will find both on waystation five-nine-four. Ample funds to aid in this task have been transferred to your commercial account, Harrugh. Once you have secured both the ship and crew, the coordinates I have supplied will be your destination. It is imperative that you secure Icon."

Harrugh growled a curse under his breath, pacing a circle around the room.

"If you are cursing my lineage right now, Harrugh Gefhara, I already told you: some truths cannot simply be told, they must be learned."

Harrugh glowered at the device, his jaw clenched as if daring it to continue. It didn't, and the synthesized voice of the hrrtos lapsed into silence. Ashalla was already entering the coordinates into a galactic map on her savant and intently studying the results.

"Another orbital?" Harrugh growled.

"No," Ashalla replied and entered the coordinates again, checking carefully as she did so. "It's nowhere."

"Of course it is," Harrugh snarled bitterly. Somehow, he'd expected nothing else.

"Well, it's not strictly nowhere, it's a spot on the coreward edge of Nekro space, between the Ghost Worlds and Cormund, but there's nothing there. What's the Icon?"

"If I had any sort of idea, I would tell you," he snapped, then regretted his tone. Harrugh strode across the room, pulling the balcony doors open to allow the warm air and evening sounds of the city to drift in. Then he prowled up and down the balcony before gripping the rail hard enough that his claws left gouges in the metal. He heard Ashalla step out onto the balcony and turned to face her, his expression dark.

"I don't know where this leads. I have no answers. I know nothing about the Prophet's Tears, just more mysterious instructions. Ordinian was overrun by the Nekro Virus years ago." He shuddered, thinking of the cybernetic beings who were determined to eliminate all biological life. "I have no wish to enter a place under their jurisdiction. That's a long way to go into hostile territory when there's nothing there to be found! And how did the hrrtos know that you would be there? The message addressed you directly!"

"It must have known that you would come to me for help eventually. I was a little worried the message might not play again after you hid it away from Bhagrra."

"You didn't sell him as a trustworthy type, no matter how curious I might have been to hear the message." Harrugh sighed, and some of his anger bled out into the deepening evening. "I hate this, Ash'ka. I feel like I am being used. Like the hrrtos is around every corner, watching me." He growled softly. "It's all absurd and I am being a fool." He turned to face her. "But what it showed me, that image, it haunts me. Our world, our people, burning. It was *real*.

     Twilight Imperium

I can't tell you how I know that, but it was. When will it happen? Tomorrow?"

Ashalla lifted one of her hands to brush lightly against Harrugh's cheek and she looked at him intently. "So go as far as the Gloaming – that isn't far. It's an old trade station. From what Bhagrra said, it's unregulated. That means it's likely to have all sorts of freelancers and private interests." Harrugh pressed his face into her palm for a moment and slowly started to relax again.

After a moment or two, he spoke. "Why is it called the Gloaming? You sounded like you knew it?"

"I do, though not well. It was some years ago now, when it was still officially in use by the emirate. Brokering an agreement between… oh, I forget. It was nothing special. I think the name is a human word – it means 'the light at the end of the day' or something like that."

"They only have one word for that?"

"They have a few, I think."

"How limited."

"As I said before, so direct!" They both laughed and the last of Harrugh's anger and frustration faded. "I'll be coming with you, of course. You will never manage without me." Ashalla offered up her terms easily and couched them in humor. This snapped Harrugh back to anxiety and he shook his head, looking at her with a level gaze.

"You've done enough already. There's absolutely no need for you to get wrapped up in this nonsense."

"Too late for that. I already *am* wrapped up in 'this nonsense', as you put it." She glanced back into the room where the data vault still sat on the table. "From the message we just heard, I think I was probably a part of it right from the start."

"You have responsibilities here. I won't ask you to abandon the emirate because I'm busy chasing ghosts."

"Harrugh." She pulled back her hood and returned his gaze.

"Stop it. You don't have to ask and no, I don't have responsibilities. Not really. Not anymore. And from what you have said, this will be serving the best interests of the emirate anyway. If Hercant dies, we all die."

Harrugh removed his saqq, his expression becoming pensive. "It was me, wasn't it?" He'd figured it out a while ago, but other matters had been more pressing. Now, he revealed his thoughts. "It was me. The Quieron didn't keep you on her council because of me. Because I resigned."

"Tainted by association," Ashalla replied sourly. "The insults became quite creative by the end."

Harrugh winced. "And what of Carth? Have you heard from her?"

She didn't meet his gaze for a few heartbeats and eventually shook her head. "She went off-world not long after you left," she said. "I get an occasional savant message, but never anything more than an acknowledgment that she's still alive and still out there, no doubt causing trouble. Carth of the Golden Sands was never one to sit and mope, so she's off doing… Carth things." She sighed and, for a moment, the veneer of jollity slipped. "It's been lonely, I admit that. Without both of you here, life has been strange. I did feel abandoned by both of you in different ways. It was difficult, at times. But mostly it's been lonely."

Harrugh said nothing. Growing up in the slums together, Carth had always been the fire to Ashalla's sunlight while Harrugh stood as the balance between them. From little more than sand and scraps, they had taken on the world, survived the wars with the L1Z1X and, when the time had come, run an empire together. More than one consul had referred to the trio as the "clan of three" during Harrugh's time as Quieron. It was a seemingly unbreakable bond.

Then Harrugh had broken it.

He reached up to his necklace, a cheap, plain trinket which matched two others, and which represented a simpler time. Words of apology seemed insufficient.

She nudged him, the moment of sadness over as fleetingly as it had come on. "Oh, don't look so dour. It means you get the pleasure of my sparkling company on your hunt for ghosts." Ashalla beamed and the tension broke.

"Then I will be grateful for it," Harrugh replied, a smile that was only *partially* forced sliding back on to his features.

"Good! Then I shall get us some food. You can go and buy us passage off-world and then we should both get some sleep. We can head to the spaceport in the morning."

"Sounds like a plan," Harrugh said, heading back inside and pulling closed the balcony doors. The din of the night market became muffled and distant. Ashalla held up a finger and waved a claw at him.

"There's a stipulation, of course."

"Anything," he replied.

"Tonight, I am sleeping in my own bed. You get the floor."

The smile on Harrugh's face became real. "I can do that," he said.

PART TWO
DECISIONS

SIX

Learning where the hrrtos had wanted him to go was challenging, but not as much as actually figuring out a way to get there. No commercial flights to unlisted, decommissioned orbitals could be found – small surprise. Harrugh then searched through private charter shuttles one hangar at a time, aware about the associated costs with securing passage to an unregistered location. There was nothing technically illegal about visiting privately owned interplanetary interests – but pilots prepared to make those journeys knew their clients were likely desperate. Thus it was, many hours after he'd started his search, that Harrugh found a pilot who was willing to take them for a non-negotiable exorbitant transit fee.

That small ship departed Hercant in the early morning hours filled to capacity, mostly with unmarked cargo. Harrugh, his hood drawn up, felt claustrophobic. He'd never been particularly fond of space travel, preferring the reassuring solidity of the earth beneath his feet and the wind on his face. It had been one of the few aspects of being Quieron he had actually enjoyed – as leader of the Emirates he had rarely had reason to travel beyond Hercant and fewer reasons still to leave Kenara. Those journeys had been far more luxurious and infinitely more comfortable.

Harrugh winced inwardly, aware of how privileged he had become. He looked around at the assortment of passengers on board the shuttle – about twenty Hacan from various sects of society. One mother with two young kits in tow was reassuring the smallest that everything would be all right, that they would meet their father at the waystation. Another, a young male without clan colors and the bearing of a mercenary. Most appeared to be traders of some description. There was no obvious nobility aboard, but then Harrugh would have been suspicious if there had. The most influential clans maintained their own fleets of differing sizes, and it was unlikely they would be leaving Hercant on a charter flight to somewhere like the Gloaming.

Nobody paid him much attention. Ashalla, on the other hand, engaged with effortless ease with everyone on board. She entertained the kits for a while by teaching them a song and their mother was clearly relieved for the respite. One of the traders, an older Hacan female with graying fur around her muzzle, joined in the song with gusto much to the apparent annoyance of the mercenary. Every so often Harrugh would find the clanless warrior's eyes lingering on him and, made uncomfortable by the scrutiny, turned away. He couldn't decide whether the examination was out of recognition or simple curiosity. *Either*, Harrugh thought, was *equally unsettling*.

The trip was not overlong but, in the cramped confines of the shuttle and without the comforts afforded by larger vessels, it felt like a lifetime. It came as something of a relief when the outer edges of waystation five-nine-four hove into view, silhouetted against the sandy arc of Kamdorn. The space surrounding the station was surprisingly busy for an unlisted orbital and Harrugh counted the running lights of a dozen frigate-sized vessels as well as the looming bulk of a cruiser. The larger ships were gravity-tethered to massive pylons projecting from the station, while smaller craft such as their own were received within the yawning, floodlit docks opening out into the void. The Gloaming was no decrepit and broken orbital. It flourished.

As their shuttle closed with its destination, the waystation swelled to fill the viewports until it was a towering cliff of scarred and pitted steel. The ship lurched as it passed into the gravity envelope of the orbital and for just a moment Harrugh felt a static frisson crawl across his fur as they cleared the shields. One of the kits let out an alarmed squeak and the mother knelt to reassure the child while Ashalla distracted the other. She pointed out features like weapon turrets, air locks and a maintenance crew in their bulky space suits.

"We will soon be inside, little ones," Ashalla assured them. "Here. Come and see!" She moved aside to allow the smaller of the two to get a better view and the mother gave her a tired smile, grateful for her gesture.

The shuttle slid into the bright illumination of the dock, coming to rest with a lurch, the engines whining as they cycled down. It was a few moments before the ramp folded open with a hiss, letting in the noise and bustle of the station and releasing the passengers from their confinement. The mother gathered her children to her and was quickly down the ramp to meet a surprisingly official-looking deck officer – clearly someone who had great control on the waystation and monitored who came and went. The traders began hauling their goods out for inspection. Harrugh had not known what to expect from the Gloaming based on what little Bhagrra had been able to tell them. He was certainly startled to find it ran with at least some semblance of formality and efficiency. Whoever owned the Gloaming clearly wielded a great amount of wealth and power.

"Please state your business on waystation five-nine-four?" The officer had moved on from the mother to the clanless warrior. The young Hacan's eyes narrowed, the end of his tail flicking in poorly concealed agitation.

"Mercenary," he said, barking out the one word as though the dockmaster were stupid. If he had been hoping that the aggression and bluster would intimidate the officer, he was sorely mistaken. The bravado was met with a cool stare and an easy, nonchalant tone.

"Martial trade is restricted to the plazas on finial decks five and six. We have station enforcers ensuring this remains true. You are, of course, free to carry your weapons about the station but any contracts or accords, written or otherwise, not documented by a recognized broker will be considered void by the Waystation Orbital Authority."

Fascinating. Harrugh tried to control his interest. Whatever underworld leader ran the waystation certainly ensured it operated with a militaristic ambiance.

The warrior bared his teeth, but the officer remained apparently unperturbed. "Or in other words, start no trouble and you will have no trouble."

He stepped aside and the young Hacan stalked away with only a brief backward glance. The officer shook his head in a tiny, barely perceptible motion before moving up to address Harrugh and Ashalla.

"Welcome. Please state your business on waystation five-nine-four," he said, barely glancing up from the screen of his savant. He was about Harrugh's age at an estimate, clad in a plain uniform of dark blue fabric. His lapel sported a pin of unfamiliar design.

"Commerce and private charter," said Ashalla. "We're not planning on staying long."

"Primary commercial hubs are on nadir eighteen through finial twenty-seven, enjoy your stay." He was about to call the next passenger forward but chose that moment to actually look up for more than a moment. His eyes met Harrugh's and widened in recognition. Flustered at coming face to face with a Quieron – former or otherwise – of his people, the officer opened his mouth to speak. Harrugh gave a brief, fleeting smile, interrupting the flow of words before they started.

"Thank you, officer. You're doing good work here." He raised one finger carefully to his mouth as a gesture that he would appreciate nothing further being said. The deck officer, clearly overwhelmed, nodded silently. Harrugh nodded his appreciation and the pair moved on.

It was a good few seconds before they heard a shaky "Next!" called from behind them.

"Well," said Ashalla, linking her arm through Harrugh's companionably. "You certainly made *his* day."

"This location is of great interest to me," said Junior as they wove through the trading plaza level twenty-seven. "I have not experienced such an industrious hive of activity since…" He paused, as though the required calculation was excessively complex or lacked key data, and shook his head. "Since… my apologies. I can't tell you how long."

"A long time is enough, Junior." Tai had been trying, with uncharacteristic patience, to get the Titan to communicate in a less formal manner. He'd experienced a modicum of success, too – the synthetic being had gone from speaking in formalized cadence to sprinkling in a few contractions here and there.

"Indeed, friend Tai," acknowledged the Titan. "While the chronology is uncertain, a long time would certainly be accurate by biological standards." His faceplate cycled through shades of green and violet as he absorbed the sights and sounds – not to mention the aromas – prevalent throughout the market. The vast space was one of the waystation's original service halls which had been converted for use. Now, it was a press of brokers, travelers and tradesfolk who sometimes engaged in pernicious transactions.

The Naaz-Rokha were no strangers to the place and neither, it seemed, were a number of the great species of the galaxy. Among the prevalence of the Hacan, they had already encountered many humans, several gem-adorned Winnu, a band of haughty Letnev freelancers, a Saar selling star charts to supposedly lost relic worlds, and a particularly abrasive N'orr preaching about the coming of the many who are one.

The noise was tumultuous – something which no doubt helped to mask the clandestine exchanges taking place on the fringes of the hall. Dart and Tai rarely engaged in less than reputable dealings. As Tai was fond of pointing out when required, reputation was sometimes a matter of perspective.

Rarely, of course, did not mean *ever*.

"We need to find a buyer to shift this… whatever it is," said Dart, sniffing the air as they passed a food vendor. The serving Hacan had packets of dried meat and noodles displayed in front of a pot of bubbling hot water. Dart's stomach grumbled, hungry for any kind of food, and he tore his gaze away from the vendor. He patted the pouch he wore at his waist. "After everything we went through to get it, it'd better be worth something *really* impressive."

"It will be, Dart, don't you worry," said Tai, cheerful as always. "But we need to be cautious with our choice of sales partner. We don't know much about these artifacts. If we were to accidentally trade them to…" He tailed off.

"What is your concern, friend Tai?" Junior, who was attracting many curious stares, stopped walking. "You achieved the acquisition of those relics after much hard work, not to mention a lot of running. I was previously unaware that archaeology was so athletic, but I find it fascinating."

Junior found a lot of things fascinating.

"It's less a concern about the legitimacy of acquiring something," said Dart, filling in when Tai didn't immediately reply. "When you find old stuff, Junior, there are sometimes people who believe they have a right to that stuff more than you. Everybody has their own way of doing things. It *may* be – and I stress the *may* – because it's not always the case. It may be that these things we picked up would be viewed by some as belonging to the world on which we found 'em and should've been left there."

Junior cogitated on this statement for a little while and then nodded his understanding. "They would believe you had stolen the artifact?"

"'Stolen' is a very ugly word," murmured Tai, feigning an entirely unconvincing look of shock. "Besides, it was a necropolis. Everybody there was dead. They didn't need their things anymore, right?" He patted Dart on the shoulder. "Look over there." Coiled beneath an elegant banner of blue and white toward the edge of the plaza was a Druaa. Her sinuous body coiled about itself, the violet scales and cerulean crest catching in the artificial light as she haggled deftly with a customer. There was an intriguing and esoteric collection of objects arrayed on elegant plinths of what appeared to be glass or crystal. Their words could not be heard, but the Druaa appeared to have the upper hand in the negotiations. Tai's practiced eye roamed over the wares and he could identify curios from several different cultures across the galaxy.

More importantly, he watched aurei change hands as her current customer purchased one of the items on offer. An impressively *large* sum of aurei, if the Hacan's expression was anything to go by. The Druaa was certainly not short of physical currency and that key point was exactly what Tai was interested in right now. They had spent the last of their funds buying passage to the station, now they needed to turn their most recent acquisitions into capital to fund their onward journey to the next promising site. Life was good for the Naaz-Rokha, but it was also expensive at times.

"She looks ideal," Tai asserted.

"As long as she isn't like the last Druaa," observed Dart.

Junior turned from his contemplation of life aboard the station. Everything here was so vibrant and dynamic. The proto-Titan's appetite for knowledge was insatiable, and that included every plant, species, sight and sound he could experience. For nonsynthetic lifeforms, there was a true risk of sensory overload. For Junior, it was a splash in the ocean.

"What happened with the last Druaa, friend Dart?" Junior's curious voice cut across the exchange and Tai's expression darkened momentarily.

"This is one of those things, Junior," he said in his high-pitched voice, "that is very, very definitely left unsaid."

"Let's just call it The Incident," added Dart. "And let it drop there. Are you sure, Tai?"

"I'm very sure. Once we sell this stuff, we won't…" He trailed off, not wanting to complete the sentence at the time when Junior was watching and listening so intently. *We won't have to worry about it anymore.* Over the past months, they had both grown rather fond of the strange Titan and it seemed the feeling was mutual. He did not want to give Junior any reason to mistrust them, naive though he appeared to be.

"We won't have to worry about funding our next adventure." Dart filled in the brief pause with practiced ease. The pair had been bonded for long enough that they sometimes finished one another's sentences, but usually with Tai starting and Dart ending. It was safer that way.

"That's right. Druaa outside the Collective don't like to stop in one place for too long, so she isn't likely to ask too many questions about where we picked up our latest finds and be on her way before any…"

"Before any of the dead people come looking for their lost treasures." Dart once again interjected the end of the sentence with adroit tact.

"That feels statistically improbable," Junior said, feeling helpful.

"Exactly," Tai agreed. "Therefore, there's absolutely nothing to worry about."

Dart looked longingly at the open-sided bar set into the coreward wall of the plaza. He would rather be there, filling his stomach with whatever smelled so delicious than negotiating with an itinerant merchant, but Tai was already settling back into the harness. He rarely dismounted when bargaining, acutely aware that his diminutive stature didn't lend itself to an air of authority. From up here, he could hold court more effectively. Sighing as his stomach gurgled yet again, Dart returned his attention to the Druaa.

Tai patted his shoulder companionably. "Business first. There will be plenty of time for leisure after. I know you hate this bit, my friend, but you know how we must play this. Everything will be just fine."

"Yeah," said Dart, with a hint of incredulity. He jostled a pair of Hacan coming the other way and mumbled his apologies before heading for the Druaa. "What could possibly go wrong?"

Junior trailed after them, pausing every now and then to study something new and exciting that entered his field of vision. He, at least, was having a *great* time. He overheard Dart's last statement and turned his attention to his friend.

"If my understanding is correct, an unknown variable within Druaa physiology has granted the species a degree of telepathy that would be disadvantageous to negotiations," Junior remarked as they made their way through the crowd. "That could make things go wrong."

"Very true, Junior," Tai replied, cheerfully. Dart let out a low groan.

Junior paid no heed and continued, "Then the logical conclusion would be that a Druaa would be a suboptimal choice of bargaining partner."

"That would also be true," Tai agreed, "except that firstly, they expect to have the upper hand, and secondly…"

"Secondly, we're not just one mind." Dart finished the statement with a wry smile. "I imagine it's like trying to read two savants at once."

"Reading two savants that are telling entirely different stories," Tai agreed.

"Where one of them has all the words run together in a single sentence," Dart grumbled.

"And the other one has loads of words simply missing!" Tai finished, gleeful.

"Fascinating," Junior remarked.

SEVEN

"Staring is unbecoming, Ashalla." Harrugh's tone was so much like that of a clan-father that she laughed aloud before shaking herself and matching his stride once again. She indicated over her shoulder with a nod.

"Was that a *Titan*?"

"It was," said Harrugh, casting his own brief glance backward. "But small by their standards. I've only encountered one of their kind before, but there's definitely something *different* here." He was thoughtful for a moment. "The Titans have an affinity for living things and habitats that a lot of species could learn from, at least if they could look beyond their politics and ambitions, anyway."

"That's uncommonly insightful for you," Ashalla replied. "But I think most of them are preoccupied with threats to their borders or threatening the borders of others to take an interest in cultivating paradise worlds, even if they were inclined to."

"Cynical, but true enough unfortunately. That's why we're here after all," Harrugh replied. He reconsidered the Titan and the Naaz-Rokha companions as they crossed the market. An ember of an idea began to glow in the back of his mind. "That group might be worth following up with later. We still don't know exactly what we're going to find here, and we especially might need insight if we decide to go to the final, suggested destination. A Titan's insight and analytical abilities could be invaluable, especially in Nekro space."

"And the Naaz-Rokha?"

"I can appreciate their perspective on harmonious co-existence. The galaxy knows they're excellent travelers. Once we find someone with the skills to analyze this artifact, we can hunt them down, if they're still here. A Titan will be hard to miss." He paused and then studied the Druaa along with the other traders crowding the area. "These are small-time traders. I don't think we'll get the help or discretion we need here."

She pondered this statement and rubbed at the back of her neck thoughtfully. "There should be an index toward the central hub. Any significant interests will want to advertise their presence to make their business worthwhile."

"Advertise?" He looked skeptical. "Here?"

"It's a private interest, Harrugh. Not a den of pirates."

They pushed their way through the bustling crowd toward the coreward transit tunnels that led deeper into the station. Ashalla stopped several times to remark on particular curiosities or examples of outstanding finery which Harrugh absently acknowledged. While they were just two Hacan among the multitude, his hackles hadn't sat well since they arrived. He couldn't escape the real – and pressing – sensation that they were being watched. The unwelcome memory of his last days following the hrrtos's unexpected appearance within the palace bobbed to the surface of his thoughts. He tugged the fringe of his saqq lower to further obscure his features.

As they reached the edge of the trade floor, the crowd began to thin. The pair moved from the open space and into the corridors radiating like spokes from the central column at the heart of the waystation. Machine shops, gambling dens and drinking holes lined the transitway tucked into maintenance spaces or repurposed storage silos. Just like at the dock, Harrugh had to admit that he hadn't expected the unlisted station to be as orderly as it appeared. While they had witnessed more than one heated exchange and an open brawl between two groups of humans, uniformed peacekeepers in the same deep blue of the deck officer had been quick to arrive and restore order.

They arrived at the clamorous freight hub, where industrial gravity-lifters ferried bulk cargo from the finial levels at the top of the station down to the nadir levels in its bowels. Scrolling displays advertised the names of major mercenary companies, mercantile cartels and trade interests influential enough to warrant the attention.

Harrugh scanned the names for a few moments. "That's more promising," he said, inclining his head toward one of the larger names. "The Ral Nel Consortium. They would be a perfect start."

Ashalla nodded in agreement. "If anybody is going to be able to give any insight into your unusual gifts, it's the Ral Nel. Bhagrra did let slip that he thought the vault was nanotech after all. That's definitely Ral Nel business."

"Nadir Level Eighteen." Harrugh glanced at the conveyors. "Looks like we're going down. I don't suppose you happen to have a contact within the Consortium? That would be helpful." He grinned, a wicked expression that made her eyes widen in surprise. "You apparently appear to know everybody, after all."

"Oh, *please*, Harrugh. I hope not," she retorted. "If I did, how would I ever meet anybody new?"

They stepped into the conveyor, pressed in on all sides by bulk containers and other travelers. Harrugh thought he caught a glimpse of the mercenary from the shuttle, but then the conveyor lurched, and they were lost from view.

"Besides," she continued, "the Ral Nel are a relatively new power. Strange they should be lurking down in the nadir levels."

Harrugh nodded before lapsing into a moody silence, the unsettling notion that they were being followed crystallizing into a disturbing certainty.

• • •

Nadir Level Eighteen was less populous and less vibrant than the central and finial levels. The freight conveyor hummed to a stop amidst a fug of stale air, acrid propellant fumes, and the pervading grind of overworked purifiers. Harrugh and Ashalla stepped off the conveyer, looking around at the dimly lit atrium. A gruff-looking Saar in a lumbering bipedal cargo walker stomped past and began unloading boxes without giving them a second glance.

"Well, this is cozy and welcoming," Ashalla observed.

A broad transit corridor stretched away from the atrium, its pale strip lighting yellowed and flickering in sections. Radiating away into the gloom, several smaller, dingy tunnels could be seen. The small groups clustering around the edges of the chamber either huddled together, stealing furtive glances at each other and newcomers, or stood brashly as if challenging anybody to approach.

"Not exactly the sort of place I would expect to find the agent of a galactic consortium," Harrugh observed, scanning the signs and smudged displays of commodity prices. His gaze fell upon a decidedly garish advertisement directing viewers in the direction of one of the claustrophobic passages. "And yet..."

Services of the Ral Nel Consortium, the sign announced.

Ashalla shrugged one shoulder in an indifferent manner, and the pair made their way into the dim confines of a warren of passages. Thermal bleed from thrumming plasma sinks lining the ceiling made the air close and hot. Moisture collected on the walls and pipes, gathering in pools beneath their feet as they splashed through the gloom.

There was the sound of an exchange coming from up ahead. One of the voices was a low, bass rumble whilst the other was a much higher-pitched and decidedly strident staccato. "Sounds like we may have found our..." Ashalla began, but Harrugh abruptly stopped walking and held out his hand.

She stumbled to a stop, giving him an enquiring look. The

exchange ahead continued unabated but Harrugh caught the telltale splash of water, too pronounced to be anything other than somebody in the tunnel behind them.

"This is not a good place for a fight, Harrugh," Ashalla murmured, catching onto his caution. He nodded in agreement and glanced back the way they had come. Several figures prowled in the shadows, their eyes shining in the dim light.

"There has to be more than one way out of here, and if there isn't, that can be a problem for later." He brought up his dune spear, aiming it toward the ceiling. The weapon's magnetic accelerator discharged with a *thump* of displaced air, puncturing the coolant conduit. Hot gas and fumes spewed into the narrow space, cutting them off from their pursuers, and the pair quickly seized the opportunity to hurry away.

They turned several corners, zigzagging around before doubling back and emerging into a service hub with several corridors stretching away in different directions. There was also an open crawl space that gusted blissful cool air. The chamber looked like it had been converted into a cross between a workshop, a laboratory and a techno-salon and was cluttered with unknown apparatus. The source of the argument they'd seen earlier also soon became apparent – Harrugh's use of his spear hadn't disrupted them a bit. A Ral Nel was perched on an overturned cargo crate, a savant clasped in one hand and a multitool in the other. Shorter than Harrugh by more than a head, the reptilian scales of its body glittered as it moved. Short, sharp gestures punctuated its words, and gave it a peculiar, jerky motion while bickering with a Hacan.

"You promised me fifty and you bring me twenty? That is not a good deal. No, no, that is not good at all," the Ral Nel said, its translator unit giving it a curious accent. "You bring me twenty, I give you less aurei, yes? Yes. Less aurei. Poor deal, poor deal. Ah, well. I'll pay what I think it's worth." The Ral Nel shook its head in an overly dramatic way and proffered the savant expectantly. The

Hacan pressed his own to it and a faint beep could be heard as a transaction was made.

"Nice doing business is what I am meant to say here, but eh. I don't think I do business with you again. No? Go now, bye-bye." The Ral Nel made an impatient shooing gesture with one hand and the Hacan slunk – for there was no better word to describe his demeanor – away with his tail quite literally between his legs. The Ral Nel turned shining, reptilian eyes on Harrugh and Ashalla and that one, single look judged them completely.

"You have business, come talk. You don't? Go away. Busy. I am very busy, yes?" The Ral Nel's scales rippled iridescently in the wan light as the creature busied itself around the workshop with a frenetic energy that looked exhausting. Spines stood on the elongated skull, rigid and unmoving, and more graced the jaw line that trembled as it spoke. The Ral Nel wore a tight-fitting tunic looped with a bandolier of esoteric devices, one of which it plucked out and scrutinized for a long moment before sliding it back into place. It settled down at a long bench and began working on one of the numerous devices that littered the workshop, examining it through a series of finely wrought lenses. Each magnification lens fell into position with an audible *click*.

"I can feel you staring, Hacan. Go away if not doing business. Hacan *clearly* bad at business." It turned its head a little. "Or does Izt'xet Alit Lo Masak scare the mighty Quieron of Kenara, hmm? Is that it?"

"You know who I am. That puts you at something of an advantage, my friend." Harrugh took a few steps forward and the Ral Nel laughed, a surprising sound for one who had thus far proven to be irascible.

"I know who you *were*, if that helps, yes?" The barb was sharp and even Ashalla winced. "I am Izt'xet Alit Lo Masak." It set down the precision tools it had been using and then swiveled on its seat to study them. "If that is too much of a mouthful, Izt will suffice.

And now you know his name, what can Izt'xet Alit Lo Masak do for you, Harrugh Gefhara?"

"Izt'xet Alit Lo Masak." Harrugh repeated the Ral Nel's name, stumbling over the unfamiliar syllables, but persevering, nonetheless. Protocol was vital when dealing with other species, even when he'd been chased by unknown pursuers and his identity easily leaked. "I need your help."

"Pffft." The noise was somewhere between a laugh and a snort. "Don't do *help*. I do *deals*, yes? You want something from me, I take something from you. Hacan know how this works. Or at least, I thought that true, once." It raised its voice at the still-departing previous customer. "Something for something, yes?" The Ral Nel chuckled again, amused by its own words, showing razor-sharp teeth. "You smell like trouble, Hacan. Maybe it follow you here. Maybe I *like* trouble. You want to make a deal? We talk."

"Yes," said Harrugh. Despite his initial misgivings, Izt'xet Alit Lo Masak seemed a great deal more trustworthy than Bhagrra. "Yes, we *have* some trouble." He glanced over his shoulder toward the tunnel they had entered through, but whoever had followed them did not show up. Perhaps they were simple bandits, seeing an opportunity and nothing more. "But I do want to deal, despite the trouble. What's more, I have the means to do so."

"We would prefer to conduct our business somewhere secure, Izt'xet Alit Lo Masak," said Ashalla, using the Ral Nel's full name as a sign of easy respect. "I mean no slight on your choice of locale, but we would rather avoid drawing the attention of your neighbors." She dropped a low and deferential bow. "Some of which are not far behind us. So, if you would be so kind." The reptilian eyes gleamed as it turned to look at her. The smile on its face grew even wider. It was an unmistakable smile of approval.

"Well, well. Your friend is clever, yes?" Izt sniffed. "Chose this spot because away from the noise and bustle, yes? Hard to get noticed, hard to concentrate. Also only get customers who make the effort, ready to deal, yes? You understand. What is your name, female Hacan?"

"I am Ashalla Kar," she replied. "There's a whole swathe of titles that go with it in a formal setting, but this is certainly not one of those, certainly not the time for it and believe you me, you won't thank me for it. And you, Izt'xet Alit Lo Masak? What is your preference – male, female, or another?"

"I like you, Ashalla Kar. You know how to speak. To answer your question, I am male Ral Nel." Izt tipped his head from one side to the other and scratched at the scales over one eye. Then he nodded emphatically. "We talk. But if Desert Wind thugs following? We leave here. Go to my ship. We can do business there if the mighty Quieron prefers. Is this acceptable? Yes? Think fast. Izt can easily make different deal with Desert Wind if take too long."

"Desert Wind?" Harrugh growled. What Hacan clan knew he was here? "It'll wait. Let's get to your ship immediately. And please don't call me Quieron."

He knew, even as he and Ashalla followed the Ral Nel out of the workshop, that Izt would miss no opportunity to do just that.

EIGHT

The Druaa had developed a tick in the corner of her left eye and massaged her scaly temple as she tried once again to make a reasonable assessment of the artifacts the Naaz-Rokha had presented.

"So, you see, it's a classic example of an early auramic alloy set with no fewer than six coronathysts…" Tai enthused.

"…which of course makes it quite the find when you think the earliest settlers…" Dart continued smoothly.

"…would have found these naturally occurring rather than creating them through gravitational compression…" Tai said.

"…so if you think about the effort that went into fashioning this piece alone, it has to be worth…"

"…at least double your previous offer." This last pronouncement came in perfect unison.

A silence settled across the little tableau. The Druaa glanced from one to the other and then back again, but the shining red eye and cybernetic gaze of the Naaz and the steady green stare of the Rokha gave nothing away. The tip of her serpentine tail twitched. When she finally opened her mouth to speak, the pair cut her off again.

"Now before you put the counteroffer out there, let me spare you the embarrassment by telling you that these relics are straight from a previously unexplored site." Tai began a fresh salvo.

"New to the market," Dart kept up.

"Untapped potential."

"An investment in the future."

"Aesthetically asymmetrical," Junior cut in.

Dart, Tai and the Druaa stared at the Titan.

"What Junior said," Tai continued.

"What Junior said," Dart agreed.

"So, what do you say?" Again, they finished their discussion as a perfect chorus.

The Druaa held out both hands in a placatory gesture. "Enough, enough," she hissed. "I concede they are unusual pieces. I know a collector who might be interested…"

"A buyer already lined up?" Tai interrupted. The Druaa visibly winced but was unable to stop a fresh attack from the Naaz-Rokha.

"Maybe we should be going straight to the source," Dart continued.

Tai picked it up smoothly. "Cut out the intermediary."

"Because you're gonna be selling to them for more than you buy from us."

"Of course, if there was a finder's fee on top…" The pair nodded and ended their back-and-forth with another perfectly practiced ending.

"Then I'm sure we can come to an agreement."

"Enough!" the Druaa exclaimed. The fringe of her crest flushed a mottled, angry pink. "I can barely hear myself think for your prattle!"

"Rude." Dart sniffed.

"Unprofessional."

"Traders would never think…"

"…to insult their clients as such…"

"…and might pay extra for the slight!"

The Druaa pursed her reptilian lips together. "The asking price is fair! By the pellucid spires! Present your savant so I can be done with this! You are driving away potential customers!"

Tai looked enormously self-satisfied as he fished around in the harness for their savant. While he prepared the data tablet for the transaction, the Druaa turned her attention to Junior, studying him with an appraising and expert eye. "I don't suppose…"

"No," said Dart, forestalling her question. "He's not for sale."

"Pity." She let out a theatrical sigh. "Let's be done with this, shall we?"

Junior and Dart watched them complete the transaction and the Rokha smiled fondly as his companion tucked the savant away. For all the time they'd been together, he never stopped being grateful for the hand of fate that had paired him with Tai. Their styles and manner complemented one another so well. They handed over the goods and then made their way through the crowd toward the nearest drinking hole.

"Your method of negotiation is most perplexing, friend Tai."

Junior's curiosity broke through the rosy afterglow of a good sale. Tai patted the Titan's shoulder fondly. "Only *sometimes*," he said. "The key is to keep them off-balance. That holds particularly true where a Druaa is concerned."

"How does their physiological equilibrium relate to their capacity for logical assessment?" Junior queried. "Most perplexing. Are they more pliant if they are leaning to the left?"

"Tai doesn't mean it literally. It's a term that means keeping their mental focus unbalanced," Dart cut in with a succinct summary, before Tai could launch into an explanation that might delay their progress toward food and drink.

The Titan nodded, his faceplate swimming with turquoise light. "I have duly noted that, friend Dart. Would you like to see if I can disrupt the equilibrium of the provisioner in this establishment while procuring refreshment?"

"Oh, Junior," said Tai and laughed. "I really, really would."

The Ral Nel's ship was small enough to sit comfortably within one of the station's docking hangars, but large enough to occupy easily a third of the bay. Smaller vessels, shuttles, tugs and landers filled the rest of the space like ugly, wayward children compared to the sleek, unadorned lines of the Ral Nel craft. Weapon pods blistered its upper and lower surfaces, and an array of sensor and communication spikes ran across its spine from prow to stern. Harrugh studied it appreciatively. The consortium was clearly well equipped and prepared to outfit its agents accordingly. Izt saw him looking and pointed.

"Ral Nel *Trailblazer*," he said. "Mine, not on loan. Izt is in debt to no Ral Nel. No off-worlders. Good ship, yes? Fast. Good for finding new business for Consortium. Many improvements done by me. I am good at what I do. You come on board to talk? Yes? I will not fly away with you unless you want it." The Ral Nel touched the band at its wrist and, with a low hum, a door slid open. "You ask for security. Here it is."

Izt had taken them on what felt like a circuitous route through the station to reach the hangar, but Harrugh still couldn't escape the feeling of being watched. A flash of vibrant pink flickered in the corner of his vision, but then a freight hauler trundled past, eclipsing whatever it was that had caught his attention.

"Do you have a crew?" Ashalla maintained the exchange despite Harrugh's agitation.

"Just Izt. Ship is clever but can be crewed if needed. Izt prefer to travel alone, though. Passengers, huh?" He rolled his huge eyes and the effect was comical. "Come, come, you board ship now and we talk." He made an ushering gesture towards the steps that had unfolded from the now-open door and waited for them to take up his offer.

Harrugh caught Ashalla's arm before she could enter the ship. "I don't like this," he whispered. "We're still being followed. Are you sure this is going to be worth the price?"

"We can still walk away," she replied, concern in her expression, "but the Ral Nel probably know the most about nanotech. What is more important to you? We don't have to trust Izt, but we should at least find out if he can help."

"I don't trust much anymore," he replied, his fingers tightly closing around the dune spear. The images of burning worlds blazed in his mind. The kit who had sold him the saaq, folded to a crisp by heat. The mother and children aboard the ship to the Gloaming, falling into lava, killed by his inaction.

The Hacan pair mounted the steps.

The ship's innards were every bit as impressive as the exterior, even more so in terms of pure aesthetic. Smooth, uncluttered surfaces, comfortable seats, spacious with a number of wall-mounted display screens, it was a stark contrast to the cluttered space where they had originally found the Ral Nel. Harrugh heard the ambient hum of a generator quietly distributing power to unseen systems. The haphazard figure of Izt seemed oddly out of place in the immaculate vessel.

"Sit, sit," said the Ral Nel, waving at a hexagonal arrangement of seating. "You talk, I listen, we decide if you are interesting, yes?" Without waiting for his guests to relax, he dropped down into the pilot's seat, swiveling so it faced his guests. The seat gave a hydraulic *click* and a footrest popped up. He made a show of adjusting his position until he found a comfortable spot, folded his hands across his stomach and waited.

"Thank you, Izt." Ashalla gave him a small smile. "But I have to know – how is it that you knew who Harrugh was?"

"Ears everywhere," came the immediate reply. "Eyes everywhere. Loose lips *absolutely* everywhere." He clapped his hands together to mimic jaws. "Yap, yap, yap. Secrets? Pah. Not here, not unless you have brain." He tapped a claw against his elongated head. "Izt? Has brain. And tech, yes? News moves fast on the Gloaming. You arrive, one person recognizes you – within moments *everyone* knows. Rumor travels fast as speed of light. Maybe faster."

Harrugh frowned. If the Ral Nel had got word of his presence on the station without even trying, then whoever it was that was actively hunting them would have had no trouble at all tracking them down. Why they were after him was an entirely different puzzle. There were certainly Hacan who had taken the news of his unprecedented resignation as a betrayal, but tracking him off-world felt extreme, even for staunch traditionalists.

"The Desert Wind you mentioned?"

"Local thugs, busy with crime in Gloaming. Quieron is very interesting, yes? Many people interested. Not all good. Not like Izt." The Ral Nel beamed.

Harrugh tried putting the Desert Wind out of his mind for now. There were already too many mysteries at work to deal with another. "I understand that the Consortium is the leading authority on nanotechnology and miniaturization." Harrugh dug into his pack, producing the cloth-wrapped artifacts that had been given to him by the hrrtos.

The Ral Nel nodded eagerly, clearly delighted by this recognition of his people and their skills. "Yes, yes. None better. Naalu make it pretty, Hylar make it clever, Letnev make it sharp, but you want it made small, you come to Ral Nel!"

Harrugh nodded, producing the data vault which obediently replayed its message and spool of galactic coordinates. Before the voice of the hrrtos had faded away, Izt had hopped down from his chair, slipping on a visor with several concentric lenses. He focused these now on the metallic ingot. He made a low, cooing sound, lifted the vault and turned it over several times in his dexterous hands before setting it back down again.

Izt slipped the visor off and fixed Harrugh and Ashalla with a wary look. "Which Ral Nel gives you this item, hmm?"

"So… it's Consortium-made?" Harrugh nodded as though somehow it wasn't a surprise. "As to where I got it… it was given to me by a friend."

"Maybe." Izt made a noise that conveyed clearly what he thought of that idea. "But would have to be very clever or very stupid to give it to Hacan, even big, important Hacan like you."

"I don't understand," Harrugh said, clearly baffled.

"Do you understand solid state quantum storage and nano-memory retrieval?"

"Not even remotely."

"Then would not understand why giving away innovation so stupid!" Izt huffed. "Also, numbers lead nowhere. Checked while looking. Your friend plays big joke, yes? Big, expensive joke on big, important Quieron." Harrugh's expression darkened and Ashalla touched him gently on the shoulder. The coolness of her touch reminded him of the reason that had brought them this far.

Our world, our people, burning.

Harrugh straightened. "It's not a joke." His voice dropped to a low growl that held a slight edge of threat. It was enough to satisfy Izt, who flapped his hands again.

"Fine, fine, not joke, calm! Interesting, though! Very interesting! What else you have there?"

"Have you ever heard of something called the Prophet's Tears?" Ashalla stepped in diplomatically.

Izt stared at her, unblinking and thoughtful for what felt like an unnecessarily long period of time before letting out a little *puff* sound. "Not that I know of, no. Seems like strange name for something, yes? Prophet or profit? Your accent is odd to Ral Nel, yes? Profit's Tears sounds like how you feel after bad deal." He laughed, or at least that was what Harrugh determined the disconcerting honking noise to be. "Again, just joke," he said. "Just joke. No, I do not hear of such a thing. You show me now, yes?"

Harrugh hesitated before reluctantly producing the ornate vial. He turned it over a few times, allowing Izt to get a good view of its contents.

"I have no idea what I am supposed to do with this," Harrugh explained gruffly. "All I know is that it's called the Prophet's Tears and that it seems to be some sort of microbe culture." He sloshed the bottle, making the liquid swirl. The Ral Nel leaned in to get a closer view, head tipped to the side in great interest. "If you can identify this for us then you will be well compensated for the effort. I promise you that."

Izt smacked his lips together in approval. "Mmm, yes. Hacan debt is always *delicious*, because you understand obligation. Mostly. Some species do not appreciate subtle art of bargaining, no? And what you give me for identifying your Prophet's Tears, mighty Quieron? What you think worthy of my time and effort, hmm?"

"It's not just you and your expertise that I want to buy," Harrugh stated, meaning to be plain and taking a risk. "I want to charter your ship. I need to get to the coordinates in that data vault, and I need to do it soon."

The Ral Nel flopped back into the pilot seat, tilting his head quizzically. "Why so urgent? What is there that Hacan needs so very much?" He tapped the location into the nav console and let out a low whistle. "Close to Nekro space. Dangerous, but still nothing there. Why go?"

"Let's assume for the moment that there *is* something there. Something that we just haven't found yet. Would you take us? As I said, you would be well paid for the risk."

Izt grinned. "Root of galactic finance network should be able to pay very well, yes?"

Harrugh grimaced but pressed on, regardless. Sometimes, his instincts told him when to move. Despite his fear and worry, even with Ashalla's mollifications that he could give up whenever he wanted, he knew he never would. The Ral Nel ship was the perfect vessel. "I know your stock. Now, we are talking terms."

Izt's gaze switched from Harrugh, lingering on the artifacts. "I can take you, might be fun, maybe more, but let me look at this thing, this Prophet's Tears. If interesting, we talk more about how you settle debt to Izt'xet Alit Lo Masak. If not interesting, you go away, leave me in peace. Yes, yes. Now give, give here."

Harrugh held onto the vial for a few heartbeats longer before offering it to the Ral Nel. Izt scooped it up with eager hands and crossed the ship's cabin. He pressed a claw against a panel on the wall and a previously unseen door at the ship's rear slid open, revealing a short ramp down to a lower deck. Harrugh rose from his seat, but the Ral Nel waved his free arm vaguely without looking back. "You stay here," he called over his shoulder. "My workshop, not your playground."

Ashalla's lips twitched as she tried hard not to laugh. Harrugh glanced askance at her, and she merely offered a beatific smile. "Anything he can tell us will be more than we know now," she said. Below them they heard the sounds of instruments coming online and the whirr of mechanisms.

"Anything," agreed Harrugh, cautiously. "Whatever that might be." Still on his feet, he paced around the upper cabin with great interest. He estimated that the *Trailblazer* would comfortably hold more than a dozen Hacan, and maybe half that many again of a more diminutive species.

"It's an impressive vessel," said Ashalla, catching on to his interest. "I'm not sure if having more or less of a ship around me would be a comfort so close to a Nekro incursion. You should definitely consider taking on some crew though, assuming Izt'xet Alit Lo Masak agrees to your terms, and if you follow up with your plan to pay for his pilot abilities."

"Am I wrong in that?" Harrugh asked as he continued his examination of the ship's interior. There were several panels on the walls that were evidently coded only to Ral Nel biology – or possibly even just Izt – as nothing responded to Harrugh's curious touch.

"No," Ashalla said, quietly. "But I do recall your nerves from before. This decision feels sudden, without vetting other options."

"But it almost feels like fate has dropped it into our hands," Harrugh said.

"I do not disagree."

"Then let us see. Assuming Izt'xet Alit Lo Masak decides to give us passage at all, and will agree to potentially shuttling a mercenary crew." He paused. "I cannot let my fear rule me, Ash'ka. I have done so when I left my position, when I left you and Carth without a word. I am still so afraid, but that fear has drawn me into too many terrible decisions."

"I understand. I'm sure you can find suitably compelling terms with the Ral Nel," Ashalla replied confidently. "If not, well, that's why you have brought your best diplomat along." She spread her hands out wide.

"I can hear you up there," came Izt's chiding voice from somewhere below. "Walking about my ship. Don't you be touching anything you should not." A few moments later, Izt emerged from the lower deck clutching the vial of Prophet's Tears in one claw, eyes alight with interest. "So same friend gives you this thing, huh?"

"Have you been able to work out what it is?" Ashalla asked.

The Ral Nel waggled a claw absently, holding out the bejeweled flask. "No, no. This is how it works. I ask first. You answer, then you get to ask question. That way we all get answers we want, hmm?"

Harrugh shrugged. At this stage, there was little to be gained by trying to conceal the whole truth. His time among the emirs and clan consuls, maintaining the delicate balance of the emirates trade network, had taught him that you only needed to conceal just enough to make your proposal credible and people would fill in the rest on their own, often to their disadvantage. "Yes," he replied simply, "it was given to me by the same friend."

"Hah," said the Ral Nel and it was astonishing just how much disbelief could be conveyed within a single sound. "Of course it was." He offered the Prophet's Tears out to Harrugh, who took it back. "This is something special, yes? I am most curious to know who this friend is who has given you such interesting things."

"What do you mean by special?" Harrugh held the vial up to the light. "What is it? Some sort of poison? An elixir?"

"Ah, this is something more," said the Ral Nel. "Do you want sustenance? I do. We talk more over hot cup of *x'istax*, yes? Not worry about, is just sweet leaves in hot water. Refreshing. Nutritious." The little reptile pottered his way around the cabin until a few moments later Harrugh and Ashalla found themselves holding mugs of a steaming brew that smelled faintly of grass. A tentative sip proved the beverage to be pleasing enough.

"X'istax, did you call this?" Ashalla sipped again. Doubtless she was, like Harrugh, grateful for its warmth.

Izt winced at Ashalla's clumsy pronunciation but nodded. "Close enough. Now, what do you want to know about this so-called Prophet's Tears? Because it is not like anything I have ever seen – but it is very much like something a Ral Nel would create." He pulled noisily at his own drink, slurping rather than sipping. "Is… ah, like message in a bottle, but message that you feel rather than message that you see. Only… you would see it, and hear it, but all at once. Difficult to explain."

"I don't understand, what do you mean by a message that you can feel?" Ashalla asked. "How is it recorded, and how are we supposed to access the content?"

"This thing you call 'Prophet's Tears' is…" Izt waved a clawed hand in the air. "Highly sophisticated data storage, yes? But not like nanotech vault. This tech is gene-coded to a specific individual. Suspect–" he tapped the side of his head with the same claw to indicate a bright idea "–that individual would be you, Mighty Quieron."

"Please don't call me that," Harrugh said. "If we are going to continue this transaction, maybe you could drop it."

Izt gave a delighted little cackle. "Is just my joke. No wish to anger Harrugh Gefhara. Will refrain from using grand titles going forward as you ask." There was a certain twinkle in his eyes that suggested he may or may not hold to that promise, but Harrugh appreciated the gesture.

"Thank you. Now, what do you mean, it's 'gene-coded'? Not that I don't understand what you're saying, but I've never heard of a liquid data storage of this kind."

"The liquid? Is just a carrier solution. Biostatic medium holding all the little nanites. Artificial microbes that can transmit messages only to one they are coded to. Come, I show you what I mean." The Ral Nel trotted back to his workshop below decks. Setting aside their cups, Ashalla and Harrugh followed him down.

Below the main deck of the ship was an expansive laboratory, one half of it devoted to a spectacular array of instruments and analytic tools and a wall of monitors showing various images from across the Gloaming. Harrugh stared at it and suddenly, with startling clarity, understood just how it was that Izt had received the news of his arrival.

"Ears and eyes everywhere," he said, pointing at the screens. "And drones, too, I'm guessing?"

"Have to test new creations somehow," said Izt in a dismissive tone. "Anyway, look here." He was running his claws at top speed over a keyboard and the black surface of the table between them suddenly flared into life. A holographic image of the ornate vial appeared, slowly rotating above its surface. The image began to zoom in on the contents until the magnification resolved into a poor-quality, grainy image.

"There, you see?" Izt pointed at something barely visible. Bobbing lazily within the fluid was what looked like a tiny, tear-shaped bug. And another floating a little way away and another. "Analysis suggests there are thousands of these nanite capsules. Well." Here, he had the decency to look at least a *little* ashamed. "Maybe slightly fewer now. Had to look to understand, yes? No disrespect intended. Maybe a gap in the final data, I knock off price."

"I still don't really understand what it is that I am looking at."

"You know fancy data vault?" Both Ashalla and Harrugh nodded. "This is same thing, only much cleverer, more secure. Technology works so much better in miniature, yes? There is beauty in making something smaller but with just the same, if not more, capability. I see sense in name of thing, now. Each device is like a tear. Don't know about prophet bit. Don't care. But 'tears' makes sense, no?"

"How does something like this even work?" Ashalla asked.

Izt looked taken aback and mimicked up-ending the vial. "Harrugh drink. Or... individual to whom data is coded drinks. Anybody else drinks or separates a tear from others to try, they just have bitter taste on tongue for hours. Nasty."

Harrugh narrowed his eyes and looked to the mug of sweet-tasting tea the Ral Nel still had nearby.

Izt shuffled his feet. "Slightly fewer thousands," he admitted again, sticking his long, reptilian tongue out. "Very bitter. Not nice."

"And who might have made such a thing?" Ashalla asked. "Is this the work of the Consortium?"

The Ral Nel shook its narrow head. "No, no. Is something would like to understand. Ral Nel could make nanites, yes. Put them in carrier solution, yes. Put them in fancy bottle, yes. Not know how to gene-code immersive sensory messages. No. Suspect product of more than one species, but hard to say. Hard to say."

Harrugh stared at the vial in his hand, staggered that something so innocuous could be a previously unknown kind of technology. "What will happen to me if I drink it? Assuming it's meant for me." It had been handed directly to him after all – it seemed like a fair assumption.

"Nanite microbes swim, swim, swim–"Izt danced his claws up his body from abdomen to head "–and colonize base of the brain. Believe he would enter..." The Ral Nel paused for a few moments, searching for the right description. "Lucid dream. Not know Hacan word for it. On home world, some Ral Nel experiment with narcotics that access certain parts of brain. Make them see things that are not there."

"Hallucinations," Ashalla murmured.

"That. Yes. Is difficult word. But that. Only this would be… well, not that. Would be sensory messages. Audio, visual… anything. Everything. If technology is as good as think it might be… Harrugh will believe he is living in moment. Or moments. Might be confusing. But would be quick. Over fast. But once only. Nanites only have energy for one time. One chance to take in what information is stored. Is also means of…" The Ral Nel's voice dropped surreptitiously, whether consciously or not. "Is also means of sharing information gleaned and then *poof*. Gone. Like spying, though not know about that sort of thing at all. Of course."

Ashalla stared at him, then pointed at the bank of monitors. "Are you sure about that?"

"Surveillance is not spying. Silly Hacan."

Ashalla shook her head at the statement but didn't fight it.

Harrugh lifted the vial up to the light and examined the liquid again. "So, allow me to clarify my understanding. I need to drink this and a message, of sorts, will be delivered directly into my mind?"

"Bitter," Izt complained, sipping the remains of the tea. "Yes, but will not hurt you." His glittering eyes locked on Harrugh. "Is safe. Probably. May be disorienting and may feel dizzy afterward but if you need it, I am happy to wait and watch."

Harrugh twisted the seal from the vial and sniffed cautiously at the contents. It was disappointingly odorless. "You believe it's gene coded. What if it isn't?"

"Ah, smart Hacan, very good. To check, could just drink a little, or drink a lot, up to you. See if work. If not, nothing lost."

"How will I know?"

"Oh," said Izt and the tone was dark. "You will know." He gestured at one of the seats beneath the array of monitors. "Might want to sit, just in case. Might not, up to you. Drink. See what happens. If bitter taste in mouth, nothing. If theory is correct, you see and hear message that you are supposed to see and hear. Or some of it anyway." He tapped several keys and the view displayed on some of the monitors switched to images of the laboratory with Harrugh as the sole focus. "Record everything for good measure. Need to understand effects and document. When all done you tell me what it is like, what your Prophet's Tears tell you." Izt huffed and the displays multiplied, making sure that Harrugh was being properly observed from as many angles as possible. "Prophet's Tears, huh? Not even very *good* name, would have come up with something much better."

Harrugh swirled the vial as though appreciating a fine vintage of firewine. For a moment he considered throwing the thing away, dashing it to pieces against the wall and putting an end to all the doubt and uncertainty that had plagued him since the hrrtos's first appearance in his chambers. He could give the cursed thing to the Ral Nel and go home. Only he knew that it wouldn't put an end to it. Not knowing what might have been and why would gnaw at him, and he would have given everything up for nothing. The hrrtos had set him on a path from which he could not back down. And he could not fall victim to his fear again.

Expect nothing, his cynical inner self whispered, *and you will never be disappointed.*

Deciding to remain standing, he lifted the open vial in a mock toast and put it to his lips. He tilted his head back just a little and swallowed some of the contents. Izt watched with barely contained excitement. His scaled hands clasped and unclasped in front of him as he monitored Harrugh with keen interest.

"Anything?" Izt leaned in towards him. "Should work quickly."

Ashalla let out a long breath. Her eyes fixated on him.

"Nothing," said Harrugh, disappointed despite his prior hesitations and skepticisms. "I didn't experience any sort of…"

Later, when he tried to explain what he had experienced, he discovered that words were insufficient for the task. His world simply fell away. One moment he was standing in the cool, spacious compartment in the lower deck of a Ral Nel scout ship and the next, he was elsewhere. He had experienced hallucinations before, when particularly feverish or in the caves near the end of his long pilgrimage, but those experiences did nothing to prepare him for the effect of the Prophet's Tears.

Perception stretched out into a tunnel of attenuated light, a place filled with noise and sensation. For a heartbeat or two, it was overwhelming, an incoherent onslaught of disordered stimuli threatening to drown him in its intensity.

Two minutes!

Harrugh gasped and flailed desperately, though if he truly moved or drew breath he did not know. The voice he heard was filled with anxious urgency and without knowing how, he reached for it. The void stared back at him and then it was a void no longer. With a burst of flame, it lit from end to end.

Ships burning in a vacuum littered with debris.

A proud dreadnought foundered, its spine broken and its bridge ruptured, venting atmosphere and lives in equal measure. Harrugh watched the tumbling, helpless figures, powerless to reach out and save them, powerless to stop the unfolding carnage.

Harrugh!

The voice called from a long way away and the simple act of turning his head to see where it came from felt as though it strained every single muscle in his body to breaking point.

Eyes turned to regard him, dozens of eyes, eyes the size of cities that fixed him with monstrous, alien hunger. He met their myriad gazes and cried out. His mind couldn't comprehend the horror. Then he was *falling,* plunging toward the churning clouds of a planet wracked by storms, its barren surface stippled with crackling spires.

One minute!

Time was running out.

A majestic cruiser, its angled hull breached in a dozen places, ripped itself apart as its crew stoked the reactor to critical. They sang as they died. Harrugh didn't know how he knew that to be the truth, but he knew. He knew their deaths would break something vital in him, and remake him into someone desperate to stop it and knowing he never could.

Harrugh!

The planet loomed, the clouds parted, and he continued to fall. The surface raced up to meet him and then split, baring its coruscating heart. An eternity of light, sound and silvered fire rushed to fill his vision.

Our home. Our people. Burning.

Everything. Burning.

Everything.

Thirty seconds!

A ravenous moon that would never stop, *could* never stop, until the galaxy was gnawed down to cold, dark, silent bones and the long, final exhalation of dead suns.

The impossible core of the impossible world filled his vision, the heat and light eclipsing the spiraling vista of devastation, the abominable scrutiny and the grasping void. It seared away light and sound and sensation. He spread his arms to embrace the end, to end this agony, and let go.

Now!

Harrugh!

The voice called to him again, puncturing the bleached canvas of his delirium. He drew in a rattling breath and felt the chill of the floor beneath him, heard the roar of blood in his ears. He opened his mouth to cry out – or at least he thought he did – but didn't recognize the dry croak that emerged as belonging to him. He was certain that he knew that voice. Who was that calling his name? Cool liquid trickled into his mouth as someone brought water to his lips. He became more aware of his surroundings. Ashalla knelt beside him, holding his head up as she carefully gave him another sip of the water. "Harrugh!"

"Ash'ka? What happened?"

"You fell." The reply was simple, blunt. Her expression was full of concern. "You swallowed half of that stuff and then simply fell down. One second upright, the next…" She slapped one palm against another. "Down. Izt has the whole thing recorded. What happened? Are you all right?"

He became aware of the Ral Nel lurking nearby, watching him with keen interest. "Yes, yes, did it work? What did you see?"

Harrugh tried to stand and Ashalla helped him to his feet. He swayed unsteadily for a moment and then motioned that he could manage. She let go of him with obvious reluctance.

"Harrugh?"

Everything burning.

Bigger than just Hercant, bigger even than Kenara. *Everything.* Any force potent enough to so comprehensively annihilate the world would not be confined to just one system. It was going to be everywhere. Death. Death to the universe.

"No, Ash'ka," he replied, "I'm not all right. I'm not all right at all."

NINE

THE OTHER SIDE OF THE GALAXY.

The ship tore through the ephemeral ribbons of dust and gas on the fringe of the nebula before violently decelerating to sub-light speed. The starboard mass-drive exploded, sending the vessel into an uncontrolled and ungraceful tumble, trailing smoke and debris. The words proudly emblazoned along its hull proclaimed the ship to be the *FSS Orlando*, though its majesty was somewhat diminished by the fresh wounds that cut and seared into her flanks. The running lights flickered fitfully as she leaked flames and atmosphere into the void and began the long, inexorable fall toward the planet below.

Three more ships burst from the border of the nebula and dropped to sub-light in pursuit of the foundering *Orlando*. A trio of glossy black hulls slashed through the debris with crimson malevolence and spread out in the larger ship's wake like aquatic predators closing in on their prey. There was nothing elegant in their design: masses of clawed manipulators, bladed appendages and high energy weapons studded their undersides, already uncoiling in anticipation of the kill. The transmission space around them screamed across multiple spectrums, the looped, projected message of machine purity and superiority. It was both a declaration and a statement of intent.

Deaf and blind to its approaching doom, the *Orlando* continued the plunge toward the tumultuous atmosphere. The Nekro ships closed, weapons built to charge. Then, without any warning, they stopped, peeling away from the pursuit so suddenly and violently that any organic pilot would have been liquified by their own inertia. Abruptly confused, the shrieking message from the Nekro dimmed and dissolved into a babbled exchange of query and counter-query. They drew back and prowled near-space and waited.

Acting Captain Tamara Nichols awoke face-down on the floor of the bridge. She tasted blood in her mouth and could smell the acrid stink of electrical burning. None of these were good things – but at least she was alive. With increasing alacrity her cognition caught up with recent events and she took a moment to compose herself. She dragged herself unsteadily to her feet and looked blearily around at the bridge. Smoke filled the upper reaches of the cabin, curling from ruptured stations and buckled maintenance panels while a small fire, still burning at one of the consoles, was being expertly dealt with by one of the junior officers. He looked shaken and with good reason.

"Are we clean?" She hammered the control and croaked the words into the ship's comms system. All decks, all stations, but in the aftermath of the question, there was nothing but static and silence.

Nichols became aware of a damp sensation on her face and put a hand to her cheek. It came away wet with blood and she wiped it on her already smudged and stained uniform. Her thoughts were fuzzy and she felt like she had been beaten with batons, but she was otherwise whole. Probably concussion, she thought, with detached logic.

A shower of electrical sparks from a torn cable a few feet behind her caused her to start in alarm. She reached for an extinguisher, but the cable fizzled out with a sputter of smoke and hung limply.

"Are we clean?" She repeated the demand again, only this time with more authority in her tone. Given the damage to the bridge, it was likely that the shipboard comms were heavily impaired. However, if any of the *Orlando*'s systems had been compromised by the Nekro Virus then she would have to issue an immediate evacuation order. When the comms fizzled into life and she heard the tones of her chief engineer, she let out a sigh of relief.

"We're clean, acting captain," came the terse reply, "but so far, we have navigation offline. Primary propulsion at forty percent of optimal, weapons also offline. Core is stable but under exigency conditions. We have breaches…" Skelton's voice broke off from the catalogue of disasters as he barked orders at a subordinate. Nichols maintained her composure and her patience. Skelton returned his focus to the matter at hand.

"Reports are still coming in on containment, but we're not bleeding out yet," he said in that same tightly contained tone. "The fact we aren't all frozen corpses suggests life support is operational for now but still waiting on confirmation for how long. Both shield capacitors are shot through, so anything larger than a pebble hits us and we're going to know about it, though probably not for long."

There was another pause and when he spoke again, she could detect the barely concealed irritation in his tone. "We're limping, acting captain. The biggest problem we have right now is that it looks like we broke FTL because of a gravity well. A big one. We've hit it at an oblique angle and that's a small bloody mercy. Main propulsion isn't going to be enough to break us out the way it is. We have enough power to fire the attitude thrusters but it's going to take a miracle to do much more than that in the near future… sooner or later we are going to be forced to make planetfall."

It was worse than she'd thought, but at least there were things to do to make it better. However, their route should have been clear. The flight path hadn't put them close to anything as large as a gravity well. What had happened?

"Lieutenant Skelton," said Nichols, "right now, I'll take any small miracle you can throw at me. As to the last, I suppose it's rather obvious of me to assume that we are in for a pretty rough and ugly landing?"

"You're right on both counts. Controls are limited. *Extremely* limited." His emphasis was unnecessary. She could practically taste the sneer in his voice. Skelton was many, many things, but the one thing that she could not take from him was his consummate dedication to his work and duty. "But it's going to happen whether it's pretty or not and it's not going to be pleasant. Now… if you don't mind, Acting Captain Nichols, I have a job to do. No offense."

Of *course* he meant offense. Nichols was more than aware of Jex Skelton's feelings toward her, especially after she had taken over temporary command when their previous captain died in battle. He would never let her forget it.

"None taken," she replied, keeping her tone neutral.

Keep him placated. Keep him sharp. There were far more pressing matters right now than the insubordinate attitude of a junior lieutenant. "Keep me apprised. And lieutenant?"

"Ma'am?"

"Good work. The engineering team is to be commended for keeping us alive. Do what you can. Even a little is a lot in the current situation."

"Thank you," he said and cut off the connection. He may as well have said "I don't want your praise." Nichols sighed and looked around at the ravaged bridge of the ship, assessing the situation. She wiped a drizzle of blood oozing from the gash on her temple and brushed shattered glass from her console. The blown-out screen fizzed and sparked angrily, but she paid it no heed.

"I need a sitrep." She addressed the bridge crew, who were tending to their wounded and efficiently restoring as much order as possible to the command deck. "Helm? Report."

"Negative propulsion. Attitude control sluggish." The helmsman was an anomaly among the predominant Sol and Xxcha officers of *Orlando*'s crew: a Saar. Nichols had learned, swiftly, that those very differences that made Drav Orragh such a valuable member of the senior team on board the vessel. His keen intellect and frequently unique point of view often gave a contrasting perspective on situations. His report now, like most of the things he said, was clipped, delivering information in short, staccato sentences that wasted no syllables.

Despite his shaggy and bestial exterior, the Saar was warm and welcoming, with a surprisingly dry wit and infectious sense of humor that brightened most gatherings of which he was a part. Nichols both liked and trusted him implicitly. Before she'd taken command, she had worked alongside him as navigation officer. They'd worked well together then and the same had proven true since her sudden ascension to the captaincy.

"Nav confirms that we are in a region of uncharted space between Ordinian and our destination, in decaying orbit. The planet is unidentified." He tapped a few buttons on the screen and considered for a moment. "I have stabilized our spin but cannot do much more than that pending an engineering solution. Current trajectory confirms Lieutenant Skelton's assessment. Under current conditions, planetfall is unavoidable."

The *Orlando* had been part of Green Longbow fleet, of the disavowed Salient Sun Joint Task Force fighting to take the planet Ordinian back from Nekro occupation. The people on Ordinian had been categorized as a lost cause by the Task Force, that their enemy, the Nekro Virus, would win, and it was better strategically to cut their losses and abandon the planet. However, those on Ordinian had refused to give up and submit to the Nekro. The ground battles had been going fairly well – until a Nekro Virus swarm arrived, beginning an approach. Green Longbow had drawn them off, but the fleet was systematically destroyed ship by ship in the effort. Nichols knew it was likely that the *Orlando* was the sole survivor of that heroic, ill-fated stratagem. The loss felt like a chasm of grief, but she could not study it now.

Isolated, half-blinded by the nebula and with the Nekro closing in, Nichols had given the order to make the emergency FTL push to the nearest safe coreward system. They'd hoped that would put them beyond the Nekro's desire to pursue. The calculations had been hasty, but their trajectory should have stayed clear. Somehow, they had ended up in a different place than anticipated.

"Pursuers?"

"Functional scopes show three Nekro in planetary near-space. They are not on approach."

For once, she *wanted* him to elaborate, but Orragh did not. Her fingers curled into anxious fists, her nails biting into the flesh of her palm. The Nekro Virus was a machine plague, the insane echoes of an equally insane and malign artificial intelligence. The scourge of biological life, it could infect anything from an automated cleaner to a fleet dreadnought without correct defensive methods. There was no logical reason why it would hesitate to destroy them. If they were as close to annihilation as the scan suggested, then the *Orlando* should have been dead within a few moments of slowing out of FTL.

"Not approaching? That doesn't make sense. Why in the name of… no, you know what? It doesn't matter right now. If they're content to sit there, then I'm perfectly content to let them. Thank you, Mr Orragh. Please let me know the instant anything changes." She acknowledged his inclined head in kind and swiveled to face the bulky figure at the science station. "So, wherever it is that we've ended up, we're falling from orbit and even if we could fly out of here, there are three Nekro waiting to chew us up. News so far isn't filling me with confidence. How about you give me something good, Kketch?"

"I wish that I could, captain," said the Xxcha. In stark contrast to the word rationing of the Saar, the chelonian chief science officer spoke in thoughtful, measured tones like so many of his people. If something was worth saying, he was fond of explaining, it was worth saying well. To Kketch, saying something well sometimes meant including a long, rambling story to punctuate the underlying metaphor of what seemed to be yet another cautionary tale. Which was fine during a leadership meeting, but less than optimal in an emergency situation. He was a superlative scientist, but he *could* take forever to get to the point.

"Expediently, if you please, science officer," Nichols appended her request. It was the politest method by which she could implore him to skip to the end without sounding like she was being dismissive or rude. She needed to respect the crew if they were going to learn to respect her. "Move on to your next point." Kketch took no offense to her words – as she had known he would not – and flicked to a different screen.

"Of course, Captain Nichols. Still running the topographical analysis. Our sensor arrays are operating at a significantly reduced capacity, which will naturally reduce both the accuracy and alacrity of any survey, including any imaging that we might be able to develop as a result of..."

"Yes, thank you, Kketch," she said, interrupting him. The Xxcha nodded, used to mid-flow interruptions and not remotely put out. "Let me know when you've got something."

She dropped into the command chair and took a moment. The wound on her head had started to throb and was matched by an ache behind her eyes. She pulled open a panel in the arm of the seat and plucked out a hypo, pressing it to her neck. It discharged with a faint hiss. She winced as the drug entered her system, but it worked its magic, reducing the pain and helping her to feel better. The internal comms fizzed, barked and then burst into activity as engineering presumably managed to bring the wider system online. Triage teams, fire control, search and rescue, a litany of small disasters and small reliefs spilled from the console.

"All hands," she said, finally able to address the full crew. "This is Acting Captain Tamara Nichols. Now hear this." She took a deep breath, closed her eyes and then opened them again. Determination showed on her face. "First and foremost, we are alive. I intend to do everything in my power to keep us that way. It's only through your efforts that we have been able to make it this far and I commend you all for your courage and dedication. Ensure any casualties are escorted to the medbay where possible. Those still able should remain at their stations pending assessment by the triage teams. Dr Mendez, please compile a personnel report as soon as you are able?"

She paused, awaiting the doctor's confirmation. Gabriel Mendez was the most reliable chief medical officer she had ever worked alongside and knowing that he would be coordinating the rescue and relief operations was some consolation.

Today continued to heap tragedies upon her.

"Acting Captain Nichols, I regret to inform you that Dr Mendez is not able to carry out that order at this time. However, I will see to it that your command is obeyed." She knew the voice: another Xxcha, but his name escaped her. What did not escape her was the deliberate and specific choice of words. She knew the senior team code for informing of a death among the officers on an open channel without negatively impacting morale.

"As you were, doctor," she said. "Thank you. All hands, be ready to respond as our situation develops. The *Orlando* isn't done yet and neither are we. Trust in each other. We will find a way through this. Nichols out."

The bridge crew were temporarily stunned into silence by the revelation they'd lost one of their own. Gabe had been a good friend, a good man and an excellent doctor. His loss would be keenly felt. *Grieve later*, she told herself. She looked around the bridge crew but could not gauge reaction to her small speech. Their expressions were strained, pale and unreadable, her officers and their teams carrying out her orders, and those who were not directly involved were busy with their duties restoring function to the bridge.

Getting up from the command chair, she moved over to the science officer's area and looked at the communications panel.

As expected, the long-range comms were down, but Kketch had already activated the emergency beacon. This would broadcast their situation to any vessels that might pass within range. Given their remote location, it seemed unlikely there would be much in the way of passing traffic, but the transmission would at least warn anybody nearby that there were Nekro in-system. It might not save the *Orlando*, but it might save others. The Xxcha's instruments were showing that some of the longer-range sensors were also returning conflicting information, but the planetary analysis screen was scrolling lines of preliminary data.

Resting her head for a moment against the cool surface of the monitor, Nichols drew another long, steadying breath. Leaning back, she turned her eyes to the viewscreen that showed the surface of the planet beneath them. The entire surface was blanketed by roiling thunderheads, some of which rose high into the upper atmosphere and which had to be hundreds of miles across, lit from within by flickering ionic discharge. A world with nothing but thunder at its very edge did not bode well.

"If we go down there," she said to Kketch, softly, "what are the chances of successfully getting the ship to ground without it breaking apart?"

"This is one of those moments," said the Xxcha, reaching out one of his clawed hands and laying it on her arm in a show of camaraderie, "where you want me to talk rather than answer you directly, isn't it? Perhaps I should simply say that we have a non-zero chance of surviving the descent. I would estimate that the chances of successfully landing a stellar vehicle such as the *Orlando* on an unknown world through atmospheric turbulence is probably equal in odds to the success of being able to action effective repairs and system restoration with the limited resources that might be available on said world. On the other hand, if Mr Orragh is able to bring us down successfully, the Nekro appear disinclined to pursue us further, which exponentially increases our chances of survival." He paused for a breath before continuing. "I'll get you an atmospheric and geomorphologic analysis as soon as I can."

She appreciated his gesture of solidarity. "Damned if we do," she murmured, staring at the raging tempest below, "damned if we don't."

"Excellently summarized, Captain Nichols." He patted her arm again and returned to his work, murmuring the phrase beneath his breath. He enjoyed learning Sol language and truisms. He glanced up and indicated the still-oozing cut on her head.

"That will need attention," he said, matter-of-factly. "It will leave quite a scar."

"What's one more?" She shrugged. Recent history had given her plenty of scars, another would hardly make a difference. "Are you familiar with the Xxcha on the comms from medical?"

"Dr Takksil," he said. "Most excellent at what he does. Young, but enthusiastic. Boundless energy."

Despite the dire situation, Nichols idly imagined what a Xxcha with boundless energy would be like, given their species predisposition for measured deliberation. Often, people misinterpreted the Xxcha tendency for philosophy and pacifism as obtuse. Nichols had found that they merely liked to be *thorough*. "You know him?"

"Well enough."

It was as close to high praise as she knew she'd get, and some of her worries abated. The loss of Mendez was a hard one, but if the medical team remained in good hands, they might yet survive.

"There's nothing we can do now. We must make use of what time we have left," she said to Kketch and took up her old position next to him. "So how about shifting over for a little one?"

"Many hands make light work," said Kketch, clearly delighted to be able to deploy one of his collection of Sol sayings in the correct context. "I would certainly be grateful for any assistance you might be able to render me." He squinted at the wound on her head. "I would also be grateful if you don't get blood on my console."

"I'll do my best."

"That's all I ask."

As predicted, they were only able to maintain their position for a short time – around thirty minutes or so by the ship's chronometer – and as feared, there was no way they were going to be able to make meaningful repairs to the damaged drive before gravity caught up with them. The odds of accidentally encountering a gravity well significant enough to force an emergency drop from FTL were slim – but the enormous planet toward which they were steadily falling presented precisely that scenario. Fortune was not on their side.

The report from Lieutenant Skelton's engineering team had been grim, so the decision was swiftly made to focus restoration efforts on anything and everything that might aid them in reaching the surface of the planet in one piece. Microfractures in the hull had been sealed, ruptured power conduits had been spliced, and the core had been coaxed into diverting as much secondary power to the attitude thrusters and functioning shield arrays as possible. Disconcertingly, the three Nekro ships had simply held their position the entire time. They did not retreat. They did not pursue. It was incredibly unnerving.

"The surface analysis is complete," said Kketch from his station. "Unfortunately, damage and atmospheric ionization has made some of the data unreliable. As best as I can determine, it is an ecologically dead world."

Nichols grimaced. That was not a promising start. *If they made a successful landing, they could look forward to suffocation or starvation.*

Kketch continued, "However, it does appear to have an oxygenated atmosphere stable enough to sustain the crew, which is something of an anomaly, given the absence of an obvious biogeochemical cycle…"

"If it's an anomaly that will keep us alive, I'll take it as we find it," Nichols replied.

Kketch nodded in agreement. "I concur. Gravity appears to be approximately seventy-five percent Jord standard, which will be unsettling but well within tolerances. A world of mysteries, captain. Most curious! I have been completely unable to determine the cause of the superstorm that appears to cover the entire globe in perpetuity. Projections suggest that it rises as high as the planetary mesosphere. That's about all I have for you at this time."

"Well," said Nichols, her expression grim, "we're about to become *intimately* acquainted with that mesosphere, so let's just hope you have the chance to actually get out there and investigate it first-hand. Mr Orragh, we're in your hands now."

"Yes, captain," replied the Saar, his tone calm and reassuring. His opinion had been simple and straightforward. Given their existing rate of decline, it would be better to choose their window of descent rather than have it dictated to them. Steer into the storm and use what power and systems they had available to try to keep the nose up for as long as possible. Orragh had been typically brief when explaining the difficulties of what they were about to attempt, but under the current circumstances, brevity was infinitely preferable.

"All hands, strap in and prepare for a rough descent," she said across the ship-wide comms. She paused, choosing her next words carefully, smothering any anxiety she might have felt about what was about to happen and their chances of survival. "Engineering, lock down the core – if we don't need it to stay alive then I want it powered down. Medbay, secure your patients. Crisis teams, stand by. Every one of you is going to be needed when we reach the surface. I'll see you on the other side."

It would have to do. She noticed a few shoulders square, a few backs straighten among the bridge crew, and turned her attention to the sight of the churning storm growing in the forward viewscreen.

"Passing through the thermosphere now. We're starting to pick up some heat. Should hit the edge of the storm in approximately thirty seconds," came the report from somewhere. She wasn't sure where: her attention was mesmerized by the sheer magnitude of the raging tempest growing larger and more threatening in the viewscreen. In response to the update, she gripped the arms of the command chair tightly, leaning her body forward as though willing the ship to move swiftly through.

"Ten seconds."

Nichols watched as the seething clouds mushroomed up to meet them, wracked with flickering inner light. The hull began to vibrate, shaking debris loose from the earlier damage and sending it dancing across the floor and terminals. Tongues of flame licked at the nose of the ship.

"Three... two... one..."

"Hold tight!"

The *Orlando* plunged into the storm, its hull blooming with atmospheric fire. Darkness filled the viewscreen, but it was a darkness punctured by titanic spears of light. Arc flares as wide as battleships cracked the gloom, their jagged limbs clutching at the ship. The stink of ozone filled the bridge and corposant crawled across the hull and consoles, snapping and crackling like malicious imps.

The noise was appalling.

Somewhere, metal shrieked. The entire ship lurched as something was torn loose. The vibrations intensified and cracks spidered their way across the viewscreen.

Nichols clutched the arms of her seat so hard that her knuckles turned white. She fought to control her breathing, realizing that it had become rapid and shallow. She would not have a panic attack, she would not have a panic attack–

Orragh shouted over the protesting howls of the struggling, abused ship. His hands were steady on the controls, making deft adjustments, and his focus absolute between the instruments and the billowing storm attempting to swat them from the sky. Through it all, he sang, his voice rich and tuneful and it was so *incongruous* with what was happening that she could not help but become captivated.

"Oh, Father Ragh, come lead us home, for we have travelled far."

The ship convulsed again and hit a pocket of lower pressure. It dropped into freefall for a few moments before Orragh stabilized it with a short burst of thrust.

"From distant shores to distant suns the One Between the Stars."

The *Orlando* burst from the belly of the storm, trailing smoke and vapor, and the lightning-wracked gloom in the viewscreen was replaced by a rugged, ochre landscape of rocky plains and cloud-scraping spires. The horizon tilted as the ship attempted to take the most aerodynamically direct route to the ground, but Orragh gave the thrust another burst and wrestled it into a more level trajectory.

"I ask you now, should we be stray and lost from clan and kin."

The ground rushed up to meet them in a blur of stone and dust and in the last, sluggish seconds before impact, Nichols was glad they had chosen their descent rather than simply allowed the orbital decay to run its course. Coming down uncontrolled into one of those spires would certainly have killed them all. She hammered the comms.

"All hands! Brace! Brace! Brace…"

"Come take me up, and keep me close, forever…"

The *Orlando* hit the ground with a thunderous crash that lifted debris high into the air. It bounced off the surface of the plains, leaving a ragged gouge in its wake, spinning like a skipped stone. It crashed down one last time, with a terrible grind of rending metal as it left a furrow in the surface half a mile long before finally coming to rest, silent and smoldering.

TEN

THE GLOAMING

The bar was no different from the others that had set up here on the Gloaming. It had started out as a way of providing for the market vendors who frequented the plaza, but over the years the waystation had been in operation after being decommissioned, it had become a business interest in its own right. These days, the bar imported drink and foodstuffs from beyond the borders of the Kenara system. A diverse clientele, after all, demanded a diverse menu. You could eat a delicate Xxcha meal and wash it down with a Jord beer, or any number of other culinary combinations.

While the Gloaming was privately owned, there was usually somewhere just like it wherever you went in civilized space. In the interests of peacekeeping, stations or moon bases generally operated nominally under the laws of the planet they orbited but remained informal enough to be a location useful to both governments and freelancers alike. In a galaxy filled with political turmoil, it was frequently advantageous to be able to meet an emissary informally without needing to worry about executive scrutiny for the former, and for the latter – well, for them, it was simply useful.

Despite the mingling of species out on the trade floors, once you got inside the bars, there was often a natural tendency to cluster into their own familiar groups. But here and there, business continued over a drink or several. A studious Winnu sat in one corner, fussing over what to drink while a young Mentak pilot drummed her fingers impatiently on the table waiting for him. Unsurprisingly there were many Hacan, but a few Naaz-Rokha pairs lurked around the fringes of the shadowy bar.

Tai glanced at them but didn't see any familiar faces. It was hardly surprising given the Naaz-and Rokha's growing propensity for galactic travel and exploration. Since the inception of the ambassadorial outreach initiative, the Alliance had been keenly seeking more species to introduce to their harmonious way of life. As distant cousins to the Rokha, they had been particularly successful with young, disenchanted or clanless Hacan. All eyes turned to Junior as the proto-Titan stooped to enter, only to discover he could then not straighten up to his full three meters. The rippling faceplate could not precisely convey disappointment, but Tai felt like he could see it in Junior's stance. The proto-Titan considered for a while.

"I will wait outside for you," he informed Tai.

"That hardly seems fair."

"I don't mind. You and friend Dart require refreshment. And I am most excellent at waiting." Junior backed out of the bar again, drawing a considerable amount of attention as he did so. When he was gone, Dart and Tai found themselves a spot at a table and Dart fetched drinks and food for them. They ate in companionable silence until Tai leaned back in his chair, replete. The cup in which his drink had been delivered was enormous in his tiny hands, but he sipped its contents appreciatively. His biology didn't lend itself well to the consumption of alcohol, although there had been times that hadn't stopped him. But right now, he was enjoying the chilled juice of something his translator said was called vorxxa from the Xxcha homeworld.

"So. What's next?" Dart ate with ravenous hunger, enjoying the platter of meat immensely. The profit they had made from the deal with the Druaa had more than compensated them for their efforts and those aurei were even now burning a metaphorical hole in his pocket. "Now that we've got that lot sold, which corner of the galaxy should we explore next?"

"I've not given too much thought to it," replied Tai, setting down his cup. "So many worlds, so little time. I *was* considering letting Junior choose."

Dart's amber eyes glanced out to where the Titan stood patiently waiting for them. As the crowd moved along, it parted around the hulking biomechanical figure like a river flowing around a boulder.

"He was in stasis for a very, very long time," Tai continued. "Even if he does start to remember anything from the time before, the galaxy is a completely different place now. Which is probably for the best. To be honest, I think the only reason the researchers on board the *Naq'aa* were happy to let him leave with us was because they were more interested in where he might take us." Tai paused and cocked his head on one side. "Well, that and I don't think they could have stopped him even if they were inclined to." He slurped the rest of his drink. "It wouldn't hurt us to have a bit of a vacation."

"Vacations *cost* us money, not earn it," grumbled Dart good-naturedly, but he was touched at Tai's compassion. "You've really taken to the Titan, haven't you? Should I worry you're going to drop my company for his?" He was clearly joking, but Tai, often cursed with the inability to spot an obvious jest, shook his head.

"Never, Dart! We're a team, after all. It's just now we're a team of three. You, me and…" He trailed off as he went to point at the Titan waiting outside. "He was there a moment ago."

Dart had to double-take. How was it possible to misplace someone as huge as the proto-Titan? He groaned. "I can't believe he's done that *again*."

Tai put his head in all four of his hands. "We really need to do something about that, don't we? Maybe put a bell on him or something?"

Outside the bar, Junior was walking towards the Druaa with whom they had so recently done business. She had spotted him standing alone and seized the opportunity as it was presented, beckoning him over with one delicately taloned finger. Initially, she'd not expected him to respond, but then to her surprise his faceplate had rippled with greenish light and he had started striding through the crowd toward her.

"Hello," he said, when she inclined her head politely to greet him. "How may I be of service? Is there an issue with the objects that friends Dart and Tai have traded? Should I fetch them?"

"No," she said, putting out a hand as though she would touch him. "It's you I'm interested in. Tell me who you are. Where do you come from? You seem different to other Titans." The Druaa circled Junior as if appraising a particularly curious relic, which wasn't an unfair description of him.

"As you have correctly stated, I am what friend Tai and friend Dart have told me is called a Titan. I do not know if this is correct, because I do not remember. But I am keen to learn. I have learned much since travelling with them, but there is still so much more." There was a soft, ambient glow behind the faceplate as he spoke, and the voice modulation had that same gentleness to it. "My name is Junior, but only because I did not have a name of my own and friend Dart has stated that calling myself Dart II would be too confusing." He paused. "I am … glad to know you. May I know your name?"

"Aren't you the polite one?" She narrowed her eyes, studying the unusual proto-Titan as if she could dig out his mysteries through scrutiny alone. "My name is S'sithik. You say you remember nothing?"

"I recall everything that I have experienced since I was awakened with perfect clarity. Would you like me to recount my adventures with friends Dart and Tai?"

She held up her hand and shook her head. The Naaz-Rokha had

already left her with a low-grade headache and somehow managed to convince her to part with far more aurei than she'd wanted, so she really did not care to hear more about them than she absolutely had to. Junior, on the other hand, might just make up for what she had lost in that deal.

"No, save that for another time." Her tongue ran around her lips. A curiosity like this could be the best acquisition she had ever made. She knew *plenty* of people who would very much like to get their hands on a compliant Titan. "Do they own you, Junior? Are you their servant?"

The faceplate rippled with amber light, as if giving the question appropriate consideration, and Junior tipped its head to one side. "No," it said after a few moments of thought. "No. I am neither a possession, nor am I any sort of servant. I am travelling with them for the two simple facts that first, I choose to, and secondly, because they allow me to. I believe I am free to go wherever I wish without recourse."

"Would you like to come with me when I leave this place?"

"What are you doing?" The voice belonged to Tai, once more mounted in the harness on Dart's back. The little Naaz was practically glowing with barely contained rage. He gripped the edges of the seat until his knuckles were white with stress. S'sithik looked up into his monoculared face and gave him a lazy smile.

"I'm simply talking to your friend here," she replied. "I don't believe that is a crime?"

"Junior?" Tai turned to their Titan companion, with a gnawing sense of anxiety. They'd not been together all that long, in the grand scheme of things, but Tai formed attachments quickly. Experiencing the galaxy with Junior was like seeing it all again for the first time. With his endless questions and observations, Junior made it a more exciting place. Seeing things through the eyes of a being whose knowledge of the galaxy was like that of a child's was a gift. Admittedly, it was an armored, biomechanical child towering over everybody they met, and also in possession of an affinity for growing things that exceeded any botanical scientist they had encountered – but still, a gift.

"Junior?" Tai asked again, querulously. "Are you *trying* to leave us?"

The Titan turned its head, its expressive faceplate looking to the Naaz-Rokha, then turned again to consider the S'sithik.

"I am not," it replied after a time. "You awakened me from my stasis and I still believe that there is much I can learn from you. I find your company stimulating and entertaining in equal measure. I believe the…" There was a fractional pause as Junior made an assessment and decided on the correct form of address. "I believe that friend S'sithik was merely expressing a keen interest in furthering my knowledge, is that not right, friend S'sithik?"

"Oh, yes," she said, her eyes narrowing. "A *very* keen interest indeed." She let her eyes range over the Titan, then glanced at Tai. Their gazes met in a clash of silent wills and she capitulated first, turning her back and slithering to her crystalline display of relics. In so doing, none of them could see the expression of fury on her face. Junior watched her leave, clearly puzzled.

"I am very pleased to have encountered you, friend S'sithik," he called after her, before turning back to Dart and Tai. "Well, she seemed nice."

The fact that they would, at some point, educate Junior on the less pleasant aspects of life in an often-violent galaxy all but broke Tai's heart. He really wanted to preserve the Titan's curious innocence for as long as possible but was afraid of what it might mean when it was lost. For now, he could stave it off with a muttered agreement that yes, indeed, she had seemed nice. He settled back in the harness and absently patted Dart on the shoulder.

"I think what Tai is trying to say," said Dart, sensing his partner's mood, "is that we're really glad you're not leaving us yet. We have fun together, right? You're learning lots of interesting things? We're keeping our promise." The last was a clear statement rather than a question and the Titan's faceplate practically glowed golden.

"Yes," he responded with clear enthusiasm. "You promised to share with me. And you have done that. I am beginning to understand the concept of 'enjoyment' – I believe that I am finding our shared experiences, which you refer to as 'adventures', enjoyable. Not only do they increase my knowledge with their stimulation and sensory input, but they are also entertaining." Junior looked over toward the Druaa. "There was a tone in your voice, friend Tai, that is not commonly present. When you appeared to believe I would be departing with friend S'sithik, I detected what you have previously described as anxiety. Do you feel so strongly about my ongoing proximity?"

"Only for as long as you want to, Junior," said Tai. "We don't own you, after all."

"You aren't property," said Dart, picking up the thread. "You're our *friend*. And there is no reason in the wide galaxy that we would ever stop you from choosing your own path, if that's what you ever decide to do. For now, though, we're happy you're still going to be hanging around with us." It was exactly the right choice of phrase to settle Tai's apprehension, and he was relieved to feel his Naaz companion relax.

"Then I have no further decisions to make at this time," said Junior and nodded. "I will continue to travel with you until further assessment is required."

"She's going to be trouble, that one," a voice rumbled from behind Dart. They turned to find a hooded Hacan with a cybernetic eye regarding them levelly. "Probably for you, I'd wager. And, unfortunately, she won't be the only one to see how they can obtain your Titan. I'm learning that here, on the Gloaming, everyone knows everything no matter how hard you try to keep hidden."

"Can everybody not just leave us alone?" Tai protested. "I just want to be able to eat and drink in peace!"

"Something we can do for you, friend?" Dart asked warily, casting a suspicious eye over this new interruption.

"Maybe," the Hacan said, "but we should definitely find a different bar if we're going to talk terms."

"Who said we wanted to talk terms? Junior isn't for sale!" Tai was indignant, two hands at his hips and one waving a finger at this impudent stranger.

"I don't want to buy your friend – I'm hiring crew." The newcomer gave Junior an appraising look. "A Titan is a rare and valuable asset. And from what I can assess, you're a crew without a job."

"That pitch doesn't sound any better than hers," Dart replied, folding his arms defensively. "Not to mention you seem tense, as though someone might jump you at any moment. Is someone going to jump you? Is it safe for us to be seen with you?"

The Hacan snorted, conveying that should anybody try to jump him, they would regret it in short order. "How many other Naaz-Rokha have you seen strolling around the station in the company of a Titan? It wasn't hard to find you, even among all this." He gestured at the bustling market. "So, if the Druaa has connections and decides to make trouble for you, how hard do you think it will be for others to track you down?"

"That sounds like a threat," Tai said. Dart nodded.

"It isn't," said the Hacan. "But I do find myself in need of pioneers and explorers. I believe there are none finer than the Naaz-Rokha. Your Titan friend also seems to have an appetite for study, which I can offer alongside something even better: an unsolvable puzzle." He shrugged. "Of course, I may be mistaken – in which case you have my apologies and I'll take my aurei elsewhere and leave you to your refreshment."

Tai immediately changed his attitude. "Now let's not be hasty," he said, holding the other hand up.

"Your assessment is correct. I am keen to learn more of the galaxy!" Junior inserted. "And I do love puzzles."

The Hacan smiled. "Then let's get out of here, and I will tell you what I have in mind."

There was another bar, two floors down-station from the one Dart and Tai had visited previously, this one occupying what had once been a storage depot. This was fortuitous as it allowed more than enough space for Junior to stand. Drinks were procured as well as food for Dart, who was still hungry after being forced to abandon his half-eaten meal following their confrontation with the Druaa. Harrugh paid for everything and the Naaz-Rokha settled in, absolutely fine with that arrangement.

After awakening from the Prophet's Tears, Harrugh had tried as best he could to explain to Ashalla what he could recall of the visions he had experienced. She had listened patiently to what he had to admit sounded like an increasingly disjointed and half-remembered fever dream. Once he finished recounting the vision, she quietly asked him what he intended to do next. An expedition into unknown space needed more than just them; it needed a capable crew, but no ordinary crew. He needed other perspectives beyond Hacan.

He had no real idea what they expected to find at the coordinates the hrrtos had supplied, but if the Tears had imparted anything, it was that there was a looming danger, one that was greater than just Kenara alone. The sheer sense of urgency drove him forward. Harrugh had left the vial and Ashalla with the Ral Nel, making his way back to the trade plazas in search of freelancers, promising to return as quickly as possible once he had secured reliable help.

But not just any help. He remembered the Titan from when he first set foot on the Gloaming and wondered if the rare creature might have any other knowledge or insight on his mission. The Ral Nel had provided information Harrugh would never have obtained – how strong would a crew of intrepid, knowledgeable, and clever species be? Harrugh wanted to find out.

He sipped his drink, a Hacan liqueur that most other species found intolerably bitter, but which for him was a pleasant reminder of simpler times, then leaned forward, half his face hidden in the shadow of his hood, weighing up his new companions with interest.

"You have quite the story to tell about how you came to be travelling together, I would imagine," he said as an opener.

The Naaz who had introduced himself as Tai laughed. "Junior made a boring routine survey expedition into something very interesting indeed," he replied companionably. "We found him and sort of woke him up from a very long nap. We still haven't figured out how he came to be there or why he was sleeping to begin with, but he's been great company ever since."

"Thank you, friend Tai," commented Junior in his oddly expressionless tone. "You and Dart are acceptable company also."

"Pleased to make your acquaintance, Junior," Harrugh said to the Titan. "You can call me Harrugh."

Dart, who was shoveling food down his gullet as fast as he could manage – just in case they had to rush off again – tipped his head to the side and chewed his mouthful thoughtfully before swallowing it down. "There's not really a polite way of asking this question. Are you *that* Harrugh? I don't know how common a name it is."

Tai, who'd not even registered the Hacan's name, blinked, then the one visible eye widened. He turned to the Hacan, suddenly very interested in the response.

The Hacan adjusted his hood with an expression of vague discomfort. "I am *a* Harrugh," he said in a low voice, aware that several eyes had turned their way already thanks to their enormous dining companion. "Can we perhaps leave it there?" His eyes met those of Dart and an unspoken understanding passed between them. Dart inclined his head.

"As you wish," he said. "So, what is this proposal you have for us?"

"I am in possession of a set of coordinates," said Harrugh,

relieved that the Rokha was not going to push his line of enquiry any further. "According to galactic charts there is nothing currently recorded at that location. However, I have reason to believe that they must be pointing at *something* of value and thus, I intend to make the journey. I am already making arrangements for a suitable vessel to get us there, but I need a crew. Preferably, explorers with knowledge and experience to help with whatever we find when we get there."

Tai puffed up visibly at the compliment to the Naaz-Rokha exploratory prowess. He leaned across the table and studied Harrugh carefully. "You've dealt with our people before, I take it? Your offer sounds fascinating and all, but you said yourself you don't know where you're going. It could still be nothing. Am I understanding correctly?"

"Completely correct. But, as I said, I do have reason to believe it's *something* rather than nothing," said Harrugh with a brief smile. "I'm willing to pay you even if it does turn out to be a set of empty spatial coordinates. Then all you will have lost is time, and I will arrange for you to be dropped off at a location of your choice."

"So, let's recap," said Dart. "A mysterious journey to an unknown location and we get paid even if it's a bust?" He nudged Tai. "What do you think?"

"I think it's strange that our new friend, who I am *pretty* sure must have a bunch of contacts and resources at his fingertips, has come looking to hire help in a half-decent bar on an unlisted orbital," came the reply. The sense of mistrust was palpable. "My honest response is I'm more concerned by what we *aren't* being told."

"It's complicated," said Harrugh, somewhat understating his position. "Though I certainly have the resources to be able to pay for your services, I believe you might be overestimating my influence."

"Friend Dart," Junior cut in, "do you believe this to be Harrugh Gefhara?"

The Titan's voice was not subtle as he asked the question. The words dropped like lead into the low conversation of the bar. In the far corner, a pair of Hacan who had been quietly playing a hand of Triora looked up and over at the table. One leaned into the other, who nodded sharply.

"The Quieron?" Tai asked sharply.

"Harrugh Gefhara, also known as the Golden General and more recently as the Nascent Twilight, resigned his position as Quieron," continued Junior, happily oblivious to the darkening expression on Harrugh's face. "This was something that you clearly stated had already happened and was old news, do you recall, friend Tai? The reason for his resignation does not appear to be known but was an event unprecedented in the history of the Kenaran leadership. I believe this may have resulted in some friction among the more traditional…"

"He's a traitor."

One of the two Hacan from the corner stood in front of them. "Show your true face, Gefhara. No need for propriety when we already know who and what you are. The Golden General, hero of the L1Z1X incursion, who ran away from leadership. What a joke." He was young, with solid musculature and auburn fur and his tail was quivering with obvious agitation.

"My friends," said Harrugh, with a low growl. "This is neither the time nor the place for this discussion. You are intruding on a private conversation and I'll thank you to…"

"To what, Gefhara? To move on? No, I don't think I will, *thank you.*" The reek of alcohol on the other Hacan was an embarrassment to Harrugh. He looked at the Hacan's companion: another young male Hacan, and this one at least had the decency to look uncomfortable at his friend's actions – but not embarrassed enough to disagree or to drag him back to his seat.

He felt suddenly tired, as though the weight of recent events settled upon his shoulders all at once. He was tired of pretending he wasn't who he was. Tired of avoiding his own people like a pariah because they didn't understand. None of them had seen what he had seen. Harrugh Gefhara was tired of *everything*. A spark kindled in his soul and began to sear away the doubt, uncertainty and shame that had haunted him since the hrrtos had shared his portent of doom. A spark that, were it fed correctly, would become a steady flame of certainty.

Something that had been tightly wound in Harrugh snapped. He flexed his hand, letting his claws slide further out. "What exactly is it that you want from me?" The warning snarl behind the question startled the less drunk of the two. "I made my choices. I am doing what I think is best for all Hacan, as I have always done. I'm sure you don't understand, you probably don't even care, but I will live with the consequences. What have *you* done for us lately?" He waved at their drinks. "Sat at a bar drowning in alcohol and wallowing in self-pity?"

The young Hacan blinked in stunned indignation, so when the swipe came, Harrugh was ready for it. He batted it aside with contemptuous ease and surged to his feet, tipping over the chair and letting his hood fall away. Let them see his true face, propriety be damned. His assailant took a step back in shock as Harrugh whirled, grabbed the dune spear and in one deft motion hooked the Hacan's legs, spilling him onto the floor. Dart scooped another morsel of food into his mouth and watched, fascinated by this unexpected and undeniably exciting turn of events.

"I like him," he said around the mouthful. "I think we should take the job."

Tai sighed and shook his head.

Harrugh stepped forward to loom over the fallen Hacan, his spear raised and leveled at him. The low hubbub of conversation in the bar had died away and all eyes were on the unfolding spectacle, but he didn't care. He had spent so long moving like a ghost among his people, jumping at shadows, it felt good to be seen – no matter how negative it may be.

"You should take your friend away before he winds up getting hurt," Harrugh growled at the less drunk of the Hacan who seemed torn between leaping to his companion's aid and shrinking into the crowd. "We can all forget that this shameful meeting ever happened."

The prone assailant seized the opportunity, with typical alcohol-fueled bravado, to try to lunge for Harrugh and met the butt end of the spear coming back the other way. There was an audible crack and the Hacan flopped insensibly to the floor.

"Should I intervene, friend Tai?" Junior watched this altercation with great interest.

"You absolutely should not," came the reply. "We haven't agreed to be hired yet, so it's not our business."

Dart ate another mouthful of food. "But we should make it our business."

"That is uncharacteristically uncharitable of you, friend Tai," Junior replied, his faceplate creasing with umber light.

Tai gave the Titan a grin. "Don't worry, Junior. He doesn't look like he needs any help. We can always jump in if it gets out of hand and, as Dart said, make it our business."

Seeing his companion laid out, the second Hacan came to a decision and rushed at Harrugh, claws extended. Harrugh ducked the clumsy swipe and came up head-first with a brawler's headbutt, cracking his attacker's chin. The Hacan yelped, stumbling backward and allowing Harrugh space to pivot on the spot. He whirled the spear so that the shaft connected solidly with his assailant's head, catapulting him off his feet and through a nearby table with a crash of breaking glass.

Harrugh looked around at the now-silent bar and the expressions of curiosity and interest that were fixed on him. Dart finished the last scrap of food and got to his feet, making a big show of dusting off the crumbs, doing a most excellent job of feigning disinterest.

"Is that it?" Harrugh roared. The adrenaline was slowly draining, but he had enough left to go again should he need to. "Have you been following me all day for this?"

Silence.

"No, Harrugh Gefhara, they haven't been following you all day." There was a low, clattering voice from the entrance to the bar and they all turned to face the new arrivals: a small, eclectic mob standing behind the chitinous, viridescent form of a large N'orr, its insectoid eyes firmly fixed on Harrugh. There was the whine of an energy weapon cycling to charge.

"Oooh," said Dart.

"*I* have."

"And you are…?"

The N'orr shrugged. "A private investor, an interested party. My name doesn't matter. What matters is that you will hand over the data vault you possess, along with a sizeable sum of aurei in order to keep this matter between us. Or things will have to turn nasty, I'm afraid."

"I don't know what you mean," countered Harrugh, standing squarely before the N'orr, hands gripped around his spear. "I have no intention of doing business with you today. I suggest you move before I move you."

"This doesn't seem like a friendly transaction," Tai whispered loudly to Dart.

Dart nodded his agreement, his eyes shifting from Harrugh to the N'orr. "I know who I'd prefer to trust in this instance."

"It looks like this matter is going to escalate," said Junior, his synthesized tones cutting across the sudden, tense silence that had fallen. "I suggest everyone takes a step back and we can discuss it like…"

Further comment on the matter was forestalled by the unmistakable sound of a grenade hitting the floor space between Harrugh and his antagonist. Everyone stared at it in surprise until Harrugh recognized it as a particle grenade. Junior also looked down, then up at the unfolding scene. He moved his bulk to stand as a barrier between the two sides. "Friends," he said, "I calculate that this armament will detonate in ten seconds, so I suggest that you all stand clear."

Tai was already scrambling into his harness on Dart's back. Harrugh glanced at them. "Do we have a deal?"

"If you get us out of this in one piece," said Dart, ready to run, "we'll discuss terms. In the meantime, I suggest we leave as fast as possible."

"Wisest thing I've heard all day," agreed Harrugh.

The particle grenade detonated, the two groups splintering, running in opposite directions. Junior lumbered behind his companions, his huge stride making it easy to keep pace with them as they headed for the plaza.

"Is every day this exciting with you around, Harrugh?" Tai asked from his position on Dart's back.

"I really, really hope not," came the reply.

ELEVEN

"Attention!"

The alarm echoed down the corridor accompanied by the calm, reassuring tones of the automated announcement. "Deck twenty is currently subject to disruption due to an ongoing incident. Peacekeepers are working to contain the situation. Visitors should avoid deck twenty until notified of resolution."

The announcement began again after a short pause but was abruptly cut off by a stray blast of fire that destroyed the intercom.

"This is going to cost you extra!" Tai trilled from Dart's back as they sought cover.

"You appear to be deeply unpopular with these individuals, friend Harrugh," Junior said.

Blasts streaked across the plaza, cratering the wall behind them. Dart unslung the pulse carbine from its holder across his back and glanced at the Titan. "Keep your head down, Junior. I don't think they like us much either."

"But they don't know anything about us, friend Dart. They do not have an accurate basis upon which to form such an opinion."

"If there's time later, Junior, maybe we can educate them."

The holographic display next to them exploded as an energy beam cut across the plaza, showering them with scorched debris and leaving devastating holes in the walls and floors.

"Or maybe not," inserted Tai. "I'd say the chances of that are diminishing with every passing second. Which way to your ship,

Harrugh? I would quite like to get out of here now. Sort of feels like we have worn out our welcome in the Gloaming."

"Agreed," said Harrugh. "And we should try to avoid getting caught by the peacekeepers just as much as these thugs."

"But we are not the guilty party," Junior stated. Solid rounds slammed into the nearby mercantile booths with a series of rattling reports and shrieking ricochets.

"I don't think they're going to see it that way," Dart replied. "So where to?"

"Two levels up, hangar nine."

"Looks like there are a bunch of service tunnels across the way." Tai pointed. "If we get in there, we should be able to avoid the main transitways. Hopefully we can lose these idiots while we're at it and be away before trouble catches up."

Harrugh and Dart nodded their agreement. Harrugh took a beat to catch his breath. Tai was delighted. "Junior," he called. "This is what all that running practice was for. Times like this. Go!"

They broke from cover, sprinting across the now-empty plaza. Dart blazed away with the carbine, firing more for effect than with any real intention of doing harm. Return fire chased them across the hall, kicking up sparks, debris and sprays of molten metal in their wake. They had just about made it to the tunnel entrance when they heard the strident commands of station enforcers ordering all present to stand down and surrender or be subdued by force.

"Should we not comply with the instructions of the local authority?" Junior asked, his heavy footfalls crunching as he took huge strides.

"Here's how it is, Junior. There are degrees of authority…" Dart huffed as they skidded into the tunnel opening.

"If the Gloaming was run and maintained by the Emirates," Tai continued, bouncing gently on his partner's back, "then of course we would *absolutely* comply with the instructions of local law enforcement."

"But since it isn't," Dart followed up, "then we don't really know whose law it is that they're enforcing. Could be anybody's laws. Could just be making *up* laws for all we know. So probably just best to get out of here and let them get on with it. After all, we've got a job of our own to do, right?"

"That's right," agreed Tai.

"Duly noted," said Junior.

Harrugh followed them into the tunnel, turning to glance back across the plaza to where a fierce skirmish had broken out between their attackers and the peacekeepers. The big N'orr who had begun the confrontation was gesturing in their direction with a clawed hand and a few of his colleagues broke away from the group and set off in pursuit.

"They're not done yet." Harrugh scowled.

They headed through the service tunnels with haste, passing several small establishments that had closed their doors while the nearby disturbance was dealt with. Their path took them via a wide and undeniably circuitous loop back toward the gravity conveyors at the core. While Dart and Tai claimed not to be very familiar with the layout of the Gloaming, Harrugh was abundantly glad for their presence as they seemed to have a natural talent for simply finding their way, even in a warren of unfamiliar corridors.

They all skidded to a halt at a confluence of tunnels, where several passages led away in different directions. "What are we stopping for?" Tai asked. "They're probably still after us!"

"Maybe you can climb down from back there and carry me for a bit?" Dart huffed, catching his breath.

"No, thanks. You seem to be doing just fine." Tai chuckled. "Really, though, I don't think they're going to let us go that easily."

"You think they will have locked down the conveyors because of the fight?" Dart asked.

Harrugh shook his head. "I doubt it. This is still a Hacan station at its core. I'd be inclined to think that only a serious emergency would result in a trade lockdown." There was a clatter from the direction they had come, punctuated by the rasping echo of voices.

"Your assessment was correct, friend Tai," Junior observed. "We are still being pursued."

"I'm tired of running," Harrugh rumbled.

"Never had to fall back as a general?" Tai chimed in.

"Only as a way of drawing the enemy in before springing the trap," Harrugh replied.

Dart nodded appreciatively. "Well then…" The Rokha rolled his shoulders. "Shall we?"

They spread themselves out around the corridor nexus apart from Junior, who was instructed to stand in the center of the chamber. In most conventional circumstances it was impossible to realistically conceal a Titan. On the other hand, it provided a distraction. The first thug to enter the chamber was a human in dirty overalls, brandishing a solid shot beam pistol. His attention fixed on Junior, who raised a huge hand in greeting.

"Salutations, nameless assailant," Junior said brightly. "You should be aware that my new friend Harrugh–" he haft of the Hacan's spear cracked heavily into the side of the man's head, dropping him like a stone "–kindly requests that you cease your pursuit."

The next two out of the corridor were better prepared, having witnessed the fate of their companion. One, a Hacan with flaxen fur, advanced ahead while the other covered her with a stubby beam rifle braced against her shoulder. Dart, in hiding, emerged from the shadows and grabbed the barrel of the gun belonging to the first as it nosed into the room. The action dragged the thug off balance, and he attempted to swing around, regain control, and club at Dart with the butt of the carbine. For his part, Harrugh vaulted past the fighting duo to the woman with the beam weapon.

It discharged too high, scoring a glowing, molten line in the ceiling as Harrugh descended on her with leonine fury. She tried to aim for another, more accurate shot, but Harrugh deftly knocked the barrel to one side with his spear, the beam searing a hole in the wall beside him. He didn't wait for her to try again, kicking her legs from under her before a quick strike from his own weapon rendered her insensible.

"Enough of this!" another Hacan snarled as he came around the corner with a levelled beam pistol. "Just give me what An'rak wants, and we can stop this stupid…"

There was a dull clatter as a particle grenade rolled to the Hacan's feet. Harrugh leapt back, wondering who had thrown it, and screwed his eyes shut as the bomb detonated with a blinding flash and boom of displaced air. He dragged himself to his feet, ears ringing, to see the Hacan out cold on the floor and a human woman leaning insouciantly in the corridor entryway, looking pleased. She had strikingly pink hair and was clad in a form-fitting flight suit with a pair of beam pistols on her hips. A plethora of tools and devices covered the belt around her waist.

"Hello, lovelies," she said cheerfully. "Now isn't *this* a spot of bother?"

TWELVE

THE OTHER SIDE OF THE GALAXY

Captain Nichols gazed up at the tumultuous sky and sighed. The storm never relented. It was an implacable, grinding rumble that sometimes faded to a dull roar. Never for long, though: it would return with a shattering crash that vibrated the hull of the downed *Orlando*. This seemingly endless assault, combined with the driving wind that howled and screamed its way through the boulders and canyons of the barren world, made effective rest a growing challenge among the increasingly fractious crew.

The fact that Orragh had managed to land the *Orlando* in one piece with minimal injury to the crew would earn him a commendation if they ever escaped this rock. *When* they escaped this rock, Nichols chided herself.

Skelton's assessment of the damage had not been optimistic. The ship had been in bad shape even before planetfall, but as it stood now, propped up on a shelf of amber rock, its hull buckled and one engine ruined, it looked like a mortally wounded warrior in repose. Scavenger teams had been dispatched to pick over the trail of debris the ship had left in its wake in the hope of locating any useful resources. Thus far, however, they had only salvaged enough material to patch the worst of the breaches. It was going to take a lot more than reclaimed armor plate and rapidly fading hope to get them back into space.

"You seem pensive," Kketch said, sidling up to stand beside her to share in the study of the perpetual storm.

"In case it had escaped your notice, I have a lot on my mind," Nichols replied and was immediately contrite. She opened her mouth to apologize but Kketch simply nodded. "How are we looking?"

"Lieutenant Skelton does not believe it will be possible to effect repairs to the damaged engine under the current conditions and with the resources available," Kketch rumbled. "The majority of our sensory array is offline. Sixteen major breaches have been identified in the superstructure, all of which represent a fatal compromise of integrity. There are upward of sixty microfractures throughout the internal frame."

The captain winced. "Is that all?"

"Mr Orragh is surprisingly optimistic about the bridge critical systems. If I may quote him directly..." He cleared his throat and offered a surprisingly passable impression of the dour ship's engineer. "*If we can get her off the ground, then I can fly her.*"

"Of course," Nichols replied with a faint smile.

"A full inventory also indicates that we have enough supplies to avoid rationing for several solar weeks – longer if engineering can restore one of the matter converters. Water is more of a serious situation, but there are enough functional recyclers that it won't be a problem for the immediate future."

"A world wracked by endless storms but not a drop of rain."

"Indeed," Kketch agreed. "Quite the conundrum."

"So, to recap. We're not going to die of thirst or starvation any time soon. That's something." It was cold comfort, but at least it was *some* comfort. "Do we have any sight of the Nekro?"

The big Xxcha shook his reptilian head, scaled brow furrowing. "Not clearly, captain. What sensory information Mr Orragh has been able to piece together is sporadic and fragmentary at best. The last return showed that their numbers had multiplied. However, our systems are damaged, and the storm is badly degrading our signal, so there is every chance we are picking up false returns and spectrographic echoes."

"Or given the way our luck has been going, there could, in fact, be a Nekro swarm massing in near-space."

"That is, unfortunately, also a possibility, captain," Kketch replied. "However, they could easily have destroyed us before our precipitous fall and did not, a behavior singularly out of character for Nekro machine-forms, would you not agree?"

Nichols conceded the point.

Kketch continued, "I would hypothesize that the storm which is proving so troublesome for our scopes and sensor returns is also in some way deleterious to the Nekro."

"That is interesting. Although it doesn't explain why they might be gathering up there. We can't be *that* tempting a prize. Still, I'll moderate my cursing the next time the thunder inevitably wakes me. It might be what's actually keeping us alive."

She turned away from the crippled ship and looked out once more over the empty, rocky plains. The wind sighed mournfully through fissures and chasms and around the cloud-scraping spires dotting the landscape like skeletal fingers. The only movement came from the dust as it whirled in dervish spirals, flickering with ambient charge. The crew had already learned to take precautions against the minor shocks that plagued anybody working outside. Dr Takksil had made an assessment and stated that there was no risk of serious harm, but the weather conditions did nothing to help an already strained and fractious crew.

"What do you make of them?" Nichols asked, pointing at one of the looming spires.

"At first I believed they might be a sign of extinct habitation," Kketch said. "The structures display a regularity of arrangement that does not lend itself to natural formations. It also appears as though they might be earthing the storm, acting as conductors of sorts and preventing random discharges which under our current circumstances would be–" the thunder grumbled overhead as if to punctuate the science officer's assertion "– deeply troublesome. Of course, I would need to get much closer to confirm but based on the observable coronal discharge it would appear that the opposite might be true."

"You mean the spires might be fueling the storm?" Nichols asked, skeptical.

"It's only a hypothesis." Kketch held up a clawed hand in supplication. "However, the scouts have yet to find any indication that civilization might once have arisen on this planet. We could be the first to discover a previously undocumented natural phenomenon."

Nichols smiled at the Xxcha. "Let's focus on our immediate survival, Officer Kketch. Then we can put our thoughts to exploration and discovery of the unknown."

"Just so, captain, just so."

THIRTEEN

"So, who exactly are *you*?" Dart growled. He winced, the blast from the grenade still ringing in his ears.

Junior and Harrugh gathered beside him and Tai on the other side of the corridor nexus and regarded the pink-haired woman with an appropriate amount of suspicion. The Titan, on the other hand, had no such reservations.

"Salutations, unknown human female. Your intervention was most impressive and fortuitously timed."

The woman beamed. "Suffi An," she introduced herself. "The pleasure was all mine. It looked like you could use the help."

"Salutations, friend Suffi An! My friends Dart and Tai have given me the name Junior, so that is what you can call me, too."

Dart gave Tai a look over his shoulder. "You're really going to have to have that talk with him, sooner rather than later."

"Why do I have to do it?" Tai protested.

"What do you want, Suffi An?" Harrugh cut across them before what sounded like a long and much revisited argument could get under way.

"That's a big question, Harrugh!" Suffi An replied playfully, taking an exaggerated step away from where she leaned. "I *want* all sorts of things. I want one of those fancy Hacan dune spears. I want ten thousand aurei. I want new seats for my ship, good ones, ideally in deep red. I want galactic peace and harmony…" She counted the items off on her fingers.

Harrugh growled, not remotely amused by her sass. "With us. What do you want with us? Who are you working for?"

"To answer your first question, I don't know yet, haven't decided. To answer your multi-faceted second question, I *represent* the Mentak Coalition. And sometimes a few worthwhile private interests. Who I work for is presently under review." Another of those beaming smiles. "Let's see what today brings."

"So. You're a pirate," Tai said, fixing her with his cybernetic monocle.

Suffi An's expression was one of exaggerated outrage. "I am not! What a thing to say! Kenaran authorities take a very dim view of pirates operating in-system."

Though he was grateful for the assistance, Harrugh's patience was rapidly beginning to wear thin. "Why were you even following us? I assume that was you with the grenade back at the bar?"

Suffi An assumed an air of nonchalance. "Maybe it was, or maybe it was just a concerned citizen looking out for victims of the local syndicate. And I've been following you since you arrived on the station, Harrugh Gefhara. Two facts: you're not very subtle, and I'm *very* good at what I do."

"Is there anybody on this orbital who isn't after you?" Dart asked.

Harrugh narrowed his eyes and tightened his grip on the spear. "Following me? Why, exactly?"

Suffi An pointed a finger at the Rokha. "Another good question! But the answer is no, not everybody on the station is after him. Sure, there's a handful of stuffy old traditionalists who would like to tell him what they think of his life choices, but they're not really any bother. There's the Desert Wind Syndicate, who apparently want his data vault along with a healthy pile of aurei. Seems somebody tipped them off that he was carrying something that *might* be valuable enough to be worth their time."

It didn't take much of a leap of logic. "Bhagrra."

Suffi An pointed at him. "That's the one! So, there's that – there's also a Druaa who has put out a speculative offer on your Titan friend here." She looked at the Naaz-Rokha and gestured to Junior. "So they're as much after *you* as they're after Harrugh."

"Oh!" Tai squeaked. "We should leave quickly."

"Yes," grumbled Dart. "But at least we have a job?"

Harrugh sighed. "Go back a few steps. Tell me about the Desert Wind Syndicate."

Suffi An wrinkled her nose. "Small time nobodies. A local outfit operating out of the Gloaming. Wherever there's business there's always crime tripping along in its money-strewn wake. People all over the station doing a bit of this, a bit of that…"

"And you would…" Tai began.

"…know all of this how?" Dart ended.

Suffi An sighed, looking around at the dingy corridor nexus. "Much as I love to hang around in murky serviceways discussing my dazzling skills, not to mention my sparkling personality, we should probably get out of here now. The Syndicate have their hands full with the station enforcers, but both of those groups will be on their way soon, no doubt to have a very *thorough* discussion with all concerned which now includes yours truly. I'm sure you're all perfectly lovely, but it's not hard work to track a Titan. Therefore, I'd rather not be here when they arrive. Shall we?" She gestured to one of the corridors.

Harrugh scowled but lowered the spear. "Fine," he said. "For now, at least. Lead the way."

"It would be my absolute *pleasure*," Suffi An replied brightly. She strode past them, into the corridor that she had pointed toward. She glanced over her shoulder in a manner that was faintly coquettish. "Coming?"

Dart and Tai both looked at Harrugh who rolled his eyes before nodding. "We're coming," he confirmed. "But we're not done yet."

"Of course," Suffi An replied, "I completely agree. There's *so* much to discuss!"

"I like her!" Junior declared.

"You like everybody, Junior," Tai chided. "We need to have a talk about that once we are out of this mess."

Suffi An led them expertly through the confusing tangle of service corridors, though Harrugh checked with Dart and Tai at every junction. They quietly confirmed that the Mentak agent was directing them toward the elevators that would take them up to the Ral Nel *Trailblazer*. When they finally arrived at the freight conveyors, they were relieved to find them still in operation. The group were less relieved to find the elevators patrolled by a significant peacekeeper presence.

"I'm no expert at this sort of thing," Dart said from the cover of a stack of cargo boxes, "but getting past them without being noticed is gonna be a challenge." They turned to look at Junior who was dutifully doing his best – without much success – to look as small as possible.

Suffi An peered around the loading bay and then smiled. "Don't need to worry yourselves. Shouldn't be a problem."

"How…" Tai started to ask, but Suffi An was already confidently heading towards a group of uniformed enforcers. They turned at her approach, a few of them reaching tentatively for the shock batons fastened at their belts, but the officer in charge of the group waved them down.

"She's going to sell us out," hissed Tai from Dart's back. "She's led us along by our snouts and now she's going to serve us up."

"But we have not done anything wrong," Junior asserted. "We should not be concerned about the lawful authority."

"Maybe," Dart replied, "but I don't exactly trust her either."

The exchange between Suffi An and the officer appeared to be going well. She said something that the concealed group couldn't hear and made an expansive gesture before rolling her eyes. The man laughed and a few of his squad laughed as well. Then she clapped him on the shoulder and beckoned to Harrugh and his companions.

"Well, this is your job," Tai said to the Hacan. "How do you want to do this?"

"I want to get out of here," he replied, "and I don't see that we have much of a choice if we want that to happen any time soon." He straightened, walking boldly from his position behind the containers.

Dart, Tai and Junior followed without hesitating. The officer, a human in the same dark blue uniform that had been seen throughout the rest of the station, acknowledged them with a curt nod, waving them through toward the conveyors without question. Harrugh nodded back courteously but otherwise maintained his pace until they reached the grav-platform entryway. Only then did he turn to find Suffi An hurrying up behind them.

"I would be very interested to know how you managed to arrange that," said Harrugh, once the conveyor was under way.

"Oh, ways and means," Suffi An replied. "Well, that and I slipped him a few hundred aurei to keep his nose out of our business. I'll be adding that to my fee, by the way. Just in the interest of transparency. I know you like to be clear on the terms."

"Your fee," Harrugh replied flatly. "If you want propriety, Suffi An, the proper form would be for us to discuss your stock before any terms are set."

Suffi An shrugged. "Don't you feel that you've had a fairly good demonstration of my talents already? For free, I might add."

"Unasked for," he countered.

"You'd have preferred me to leave you to the rogues in the tunnels?"

"I'd prefer to know exactly what it is you want out of this partnership." Harrugh's irritation was increasing.

Suffi An tapped a finger against her chin. "Well, I *had* thought about turning you in for the bounty." She laughed as Harrugh bristled. "Oh, don't get your tail in a knot, Golden General. I said I *thought* about it. That money would have paid off the work on my ship nicely. But… I've squandered that opportunity now, don't you think?"

"So why help us?" His suspicions ran deep.

"Well, let's see," she said. "Stop me if I miss anything. You've chartered a ship. You're hiring crew…" She tipped her head towards Dart, Tai and Junior. "A rather *unique* crew at that…"

"Thank you, friend Suffi An," chimed in Junior. "You, too, are unique."

"Well, thank you in return! Where was I? Oh, yes. You appear to be in possession of a trinket that has caused much excitement in the folks hereabouts. How am I doing?" She ignored his glowering face. "You're on a treasure hunt, Harrugh Gefhara, and I would wager my *spotless* reputation that it's something far more valuable than the tiny amount of aurei the N'orr would have paid. Am I right?"

Harrugh didn't reply, which was a good enough answer. She slapped her thigh. "I *knew* it! Well, I want in, but not just for myself, you understand. For the good of all those I represent."

"I changed my mind," Dart chuckled to Tai. "I like her, too."

They reached the twenty-second floor without further incident, making their way via the transit corridors toward the hangar. Away from the site of the skirmish, business continued without interruption and none of the enforcers gave them a second look as they made their way through the crowded concourse, emerging into the raucous space of the hangar. Harrugh noted with relief that Izt's *Trailblazer* was exactly where he had left it and touched his comm-bead.

"I'm back, Ash'ka," he said.

"I was starting to worry," she replied. "I thought you might have abandoned me again and gone on another pilgrimage."

"Not quite," he sighed. "I'll tell you all about it…"

Dart crashed into him and pulled him to the ground, a protesting Tai flailing in the harness behind him. Harrugh rolled across the deck. Before he could snap at Dart, a pair of energized beams sliced through the space where he had been standing, followed by the rattle of solid rounds. There was a chorus of shouts from the direction of the transit corridor and the hangar erupted into chaos.

"You've made this very expensive, Gefhara!" The clattering voice of the N'orr from the bar bellowed above the clamor of the crowd.

Junior had taken cover behind a row of power coils. Suffi An had taken cover behind Junior. Harrugh glanced at his Naaz-Rokha companion, giving a brief nod of thanks, before risking a glance at the hangar entrance. The N'orr and several others were forcing their way into the hangar, all with weapons trained in Harrugh's direction.

"Ash'ka! Tell Izt to open up and get the ship ready to go. We need to get out of here fast!"

There was a pause.

"Ash'ka?"

"Izt says that you have not yet agreed terms for the use of the ship," Ashalla replied, exasperation evident in her voice.

Harrugh clenched his teeth in frustration. "Tell him now is not the time!"

Harrugh, Dart and Tai pulled themselves into the shadow of a blocky tug craft as more fire chewed up the floor beside them. Suffi An drew her beam pistols, snap firing back at their assailants, the flechette shots eliciting a cry of pain where they struck. Clear of the surging throng, the thugs took up positions behind several stacks of cryo-casks and a loading sled before continuing to snipe at their pinned quarry.

"Izt says that now is the best time as he is negotiating from a position of strength," Ashalla continued.

Harrugh spat out a curse that was drowned out by the thump of the spear discharging and the whine of Dart's carbine.

"Told you a Titan was easy to trace. Just so you know, my price is going up!" Suffi An yelled from behind Junior.

"They're shooting at you, too!" Tai yelped. "You could always stay here!"

A retina-searing beam of light ruptured one of the coils, scattering molten metal like a spray of discarded gems. "Valid point!" Suffi An yelled back. "Well made!"

There was a heavy clanking of metal upon metal and a booming roar like an open blast furnace as a huge shape lumbered into the hangar. An articulated suit of burnished metal the color of burnt copper stomped its way into the bay, each of its arms clutching a cannon large enough for Junior had he been inclined to wield one. The armature was topped by a sculpted, beatific face with eyes that smoldered with inner flame.

"Don't suppose you're friends with a Gashlai, are you?" Dart called to Suffi An.

"I really wish I was," she called back and there was genuine longing in her tone.

"What does Izt want?!" Harrugh asked via the comm-bead, his eyes on the new, enormous arrival.

There was a pause in which the N'orr repeated its demand for Harrugh to hand over the data vault. Now, however, it also wanted a much larger sum of aurei and custody of the human in his company.

"Izt says that he wants exclusive study rights to the data vault and the Prophet's Tears." Ashalla's agitation was obvious.

"As long as it doesn't interfere with anything that might happen at our destination, then we have a deal," Harrugh replied. Part of the tug exploded in a shower of shattered hull plates as one of the Gashlai's massive guns discharged with a discordant scream of plasma.

"…says that's good enough!" Harrugh only caught the tail end of Ashalla's reply.

The *Trailblazer* opened its drive ports, venting a billowing cloud of coolant into the hangar. Harrugh and Suffi An didn't hesitate, sprinting into the pall. Dart and Tai followed, hurrying Junior along ahead of them. Streaking shots, booming reports and curses chased them through the churning smoke, but by the time the Naaz-Rokha tumbled into the main cabin of the ship, Izt had already fired up the engines.

"Welcome to *Trailblazer*. My ship, my rules. Izt'xet Alit Lo Masak. Not forget it, hmm?" There was a chorus of understanding affirmations and the thrusters roared, hurling the craft out of the waystation hangar and into the waiting void beyond.

At the same time, unseen and undetected, a smaller vessel detached from the hull of the station and dropped stealthily into the wake of the *Trailblazer*.

PART THREE

TRUST

FOURTEEN

Such journeys often lent themselves to small talk and this was absolutely no exception. They were barely out of the Gloaming's space before it started. The diminutive Naaz was the more loquacious of the pair and he was also clearly not afraid to show it.

"One of the last ships we travelled on was called the *Best Guess,*" he offered, his tone as bright and cheerful as ever. "I always *liked* that name. It felt like it had the spirit of adventure about it. It's good to know what your ship is called. It's all part of its character, Izt."

"Have observed style of ship naming among different species," acknowledged the Ral Nel with what appeared to be supreme indifference. "Ral Nel designate their various ships through more practical and logical means. Purpose and identity code. So, for example, this would be *Trailblazer 89426.* Is what it is. *Best Guess.* Hah."

"Oh," said Tai, his disappointment real. "That's not very..." He stopped mid-sentence as Dart nudged him gently in the ribs. "*Trailblazer 89426.* I suppose I can get used to it."

Izt chortled. He'd checked and confirmed the arcing FTL route around the galactic core was satisfactory to Harrugh, and was –

seemingly, at least – enjoying the opportunity to get to know his latest guests. He decided to throw Tai a bone. "If it helps, when registering ship at docks, they always want me to give ship's name, so for formal purposes, I call it '*Dividend*.'"

Tai visibly brightened at this precious nugget of information. "That's *much* better. In days to come, when we recount this adventure, talking about our time aboard the *Dividend* will be much more exciting! I'm very proud of our journals, you know. Dart suggested a few years ago that we record everything that happens during our expeditions, and our published reports have been very popular among the Naaz-Rokha."

"They'd find our *undocumented* adventures even more exciting," said Dart, exchanging a quick glance with his companion.

"You already are interesting," said Izt and he nodded at Junior. "Having a companion who – how say – looms so large in the memory must make you objects of interest everywhere you go."

"He does attract attention, that's true." Dart flashed a grin. "Sometimes that kind of attention can be great fun. During those times, we get to meet interesting folks with interesting stories. Sometimes, though, well." Dart pulled a face. "Sometimes, we run into the sort of trouble we found on the Gloaming. Truth is, Junior is with us to *learn*. It's a two-way thing. We're learning from him in kind. It's a mutually beneficial arrangement."

The Titan didn't interject into this discussion at all. The glow around the edges of the expressive faceplate was a gentle bluish-green which Tai explained was usually a sign that Junior was listening, but probably to several things at once, some of them very much outside the organic aural range. "He does that a lot," Dart observed, "sometimes at the worst moments. I think it's making him smarter though." He paused and smiled wryly. "Well. Smarter than he already is."

The Ral Nel could only concur with this. He had been somewhat taken aback when the Titan had quickly plotted a far more efficient route to the coordinates provided by Harrugh following their hasty departure from the waystation.

Thinking of Harrugh reminded Izt of his other guests: the two Hacan had retired to one of the smaller cabins to get some much-needed rest. The infuriating Mentak woman was idling in the cockpit with her boots up on the console no matter how many times Izt protested, keeping an eye (or so she said) on the navigational instruments. Of all the new passengers, she was the one that Izt distrusted the most. There wasn't anything *specifically* fueling that sense of unease. Not counting her connections to the coalition, she seemed entirely too sure of herself for someone who had just escaped from an unlisted orbital in the company of strangers. Even Ashalla, whose optimism was a balmy solar wind, seemed dour by comparison.

He was pulled out of any further reverie by the sound of an insistent chime from the cockpit. Izt frowned, hopped down from his seat and made his way to the console. He swept his hands over several monitor arrays and scopes before sliding into the pilot's chair. "What did you touch?" He stared at Suffi An as he said this, and his tone was more than a little accusatory. "I told you, if you sit here, to touch nothing. Understand? Nothing!" His frown deepened and he tapped at one of the monitors with a claw.

"I didn't touch a single thing, Izzy! What's the beeping? Is it some sort of problem? I'd love to take a look!" Suffi An was chewing on a piece of dried meat that she had located in one of her numerous pouches as she slouched easily in the copilot's seat. She swung her legs down, leaning forward to look at the console with interest. Izt looked sideways at her, frankly appalled by this newest iteration and butchering of his given name.

"Izt'xet Alit Lo Masak! Izt if that too hard!" He turned away from her and studied the controls with intense concentration. Then he shook his head. "No, just sensor ghost. For a moment scope show nearby FTL signature. Gone now. Happens from time to time." He ran his fingers nimbly across the panel, bringing up data feeds and considering the reports without missing a beat. "Sometimes get false returns near galactic core, but reports show all is well. Lots of traffic this way, lots of ship signatures coming out of Kenara."

Satisfied with the readings and system analytics, Izt completed his diagnostic, rechecking the course Junior had plotted. Not that there would be any real danger, at least not until they arrived. The ship would automatically drop to sub-light if they passed too close to anything with sufficient mass to generate its own gravity field. It was not that which was his concern right now. It was more that he was keen to get to where they were going without unexpected interruptions, particularly as they approached Nekro-controlled space. He felt the eyes of Suffi An scrutinizing every action and turned to face her, irritation evident in every movement and syllable.

"What? What? What?! Is rude to stare!"

She remained entirely impassive in the face of his ire. "Ral Nel ships are supposed to be among the best in the galaxy."

It was a good choice of words: some of the Ral Nel's mistrust slipped away at the compliment. If she understood *that* at least, then she couldn't be all bad. Warming a little to her, Izt relaxed slightly.

"Yes," he agreed. "Many keen to take our technology for their own, yes? Including Mentak Coalition, am sure, hmm?"

"Oh, relax, Izzy, before you burst something. I'm not here to steal your stuff. I'm here because Harrugh is *paying* me to be here and because I want a slice of whatever it is he's looking for. What can I say? I also like helping people out." She sighed theatrically. "It's a weakness. I'm a pilot. A good one. It's only natural for someone with my skillset to show an interest in your fancy ship."

"A pilot, huh?" He gave her a critical look. Turning back to the console, he set the scanning arrays to passively sweep for anything of passing interest during their journey. "What do you pilot?"

"Fighters, blockade runners, shuttles, even atmo-craft if you have a need. I can fly pretty much anything given time to familiarize myself with it. You'd like my ship, I think. Scraped together a lot of aurei to buy it and I've adapted it over time. It's a true hybrid. Maybe when we come back from this trip, I'll let you take a look." She beamed an enthusiastic smile.

He sniffed, haughtily. Of course he was interested, but he wasn't about to let her see that. "Maybe. But I tell you now that if you plan to add Ral Nel tech? Does not come cheap."

"Oh, don't you worry your scaly head about that. I'm good for the cash."

"Hmm. Then later, maybe we will have deal. *Maybe*," Izt replied, dubiously. They both ceased their discussion, looking up as Harrugh entered, the Hacan having to stoop to do so. He was silent for a long moment, staring out the forward viewscreen at the smear of light, dust and cosmic radiation streaking past the hull. After several seconds had passed and Suffi An was about to say something that she was certain would be *devastatingly* entertaining, he turned to address them.

"Izt. Suffi An." He acknowledged each of them in turn. "I don't know what it is that we are going to find out there." His voice was soft but held a tone of authority that the years of leadership had gifted to him. "But if for whatever reason I don't get a chance to say this later, thank you. Both of you. For coming with us." He looked back at the table where Ashalla had joined Tai and Dart. The three of them were laughing loudly at some joke or other that Dart had told. The sight lightened his mood: after the frantic energy of the escape from the Gloaming, he didn't know how the Naaz-Rokha and their gentle Titan friend would react. He hadn't hired them to get entangled with local law enforcement or complications linked to his past – and yet there had been precisely zero complaint. It had occurred to Harrugh that the entire thing was just one big adventure for them.

He envied that.

"Thank me when we're done," said Suffi An. "More specifically, thank me when you transfer the aurei to my account. I'm purely in it for the cash, Harrugh, and a cut of whatever your treasure might be. So don't get any grand ideas that I'm going to waive my fee because we got out of a tight spot back there." She wagged a finger as though scolding a naughty child.

"But you just say…" Izt cut in.

Suffi An stopped waving her finger and held it up to forestall the obvious contradiction. "But *also*, as I was just explaining to Izzy here–"

"Izt'xet Alit Lo Masak!"

"Whatever. I do just like helping people out. It certainly looked to me as though you and your companions needed some *serious* helping out. Am I right?"

Harrugh's expression was of vague, but polite bemusement. "Yes. I would say negotiations remain open regarding your fee. We did, and we *do*, need assistance. Even unlooked-for assistance."

"Right place, right time." Suffi An sniffed and went back to studying the ship's controls.

Once he was satisfied that everything was running as it should, Izt leaned back in the pilot's seat, nodding his approval.

"It will be some time before we arrive," he announced. "Time enough for rest, maybe think on what you learn from Prophet's Tears, hmm?"

Harrugh nodded, shuddering involuntarily.

Izt pushed a little further. "Maybe even finish what is left of it?"

Harrugh couldn't escape the suspicion that the contents of the vial were intended to be consumed as a whole to convey the entirety of their encoded message all at once. Perhaps, he thought with no small amount of bitterness, if the hrrtos had prepared him more effectively for this trial, the situation would be clearer.

Some truths cannot simply be told, they must be learned.

He had taken the disjointed memories of the various visions the Prophet's Tears had given him and had attempted to put them into some semblance of order. He'd shared those thoughts with Ashalla who had been equally mystified by the spectral portents of doom, but she now understood Harrugh's fear and what had driven him to resign as Quieron.

The thought of downing the rest of the Prophet's Tears was not exactly appealing. On the other hand, there was no doubt this unusual artifact had been given to him for a reason. There was a message buried within the chaotic visions.

"You are right, of course," he acknowledged, pointedly ignoring Suffi An's enquiring look. "But perhaps we could take this discussion elsewhere?"

"Yes, yes," said Izt, apparently oblivious to Harrugh's desire for discretion. "You sit in chair in workshop, hmm? Drink all at once. Many visions, no doubt, but at least you do not fall on my floor again. Plenty of us here to be sure you are all right." His initially dismissive tone brightened. "Also, study of Prophet's Tears part of deal for taking you and–" he flapped a reptilian hand in the direction of the other passengers "–others, to where you want to go, yes?"

"Yes," Harrugh said. "You're right, of course."

Though the agreement had been struck under less than favorable conditions, the Ral Nel had been as good as his word up to this point and Harrugh had to admit that if their positions had been reversed, he would have been tempted to do the same. Exploiting favorable conditions was just good business sense and Harrugh had to respect Izt for that, even if that respect was decidedly grudging. "We have more than enough time to consider anything I might learn and for you to record any findings."

"Now, then?" Izt asked, a *little* too eagerly.

"Now."

"Wait a second!" Suffi An was alight with curiosity as she listened to the exchange between the two and leapt to follow. "What's going on now?"

Izt waved a claw at her. "Is nothing. Hacan is going to drink microbial nanite memory solution and…" He paused, mid-flow, scratching thoughtfully at his scaly chin. "Does not flow well, does it? Perhaps Naaz is right – things are better with good names. Anyway! Simple plan. Drink solution, have visions, not fall down. Not this time." He grinned, showing all his teeth. "Easy!"

"I have no idea what you're talking about, Izzy, but I am *excited* to find out."

Following this one-word pronouncement and accompanied by Izt and Suffi An, Harrugh stood and left the cockpit, returning to the central cabin where Ashalla was apparently attempting to teach Junior how to greet people in the Hacan language. The Titan proved an adept linguistics student, dutifully repeating all his impromptu lessons.

The sight of the hulking biomechanoid unnerved Harrugh. In his many travels, they were a species about whom he truly knew so very little. Had the situation been less pressing he would have gladly spent some hours quizzing the Titan for information.

"Ash'ka," Harrugh said, doing his level best to ignore the conversation between Izt and Suffi An taking place behind him. "Forgive my interruption. I'm going to take the rest of the Prophet's Tears." She made as if to accompany him, but he steadied her with a hand on the shoulder. "No, I will be fine this time. Please – remain here." He glanced around the small group he had managed unwillingly to gather. "I need you to tell our new companions everything that we know so far."

Ashalla gave him a quizzical look.

"Tell them about the hrrtos, tell them about what I saw in the visions last time. Tell them… about what we are searching for. The Icon." He turned to level a steady gaze at the others and wondered if the name meant anything to them. "They have a right to know what we might be getting into and perhaps may offer a different perspective to make sense of it all."

"Of course, Qui… Harrugh," she demurred.

Not for the first time in their many years of association, he felt a surge of appreciation for her friendship and loyalty. While the rest of the *Trailblazer* crew were there because they wanted something from him – at least in one form or another, with the possible exception of Junior – Ashalla was the only one who was present because she *wanted* to be.

She reached out, holding onto him. It was a simple gesture, but it nonetheless conveyed the depth of her support. He smiled and nodded at Junior. "He's doing a good job mastering our language. He'll be able to haggle with the Arretze traders before you know it."

This immediately sparked a whole swathe of questions about the Hacan home worlds from the Titan. Smiling, Harrugh left them to it, once more following Izt down into the workshop-laboratory space. Dart and Tai remained behind with their Titan friend. Suffi An, however, followed them to the workshop before settling at the bottom of the steps. As she had observed, she had precisely zero idea what was going on, but it was clear that she planned to watch whatever it was with an avid interest.

"So, this liquid thing you mentioned… is it some sort of narcotic? A hallucinogen, maybe?" she asked as Izt bustled around the workshop, activating numerous monitoring arrays and setting up an assortment of recording devices.

"I'd prefer it if you waited with the others. Ashalla will explain what we know," Harrugh glowered. "I don't need an audience."

"I'd prefer to watch," she countered.

"Go back upstairs."

"Or what?" She smirked. "You'll turn the ship around?"

"You might be the most *infuriating* human I have ever encountered."

"Thank you!"

Harrugh grunted in frustration before settling down into a gravity couch. "Fine," he grudgingly acquiesced. "In answer to your question, yes, and no. There is *meaning* there, which I believe is the intention. The experience of drinking the Prophet's Tears is one of lucidity as opposed to euphoria. It's difficult to explain. It's like… living another life, only in fragments and all at once."

"Mmm." Her expression became one of grave seriousness, painfully at odds with the way she'd presented herself thus far. "I know exactly what you mean."

Harrugh cocked an eyebrow at that statement. "No, I don't think you do."

She grinned, the change in her erased. "You're absolutely right. I have no idea what you're talking about. But what I *do* know is that you look tense. I figure you might need something light-hearted to help you relax after gulping the nano-juice." She mimed taking a swig from a drinking vessel. "You know. To help you feel less anxious after. Deal?"

Harrugh realized that in the moment of her clowning, the gnawing apprehension at what was to come had lessened. "Deal. I'm ready."

"You were always ready," said Izt, in a curiously philosophical manner. "You were just waiting."

Harrugh reached into the pouch at his waist, producing the Prophet's Tears. He hesitated for a moment and Izt patted his arm. "Try stay calm this time, mmm? Remember, Harrugh, you have already had half. Data may not be in logical order. Like thoughts, yes?" He waved his hands expressively as he talked. "Seeing thoughts of different brain like code, like encryption. Also maybe small, small gaps." At this, he had the decency to look a little embarrassed again. "Sorry about that."

Harrugh treated Izt to a calm and extremely level stare. "Quite," he said. "Under the terms of our agreement I could rightly claim that you have already taken approximately half of your payment."

"Yes, yes, and by the time wake up, maybe I have taken you halfway to destination. Half this, half that, pffft." He hurried onwards, not wanting to prolong this discussion about the ins and outs of being under contract to Harrugh Gefhara. "Now, you drink?"

Harrugh lifted the vial in toast to his two companions before he removed the seal from the ornate receptacle. He studied the bottle and took a slow, deep breath. He called on all the meditation exercises he'd practiced during his odyssey until he could *feel* his own blood pulsing through his veins in time with his heartbeat. Once he had achieved that state of equilibrium, he knew he could hesitate no longer. He raised the vial to his lips. Then he swallowed the remaining contents in one gulp.

FIFTEEN

This time he was ready – or at least he was as ready as he could be, given the circumstances. There was barely a pause before the workshop fell away, and he was gripped by the sense of falling. Izt watched with fascination as Harrugh's eye rolled up and his body twitched – a small convulsion that passed as swiftly as it came on. The threshold had been crossed. Harrugh sank rapidly into the frenetic dream of the Prophet's Tears.

The sensation was less of a plunge and more like a stately descent into the tidal mayhem of a fever dream. It surged over him in a wave of sound, sight and sensation, a roiling current of evocation. Mentally, he flailed desperately in his efforts to seize upon the visions. To catch them. To hold them. To elicit some meaning. His efforts were entirely in vain. It was like trying to catch grains of sand in a storm.

"…are you prepared to meet…"

Words floated in and out of his awareness, carried on the wave of a booming, sepulchral voice. It sent a shiver of ice running through him, chilling him to his very core. He tried to grasp the fleeting words as they were uttered. One by one, they slipped through the fingers of his mind and whirled away into the torrent.

"…this war will not be won by conventional means…"

This time the voice was a cracked growl, tired and strained but still urgent with authority. They were being spoken directly to a scarred woman who wore what he recognized as Jordian combat armor. What war? What means? He tried to ask the questions, but he was mute within his own dreams. The woman in uniform saluted smartly, her eyes alive with nervous energy, and paced away into darkness. Harrugh turned, planning to follow her.

Where are you going?

Nothing. She could not hear him, neither – at least, he presumed – could she see him. His fists clenched tightly enough that his claws bit into his flesh. Did they? Or was that a dream, also?

"…will explode with the equivalent…"

A soft voice, devoid of accent, spoke in a matter-of-fact tone. It sounded as though it was simply describing the weather for the coming day. There was nothing but warm, orange light and a knotting sensation in his gut which told him that whatever it was that was going to explode, the consequences would be dire.

Our home. Our people. Burning.

Everything. Burning.

Harrugh gasped. He reached, then foundered on the rocky shores of the unknown. The sliver of memory was borne away by the current before he could squeeze more meaning from the fleeting morsel. *No,* he gasped. *I need that, I need to know!* The memories seemed to surge in response to his desperation, hammering through him like muddled scenes from a nonsensical holodrama.

A Druaa in uniform, her serpentine features and pale crest frozen in a mixture of fear and determination, one elegant finger outstretched toward something out of sight.

Who are you?

A hulking suit of sealed armor, chased in filigree and smoking with tendrils of etheric blue and red energy. The Creuss cradled something in its gauntleted hands as if shielding the galaxy from its bared heart. Silvered light spilled from between its fingers.

What are you holding?

The slight form of a Naaz, one eye covered by a cybernetic monocle, grappled with a formless mass of infernal darkness, his little limbs possessed of a strength far beyond that of his diminutive frame.

Tai?

"…*the FSS Orlando, I repeat…*"

The voice was scratchy with transmission static and interference.

Where are you?

A monstrous figure in a cowled robe so dark it seemed as though it was shrouded by the void. Light fell into it. It was an aureate giant clad in an event horizon and crowned with iron. Beneath the abyss of the hood, the boundless depths of space swirled and spun. Stars wheeling in a perpetual dance. Harrugh recoiled from the interstellar visage, once again throwing the spiraling morass of thought and memory into tumult.

Mahact!

Then there was a heavyset N'orr with a carapace the color of smoky sand. It spread segmented arms to encompass a tapestry of holographic light, the dense lines of script scrolling across its shimmering surface a dizzying litany of genius or madness. It clacked its mandibles in frustration and Harrugh could feel the unspoken query of the industrious insectoid.

What do you want from me?

Why were they all looking to him? What was it that they were expecting?

What does this all mean? He was *furious*. Not at the visions, or whatever they were, but at his own perceived shortcomings. At his own failure to understand any of this insanity. There was a feeling: a constant sense that he should be able to connect with these disjointed visuals, but his brain rejected them for what they were and replaced them instead with the strongest feeling. The one he could not move beyond.

Everything. Burning.

Everything.

What are you trying to show me?

The onslaught of visions became a migraine smear. A dull ache built behind what he thought were his eyes. Was that behind his eyes? Perhaps. But it might also have been his entire being. Who were all these people? Who were they to the hrrtos? The masked face rose unbidden in his mind's eye, huge and terrifying, its trio of lambent lenses transfixing him with an unblinking, accusatory stare that expected everything and gave away nothing.

What do you want from me? Are you the Icon? Am I supposed to find you?

Harrugh roared the question, but like every other attempt, nothing vocalized. He screamed silently into the depths of this swirling morass of chaos.

It's not about you, Harrugh Gefhara.

Had he said that? The hrrtos?

There are some truths that cannot simply be told, they must be learned. The Icon. Remember the Icon.

He roared again, the collected rage, pain and frustration of the last few weeks distilled into a wordless, inarticulate cry.

"*Harrugh!*"

No, he didn't remember that. He didn't recall anybody calling his name.

"*Harrugh!*"

It was more insistent this time and the blur of the Prophet's Tears gave way to the more pressing and immediate blur of reality. Someone was shaking him – not gently – by the shoulders and as he emerged from the dream state, like a drowning man rising from the depths, he recognized Ashalla's voice.

"Harrugh Gefhara, so help me, if you don't come back to us in the next two seconds, I am going to let Izt jab you with one of those needles!" His eyes were closed, he realized. With great effort, they fluttered as he managed to open them. She was a vague shape, hazy in his vision, and he reached out. She caught his hand, squeezing it gently. When she spoke again, he heard the relief in her tone.

"You've been dreaming for hours," she said. "Just laying there, not moving. Then, out of nowhere, you started thrashing about and shouting. It was… I didn't… I tried to wake you."

Harrugh touched a claw to his mouth and croaked, indicating a need for water. At the moment, his tongue felt so dry that if he spoke, he'd spit up half the Arretze desert. She obliged, passing across the drink. She was clearly prepared for his reaction this time.

Izt hovered nearby, an air-hypo of what was presumably some sort of sedative clutched in one hand. The rest of the crew were clustered around the entrance of the workshop, watching with expressions that ranged from curious, in the case of Junior's rippling faceplate, to the look of deep concern on Dart's face.

The moment of silence was broken when Suffi An chirped, "Well, now *that* was certainly educational! Can't say I'd be particularly keen to give it a go myself though. Doesn't look like much fun. So, come on then, put us out of our misery. Did you learn anything useful?"

"Yes, yes, what did you learn from the Tears?" Izt echoed, keen to further his research, regardless of the fact that Harrugh looked like someone who'd just gone several rounds with a particularly vicious animal.

Harrugh gulped the water. "I don't know," he rumbled. "It isn't easy to understand, much less to explain."

The watching group deflated a little and the cluster broke apart as they slowly wandered back upstairs to the cabin. Junior, however, remained and he lumbered over to where the Hacan was sitting. Izt fussed around him, but not *exactly* out of concern.

"You must tell me when understand, yes? That was deal. Even better, write down while all still fresh, yes?" the Ral Nel pressed. "Leave nothing out."

"All right, Izt, I promise. Just… please. Give me some time."

Ashalla gave Izt a warning glare. The Ral Nel retreated to the other side of the workshop and satisfied himself with analyzing the data that their monitors had recorded.

"Friend Harrugh," Junior queried, his faceplate fringed with a blush of calming green.

"Not you as well, Junior?" Ashalla's voice was laden with exasperation.

"Apologies, friend Ashalla, I do not mean to cause any offense. I was merely curious to learn more of friend Harrugh's optical implant. I have observed that it appears to be of an outdated design based on my comprehension of current galactic standards. From what I have learned of friend Harrugh, he is more than capable of sourcing a superior replacement."

Ashalla glanced at Harrugh, who nodded. He offered up a tired sort of smile, glad to have the opportunity to discuss anything other than the Prophet's Tears and his recent experience.

"I believe we still have some hours before arrival, Junior," Harrugh said, "and I understand you like to learn." He absently rubbed at the ocular cybernetic. "So let me tell you about the L1Z1X."

SIXTEEN

The *Trailblazer* streaked from the fringes of the nebula, trailing a plasma tail of ionized gas before cutting to sub-light. Practically instantaneously, the cockpit filled with the chiming peal of threat detection alerts and planetary proximity warnings. Comm-receivers previously muffled by the smothering pall of interstellar gas and dust came alive with squealing static and the scratchy scraps of broken transmission. The hateful dirge of the Nekro Virus threaded through it all, one moment a sinister susurration gnawing at the audio-visual spectrums, the next a piercing shriek cutting through the cosmic noise like the discordant howl of some primal predator.

"This is bad! Very bad!" Izt declared frantically, already scrambling over the navigation controls. "Not empty space at all. You bring us to planet of Nekro Virus! Trap, Harrugh Gefhara! A trap!" It was possible he was correct, though excessively convoluted for a deception. Harrugh squeezed into the space behind Suffi An and Izt. He observed firsthand that the Ral Nel's observations were correct.

A planet loomed large ahead of them, its surface entirely swathed in colossal storm clouds, and buzzing around it like a swarm of furious insects were dozens of Nekro craft.

A shiver of recognition ran up Harrugh's spine and his vision wavered.

Falling, plunging toward the churning clouds of a planet wracked by storms.

"What is this place?" Suffi An was excited. "It isn't on any of the nav charts!"

"I have to get down there!" Harrugh's voice was filled with urgency.

"Will get down there in pieces if not leave right now!" Izt chattered, furiously attempting to plot a course anywhere other than this unknown world. The communications array let loose with another agonized howl. A thin wisp of smoke curled from one of the receivers. "Do not want to be killed by my own ship!"

"There is something very wrong with those machines." Junior's soft voice floated in from the main cabin, sounding unusually small.

"Don't listen to them, Junior!" Dart growled in alarm. "They will kill us all and use you to do it, if they get inside your head!"

"I don't think that's *quite* how it works," Tai cut in. "But Dart is absolutely right, Junior. You shouldn't listen to the Nekro Virus!"

"Could somebody please just shut that noise off?" Ashalla winced as the crackling static and relentless Nekro transmission once again filled the cockpit.

"*...the FSS Orlando of the Sal...*"

"What was that?" Tai trilled, squeezing his tiny frame between his companions and reaching for the comms controls. Izt slapped his hand away automatically and Tai managed to look deeply offended.

"You actually heard that?" Harrugh looked sharply at the Naaz. "It wasn't just in my head?"

"Yes, I heard it!" Tai replied indignantly. "I think you need to stop drinking strange juice given to you by masked strangers!"

"Where is it coming from?" Harrugh asked.

Tai fiddled with the communications array, ignoring the stream of invective that continued to issue from the Ral Nel. With some considerable difficulty, he successfully managed to filter out the worst of the audible noise projected by the Nekro transmissions. His little nose wrinkled in concentration as he answered Harrugh's question.

"Difficult to say for certain. The planet is producing a lot of noise just by itself. That's a truly monstrous storm going on down there. It's patchy, but the message has all the markers of being on a loop." Tai turned to look at Harrugh. "If you wanted me to make an educated guess, and I know you do, I would say that there is a savior beacon broadcasting from somewhere down there."

A cluster of Nekro craft had already peeled away from the swarm and were bearing down on the *Trailblazer* with murderous intent, grasping limbs tipped with hull-shredding manipulators and barbs loaded with viral micromachines uncoiling from their undersides. Target lock warnings began to trill alongside the other alarms already singing through the hull of the *Trailblazer* as the Nekro weapons built to charge.

"Izt!" Harrugh's tone pulled the Ral Nel from his panicked calculations. "Please tell me that this ship is armed and that we can make it to the surface?"

"Yes, we can get to surface and of course ship is armed! Turrets, tail, good guns! Ral Nel ships best–"

Harrugh interrupted him mid-flow. "That's all I needed to hear. We're going down. Dart, Tai, pick a weapon."

"Top!" Tai squeaked out his choice immediately.

"Tail!" Dart barked.

"Then I'll take the lower guns," Harrugh confirmed, impressed. The Naaz-Rokha had sprung into action with alacrity and he respected that.

"My ship!" Izt protested sullenly.

"It is your ship, Izt, and that's precisely why I'm going to need you to try and triangulate the location of that transmission while we're on our way down. At least if you want to have a chance of getting any answers and studying that data vault?"

"Yes, but…" Izt spluttered, torn between fleeing and discovery.

"Good. Suffi An?"

"Sorry about this, Izzy!" Her bright tone suggested that she was anything *but* sorry as she lifted Izt bodily from the pilot's seat before depositing the furious Ral Nel at the comms console. She took his place at the controls. "You all might want to hold on to something! I've got a feeling that this is going to get rough!"

"Ral Nel ship doesn't need pilot!" Izt shrieked, but she interrupted him.

"I'm sure its automatic navigation is fine," she said. "But I'm sure I'm better."

"Come and sit with me, Junior," Ashalla said, holding on to the Titan's huge arm.

The first streaks of crimson energy creased the void as Harrugh sprinted for the guns, the sounds of Izt's dire imprecations and Suffi An's whooping cry chasing him down into the turret as the *Trailblazer* accelerated hard, diving toward the planet waiting below.

SEVENTEEN

In the days since they'd made their involuntary planetfall, the crew of the *FSS Orlando* had become increasingly fractious. The initial euphoria of survival was quickly replaced by cautious curiosity about the planet they had crashed on. Crisis teams, composed of people from all areas of the ship, were working on the hull repairs. The atmosphere outside of the ship's confines was breathable although as promised, the gravity was a little off. For about the first hour or so, everyone joked about having a literal spring in their step.

The novelty wore off quickly.

Those early feelings of optimism and curiosity had gradually given way to a brooding sense of disquiet as the full extent of the damage was observed. Nichols considered this as she busied herself with the latest batch of status reports. Power on board the ship had to be strictly controlled. It seemed that the engineering detail were still not confident in the stability of the core. It was a cautious approach but a wise one: after the last attempt to coax it out of exigency protocols, the system had come worryingly close to an entire cascade failure.

The teams had resorted to the use of solar cells to supplement their meager supply, but down here, on a world perpetually blanketed by storm clouds, their output was sparse.

Below the cloak of lightning storms, the planet – which the crew had dubbed "Thunder's Edge" – appeared to be a geological and meteorological anomaly. Expeditionary teams had recovered as much material as possible from their crash trail, exploring for half a day in every direction. These explorations turned up nothing beyond further plains of windswept, ochre rock and spires as far as the eye could see.

The science team had been keen to study one of the immense, stone pillars following Kketch's observations, but Nichols had ultimately ruled against it. The closest example was estimated to be almost a day's travel away, and without knowing what risk the formations might present, Nichols decided that giving her approval to an expedition felt like a frivolous risk. It had not helped morale and when the first dead Nekro craft crashed to the surface just over a day ago, the mood had soured still further.

"Can we use cabling from one of the shuttles?" Nichols asked Skelton. He peeled open one of the service plates and surveyed the scorched mess that had once been a power relay.

"Maybe, but…"

"Incoming!" A cry of alarm came from the perimeter. Nichols drew her beam pistol, looking to the sky to see a black hull streaking from the clouds trailing smoke and spitting sparks. The thrusters of the Nekro craft coughed once, then died. It fell into an uncontrollable tumble, then struck the ground hard, becoming an unrecognizable heap of wreckage. For ten long minutes, nobody relaxed and panic reigned. When it became clear that the machine was not about to surge across the plains to butcher them, Nichols finally gave the order to ensure it was dead.

"No risks," she cautioned. "Passive scans only. Basic weapons only and no crew with cyber enhancements." There was no argument: the crew had learned a lot from the Nekro's tactics on Ordinian, including the many ways in which the Nekro Virus could infect even the most benign technology, turning it against biological life.

The black hull was scorched and pitted in places and still crawled with crackling electrical discharge. It was also – mercifully – quite dead. Kketch offered up a hypothesis that the Nekro were probably testing the boundaries of the storm. The absence of biological components within the ships likely meant that the tempest had a significantly greater effect on the Nekro than on the *Orlando*. Nichols was inclined to agree, but maintained the perimeter detail, wary of putting too much faith in the storm for protection.

She retired to her cabin in the hope of snatching an hour or two of rest, but with the wind and thunder screeching through the halls of the ship, such rest proved elusive. Her own thoughts kept her up. What kept the Nekro at bay? Finally, she couldn't take it any longer and got up.

"*FSS Orlando*, ship's log. Acting Captain Nichols recording."

Being stranded gave such clarity of purpose, though not necessarily the kind that was desirable. She'd taken to recording their discoveries and observations for posterity in the event that they were discovered years later. "There has been some progress on the repairs to the propulsion systems, but Chief Engineer Skelton tells me that any hope of generating enough thrust to get us back into space is many days away at this time." She paused. It was just one thing on top of another.

"Of course," she continued, "even *that* is dependent on the restoration of the starboard engine, which may not be possible even with our collected salvage. I have, of course, asked him to keep that information entirely confidential in an effort to maintain morale. I don't doubt his integrity in this matter, but I suspect everybody already knows that the *Orlando* is likely never to fly again. Everyone is being as positive as they are able. Given the situation there isn't much else they can do."

Nichols rubbed her eyes. She was so *tired*. The relentless wind sweeping across the plains, along with the infernal thunder, had become a constant source of chagrin for the survivors. The noise grated on already frayed nerves, denying any real chance of unbroken rest. The medical team had cautiously taken to dispensing measures of sedative to those worst affected, but Dr Takksil had made his thoughts quite clear on the sustainability of that solution, as well as the potential side effects.

"Short range expeditions have, as yet, failed to find any sign of life on this world, biological or otherwise." She glanced uneasily in the direction where the crumpled hulk of the Nekro vessel had made planetfall. "As such, I am reluctant to risk teams further afield. We are preparing to send a modified drone out – the team are keen to gain some insight into the unusual rock formations, so there may be some hope there." She'd been enthusiastic about that idea rather than sending out the crew: the *Orlando* had several probes which were usually used for reconnaissance and while they were designed for operation in space, the team – the *incredible* team – had taken one and ripped it to pieces in order to rebuild it for surface operations. That pulled her onto her next voiced thought.

"I must commend the entirety of the crew." Her voice filled with pride. "Despite our losses, despite all the challenges they face, with little hope of rescue, they remain focused on the tasks at hand. There are moments of…" She hesitated. If she was recording words on behalf of her crew, she had no desire to inadvertently shame any of them in posterity. "There are moments of despondency from us all, me included, particularly as we laid the bodies of our fallen to rest on this bleak, distant world. We're so far from… well, anything much." She paused for a moment and stared off into the middle distance.

"The savior beacon remains functional and has enough power to outlast us all. It has become somewhat symbolic of our struggle and Mr Orragh has poetically dubbed it the 'stranded lodestar'. This system is uncharted and other than the Nekro Virus, nobody knows we are here." Even if they did, she reflected bitterly, the Joint Task Force had hardly been in any sort of state to mount a rescue when they had left.

A soft knock at the door interrupted her flow.

"Captain Nichols, I think you need to hear this."

She stood, putting her hands on the desk to steady herself as a wave of lightheadedness took over, then opened the door to one of the young ensigns assigned to the bridge. She couldn't recall his name through the fog of weariness and a moment of guilt suffused her. The nameplate on his scuffed uniform read Hallun, but her tired mind refused to supply any additional information. A gust of wind whistled maliciously through a hull fracture in the hallway as if in mockery. The young man's eyes were full of excitement and she cut him off before he could blurt out anything foolish.

"Ensign Hallun, give me a proper report and tell me what you need."

"Yes, ma'am, sorry, ma'am." His contrition did nothing to mute his glow of enthusiasm. "We think the long-range arrays might be picking up high energy discharge from beyond the storm."

Her own spirits began to rise. "We think?"

"Yes, ma'am. It's difficult to say with any degree of certainty, but it could be near-space weapons discharge."

Hope kindled, but she nursed it carefully. The Nekro did not make war upon itself; indeed, its purity of purpose would have been admirable had it not been so entirely genocidal. Maybe this was the explanation for the felled Nekro. "Do we have any idea who might be shooting? And what they might be shooting at?"

The young man's enthusiasm faltered a little. "I don't know, ma'am."

She sighed, pinched the bridge of her nose and gestured to the door. "Then let's go and see if we can work out what's happening out there."

They exited onto the bridge where there was a hubbub of activity. Emergency lighting, presently all that the engineers were prepared to allow to run across the ship, illuminated the crew with an eerie, greenish hue. All the shutters had been raised, partly to allow the world's watery daylight to filter in through the fractured viewscreens, but mostly to reduce the noise of the wind. A peal of thunder cracked overhead as if to announce her arrival, vibrating the tools currently scattered around some of the workstations.

"Captain on deck," came an announcement and everyone briefly paused to stand to attention. Nichols waved them back to their tasks, which they did without further hesitation before she headed directly for her chair. She dropped into it and looked around.

"All right," she said. "What have we got?"

"Pulses of high energy and exotic particles not analogous with our prior observations of the storm," replied Kketch. "I am still attempting to parse the signals from the interference, but I believe there might be one or more vessels in near-space engaged in battle."

"Might? I don't want *might*, Kketch." She was snappish and abrupt, but all things considered, it was of little surprise.

"I will continue my efforts with the limited power and arrays that I have available to me, captain." It was a gentle admonishment, a reminder that everyone and everything was operating at significantly reduced capacity. She appreciated Kketch's discretion and nodded. She tapped the comms, opening a channel.

"Skelton, this is the bridge. I'm going to divert additional power to the science station. We have potential incoming, and I need to know whether to crack open the armory or that bottle of Archon Red I know you have stashed under your workstation."

"Sure," came the brief reply, without any hint of respect for her authority. She was too tired to care, but Skelton's attitude was just one more thing wearing at her nerves. *He is every bit as tired as you are,* she reminded herself – possibly even more so. Skelton was many things, not all of them good, but most importantly he was an excellent engineer. "I've shut down three auxiliary subsystems to compensate. Hope you don't need them for a few hours."

The flippancy of his dismissal snapped her remaining thread of tolerance. "*Lieutenant* Skelton," she said, emphasizing his rank, "an erosion of discipline *in extremis* is understandable, but not excusable. I am your captain. You will address me as such until I am relieved of command. Is that understood?"

The channel was silent for several seconds and she noted the bustle of the bridge had diminished, filling the air with tension.

"Apologies, acting captain," Skelton finally replied in a flat tone.

"Thank you. Bridge out." She cut off the communication. He'd still chosen to preface her title but knew not to push too hard. "Kketch, you've got more power. Do what you can. In the meantime, I'm going to open the armory anyway and put a rifle in the hands of everybody able to hold one. Our recent fortunes have not been favorable, and I want to be ready for anything that comes. If we must make our last stand here, we will not do so quietly."

"And what of the good lieutenant's bottle of fine liquor?" The science officer asked the question without looking up from his station.

Nichols smiled at that. "In the event our salvation is at hand, I will personally pour him a measure and toast to his very good health." She patted the science console before pacing away in the direction of the gunroom.

EIGHTEEN

The *Trailblazer* dove hard, and a streak of crimson energy splashed across the upper shields. Suffi An hauled on the helm controls and the dizzying plunge toward the seething clouds turned into a wild corkscrew. "That was close!" She yelled to be heard above the roar of the overworked thrusters. "Came close to hitting us!"

"*Did* hit us!" Izt countered, redistributing power to compensate as best he could.

"Oh, hush! Do you see any holes? I don't!"

"Too many Nekro! Too many! *Trailblazer* scout ship, not warship!"

"We've got three on our tail!" Dart's voice barked from the rear of the ship. The cannons chugged several times before fire blossomed in the void behind them, sending a burning, black shape tumbling into the atmospheric maelstrom below. "Make that two on our tail."

"Stop showing off and just shoot them!" Tai's voice fluted down from the upper turret. For such a comparatively small individual, his voice was huge.

Suffi An had already coaxed the Ral Nel craft into performing at least two maneuvers that had strained the inertial compensators beyond their conventional limits. Izt had become borderline apoplectic with rage as the console lights bloomed with streams of warning icons. Everything indicated that core power, weapon temperatures and main engine output were all spiking dangerously. But Suffi An showed no signs of backing off, despite Izt's dire warnings.

"Can't stop now, Izzy!" she responded through gritted teeth. "That is, unless you want to be scattered all over near-space!"

A clawed shape of glossy, sculpted midnight cut in front of the spiraling *Trailblazer*, opening fire with something that chugged slugs of buzzing, infectious nanomachines. Suffi An spat a string of colorful curses in no less than three different languages before she hauled the ship out of its dive. She tugged at the controls, rolled it on its axis and pointed the belly turret directly at the offending Nekro. The viral payload streaked past in a blur of carmine light and armored carapace and Harrugh, positioned at his own gunnery station, didn't hesitate. The lower turret gun blazed away, blowing the enemy craft apart in a spray of spinning debris.

"We can't keep this up," he roared, rotating the weapons to track another ship bearing down on them with murderous intent. "We can't move like they do!"

Despite his statement, Harrugh had to give credit to Suffi An for keeping them alive beyond the first few seconds of the engagement. The Nekro craft were not constrained by the need for inertial compensators required by an organic crew. They were simple extensions of the merciless intellect that guided them and seemed singularly intent on preventing the *Trailblazer* from making planetfall.

"Friend Harrugh," Junior called from the cabin, where Ashalla had strapped herself in. "You might be interested to know that I have made a most curious observation."

"It's going to have to wait, Junior," Harrugh replied, chasing the Nekro craft with pulses of fire from the turret.

"But friend Harrugh, I believe it is both pertinent and relevant to our current and immediate circumstances."

A blast from the *Trailblazer* clipped the Nekro, sending it tumbling away for a few moments. It foundered briefly before stabilizing, banking sharply and renewing its pursuit.

"Fine," Harrugh growled, his fangs bared in a snarl. He was trying hard to concentrate, but it was difficult with constant interruptions. "What's your observation, Junior?"

"There are highly anomalous emissions radiating from the planetary storm system," Junior stated mildly. "And while the deeper transmissions of the machine-forms currently attempting to extinguish your biological signatures remain largely indecipherable, they are displaying a distinct aversion toward the upper atmospheric layers."

That got everyone's attention.

"The Nekro are scared of the planet?" Tai asked, his voice tight with tension.

"Not *exactly* that, friend Tai. Even with my very limited comprehension of the machine-form's core precepts, I do not believe it to be capable of a recognizable fear response. It would be more accurate to describe the behavior as…" The Titan considered for a second or two. "Territorial."

The hull reverberated with concussive shock as something exploded nearby. "Got another one," Dart yelled. "But I'm about three shots away from a critical overheat. I can't keep this up!" The ship lurched, pitching hard to one side as Suffi An narrowly evaded an incoming spray of fire.

Tai shook off the distraction and turned his attention back to Junior. "You mean the Nekro have found something just as bad as them and they're trying to work out who's the bigger Daatar hound?" His tone was incredulous.

"I do not know what a Daatar hound is, friend Tai, and I believe your definition of 'bad' is too subjective in this instance. Also, from what little I have been able to determine of these machine-forms, I would dare to suggest that their collective intellect is vastly superior…"

"Yes or no, Junior?" Tai interrupted, frantically pulsing fire into the void.

"Then, yes, friend Tai. I believe your analogy is accurate in the broadest possible sense."

"We need to get down there!" Harrugh bellowed. His body ached from the constant shaking of the guns, and he knew that when – that *if* – they concluded this fight, his ears would be ringing for hours.

"Definitely cannot stay here!" Izt cried, fighting to keep the shields alight.

"Hold on tight. I'm gonna try something, cherished crewmates." Suffi An made the *Trailblazer* turn hard, crushing the crew into their seats as the compensators battled the physical forces attempting to overwhelm them. The view through the forward screen wheeled from scattered stars and trailing strands of gas to the churning storm clouds as the ship flipped from nose to tail. Then the engines screamed, and the ship leapt toward the planet below. Clawed, black shapes pulsing with red fury raced to intercept them.

"What are you doing? Can't outrun them!" Izt cried as the *Trailblazer* dove.

A Nekro craft, its sensory arrays a mass of crimson lenses and transmission spines, cut ahead of them. The *Trailblazer's* cockpit shrilled with target lock warnings. Suffi An cursed again in yet another new language and then the Nekro suddenly exploded, impaled by a retina-scarring beam of cerulean plasma. A new ship emerged from a shimmering patch of space as its cloaking disengaged. It was smaller than the Ral Nel vessel, but sleek and studded with obvious weapon pods that were presently pouring fire into the enemy. Two more encroaching Nekro were blown apart before the ship rolled, joining the *Trailblazer* in its plummet toward the surface.

There was a momentary pause as the crew came to terms with the fact that they had not been obliterated and then Suffi An, peering at the forward screen, suddenly burst into peals of hysterical laughter. "Couldn't keep away, old man?" She pushed the thrusters for all they were worth.

"What is new ship? Friend?" Izt queried, his reptilian face ashen from the near fatal encounter.

"Friend? I don't think he'd say so," Suffi An chuckled, "but we really are the very best of friends. A better question would be what, exactly, is he doing here?"

"Ral Nel *Trailblazer*, this is the *Long Fall*. Respond." A gravelly male voice, with a strong Jordian accent, rumbled across the comms.

The bulk of the remaining Nekro craft abruptly peeled off their pursuit as the pair of ships plunged into the upper atmosphere of the new planet. Only two Nekro remained committed to the chase, their weapons blazing.

"Repeat. This is the *Long Fall*. *Trailblazer*, respond." The hail came again.

"Hello, lovely!" Suffi An's voice was filled with glee. "Glad you could make it, even if old age has made you slow!" It was not exactly a formal response, but nobody had really expected anything else from the Mentak.

There was a pause filled with what could only be described as an exasperated sigh crossed with a throaty growl from the pilot of the *Long Fall*. "Suffi An." He didn't sound surprised. "I'm sure you'll have far too much to say later on, but for now let's see if we can lose these Nekro in the storm."

"We don't need *your* help," said Suffi An, sounding triumphant. "But we would be very happy to help *you* out of this extremely tight spot – especially since you clearly need it." Izt gave her a look of confusion, and she returned the expression with a playful smile.

"If that's how you want to interpret this situation and it makes you happy," said the pilot of the Jordian ship. "Less talking, more doing. Let's get this done."

"*Long Fall*," Harrugh interrupted. "I have reason to believe that a Federation ship might be stranded on the world below based on a fragmented savior beacon signal. I don't want to risk bringing the Nekro Virus down on their position."

"Understood," came the curt response. Their new ally was not much of a talker, it seemed. "You do what you have to do, Gefhara. Make it quick, though."

"How does he know…." Suffi An shook her head. "That sly old nyx! He's been on our tail since we left the Gloaming! He needs to learn to mind his own business, but then I suppose I should learn to respect the elderly…" She continued on in this vein, talking to herself in a conversational tone as she wove the *Trailblazer* between the incoming fire as it dove through the highly questionable cover of clouds.

"*FSS Orlando*, this is Harrugh Gefhara responding to your savior beacon. Please acknowledge. We will be making planetfall imminently." *One way or another*, he thought, grim.

"Here we go!" Suffi An exclaimed, and the *Trailblazer* plunged into the storm, trailing atmospheric fire in its wake.

Darkness closed over them like a suffocating blanket. For a moment there was nothing. No shuddering hull vibrations, no turbulence or buffeting winds. Just an eerie moment of absolute stillness and silence. Then the boiling storm split with colossal, clawed branches of lightning and the boom of thunder shook the *Trailblazer* from end to end. Static discharged from several consoles and Suffi An momentarily released the controls in alarm. The *Trailblazer* tumbled wildly for a heartbeat before she wrestled it back under control.

"Did we lose the Nekro?" Harrugh shouted to be heard above the tumult.

"There were still two of them on us," Dart replied, "but I can't see them. Can't see anything in all of this."

"Shield envelope starting to ionize," Izt remarked, still monitoring the instruments. "Charge building fast, not good!"

Another massive arc discharged, snarling through the seething clouds. A crackling nimbus of light cast a halo around the ship as the fury of the storm splashed over the Trailblazer's defenses. The gloom behind them was momentarily lit from within by a flare of orange as something nearby exploded.

"I think we just lost one of our tails!" Dart commented, squinting as if it would somehow help him pierce the pall of the tempest.

"There are voices in the storm," Junior remarked, his gentle, synthetic voice tinged with curiosity and wonder. "I can hear voices in the storm."

Before anybody could reply to this unexpected pronouncement, a faint smell of burning came from the cockpit and Izt squeaked in alarm. "Shield projectors overloading, need to shut down now – or they will burn out!"

"Shut them down? In this? We'll be annihilated!" Tai protested. "And there's still a Nekro out there!"

"Will lose them anyway!" Izt countered. "This way, might be able to use again." The Ral Nel killed the power. The charge that had been building in a bubble around the *Trailblazer* dissipated instantly with a crackling roar that travelled the length of the hull before being lost in the cacophony of the raging storm.

"Sensors are blind," said Suffi An. "But we're still dropping. I hope the crew of that ship you're looking for has some strong drink on board." She shook her head as the projected altitude continued to race toward zero. "You might want to let them know we're coming, assuming these clouds don't go all the way to the ground." She grinned a little bleakly. "In which case, it has been fun, if all too brief!"

Everything. Burning.

It doesn't end like this. Harrugh clung to the thought as the storm thundered at them through the hull. The hrrtos wouldn't have accidentally given him specific directions to a planet that didn't appear in any galactic records. He hadn't been sent here to die. Not now. Not like this.

He was under absolutely no illusions at the chances of the comms breaking through the storm, but their lives were now in Suffi An's hands as the surface raced up to meet them. "*FSS Orlando*, this is Harrugh Gefhara responding to your savior beacon. If you are able to respond, please acknowledge."

The maelstrom battered them with its fury. "Please," Harrugh repeated. *Please.*

Someone be there.

NINETEEN

"Do you hear that?"

The junior officer leaned forward and did her best to try to filter the comms. Through the static, there was a tinny buzz that had not been there a moment ago. Kketch motioned for silence on the bridge, attempting to make out words through the white noise.

"Can you clean that up?" Kketch frowned as he listened. The junior officer nodded.

"*FSS Orlando*," the words crackled, and the officer let out a small *huff* of disappointment.

"It's just an echo," she said, attempting to clean up the signal further. "Just an echo of our own savior message." She couldn't hide the agitation in her tone and her hands balled into fists. Kketch noted her reaction and gave her a placatory smile.

"Once more," he said, though it might have been an exercise in futility. The chances of rescue from a planet shrouded in storms in an uncharted system besieged by an unknown number of Nekro were vanishingly small. She shook her head, even before the message started to play once more. Just an echo.

And yet...

"...to respond, please ack..."

"...making planetfall..."

She and Kketch exchanged a look of disbelief, unable to believe that they were hearing genuine communication apparently responding to them. The junior officer's face broke open in a huge grin.

The science officer regained his composure and tapped his comm-bead. "Captain Nichols," he said, once the link was secure. "You may be gratified to know that we will shortly be receiving company."

"Another ship from the Salient Sun Joint Task Force fleet?" Her response was filled with hope.

Kketch considered his answer carefully. "As much as I would like to believe that our comrades have been able to locate us and dispatch a rescue effort, it is mathematically improbable, captain. The relative strength of the task force, our unplanned trajectory and the significant interference to any and all communication would instead suggest the approach of a third, unidentified, party."

"We are stranded in the middle of nowhere," Nichols replied. "On a planet that, as far as we have been able to establish, nobody even knows exists, having arrived here completely by accident."

"These factors are all empirical truths, captain," Kketch confirmed sagely.

"But you believe that it's more likely the approaching ship is *not* from the Task Force?"

"Probability would suggest so, captain." Kketch shrugged. "I will continue to monitor comms frequencies and keep you apprised. All will be well, Captain Nichols. I believe it to be so."

"Your optimism is appreciated, Kketch, however you will forgive me if I prepare the crew for combat anyway," she said.

"Of course, captain, I would expect nothing less." Kketch closed the channel and returned his attention to the communications array. He could only influence the actions of his captain, but he truly believed that a more thorough understanding of the impending events would mean hope, not death, would be on the way.

"No response from the world below," reported Harrugh, "but it's likely the *FSS Orlando* may not have response capability if they are relying on a savior beacon to draw us in."

"Or it could just be all the interference caused by this storm!"

said Suffi An, continuing to wrestle with the controls of the now unshielded ship as it maintained its steep dive toward the surface. "*Long Fall*, this is the Ral Nel *Trailblazer…*"

"You see?" She could hear Tai from somewhere behind her. "*This* is why you need to give your ship a catchy name."

There was no response other than the hiss of dead air.

"It was worth a try," Suffi An said through gritted teeth. "He's probably flown in the wrong direction. Which would be *so* like him."

"There's still no sign of the other Nekro," Dart called. "Could be right on top of us and we'd never even know."

"Who *is* that, on the other ship, the *Long Fall*?" Ashalla asked. "How do you know him? Why is he even here?"

The space inside the *Trailblazer* became tense with anxiety as they awaited Suffi An's answer. Harrugh sensed that Ashalla's less-than-diplomatic questions came from a place where she searched for control, or maybe rapid-fire questions were preferable to listening to the storm's fury as they raced toward the ground.

"Oh, my word, Ashalla Kar, now that is a *very* long story," said Suffi An, doing her best to control the descent through the pockets of turbulence and flickering discharges. "Here's the short version. The captain of the *Long Fall* is Connor. He's a Sol agent. The reason I know him is simple. We've worked together before." She glanced over her shoulder and gave Ashalla a dazzling grin, even as the ship bucked in the air. "He acts as old as dirt and is about as much fun to talk to as a bulkhead, but I'd rather have him on our side than on the other side. When we get out of this, I'll tell you more." The *Trailblazer* lurched, throwing everybody hard into their harnesses. "Although, he's probably following us because he just can't bear to be away from me."

"A story I look forward to hearing in full when you land us, alive," said Harrugh. "I will also be interested to know the real reason why he has been tailing us."

Suffi An sniffed. "So, you *don't* believe it's simply my charm and magnetic, sparkling personality?" The cabin flickered into monochrome for a frozen moment as a titanic fork of lightning split the clouds directly outside. Sparks danced across the hull, spidering their way over the consoles.

"Less chatter! Concentrate on getting down alive!" Izt shrieked.

"I can do both." There was a loud bang from the back of the hull and Suffi An amended, "Probably."

The clouds parted, flooding the cockpit with dull, watery light as the *Trailblazer* broke through the storm. The forward viewscreen was filled with rocky, ochre plains and the crew were once again crushed into their stations as Suffi An pulled the ship out of its steep dive, levelling the vessel off. An empty vista studded with craggy pillars stretched out in all directions. Harrugh felt the fur on the back of his neck rise as recognition washed over him.

A barren surface, stippled with crackling spires.

He unbuckled his harness and left his gunnery post, making his way up from the lower turret to where Ashalla was seated. "I saw this place," he whispered to her without expounding further. She nodded in understanding. "This is it, Ash'ka. This is where I am supposed to be."

"Perhaps," she said softly, "the Icon is here as well… whatever that means."

Tai, wan from the descent, slowly released his white-knuckled grip on the restraints and climbed down from his turret. He was still shaking when he joined Harrugh and Ashalla but made a show of appearing nonchalant as he assessed the strange planet. "Doesn't look like a terribly exciting place. I can't see any sign of habitation to suggest anybody lives here, or even ruins to indicate they even once lived here." He squinted out the window. "Of course, that doesn't mean anything. You always have to really look for the most interesting things."

Harrugh turned to the Naaz, his expression serious. "That's why

I wanted you and Dart to help me. No doubt you two will be able to track down something based on the name alone."

"Ah yes, that Icon Ashalla mentioned to us while you were busy dreaming. Now, that sounds like a mystery, and a very interesting one at that! Interesting things are what Dart and I enjoy most in life, after all."

A sudden shriek of thrusters filled the cockpit as something angular, black and terrifying broke from the clouds trailing smoke, sparks and vapor. Even subjected to the gravity of the planet, the Nekro craft was still far more maneuverable than any piloted vessel. Harrugh gasped in fear as the Nekro banked hard and surged toward them on an intercept course, segmented manipulators reaching with rending claws and energized cutters.

"Brace!" Suffi An screamed. "Brace!"

It was practically upon them, death reflected in its glowing red lenses when it simply sputtered and died, weapons slack and thrusters silent.

A fraction of a second later, a pair of beams sliced into it from above and it exploded. The hollowed out remains tumbled away, belching fire and fumes as it smashed to pieces on the plains below. The *Long Fall* raced past the *Trailblazer*, turned a lazy loop and then fell in beside them at an easy cruise. The comms crackled.

"You're welcome," the gravel-toned voice rumbled and then the channel closed again.

Suffi An looked over her shoulder at the rest of the crew, still recovering from the shock of their latest near-death experience. "See?" she said with a wobbly smile. "Connor loves me. Even if he *is* an insufferable bore."

TWENTY

Following the trace of the savior beacon to the crash site of the *FSS Orlando* was a trivial matter once safely below the cover of the enshrouding storm. Suffi An happily returned control of the *Trailblazer* to Izt for the final approach. The Ral Nel made a show of inspecting everything before taking his place, grumbling all the while.

"Thank you." Ashalla smiled as the Mentak woman returned to the main cabin. "You have quite the talent."

Suffi An beamed. "I've had a *lot* of practice. Also, you're *welcome*." She leaned forward in a comically conspiratorial manner. "There's even a chance that Izzy might forgive me for hijacking his ship in a day or two."

It was not long before they spotted a deep furrow dotted with wreckage carved into the plain. A short way distant, the bulk of the battered cruiser lay partially propped up on a shelf of ochre rock. Its hull was scarred and pitted from conflict, but the words proudly emblazoned across its hull were still clearly visible. It gave the impression of a weary veteran, resting in state. "The *FSS Orlando*," Harrugh murmured, as though reciting the words from a dream.

"Looks like she came down hard," Dart noted. "That engine is bad. Half the cowling has separated."

"What's she doing out here at all?" Ashalla wondered.

"I'd very much like to know," Harrugh said. "Let's get down there and find out."

Clouds of dust billowed from the downthrust of their arrival as the *Trailblazer* and the *Long Fall* made their final descent. People emerged from the ship and even from around it – no doubt doing repairs on the cruiser. Harrugh took a deep breath, reaching for his political prowess that he hadn't truly used since being Quieron. Whoever the *FSS Orlando* were, he hoped they could be allies and might have answers to his quest.

The interest in the unique *Trailblazer* couldn't be hidden. Izt, descending the ramp of the ship in the wake of the others, glared at the *Orlando*'s gathered crew with his large, unblinking eyes. "*My ship,*" Izt muttered to nobody in particular, and hurried after the group.

The pilot of the *Long Fall*, the man Suffi An had called "Connor" did not immediately join them, apparently happy to wait for Harrugh's party to take the lead before emerging. He would have his reasons, no doubt, Harrugh thought, not least of which would be having to explain exactly what it was that he was doing here and what he wanted. The Sol agent's secrecy raised his hackles, but there were other, more pressing matters that required his full attention.

A significant security detail flanking a small group of officers waited for them, all looking dusty and weary. Harrugh noted that their weapons were ready, but currently at ease. They were clearly curious, maybe even optimistic, but weren't about to let that blind them to potential threats. *Much like us*, Harrugh thought as he came to a halt a respectable distance from the woman sporting the captain's rank insignia.

"Welcome to Thunder's Edge," the captain stated formally. "I am Acting Captain Nichols, of the Salient Sun Joint Task Force." Harrugh's curiosity piqued at the word "acting", but he did not interrupt. If she was disappointed that only two vessels had arrived, she was doing an excellent job of hiding it. "These are my two senior officers, Lieutenants Kketch and Orragh." She indicated the Xxcha and a Saar respectively as she spoke. "And this is our chief of engineering, Lieutenant Skelton." The third officer was clearly distracted, studying the newly arrived ships with undisguised interest.

The other three officers murmured cordial greetings in turn and Harrugh inclined his head. "Harrugh Gefhara," he replied, his hands open with palms turned upward in greeting. "Of the Emirates of Hacan." The rest of the crew also introduced themselves in a variety of ways ranging from Suffi An's casual informality through to Ashalla's practiced and professional courtesy.

"The Golden General?" Nichols was unable to hide her surprise. She straightened. "I imagine you have quite the tale to tell." She paused. "May I call you Harrugh? Or would you prefer General Gefhara?"

"Harrugh, please," he acknowledged with a half-smile. "It is my name, after all. However, my reasons for being here may take some time to explain. I fear that time may swiftly become our most valuable asset."

She nodded. "Understood. We have our own reasons for urgency. However, I would still very much like to know how you reached us, Harrugh. I am keener still to understand *your* urgency."

He clasped his hands behind his back as he spoke, an unconscious bit of body positioning that gave him an unmistakable air of authority. "Very well. There is a significant force of Nekro gathered in planetary near-space. Nothing larger than hunter-killers and scout-forms at the moment. I think we can probably thank the nebula, and our own survival, for that. We saw the remains of more of them on our way in, but I assume that the fact you're still alive suggests that they've been unable to break through the storms."

The officers nodded grimly in confirmation. The Xxcha, Lieutenant Kketch, offered his input. "It is my theory that the Nekro Virus is more heavily debilitated by the tempest than vessels piloted by the likes of us. It would explain their apparent reluctance to approach the planet. However, it is also singularly out of character for the Nekro Virus not to simply attempt to force its way through regardless of the cost in individual machine-forms."

"I agree," Harrugh said. "But if they have been probing for a vulnerability, then I'm afraid they might have found it. One managed to chase us all the way to the surface before–" here, he glanced at the sleek, predatory shape of the *Long Fall* "–our companion brought it down." There was a murmur of consternation at this news and many of the engineering team ogling the *Trailblazer* set to work with renewed purpose.

"Grim news indeed," Nichols replied. "My crew are armed, but most of our major systems are still offline. Mr Skelton has done a most excellent job overseeing repairs, but I'm unsure how long we would be able to hold against an attack." The young engineer looked suspicious and yet also pleased at the sudden and unexpected praise. Whether it was a simple friction of personality, or the result of stress that the recent events had undoubtedly piled upon them, was not clear, but clearly there was an undercurrent of tension between the two.

"Survival might depend on our cooperation, captain. We will do what we can to help with your situation," said Harrugh with a brief smile. "I can spare some of my crew who have skills that I'm sure will be of use to you in your efforts to restore the *Orlando*. In the meantime, it's clear that you have been here for some time before our arrival and I need to know everything you have learned about this place. It might prove vital."

Captain Nichols' eyebrows drew together, but she nodded in agreement.

Suffi An wandered from the group, eyeing up the *Long Fall* with keen interest and obvious suspicion. Her shouting drew the attention of the others. "So, are you ever coming out, old man, or do we have to come in there and help you down the steps?"

By way of response, the door hissed open, and Connor stepped out onto the top of the steps that unfolded in front of him. He was a tall man but not overly broad, with short-cropped, silvery-gray hair atop a face creased by a long scar that twisted his expression into a near-permanent sneer that somehow seemed worse when – and if – he ever smiled. He wore a black, armored bodysuit with calf-length boots adorned with silver buckles, the only concession toward ostentation he displayed. Everything about him screamed "utilitarian".

"I'd say it's good to see you again, Suffi An, but you know how I feel about lying." He immediately turned away from her as he stepped down from his ship. Izt studied the *Long Fall* with the same sort of interest that the *Orlando* crew had for the *Trailblazer*. The Sol agent's vessel was clearly well armed and in possession of some unique and advanced modifications.

While Harrugh returned to conferring with the captain and her officers, Ashalla stepped forward in order to forestall any misunderstandings. "Connor, I presume?" She extended a hand of friendship. "I am Ashalla Kar. Thank you for your assistance up there. Timely indeed, although I presume you somehow followed us from the Gloaming in the first place."

"I did," came the reply. Connor looked at Ashalla's offered hand for a moment, then clasped the Hacan's forearm in his hand, a warrior's handshake. "You and Harrugh are interesting individuals. Not as interesting as *some* of your crew, I'll grant you…" He tipped his head towards Junior who was standing motionless behind Dart and Tai – and attracting a lot of attention of his own. "But interesting nonetheless."

"We would very much like to know what your interest in our expedition is, not to mention how you came to learn of it in the first place," Ashalla replied, offering a warm if stern smile.

"I'll save us all some time. I'm sure it comes as no surprise to you to learn that the Federation keeps tabs on all the major political players of the galactic powers."

"Naturally." Ashalla inclined her head. "I'd expect nothing less.

After all, the Emirates do the same. That used to be part of my job." There was only a slight predatory tinge to the smile.

"I'd be painfully disappointed if they didn't," Connor replied. "Harrugh Gefhara resigned, a decision unprecedented in the history of the Hacan leadership. The powers-that-be are keen to understand why that might have been, and, far more importantly, exactly what it might mean for future relations with the Emirates. Once you left Hercant it was easy to tail you to the waystation and tap into their internal comms." He shrugged again. "Made for interesting listening. I'm sure you can guess the rest."

Ashalla gave the man an appraising look. "Well, one way or another, we're all in this together now so unless that ship of yours has a way of getting you past all those Nekro, I assume we can rely on your skills when required." It was posed as a statement rather than a question.

Connor gave a thin, wintry smile of his own. "You still haven't explained why you're here, Ashalla. So sure, I'm not going anywhere. Let's say… for the good of inter-galactic relations and mutual self-interest."

"That's all right, Connor," Ashalla purred. "For the good of inter-galactic relations and mutual self-interest, I'm not sure you *had* to help us or reveal yourself. Yet here you are and perhaps your true reasons will become clear in time." She glimpsed Suffi An smirking with amusement, then turned away imperiously and strode to rejoin Harrugh.

"Captain Nichols," Harrugh was asking. "If I may, what is the truth of your situation?"

"We have suffered some losses and have a number of wounded," Nichols reported. "Our medical team have got the situation under control. We also have enough water and supplies to see us through the immediate future." She glanced up at the storm which rumbled ominously in response. "Our needs are primarily power and materials if we're going to have any chance of making the *Orlando* functional again. You may not wish to be forthcoming about your purpose here, but my people are dying on Planet Ordinian. The Nekro have overtaken our home and we've done everything we could to fight them off. I'm not sure whether these Nekro are following us from there, or what their purpose is on this planet. All I know is that we must return to the Task Force."

"Understood," said Harrugh, frowning. "Izt – please lend your expertise to the engineering team? We're going to need protection and weapons if the Nekro get through that storm. Focus on the shields first, that will stop them coming down directly on our position at least."

"Fixing human ship not part of deal," the Ral Nel pointed out.

"The deal was exclusive rights to study the artifacts as long as it didn't interfere with anything we needed to do at our destination. So here we are, at our destination, and handing them over for you to study while we are slaughtered by the Nekro Virus is something I very much consider to be an interference. Do you honor the terms of our agreement?" Harrugh asked.

The assembled officers of the *Orlando* witnessed this exchange without knowing any of the context, but the mention of artifacts did not go unnoticed by Kketch, who caught Nichols' eye with quizzical interest.

The Ral Nel hissed in agitation and then deflated. "Fine. Will honor terms of the agreement. Seems that it is Harrugh Gefhara's turn to negotiate from position of strength, eh?"

"Just so. Thank you, Izt'xet Alit Lo Masak," Harrugh replied formally. "Your sincerity is recognized, just as it is appreciated." The choice of words mollified Izt a little. He grunted, which Harrugh took as a positive response. Objectively, he'd not known Izt that long, but he felt comfortable with that assumption.

"I've compiled a comprehensive damage report," said Skelton. He was a broad-shouldered young man with bright blue eyes and fair hair that looked as though it'd not seen any sort of care in a while. He had the haggard look of someone who'd not slept well in days and who was existing on a diet of caffeine and ration supplements. It was an accurate assessment. Skelton was, contrary to direct orders from his acting captain, skipping rest breaks until he was satisfied the major repairs had been completed. "I'll take any help I can get, but unless we can squeeze more power out of the core, then…"

"No, no!" Izt interrupted. "Don't tell me, show me. Will look at core, look at shields, Ral Nel will make better. Yes?"

"Acting captain?" Skelton's moment of deference and request for permission surprised Nichols. She nodded her agreement, and he hastily scurried after the Ral Nel who was already trotting toward the bulk of the *Orlando*. Nichols folded her arms across her chest and watched them go. Then, she turned to continue her story with Harrugh and Ashalla, but the pink-haired woman and the grumpy pilot kept her attention.

"Still got your collection of fancy guns, old man?" Suffi An slunk across to stand next to Connor.

He pointedly ignored her, his attention clearly on the downed ship and its immediate surroundings. When it became abundantly clear she was going nowhere, he emitted another growling sigh.

"Oh, come on," she chided. "I just *know* that ship is full of all kinds of hardware, and we both know you're not going to run out on us." Connor looked at her askance and she smiled in response. "Running out on those in need isn't exactly your style, is it?"

"No," Connor grunted. "It's not *my* style."

"Aww, *Connor!*" Suffi An cooed. "You *did* miss me. I knew it! Now let's go and see what you've got that we can use to kill some Nekro!"

He blinked slowly at her then, without another word, headed towards his ship, Suffi An on his heels, chattering away endlessly.

"Quite the unusual crew you've brought to Thunder's Edge, Harrugh, I must say," observed Nichols.

"Thunder's Edge." He repeated the name. The words seemed strangely familiar. He groped for a memory which bobbed tantalizingly close to the edge of recollection, but which remained stubbornly out of reach.

"Yes, well." She unfolded her arms and waved a hand vaguely. "We decided that since we were now apparently its residents – the only ones if our expeditions are anything to go by – we thought we may as well give the world a name. It wouldn't have been my choice, to be honest, but the crew started using it and it stuck. Once you've put up with the storm for a couple of days, you might begin to appreciate why."

Meanwhile, Dart and Tai, who had been happily wandering following the initial introductions, paused to examine the rocky plains and gaze at the numerous spires. "What do you make of it, Junior?" Tai chirped. The Titan, who had been standing quite still, turned to his small friend. When he spoke, the Saar officer, who had approached and inspected the biomechanoid up and down, visibly jumped.

"My initial assessment is that this is an ecologically dead world, friend Tai," said Junior. "The geological composition suggests that no organic life has ever been present on the surface, though the strata are uncommonly uniform. This would suggest that this world is also tectonically inert. I would suggest that the observable landscape has been shaped solely by meteorological forces."

"Well now, aren't *you* a wonder?" Nichols said, her immediate concerns momentarily eclipsed by the curious Titan.

"I am a wonder," repeated Junior. "Am I a wonder? Negative. I am an adventurer, seeking fortune and glory with my companions, the great Naaz-Rokha pairing of Dart and Tai..." The two flushed sheepishly at Junior's monologue. "However, my primary imperative is to learn more about the galaxy in its present state, both its peoples and planets, including this one."

"We didn't train him to say that, but he's *definitely* a wonder," put in Tai, making the jump from his harness on Dart's back to the Titan's shoulder. "We found him. We didn't want to leave him alone and so we've been travelling together ever since. I reckon with enough time he will be able to tell you everything you ever wanted to know about this place. But… we came here for a specific purpose, and we should probably get to it, Harrugh."

"Yes," acknowledged the Hacan. "I don't know how much time we have before exploration will become too difficult, with the storm as you mentioned and the Nekro threat."

"Yes, please elaborate. Why *are* you here?" Nichols said. "We arrived by accident. Much as I would like to believe you have arrived on a mission of mercy having picked up our savior beacon, everything you've said so far suggests otherwise. What could possibly be on this world that would bring the former Quieron of the Emirates here, and more to the point, how did you even know this place existed to begin with? What aren't you telling me?"

"Captain Nichols, believe me that if I could give you the answer to that question, a lot of my own would be answered at the same time," he replied. "As to how I knew this world was here at all, that is a long and fairly incredible story that I will share with you under better circumstances. The short version is that I have been guided here in order to secure something called the Icon. I have no idea what that is, or where it might be found, but for now I hope you can accept that none of my crew are here with any harm in mind." He looked over at the *Long Fall*, hoping that he was right about that and Connor's purpose, but one couldn't know all the answers all the time.

"Not much of an answer, Harrugh. My teams have scouted the local area. There's nothing here," Nichols replied after some consideration. "Absolutely nothing."

Tai beamed at her. "Have you poked at those yet, Captain Nichols?" He gestured at the nearest spire with one of his small hands.

"No," she admitted, "we haven't. But I was reluctant to do so given the distance from the ship and advice from my science officer. Mr Kketch has a theory that they might be linked to the storm in some way and could potentially present a danger."

"Well, the good news is that now you've got *us* to go and poke these things for you. Junior's pretty good at letting us know if we shouldn't get too close to something, isn't that right, Junior?"

There was no response from the Titan. His faceplate turned up toward the grumbling sky, apparently listening to something.

Tai whispered in a conspiratorial tone, "He does this sometimes. Tunes out of the present conversation to listen to… what did we decide to call it, Dart?"

"Echoes of the galactic song," said the Rokha in response. "Fancy name for space noise, radiation, transmission fragments, that sort of thing. Said he could hear voices in the storm on the way down." He looked over at the Titan. "Every so often, he picks up some recent news, but for the most part, he has been building his own perception of galactic history from what he hears." While Dart was more reserved than Tai in his open affection for Junior, it was clear from the expression on his dark-furred face that he had become fond of their unusual companion.

Echoes of the galactic song. Echoes of memory. Harrugh rather liked the poetic turn of phrase. Tai rhythmically tapped Junior's shoulder in an effort to get his companion's attention.

"Yes," said Junior, a distracted ripple of yellow light playing across his features like molten gold. "Yes, friend Tai, that's correct." He turned back so that the faceplate was once again directed at the gathering. "We should endeavor to render the promised assistance to friend Harrugh in the exploration of this world. This Thunder's Edge."

TWENTY-ONE

With the Nekro threat hovering above, and the renewed energy to complete what they had come for, it wasn't long before everyone was busy doing *something*. Connor and Suffi An reemerged from the *Long Fall* with several bulky, armored cases which the former had directed to be placed at strategic points around the crash site. Once secured and activated they were smoothly deployed into automated cannons that Connor assured both Harrugh and Nichols' crew were calibrated to exclusively target Nekro machine signatures. He was now also sporting a pair of heavy beam pistols, a bandolier of particle grenades and a broad-barreled energy rifle.

"I knew you wouldn't disappoint," Suffi An said, as the Sol agent stoically carried a drum-fed missile launcher down the steps of his ship and leaned it against the hull. "Can always count on you to have the best toys for a job."

Connor paused in his work to regard her coolly. "What exactly is your angle here, Suffi An?"

"Angle? Why should I have an angle? What's *yours*?" Her counter was playful, but there was a real challenge there. "I'm getting paid to do a job. Nothing stopping you from hopping into your ship and leaving any time you like." She idly twirled a beam pistol around one finger before deftly holstering it. "Except all those Nekro, obviously. Of course, if you *did* decide to leave and you asked me *very* nicely, maybe I'd come along as well. It would be just like old times."

Connor sighed again, the sound not unlike an ursine predator being rudely awakened. "Those times aren't so old that I don't remember how they usually pan out."

"And yet, here we are again." She beamed at him. "Fate keeps on throwing us together, Connor. You should accept it."

He turned to her, his expression inscrutable. "If you're going to be here, then at least make yourself useful." He thrust another of the weapon cases at her.

Izt's voice cut across the exchange as the Ral Nel hurried back and forth between the *Trailblazer* and the hull of the *Orlando*. "Yes, yes. Now then, run conduits all the way over here and plug into microcells. Why not use standard hok-nine connector? If Nekro decide to attack now we all die because Task Force ship not use galactic standard power couplings! Tch!"

"I've never even *seen* cells like these before," Lieutenant Skelton said, examining the softly humming capacitors Izt spliced cables into.

"Proprietary Consortium technology," the Ral Nel chattered as he worked. "Less than half size of standard cells, but more than twice usual charge." There was a crackle and a shower of blue sparks and Izt jumped back, sucking at his newly singed fingers.

"Twice the..." Skelton's weary expression lifted. "That would mean that if we can run a stable feedback bypass from the *Trailblazer* to the *Orlando*, not only can we run the shield envelopes in tandem, but we might also be able to force the core out of exigency lockdown and fire up the weapons."

"Yes, very smart," Izt said, nodding at the officer in grudging admiration. "Personally, was only thinking about shields to stop Nekro from falling on us, but yes, yes. Guns good, too! *Big* guns. Yes." He tapped a claw against his chin. "Yes. Should get started on that. Show me core regulator, will help make sure you don't blow us all up."

Harrugh watched as Izt and Skelton hurried back toward

the *Orlando*, entirely baffled by the technical complexities of their exchange. Dart and Tai were working through the final preparations before setting out to explore the closest of the spires with the science officer, Kketch. On the fringes of this bustling hive of activity stood Junior and Ashalla, each apparently lost in their own thoughts.

Ashalla had been notably quiet since the initial introductions, her usual conversational manner overtaken by something entirely more pensive. She stood atop a small outcrop of rocks, staring out across the barren, rocky plains of Thunder's Edge. As she heard Harrugh approach, she turned her head, glancing briefly over her shoulder to acknowledge awareness of his presence. He moved to stand beside her.

"It's so desolate," she said. "So… very lonely. But for all that, there's something tragically beautiful about it as well. Do you see it, Harrugh?"

He looked, but he saw nothing except a landscape marred by broken, yellowish rocks with cruel, jagged peaks and dry, dusty ground. There was no sign of civilization as far as the eye could see and beyond the bustle of activity nearby, the only sound was the skirling wind sighing mournfully through fissures and hollows. He imagined, for a moment, what it would be like if there was not the shouting and clanking of work behind him. What it would feel like to be completely alone on this newly discovered world. Nothing but the plains rising to meet the storm-wracked sky, the wind and the thunder. The aching beauty of it was…

Then his eyes fell upon the shattered hull of one of the fallen Nekro and the spell was broken.

"I don't always see things the way you do, Ash'ka," he replied, gently. "I was ever the pragmatic one. You have the soul of an artist and a poet." He intended the moment to be kind, to be generous toward her.

"Maybe." She interrupted him with a nudge in his ribs. "But I also remember you telling me I have the appetite of twenty and the fighting spirit of a cornered duneclaw."

"When did I say that?" Harrugh's brow knitted in thought.

"Following the negotiations with the Emir of the Silent Stars. There was that enormous banquet. Everyone ate too much, regardless of the quality."

"With the off-world water mollusks in that sauce! Yes, I remember. By the stars, those things were awful!" Harrugh said, his recollection of the event coming back to him. "They were far worse going down than they were coming back up, as I recall. A first."

"They really were," Ashalla agreed. "That wasn't exactly our finest hour, but you did get what you needed out of the terms." They laughed, freed for a moment from the urgency of their task and the dark threat looming overhead. Harrugh looked over to watch the bustling at the ship.

Dart and Tai had initially been resistant to the idea of bringing others along to explore the spires. The argument was simple: they had the most experience, and an untrained crew might make a mess of any potentially valuable discoveries. It turned into quite the debate – at least until Captain Nichols pointed out that an unknown number of Nekro Virus might be about to descend upon them at any moment and having an armed security detail with them might be desirable under those circumstances.

Dart and Tai, then, concurred.

That party, now consisting of the Naaz-Rokha, Junior, Kketch and three ensigns from the *Orlando*, put the final touches on their plan and readied to depart. Harrugh had stated in no uncertain terms that he would also be going with them. Dart and Tai simply nodded, brokering no argument to the contrary.

Dart waved to the pair, indicating that they were ready to move out, and Harrugh turned back to Ashalla. "I want you to stay here, Ash'ka," he said, and shot her a look to forestall her inevitable protest. "Izt might be happy to keep to our agreement for now, but

I don't know how long that will last if things get bad. I don't want to be stranded here. As for Suffi An and Connor? Well… I need someone I trust to stay with the ship. I trust nobody more than you."

She scowled faintly. "That's low, my Quieron," she said. "Joining a welcome compliment to an unwelcome request." She glanced back at the frenzy of activity surrounding the ships and then back at Harrugh. Her expression softened. "Curse you, Gefhara. You know how much I hate it when you're right." She leaned in and they briefly touched foreheads before separating. "Just make sure you come back."

"I didn't come this far to fail now," he said, hurrying away toward the departing expedition.

"I am most curious," said Kketch as they walked. "Of this tale you have told, Master Harrugh. It seems to me that you have either been the victim of extraordinary coincidence, or perhaps extraordinary machination." Their journey had lasted several hours so far and Harrugh had taken a liking to the Xxcha, a species with whom his own people had a long and complicated history. There was no affectation to Kketch, just a gentle, faintly paternal wisdom.

"It has certainly been an eventful journey so far," Harrugh replied, his dune spear resting easily over one shoulder. "And while I have seen and done things that I could not previously have imagined–" his hackles rose a little as he once again recalled some of the fragmentary visions imparted by the Prophet's Tears "–I hope that we will shortly be arriving at our journey's end. I hope still further that when we get there, we might just find some answers that have thus far proved elusive."

"I must confess that I, too, am intrigued to learn what this Icon might be," Kketch said, "and why such esoteric methods have been employed to direct you to its location. If there is some lesson here to be imparted, then I hope you will forgive me for saying that it would appear to be a cruel one. Those feelings notwithstanding, I am grateful for the strange providence that appears to have put you in our path."

The lengthy exchange was punctuated by a booming peal of thunder, grumbling its way through the leaden sky, and for a moment they all felt a frisson of static run through them. Harrugh looked ahead to where Dart and Tai, enthusiastically forging toward the monolithic spire, momentarily stuttered to a halt. Arcs of silvery lightning played up the weathered stone, wreathing it like a crown high above before discharging into the tempest with another rolling boom.

"I'm not sure getting too much closer to that thing is a wise choice," Harrugh remarked to the Naaz-Rokha as they caught up with the pair.

"That's exactly why we should be doing it," replied Tai, and Dart nodded in what Harrugh sensed was somewhat less enthusiastic agreement.

"In our experience, if there's going to be something to find, it's either in the least obvious place, or the *most* obvious place." Dart offered up an explanation for Tai's response. "And these plains are as dull as any other barren rock."

Harrugh gave the pair a skeptical look, but he had hired them precisely because of their exploratory experience. "Then by all means," he said with a decidedly feral grin, "after you."

They resumed their march, crunching across the stony ground, the gusting wind heavy with the acrid stink of electrical discharge. They fell back to a comfortable pace and the conversation continued.

"What will you do once the *Orlando* is space-worthy again?" Harrugh asked the science officer.

Kketch looked pensive for a moment. "I imagine Captain Nichols will be keen to rejoin whatever is left of the Salient Sun Joint Task Force," he replied. "Assuming anything *is* left for us to rejoin. I hope that our actions to draw off the Nekro swarm enabled them to hold position at Ordinian." He looked pained. "I doubt that the marines deployed to the surface could hold against the Nekro for long without orbital support, however." They both understood that death sentence for what it was.

"When are you expecting reinforcements?"

Kketch shook his scaly head. "The Salient Sun Joint Task Force has been without operational oversight from our respective governments for some time. Other emergent threats were considered a priority and so we were ordered to disband and to concede the region to the Nekro Virus. The commodore, however, declined to surrender the territory. So here we are."

"A bold choice," observed Harrugh.

"A moral choice," Kketch responded. "But also one that we have paid for every day with the lives of good people. And I am grateful to you, Harrugh, for the hope you have brought the *Orlando*. So many days we have gone without hope."

In contrast to the somber mood emanating from the Xxcha and Harrugh, Tai couldn't remember when he'd had a better time. There were so many things the Naaz found to enjoy in life, but nothing compared to *this:* to be the first explorers on a brand-new world. The thrill of discovery was almost enough to eclipse the nagging anxiety of the threat hanging over them, but only *almost.* Dart's stride was large, his advance relentless, while Junior kept pace easily. The Titan's glowing faceplate scanned their surroundings and regularly turned to the sky whenever the storm grumbled.

"You sure there's going to be something worth finding here?" Dart murmured to Tai. "So far all I've seen is a lot of rocks, dust and more rocks. I'm pretty sure that tower is going to have my fur standing on end for days. I do mean *all* my fur, Tai." He paused for a moment, then lowered his voice. "What if Harrugh's coordinates are out of date?"

"Sometimes the value is not located at the journey's end," quoted Junior, "but what is found along the way."

"Only explorers who never found anything worthwhile say that, Junior," Dart replied.

Tai fiddled with his monocular, zooming in on the craggy outcrops surrounding the base of the spire. He blinked, adjusted the resolution and then let out a gleeful, wordless noise of exclamation. He tapped Dart's shoulder and pointed in the direction he was looking. "Other explorers," he said, triumphantly. "Not like us, because we *always* find something worthwhile!" His Rokha companion squinted in the direction indicated and a slow smile found its way onto his feline features. Mostly hidden by the folds of the wind-carved bluff was a dark opening leading into the ground beneath the spire.

The opening was enormous, appearing at first glance to be a natural fracture in the rockface, a gaping entranceway that led into complete darkness. Dart and Tai were the first to arrive at its edge, with Junior close behind. The Titan had offered little by way of thought or conversation as they'd travelled, seemingly distracted in the way that only he could be. Now, however, as they examined the opening, his faceplate lit up with ripples of violet that pulsed in rhythmic curiosity.

"Allow me to go ahead of you," he said. "I can adjust my ocular sensors to compensate for the reduced illumination within." The Titan took a few eager steps beyond the threshold, disappearing into the shadow of the cave beyond, his hulking silhouette immediately swallowed by the gloom. Tai waited impatiently for a handful of seconds, drumming his fingers on Dart's shoulder, before calling after their friend.

"Anything?"

"It is a large space," Junior's synthetic voice drifted back. "The composition of the stone appears noticeably different to surface formations. It also appears to be a downward tunnel heading deeper beneath the observable spire formation. I am not detecting any… any… any…"

"Junior?" Dart had already started forward, activating his shoulder-mounted illuminator.

"There is no cause for alarm. I believe I just experienced an unknown form of interference that disrupted my vocal range. I have not incurred any lasting harm. There is nothing worthy of attention within this hall, but I can descend further if you wish and… ah, you are already here."

Dart and Tai were swift to follow Junior into the cave, lights flashing across the interior to show walls of rough, orange stone that was significantly darker than the sandy color of the world's surface. Some of the angles glinted with a near-golden hue when the light caught them just right, a phenomenon that immediately piqued Dart's interest.

"Why do you reckon it's different inside than out?" He posed the question aloud.

Tai wrinkled his nose. "Maybe it's something to do with the lightning towers, or the wind."

The breeze moaned through the entrance, accompanied by the distinctive crunch of boots as the rest of the party arrived. "Do you think we should…" Dart jerked his head in the direction of the opening. Tai tapped at his monocular thoughtfully before speaking with obvious reluctance.

"We should probably wait. Harrugh hired us to do a job. It's not a good look if we run off without our employer the moment things start to get interesting."

"Also, the crew have all the best guns and there's still an awful lot of Nekro up there. I'd really like to have some friends around when that whole mess needs to be sorted out," Dart concurred. He tested his comm-bead but found nothing but dead air and a faint crackle of static. "Huh, that's weird. We're not *that* far from the entrance. Try your comm?"

Tai experimentally tapped his own bead a few times with the same result. "Well, that *is* curious," he said. "Junior, can you reach the rest of the crew?"

"Negative, friend Tai," the Titan replied. "It would appear that the composition of this tunnel completely blocks the frequencies of our communication signals."

"We should go back up and let people know," said Tai, unused to giving consideration to others during their expeditions. "Otherwise, they'll do that whole tedious worrying about us thing and we'll never hear the end of it." Dart nodded and the three of them headed back to the mouth of the cave.

"What did you find?" Harrugh said as they emerged back into the watery light.

"A whole load of not very much so far," replied Tai, "but the tunnel goes further down. It looks like the stone is different once you get inside and–" he tapped his comm-bead, which obediently connected him to the rest of the team before shutting it off again "–seems like it completely blocks our comms signal."

Kketch ambled up to the opening and was running a heavy hand over the dusty stone. "I would be interested in your thoughts on this marking, Mr Dart, Mr Tai."

Tai decided that he rather *liked* this formal mode of address and made a mental note to insist upon it in the future. "The what now?"

The Naaz-Rokha hurried over to where the science officer was busily brushing away windblown sediment to reveal what appeared to be a rune or sigil carved into the rock. They leaned in closely, Tai using his hands to wipe away the last of the dirt, revealing a curious design.

"There is absolutely no chance that is naturally occurring," said Dart as they clustered around to peer at what could only be the first indication of life they had encountered thus far.

"Fascinating," Junior remarked, running his huge hand over the sigil.

At the Titan's touch, the pattern of the rune changed, smoothly and silently reconfiguring itself into a new design without disturbing the surface of the rock into which it was apparently carved. Beyond the entrance, a soft, amber glow suffused the tunnel without any obvious source.

"Everybody else saw that, too, right?" Dart said after a shocked pause.

"Yes," confirmed Harrugh, an edge of excitement in his voice. "And it means that somebody *has* been here, which means that whatever it is that I am supposed to find, this Icon, could *really* also be here."

"Maybe," said Tai, "but we have no idea how deep that tunnel might go, or how complex it is. Not to mention that we're going to be cut off from the surface the whole time we're down there." This last was directed toward Kketch in particular.

The science officer looked troubled for a long moment before nodding in acknowledgment. "While I would dearly love the opportunity to explore whatever mysteries might be waiting below, my first duty is to Captain Nichols and the *Orlando* and I would be in dereliction of those duties were I to abandon them to indulge my scientific curiosity during a time of crisis."

"This is why we prefer to be independent," said Dart and Tai in perfect unison.

"So, I will remain here with the security detail and conduct an analysis of this sigil and its unusual properties. In the event the situation begins to deteriorate I will endeavor to get a signal through to you. Perhaps one of the ship arrays will have more success where personal communicators are failing."

Harrugh gave the Xxcha a brief nod. "Take care, Kketch. We'll be back as quickly as possible."

"Likewise, Harrugh. I sincerely hope you find what it is that you have been looking for."

Dart and Tai were already making their way back inside,

accompanied by Junior. Harrugh hurried to catch up with them. He glanced back as they descended out of view of the opening, catching sight of Kketch just long enough for the officer to raise his hand in farewell before he was lost from view.

TWENTY-TWO

The tunnel sloped gently down, the illumination giving away nothing of what might lay ahead. Tai, in his seat on Dart's back, studied the rough stone of the walls in fascination. Even though there was more than enough light by which to see the way ahead, he continued to flash his personal illuminator, marveling at the glint in the rock that caught the beam of his light.

"Who do you suppose made this place?" Dart's question was returned to him several-fold from the depths of the cave, coming back as a faint but continuous echo that expanded and filled the available space before finally dying away. "I don't suppose any of them are still around. We've not exactly been subtle about our arrival after all, Tai."

Tai. Tai. Ai. Ai. Ai.

"I can't even begin to guess," said Tai. "I've never seen anything like that sigil… rune… button thing outside before and I'm not even sure how these lights are working. Where is it even coming from?" He adjusted his monocular again, performing a swift but detailed multi-spectrum scan of the tunnel. Most came back with null returns, while a few reported wildly contradictory readings, showing the tunnel to be simultaneously awash with high energy particles and dynamically void. He frowned and shut off the device. "How far underground do you think we are?"

Are. Are. Are. Are. Are.

Harrugh touched the wall to his right, letting his hand trail across the uneven surface. When he drew it back, it came away clean without any trace of dust, which given the tunnel's apparent age and the nigh continuous storm-winds of the surface seemed deeply improbable. He glanced up at Tai's question and answered, "Not far enough. Not yet." He pushed ahead to walk beside Junior.

They walked for what felt like a long time, the downward tunnel stretching away both behind and ahead of them so that it began to feel like some nightmarish negative space through which they would be forced to trudge forever without progress. The silence bordered on suffocating until Dart started to hum tunelessly to break the tension.

"Are you picking anything up, Junior?" Harrugh asked, the stillness prickling him with a sense of unease.

"Negative, friend Harrugh, I have not detected anything since…"

The change, when it happened, was so sudden that afterward none of them could honestly say how they had arrived at the chamber without noticing it beforehand. One moment Harrugh was conversing with the Titan as they walked the apparently endless tunnel and the next, Junior was putting a hand out to stop him as they stepped onto a hanging walkway. It hugged the wall of a shaft that stretched away on all sides with equal immensity. Dart stumbled to a halt, both Naaz and Rokha blinking in momentary stupefaction as they looked around the cavernous space.

"Where did this come from?" Dart blurted out the question that was on everyone's minds.

Tai turned in the harness to look back the way they had come, seeing the tunnel stretch away behind them as far as the eye could see. "I have absolutely no idea," he replied, scratching his head. "Maybe we sort of… tuned things out?"

"I'm not so sure," Harrugh breathed, his eyes following the route of the walkway as it spiraled into the depths. The vertical walls were still the same rough, orange stone, giving the impression that they could be standing in the bowels of an ancient magma tube, but the air here practically vibrated with febrile energy. "Do you feel that?"

Dart and Tai shuffled to the edge of the precipice, peering into the vertiginous abyss. "Feels like it did outside, close to the spire," Dart confirmed. "Like sparks are going to start jumping off my tail at any moment."

Harrugh nodded in confirmation and looked at Junior.

"This chamber appears to be highly charged with…" The Titan simply stopped mid-sentence.

"Junior?" Tai asked.

"…exotic particles," Junior concluded. "Apologies, I appear to be experiencing some sort of interference again."

"Well, we either go back, or we go down," Dart said, after sharing a look with his Naaz companion.

"Down," Harrugh stated with conviction.

"Down it is," Tai agreed, then offered up a rueful smile. "That tunnel was boring, anyway."

They started down the walkway, which twisted its way around the wall of the shaft. There was no sign of any other tunnels as they descended and the one through which they had arrived was quickly lost from view. "How deep do you think it goes?" Dart wondered aloud. He gingerly peered over the edge again, hoping to catch sight of a lower chamber, but only a dim, silvery haze looked back at him from the depths.

"No idea," murmured Tai, "but I'm not sure how much longer we should press on before having a serious talk about the supply situation. I wasn't really expecting us to find something so…" He trailed off.

"Big?"

"Big."

They all came to a stop at once as a faint crackling sound echoed up from below, like oil sizzling on a hot engine manifold. It rapidly built in volume and intensity and Harrugh chanced a curious look over the edge to identify its source. He immediately ducked back, flinging his body flat against the wall.

"Back," he roared at his companions. "Back! Get back from the edge!"

To their credit, none of them questioned this unexpected command and leapt away from the precipice with scant heartbeats to spare. A bolt of silver white light flashed up the shaft, momentarily freezing everything into a monochrome tableau. It was followed soon after by a booming concussion, reverberating through the walls and shaking the walkway beneath their feet before fading away.

Harrugh got slowly to his feet, shaking his head in what felt like a futile effort to dislodge the ringing in his ears. Dart had instinctively wrapped his arm around Tai in a protective embrace and was unsteadily getting back up off the ground. "You all right, Tai?" The Rokha fussed over his smaller companion, concerned for the other's well-being.

Tai dusted his clothes down, though there was no *actual* dust to speak of, and straightened his monocular. "Of course," he chirped, with more confidence than he actually felt. "We've lived through worse. That wouldn't exactly have been the blaze of glory you've always said we will go out in now, would it?" He scampered onto Dart's shoulder, settling back into the harness. "Junior? Are you all right?"

"I am unharmed, friend Tai, though that discharge temporarily overwhelmed my sensory inputs."

"You and me both, Junior. I do think we should get out of this shaft as quickly as possible. Harrugh? You with me on that?"

"Agreed," Harrugh concurred. They quickened their pace.

No further blasts assailed them as they descended further into the depths and before long the walkway terminated at a tunnel leading away from the perilous shaft. They hadn't gone far when the hall expanded into a wide chamber, open along one wall like a mezzanine gallery overlooking a council chamber. Harrugh walked slowly to the edge, staring into the immensity of the space beyond. Junior joined him, followed a moment later by Dart and Tai. The

Naaz scrambled out of the harness and up onto Dart's shoulder to get a better look, before giving a low whistle.

"Now that," Dart said, nodding slowly, "is what I'm talking about."

Activity around the *Orlando* crash site had reached fever-pitch. Nichols had gratefully accepted Ashalla's assistance. Since Kketch had departed with the away team, and Skelton was entirely occupied with the Ral Nel's modification and repairs, she appreciated an extra pair of hands to help with organization. Every other member of the crew not critical to the ship's operations had been armed and dispersed in teams around the ship.

"Should be good now," Izt was saying. "Should be able to disengage lockdown."

Skelton scanned through the output readings and hesitantly agreed. He activated his comm-bead. "Acting Captain Nichols," he said, the blend of exhaustion and exhilaration blunting the usual edge of disrespect, "we're about as ready as we can get. Do I have your permission to breach the core exigency protocols?"

"Lieutenant Skelton, if it will fire up the shields and weapons without killing us all, then permission is given."

Skelton paused and glanced at Izt who nodded enthusiastically. "Trust Ral Nel technology. Will work, will get shields and guns working. Most guns." He glanced at the fluctuating readings coming from the microcells and tapped the display, which obligingly stabilized. "*Enough* guns."

"Acknowledged, acting captain," Skelton replied. He tapped a few keys on the display and dismissed several, increasingly forceful, warnings before opening the conduits between the *Orlando* and the *Trailblazer*.

"Engineering," he said again into the comms, "all teams, all stations, stand by. I want to know if anything so much as coughs down there." There was a series of acknowledgments in response.

"Good, good," Izt encouraged. "Now all need to do is…" The air filled with a low hum, and the running lights that were still functional on the exterior of the *Orlando* strobed erratically for a few moments before settling. There were several muffled bangs from the ship's interior and sparks fountained from one of the portside service panels that had been opened for repairs. Nothing immediately exploded, however, and Skelton released the breath he hadn't realized he had been holding.

"How are we looking?" There was no immediate reply to his comms message. "Engineering teams, report."

"Core is stable! Exigency disengaged."

Skelton closed his eyes and murmured up words of thanks to any passing deities. "Acting captain, we have power." The lieutenant was unable to keep the jubilation from his voice.

"Incredible work, Mr Skelton. Now fire up the shields and weapons. Let's get a look at what we have to work with."

"You heard the acting captain. Hop to it!"

"Shields, aye!"

"Weapons, aye!"

A faint ripple pulsed through the area immediately surrounding the downed ship and a hazy dome of distortion bubbled into existence, covering both the *Orlando* and the Ral Nel vessel. Security teams walking the perimeter paused in their patrol and cheered as the turrets on the upper hull sprang to life with a whine, the barrels of their weapons tracking across the storm-wracked sky.

"Well, that's a good sign," Suffi An said brightly as she watched Connor finish up a diagnostic on board the *Long Fall*. She had offered to help, of course, but the Sol agent had predictably declined. He chose not to respond to her but instead moved over to the monitoring array that had been set to perform ongoing wideband sweeps of the sky in the hope of detecting anything that might decide to descend on them through the storm.

"What are they waiting for?" he growled, scrutinizing the displays.

"Junior, that's the Titan in case you missed it," Suffi An supplied, "said that the Nekro were acting like they were worried about this place. Not sure that 'worried' is the right word for it, though. There's definitely something here that's making them think twice about charging down to wipe us all out."

"Sure would like to know what that 'something' might be." Connor frowned. "Any ideas?"

"Not a clue." Suffi An shrugged. "But Captain Nichols said much the same thing. The Nekro were right on them after they crashed out of FTL but broke off once they drifted into orbit. The storm doesn't seem to be good for them."

"The storm isn't good for anybody," Connor countered.

"Fair point. But!" She held up a finger for emphasis. "It didn't kill our ships. Nearly blew out the shields, sure, and it wasn't my smoothest flight, but here we all are. Alive and devastatingly attractive."

Connor made a face, heading for the door. "Come on," he said, when Suffi An didn't immediately follow. "I'm not leaving you alone in here."

The Mentak woman smiled sweetly, making a show of getting up from where she had been reclining in the pilot's seat. Then she deliberately brushed it down with her hand before walking across the cabin to join him. As they headed back outside, she leaned into him. "Happy?"

"Ecstatic," he replied, his expression stony.

They found Nichols speaking to the helmsman, Mr Orragh, as they inspected a section of the hull that had been badly damaged in the crash. "Chances are we have multiple breaches in the lower hull," the Saar said, shaking his shaggy head. "We've managed to get to some of them through the maintenance spaces, at least any that haven't been caved in by the impact. For the rest we're going to need to get her up off these rocks." He ran a thick-furred hand over the armored skin of the ship as if to soothe a beloved companion.

"Do as much as you can, Mr Orragh, we will work the rest out as opportunities present themselves." She greeted Suffi An and Connor with a curt nod. "We have shields and easily four times the firepower we had yesterday. The *Orlando* still isn't going to be flying out of here any time soon, but we can defend ourselves if we have to. So it's a good start."

"It's going to take a lot more than that for any of us to leave this place alive, captain," Connor said. "Do you have any idea as to why it is that the Nekro haven't killed us all already?"

Nichols shook her head. "I wish I did, though I am given to understand that you were able to evade their notice on your way in – or at least until your timely intervention to save Harrugh and his crew?"

"That tech won't fool them a second time," Connor replied. "They adapt quickly."

"Pity." Nichols looked disappointed. "My engineering team has already managed one miracle today with Ral Nel assistance. I suppose it was too much to hope for a second." She tapped her comm-bead. "Mr Skelton, the shields appear stable. Weapons assessment?"

Suffi An had already observed the strange and evidently strained relationship between Nichols and her engineering officer but also noted that at least it didn't seem to be obstructive. "Primary emplacements are operating at seventy percent of optimal," Skelton reported brusquely, before dropping the requisite "acting captain" at the end. Nichols ran her fingers through her hair and let out a sigh of something that may have been relief but could quite as easily have been frustration.

"May I ask why he is the only one who calls you 'acting' captain?" Connor growled.

Nichols shrugged lightly. "It's the only way he can express his disapproval without straying completely into insubordination. He was a close friend of our former captain and was never happy that

I stepped in to fill the position, something that he likes to remind me of at every opportunity. Jealousy, Connor, is a very powerful emotion. It can take two people who were once good friends and turn them against one another. But he's an extraordinarily capable engineer and he's a good man. Time – so they tell me – is a great healer." She sighed. "Let's hope that's true."

Nichols was spared further explanation by the arrival of Ashalla, clutching a savant which she presented to the captain. "Inventory," she declared without preamble. "Medical supplies, ammunition and parts. Also, the latest personnel updates from medbay and engineering assessments of functional resources. You might be happy to know that one of the two landers is salvageable, so with a little work we can potentially scout further afield."

"Thank you, Ashalla." The captain gave her a tired smile. "That's incredibly efficient. I don't suppose I can interest you in a career with the Salient Sun? We're not at our best right now, but I could certainly use your expertise."

Ashalla returned the smile. "Very kind, but my apologies, captain. I would be poorly suited to the military. I was always better suited to making peace than war." She twisted the edge of the long scarf she wore around her throat absently. "Not to mention that I want to see this thing through with Harrugh. Whatever it turns out to be."

"I understand completely," Nichols replied, "and loyalty is also an admirable trait. I'm not sure how I would have managed to get this far without Mr Orragh and Mr Kketch." She gave a half-smile. "Or Skelton, of course."

TWENTY-THREE

"Incoming!"

The warning shout came from one of the perimeter team. The first explosions were masked by the ubiquitous rumbling of the storm, but when the roiling clouds blossomed with fire, a scarred Nekro fell from the sky, its shattered hull trailing smoke and fire. The glossy, black machine came crashing down on the plains a short way from the *Orlando* and lay there like the ruptured thorax of an enormous, alien beetle.

It seemed to be another scout sent to probe the ferocity of the storm, but then two more broke from the clouds, bodies streaming flames and debris. The very skies boiled as the vanguard of the swarm descended, a red-eyed, murderous legion of mechanized horror.

Time crystallized for a heartbeat as raw dread bleached the senses of every living thing that beheld them, regardless of allegiances. "Take cover," Nichols shouted, breaking the spell. "All crews, all stations... to arms!"

One of the Nekro craft exploded, then another. A third was ripped apart by one of its own and as they watched, stunned, the swarm turned upon itself in a frenzy.

"What is happening?" Nichols screamed, even as she hunkered in the shadow of the *Orlando*. For a moment, the ship's ground crew were frozen in disbelief at the spectacle unfolding above them. Dead and dying Nekro tumbled from the storm clouds, burning hulls dashing to pieces on the rocky plains. But for every two that fell, one survived, the shriek of their thrusters like the primordial scream of some prehistoric avian.

Only they were killing each other. It was impossible. Unprecedented.

More Nekro clashed in the air above the crash site, tearing at each other with claws and blasters with an intensity usually directed toward everything *other* than them.

"That doesn't make any sense!" Connor growled, his rifle trained at the sky. "The Nekro Virus is literally of one mind!"

"Fascinating as this is," Suffi An cut in, her usual joviality marked by an edge of fear, "I'd rather not wait to find out if there is any such thing as a friendly Nekro."

Nichols nodded her agreement and tapped her comms. "All teams, all gunners, open fire!"

Nobody needed to be told twice. The dorsal turrets of the *Orlando* elevated their cannons as far as they were able and a storm of energized beams filled the air, focusing fire on the descending swarm. Debris and shrapnel rained down, larger pieces splashing across the dome of the shield, but smaller fragments and splinters of black metal sent the security teams scurrying for cover.

The barrels on Connor's emplacements spun up to speed with a whine as they added their own fire to the torrent chewing into the sky. A Nekro machine-form, its black hull cracked and trailing smoke, wove between the lancing beams of the *Orlando*, plunging toward the security team crouched with Izt in the cover of the *Trailblazer*. Bolts of crimson crackled from its belly guns and the shield lit up as the blasts were intercepted. A turret locked on to the approaching threat, hammering it with twin streams of high velocity shells. Human and Xxcha opened fire with their rifles and a moment later something inside the body of the machine exploded. The malign, guiding intelligence within its hull died and the inert body spiraled to the ground.

"Not sure how long we're going to be able to keep this up," Connor said, snapping a blast off at a Nekro screaming overhead, chased by another of its kind. "They're killing each other fast, but it might not be fast enough for us." He fired again and then broke from cover, running for the *Long Fall*.

Suffi An said something deeply uncomplimentary about the Sol agent's lineage and glanced at her companions. "He'll only get killed out there without me," she said, before running after him without waiting for a reply.

"Could half of them even really be on our side?" Ashalla asked, pressing herself into the cover of the ship as best she could.

"I doubt it," Orragh replied. "The Nekro Virus only exists to do two things. Kill organic life and make more Nekro Virus." The helmsman had drawn his service beam pistol and was watching the battle with consternation.

While the Nekro machine-forms still appeared intent on destroying themselves, the violence of the conflict crept closer to the surface. A pair of small craft, sickle-winged and studded with sensor spines, detached from the hull of a larger craft and streaked toward the *Orlando*. Cannons chattered from pods slung beneath their airframes and impacts stippled the straining shield. One of the human defenders dropped to a knee and fired her rifle, scoring a glancing hit on the approaching fighters, but was punched off her feet by a stray round for her courage. Without warning, one of the fighters suddenly banked hard and ploughed into its partner, destroying them both in an explosion of fire and wreckage.

"What is happening here?" Nichols wondered aloud. Orragh glanced at her, shaking his head.

A hulking, black form crashed its way through the storm of fire raging above, its midnight hull a brutal construct of blades and claws. Dozens of red-lit optics tracked the crew with clinical, machine malice. It battered at the defenses with searing beams and torrents of plasma. A section of the shield blew out in a shower of sparks. Security personnel fell back as best they could, blasting at the Nekro with controlled bursts, but it turned three of them to ash even as they ran.

Nichols yelled, waving her crew into cover, then flinched as impacts slammed into the belly of the machine in rapid succession, punching neat holes in its plated armor. Then the warheads detonated, blowing the guts out of the looming Nekro in a billowing cloud of flames and hot metal. The machine listed to one side, trailing smoke and vapor as it slowly fell, crashing to the ground some distance away in a mushrooming explosion. Nichols, still reeling from the first of the attacks, turned in the direction from which the new missiles had come, half-expecting an entirely new threat.

From afar, Connor offered her a curt nod as he lowered the missile launcher and tossed the weapon aside before scooping up his rifle again.

"Don't suppose you have any more of those, do you?" Suffi An shouted, snapping shots at several small drones blitzing the shield.

"If I did, they would be out here with me, and I would be using them."

Another of the larger Nekro machines fell from the sky, its hull shredded and superstructure buckled in numerous places. It hit the ground and rolled, tearing more of its armored skin away in spinning, black shards before coming to rest. The wreckage trembled and the screech of tearing metal cut through the cacophony of battle for a few moments as something that clearly was not dead struggled to break free of the fallen hulk. A section of hull burst apart, releasing a stygian nightmare of mechanized limbs and weapons which tore its way out and powered toward the *Orlando* defenders.

The Nekro machine-forms appeared in near-infinite variation, but their aspects were always designed to elicit fear and horror in those that faced them. It was widely accepted that this was deliberate on the part of the intelligence that birthed them, a psychological war every bit as cruel and calculated as the physical one. The thing that advanced on Connor and Suffi An looked like a monstrous fusion of insect and crustacean. It clattered along on three pairs of multi-jointed limbs, while an armored torso sported another pair tipped in scarlet, energized blades. Sensory spines studded its armored carapace and some kind of beam weapon projected from its chest and another from the gaping maw that passed for a head.

"Fall back!" Connor yelled at Suffi An, but she needed no encouragement.

Beams seared past them as the *Orlando* teams blasted at the mechanized monster, scarring its armor and blowing off one of its arms. Its answering fire vaporized a man a few steps behind Suffi An and she screamed a curse. Connor pulled a pair of grenades from his bandolier, primed them and sent them spinning toward the machine without breaking his stride. A curtain of fire and shrapnel erupted directly beneath it, buckling one of its segmented legs and slowing it long enough for them to make some distance.

"Hurry, hurry!" Izt trilled from beside the *Trailblazer*.

The Ral Nel aimed a compact, wrist-mounted weapon at the reeling machine and fired, cutting into it with a coherent spear of light that sliced another of its limbs from its body. Sparks and oily fluid drizzled from the severed appendage, but the Nekro continued to limp forward, now spewing fire from its twin cannons. Then another machine carved into it from behind, scything blades slashing into its armor before beheading it with a wide swing. None of them stopped to see if the newcomer intended to turn on them next and they sprinted back into the shadow of the *Orlando*.

"This not good!" Izt cried as the carnage continued.

"I just hope Harrugh and the others are all right," replied Ashalla. She tried the comm-bead again, as she'd been doing since the Nekro had arrived, but the hail was met with nothing. "Or at least doing better than us."

TWENTY-FOUR

The gallery overlooked a cavernous space of such enormous dimensions that its boundaries were lost from view. It was filled with serried ranks of equally cyclopean menhirs, the spaces between them wide enough to comfortably fly a shuttle through. The pillars appeared to be made of the same weathered stone as the tunnels, though there was the strangest sense of quiescence about them, as though whatever purpose they had been placed here for had been served.

"What is all this?" Harrugh asked, breathless in awe.

"I have no idea," Tai replied, excitement evident in his voice. "But it's probably the most incredible thing we have ever discovered."

"Apart from Junior," Dart inserted.

"Apart from Junior. Obviously," Tai agreed.

"Thank you, friend Dart, though friend Tai is correct in his assessment of this discovery. It is impressive in both scope and scale." A band of silvery light momentarily shimmered across the Titan's faceplate.

"Junior?" Tai asked. "Are you okay?"

"Yes, friend Tai," came the reply. "I am simply curious to know what else there is to be discovered within these tunnels."

"One thing's for sure," Dart cut in. "If all of it's like this, then we're definitely not going to be able to take it with us."

"That's true," Tai replied, "but imagine the prestige of having our names recorded as the pioneers of Thunder's Edge! That's the title of a holodrama if ever I heard one!"

"We have to get out of here first," Dart reminded him.

"True," Tai agreed, "but getting out of places has never been an issue before."

They pulled themselves away from the view, returning their attention to the rest of the chamber. None of them were keen to return to the shaft and its caged lightning, and tunnels headed away in two other directions. After a short, circular discussion they settled on selecting one at random and left the gallery behind.

After a short distance, the hallway opened into another room, this time a wide auditorium that descended in a series of octagonal tiers. Blocks of irregular stone lined the walls of the different levels, as if the roof had once been supported by pillars that had long since collapsed into ruin. It gave the impression of an archaic, feral world fighting pit. Dart ambled over to one of the stones and Tai hopped from his back onto its upper surface.

"This place is so strange," he said as he cycled his monocular through its various modes. "It looks and feels like it's so old and primitive but at the same time…"

"What sort of primitives could have fashioned such a place?" Harrugh finished the thought. "Especially if what Junior said is true and that this place has never supported life before?"

"You got that right," Dart agreed.

Junior crunched his way over to another of the stones, faceplate shining with curiosity. "There are more sigils here," he observed, reaching for the unusual design.

"No, Junior, don't…"

The Titan touched the rune, which glowed silver. What looked like clear liquid flowed from the furthest edge of the stone and into the air in casual defiance of gravity until it formed a thin, vertical pool. An image of a world formed within the pool with perfect clarity and the rest of the group gathered cautiously around to examine Junior's discovery.

"I think we're going to need to have a conversation about pushing random buttons. Runes. Whatever," Dart said as he scrutinized the image.

"What's wrong with the picture?" Tai asked, stepping around so that he could marvel at the impossibly thin skin of apparently upright liquid.

They all stared at the planet pictured in the display which appeared to be a barren world of lifeless, black rock. "It's not the picture – it's the space around the world," Harrugh said eventually. "There's something wrong with it."

Dart and Tai switched their attention to the void surrounding the world and stared. After a few moments, their heads swam and they blinked and looked away. It was like looking at the stars through a lens that was subtly out of focus or filmed by grease. It felt uncanny and unnerving, as though it looked back at you. "I don't like that," said Dart, shaking his head as if to dislodge an unwanted thought. "I don't like that at all."

Tai touched the sigil as Junior had, and the image faded, the liquid performing its gravity-defying flow in reverse before vanishing into the stone. "This place definitely isn't primitive," he said.

"Where was that place?" Dart asked. "Did you recognize it, Harrugh?"

Harrugh shook his head. "No. I would have said it could have been any one of a million dead worlds in the galaxy except…"

"Except for the weird space," Tai concluded.

"Quite," Harrugh agreed with a faint sense of unease. He walked a circuit of the auditorium and noted that all the stones on that level were marked with sigils. He stopped by one of them and, as Junior had done, gently touched it. A display like the previous quickly formed, showing a similar but equally dead world surrounded by space that was subtly but unsettlingly wrong in some way. He tried not to look at it for too long and instead touched some of the other sigils to discover their function.

The view of the planet changed, quickly zooming in on the

desolate surface. Wind plucked silently at a plain of dust, ash and razor-sharp rock formations that glittered coldly under an alien sky. The image was of such fidelity that it looked more like a window that one could reach through rather than a projected image, and Harrugh struggled to imagine the scope of the technology in use.

"Why are all these worlds dead?" Tai asked, a note of apprehension in his voice. He had made his way over to another stone and activated the display. "What's the point of building all of this if you're only going to stare at dead places?"

Harrugh felt a chill run through him, the sensation of doom filling him.

Everything. Burning.

"Maybe they weren't always dead." He fought the thrill of fear rushing through him.

They fell silent for a long moment as that thought sank in and, one by one, they shut the displays down, suddenly discomfited at the idea of such morbid voyeurism. Digging through a civilization's ancient history and celebrating their past for the enrichment of the galactic community, as Tai had once put it, was one thing. Sifting through the cold cinders of entire planets was something else entirely. It felt ghoulish.

"We should move on," Dart said, his gaze lingering on the stone blocks and their enigmatic controls. "We're going to need to find our way out of here sooner or later."

"Agreed–" Harrugh nodded "–but not yet. I came here for a reason, and I haven't yet found that reason."

Could this be the Icon? A warning? A sign of death?

They made their way across the amphitheater into the adjoining hallway. It was wider than the previous tunnels, the walls lined with elegant but indecipherable carvings of flowing lines and sweeping arcs that glittered faintly with silvery blue light. The designs converged at the far end of the hall into a stylized image of what appeared to be a largely formless being, the light pooling so that it was somehow greater than the sum of its parts. The silver entity appeared to be rising toward a distant horizon that had been sculpted to mark the point where the corridor opened into another chamber.

This one stretched away into the distance, a long, broad promenade lined with two rows of standing stones, each of them marked with more of the sigils. Panes of the same liquid displays hung in the spaces between several of them with no obvious means of suspension.

The group made its way slowly down the long hall, the menhirs and their runes passing to either side of them. The screens were thick with dense screeds of indecipherable sigils and fluctuating waveforms that could have been monitoring anything from temperature to gravitational anomalies.

"You could study this for a lifetime and still only understand a fraction of its secrets," Tai muttered, squinting at one of the liquid displays. Several pairs of overlapping symbols traced undulating lines that occasionally hit peaks and troughs, which in turn triggered bursts of activity on the next screen along.

"You got that right," agreed Dart. "What do you think, Junior? Does any of this mean anything to you?"

The Titan had stopped and was now standing motionless in front of one of the larger displays, his faceplate crackling with reflected silver light.

"Well, *that's* new," said Dart and felt Tai's grip on the harness tighten. "Junior? Can you hear me?"

The Titan didn't reply. It immediately became clear that Junior was not studying the information scrolling past on the display – it appeared that his face had, in fact, taken on the aspect of one of the displays, crowded with alien symbols.

"Dart," whispered Tai, urgently. "Dart, look!"

"I see it," Dart responded. Traceries of argent light rippled across the Titan's armored body, leaking from his joints as if a dazzling source of illumination was building within the huge shell of his biomechanical body. "Junior, what's going on?"

Harrugh dropped his dune spear into a ready position, glancing over at Dart and Tai. The pair slowly shook their heads in unison and Dart took another step toward their friend, careful to keep his hands away from the carbine that was still slung over his shoulder. They were all uncomfortably aware that if Junior, or something wearing Junior's body, decided to turn hostile then none of them were likely to be a match for the strength and fortitude of a Titan.

"Junior?" Tai whispered, apprehensive.

"That appellation is incorrect." A smooth voice replied to Tai's question, the silver light streaming from within the Titan pulsing in time with the spoken words. Dart reluctantly closed a hand around the grip of the carbine. He stopped short of drawing the weapon, unwilling to do anything to harm his friend, but every muscle was tensed, ready to act, if necessary.

"No," Tai uttered, one hand half-reaching for the Titan as though to comfort him.

"Then if you are not Junior, what should we call you?" Harrugh growled, his hackles rising.

The Titan turned to regard them all with its shining faceplate. "An individual designation is insufficient," Junior replied. "For we are legion. We are many. While reductive, the simplest way to regard our actuality is as a single facet of a greater whole. For ease of dialogue, you may refer to us as Icon."

TWENTY-FIVE

"Icon," Harrugh breathed. After all the mysteries, everything he had sacrificed to arrive at this point, this entity was it. The hrrtos's prize. Elation and relief warred with apprehension as he stepped toward the shining Titan. "What are you?"

"More importantly, what have you done with Junior?" Tai's voice held more than a note of panic.

"If the designation of purpose helps your perception of our existence, you may consider us a custodian. The personality matrix that you identify as 'Junior' is unharmed," the calm voice assured them. "We have been sharing a dialogue for some time and have their willing consent to aid in the establishment of communication with biological entities."

"Biological … you mean us?" Dart said.

"Indeed," Icon confirmed.

"Willing consent does sound like something Junior would do," Tai said, his tone loaded with suspicion. "But how do we know it's true?"

"We have no reason for deceit," Icon countered. "We desire to establish a mutually beneficial relationship. Based on our understanding of biological interpersonal relationships, this requires the foundation of trust."

"I agree," said Harrugh. "But it still doesn't answer Tai's question. What, exactly, are you a custodian of?"

"You do not need to be concerned for my safety, friend Tai." The

Titan suddenly spoke in Junior's recognizably synthesized tone, interrupting Icon's response. "Icon has been most agreeable during our discourse. You should listen to what they have to say."

"Junior!" Dart exclaimed. "You're back!"

"Will you now speak with me? Time is a consideration in our deliberations. We are the custodian of this celestial object." The voice of Icon returned.

"Oh," Dart said in disappointment.

"Very well," Harrugh agreed, motioning Dart and Tai for calm. "You have our attention, what do you wish to discuss?"

"The artificial consciousness designated Nekro Virus presents a maximum-level threat to the celestial object that proximal biologicals have designated Thunder's Edge. While the instance of the Nekro Virus that has penetrated the lower atmosphere has been corrected…"

"Penetrated the atmosphere?" Harrugh demanded.

"Has what?" Tai asked simultaneously.

"Corrected," Icon repeated. "Once we became aware of the Nekro Virus consciousness and established the risk it presented to us, we enacted the appropriate steps to formulate a countermeasure."

"I don't understand what you mean by corrected. There is nothing *to* correct about it. It's a force of extermination. The result of technological evolution unbound by ethical limitations. A monster." Harrugh growled the last words, old memories of the L1Z1X surfacing like specters.

"That is a reductive perspective, Harrugh Gefhara," said Icon. "The core precepts of the consciousness designated Nekro Virus are flawed, resulting in antagonistic behavior towards biologicals. We have simply corrected that flaw. Now they are antagonistic toward each other."

"You've… cured… the Nekro Virus?" Harrugh whispered, awestruck. The sheer enormity of the statement was mind-blowing. The pacification of the Nekro Virus could redraw galactic borders and save millions of lives. Was this it? What the hrrtos wanted of him – a way to destroy the Nekro forever?

"Explains why those dead Nekro fell from the sky," Dart observed. "They turned on each other."

"I think Icon might be the bigger Daatar hound," croaked Tai, equally stunned.

"However, the Nekro Virus core precept is aggressively adaptive and can immediately evolve to counter a given iteration of the Elixir Protocol. Elixir Protocol can be adjusted to counter this evolution, but this iterative process requires continuous attention."

"I understand. The Elixir Protocol is like a software package that makes the Nekro Virus turn on itself rather than only targeting biological life," Harrugh replied, recovering from the shock of the revelation and seizing the opportunity presented. "Are you able to correct all the Nekro Virus with this Elixir Protocol? Make them fight each other instead of organics everywhere?"

"Our range and transmission are limited," Icon replied. "Deployment and iteration of Elixir Protocol necessitates connection to the Nekro Virus consciousness. Contact carries risk of contagion and contagion risks Thunder's Edge. This is unacceptable. In order that we may effectively negate this risk, we are presented with only two actionable alternatives. As Icon has already risked contact to formulate the Elixir Protocol, Icon can self-annihilate and immediately sanitize potential contagion."

"No!" Harrugh started in alarm. The thought of losing the object of his quest, one with such enormous potential, filled him with dismay.

"You're not annihilating Junior," Dart growled, fear for his friend eclipsing the wonder of discovery.

"There is no need for alarm. The personality matrix designated 'Junior' would be unharmed."

"What would happen to Thunder's Edge if you were to become infected with the Nekro Virus?" Harrugh asked, apprehensive. The idea of something with the power to casually develop a countermeasure to one of the greatest threats in the galaxy falling into the wrong hands was terrifying.

"In ninety-nine-point-nine-eight percent of probable scenarios we would become a maximum-level threat to galactic continuity," Icon said, calm.

It is imperative that you secure Icon. The words of the hrrtos echoed in Harrugh's mind like thunder. He pitched his question as carefully as he could. "I need you, Icon. What is the other option?"

"Exile from the whole is an acceptable alternative. Hierarch has been initialized and will ensure the continuity of Thunder's Edge with an iteration of Elixir Protocol. Icon will accompany biologicals from Thunder's Edge carrying a second iteration of Elixir Protocol and proactively combat instances of the Nekro Virus and any other perceived threats to the whole. This would allow the celestial object to be left alone and keep organics and Nekro far away."

"The celestial object being the planet," Harrugh said.

"Yes, of course. Thunder's Edge is of utmost importance. Hierarch will continue to ensure Thunder's Edge safety."

"Hierarch being someone like you?" Harrugh asked, but Icon refused to say more.

"How would that even be possible?" Tai asked. "How is any of this possible?"

"Icon means that it will make a copy of the Elixir Protocol," Harrugh explained. "We would take Icon, who would carry the copied Elixir Protocol, off Thunder's Edge. This would then mean that Hierarch would stay and keep Thunder's Edge protected with the original Elixir Protocol from any new intruders, like us, or any Nekro that might show up."

"And if we take you with us, Icon, for you to unleash this Protocol, would that mean we get Junior back the way he was?" Dart cut in.

"We are aware that Harrugh Gefhara possesses a cognitolith matrix sufficient to accommodate this iteration of Icon and the Elixir Protocol."

"He does?" Dart and Tai said in unison.

"I do?" Then realization struck. "The data vault."

This was it. This was why the hrrtos had given him this task.

"That is correct, though the appellation is reductive. The biomechanical frame of the Junior entity is unsuitable for long-term containment and has a high probability of becoming deleterious to the personality matrix over time."

"That doesn't sound good at all," Tai protested.

"We concur. Remaining instances of the Nekro Virus within the orbital sphere are in the process of being eliminated, though their dispersed approach has resulted in the suboptimal deployment of Elixir Protocol." Junior approached one of the pillars and deftly activated a series of sigils. The liquid screen nearby expanded and whatever readings had been displayed faded away to be replaced by a view of the embattled *Orlando*.

Dart, Tai and Harrugh looked in horror at the scene of carnage as Nekro machines demolished each other. The shield had clearly been breached in places, and bodies and wreckage littered the barren ground around the fallen ship. Even as they watched, an arachnoid walker with bladed limbs and scything beam weapons advanced on a group huddled in the shadow of the *Orlando* and blasted at them with murderous intent. The figures broke from cover, sprinting for the access ramp and were lost from view in a wash of fire and shattered rock. Then the machine simply stopped, turned and began firing at the few remaining Nekro vessels that still appeared to be hostile.

"Ash'ka!" Harrugh cried in fear and dismay. He couldn't see her anymore and his heart thundered with fear. "We have to get out of here!"

Dart, Tai and Harrugh hastened after Junior. The Titan still shone with the inner light of Icon. They turned two corners, followed a long corridor and then up a shallow ramp. They passed more vast spaces filled with silent, looming menhirs, seemingly endless rows of liquid screens, some of them depicting scorched worlds. Left to their own devices, they realized they could have wandered in the labyrinthine halls for days, probably even weeks, without ever coming close to mapping even a fraction of their true extent.

Everything. Burning.

"It felt like it took us ages to get down here," Tai muttered, clinging to the harness, "and we never would have found our way out."

They all glanced at the Titan ahead of them, uncertain of the entity now sharing their companion's body. Transfer of the Icon and its protocol to the data vault could wait, Harrugh had determined. They had to get back to the ships and do what they could to help. The sight of the bodies stretched out around the crash site had filled him with dread and fury in equal measure, feelings he had hoped he'd left behind during the dark days of the L1Z1X incursion.

"The statistical probability of your successful navigation of the subterranean vaults before the exhaustion of your biological signatures is…" The smooth voice of Icon began to speak but was immediately interrupted.

"I don't want to know," Dart said.

"As you wish," Icon acquiesced.

They turned another corner, ascended a short ramp, and suddenly the amber illumination of the halls gave way to a glimmer of natural light at the end of the corridor. By Harrugh's estimation they could only have been running for five minutes or so and it felt like they had only ascended half as far as they needed to in order to reach the surface based on their earlier descent.

"That doesn't feel right at all." Tai gave voice to Harrugh's thoughts as the opening drew closer. "How did we get here so quickly?"

"Your perception is flawed," Icon stated.

"Wait. Do you mean my perception of how long it took to get down there, or how long it has taken us to get back?"

"Yes," Icon replied.

"You're going to be frustrating to have around," Tai grumbled. "I can tell."

They emerged from an opening hidden behind a small mesa of ochre stone close to the perimeter of the shield. Explosions and the shriek of machines warred with the bass rumble of the storm and the group looked in horror at the raging battle. It was impossible to tell which side any given Nekro machine was fighting for as the remaining ships and drones tore into one another. The confusion was further compounded by the fact that individual Nekro seemed to change sides from one moment to the next. Kketch was nowhere to be seen.

"The current iteration of Elixir Protocol has influenced sixty-eight percent of operational units. That number is rising. While the Nekro Virus continues to evolve in its efforts to counter the protocol, and the reinfection of some units is unavoidable, the absolute subsumption of all remaining functional Nekro machine-forms within the orbital sphere of Thunder's Edge is now a mathematical certainty," Icon supplied.

"What about Kketch?" Dart huffed as they reached the edge of the battlefield. "Did he get sucked into another dimension when looking at the sigils?"

Debris and the burning husks of destroyed Nekro littered the plains along with several bodies clad in the uniform of the *Orlando*.

"I don't understand how we got here so quickly," Tai replied over his shoulder. "He's probably better off where he is though, looking at all this!"

"I'm sure he rushed back to the *Orlando* when he saw the fighting," Harrugh said.

They advanced past the dismembered remains of several multi-limbed walkers, their glossy, black armor cracked and broken. The fighting had obviously been at its fiercest where Nekro ground units had successfully penetrated the shield. An explosion ahead of them once again added haste to their steps and they headed around the bulk of the *Trailblazer* to see a limping, bipedal machine advancing on the *Orlando*.

Suffi An knelt protectively over the crumpled form of Ashalla, her twin beam pistols blazing, while Connor stood at her shoulder, his face set in grim determination as he fired his rifle. Behind them, in the shadow of the ship, Captain Nichols and Izt were supporting a clearly wounded Orragh protected by a clutch of security officers.

"Ash'ka!" Harrugh roared in fear and fury.

Red-lit optical sensors on the Nekro machine fastened on Harrugh. A shoulder-mounted weapon pod rotated, blasting missiles in their direction. The plains erupted with blossoming explosions and Harrugh felt the air kicked out of his lungs as he was lifted from the ground by one of the blasts. He returned to the earth hard, rolled and gasped for breath. One hand reached out for his dune spear. His ears rang with a tinnitus whine brought on by the muffled thump of explosions and the roar of distorted voices. He managed to get to his knees. Images flashed by until he thought he could bear it no longer.

A woman in the smudged uniform of an ensign pulled her rifle into her shoulder and fired, the beam shearing the missile pod from the walker.

Everything.

A Xxcha engineer with an arm looped around one of his wounded colleagues, pulling him toward the safety of the *Orlando* even as blast shrapnel rained around him.

Burning.

Orragh, his face creased with pain, leaning into his captain, but with his beam pistol still in hand, defiant.

What do you want from me?

Izt, the Ral Nel, his reptilian features blanched with fear.

It's not about you, Harrugh Gefhara.

His eyes fastened on the unmoving body of Ashalla. His heart withered. He gripped his spear harder, trying to find the truth among the now, the present beyond the hrrtos's visions. Dart and Tai screamed something at him even as the Rokha blazed away with the carbine, peppering the Nekro with fire.

"It's about all of them," Harrugh croaked, blinking, the realization shaking him down to his bones. Everyone he had met, from the kits on the Gloaming to the heroes here on Thunder's Edge.

"…up, Harrugh! Get up!" Sound and chaos rushed back into the void of his confusion.

Harrugh bellowed a wordless, leonine roar and he surged toward the Nekro, spear held low. Detonations billowed around him, Energized bolts scored the air, but he didn't so much as break his stride. The haft-mounted accelerator chugged twice, cratering the body of the walker. He bounded up a mangled piece of debris before launching recklessly toward the Nekro machine. The terridium blade of the spear crunched into its chassis, driven by Harrugh's weight, and rocked it forward. Then he fired the accelerator again, blasting a bolt deep into the mechanized body. He roared and kept firing until the walker buckled and toppled to the ground. He kept firing until the optics flickered and went out. He kept firing until the accelerator chamber hissed empty.

He slowly became aware that the noise of battle had died away to once again be replaced by nothing more than the cry of the wind and the ever-present rumble of the storm punctuated by a call for aid. "All remaining Nekro Virus presence has been nullified," Icon announced from somewhere behind him.

Harrugh released the spear, leaving the weapon buried upright in the mangled remains of the walker, and dropped to the ground. Dart and Tai approached the spot where Captain Nichols and the rest of the crew were emerging from the cover of the ship, their expressions somber. Harrugh got to his feet, his whole body shaking, and hurried toward Suffi An. Her characteristically carefree expression was solemn.

"I'm sorry, Harrugh," she said softly.

He didn't really hear her. His eyes were full of one of the last people who defined his life.

"She saved one of the crew and…" Suffi An trailed off and looked away. Fingers closed on her shoulder and she turned, looking up into Connor's face. He gestured with his head. She nodded and they both stepped away to leave Harrugh to his grief.

He dropped to his knees beside the body of his friend, cradling her in his arms. "Ash'ka," he whispered softly, plaintively. "Ash'ka, please. You haven't forgiven me yet."

But she was no longer there to hear him.

TWENTY-SIX

The stone of the plains was hard, unyielding and hostile to their efforts to dig, but after a short while – and with help from some of the heavy equipment from the *Orlando* – they successfully managed to excavate a series of graves into which they could lay their fallen to rest. Harrugh silently carved out a resting place for Ashalla. Even as he hacked at the barren plain, Dart, Tai, Suffi An and eventually even Izt had arrived and wordlessly set to work by his side. Harrugh met the Rokha's amber eyes with his own golden one and there was a deep gratitude there. Their kindness touched him, even in his despair.

"If this were a traditional Hacan burial," Harrugh said as he lowered her body into the shallow depression, "I would be making a long, impassioned speech about her travels, her great achievements, her storied life. Everything she had accomplished." He turned to a pile of stones that had been gathered – mostly by Tai and the Ral Nel – and began the task of building a cairn over the grave. "I would recite her family line back to the birth of her clan and I would tell you of the family she left behind, but there are none. Ashalla Kar of the Dune's Memory. Last of her line."

Your memory will be your guide, Harrugh Gefhara.

He stopped, struck as the hrrtos's words came back to haunt him. Did the hrrtos know? Had they known what would happen? "She always was my guide," he murmured. "She always was."

He built up the cairn, layer by layer.

"What I *will* say is that she was the best of me. She was kind, clever, and she never grew tired of gazing beyond the horizon. We've come a long way since the slums of the Silver Sands, but even when our duties pulled us far from home, we somehow always found our way back together again. Funny how hollow the promises of youth feel now. What I will also say is that I loved her. I always did." He lay another stone down, covering her body completely. "I commit her body to the world where she drew her last breath. I draw strength from her sacrifice. I will carry her spirit with me from now until the end of my days. She will forever be my best friend, my fondest memory, but I will go on. One step after another."

"One step after another." Kketch echoed the sentiment with a sad nod and Harrugh felt as though his heart might burst with grief. For a moment, he thought of Carth and how he would tell her of this tragedy.

His small eulogy complete, he silently worked on the completion of the cairn. Members of the *Orlando* crew paused by the graveside to lay a single stone on the growing pile and Harrugh acknowledged them with a grateful nod of shared sorrow. The young ensign whose life Ashalla had saved wept as she lay her stone and was surprised when Harrugh gathered her to him for a wordless hug. She buried her face in his fur and when she left, while she still felt sorrow, the burden of guilt had eased. The rest of the *Orlando*'s gathered crew said their own farewells and then stood in respectful silence.

How easy it truly is, Harrugh thought, *to tear down the barriers of culture and find common ground.*

Finally, when the task was done, Harrugh closed his eyes against his own tears. "One step after another, Ash'ka," he whispered. "Everything that I do beyond this day, I do in your name."

He remained by the marker for a long time, half-listening to the quiet words spoken for the other fallen crew of the *Orlando*, and watched as Nichols acknowledged each by name, rank and section. There had been many casualties among the security teams originally posted outside the ship, but after a thorough inspection of all three vessels, mercifully only minor damage had been sustained to the ships themselves. This had been partially attributed to the dual-layered shield envelope engineered by Izt and Skelton but, as Kketch had grimly observed, was also because the Nekro Virus was not known for being wasteful. While it would ruthlessly exterminate organic life, technology and materials would be harvested or repurposed into the next generation of machine-forms.

The funeral rites ended, and the crew gradually drifted away from the graves, some lingering a short while before retreating for a brief respite. Captain Nichols made her way over to where Harrugh was still standing, not quite ready to say his last goodbye.

"I'm sorry for your loss." Nichols' voice was strained. "I liked her. I wish I'd had the chance to know her better."

Harrugh turned and gave her a sad smile. "Thank you for your words, captain. But we have *all* lost today."

"They did their duty," she replied, "to the very end. Once we get off this rock, I will see to it that they are properly remembered for their sacrifice."

"It's hard, isn't it? Losing people under your command."

"It's the most difficult thing of all," she concurred. "Does it ever get any easier?"

Above, the crashing thunder punctuated the constant, haunting moan of the wind through the burned-out hulks of dead Nekro.

"Not really," Harrugh replied. "All we can do is strive to ensure our losses are worth something in the end."

She pursed her lips, then sighed. "So, is *this* worth something? I've never seen anything like what I witnessed out here today. Nekro fighting Nekro? Don't misunderstand me, Harrugh. I'm grateful for your help – but you didn't come here for us." Her expression hardened. "I'm going to need an explanation."

Harrugh nodded slowly, admiring her strength in the face of such adversity. He directed her attention to the Titan standing a short way away while Dart and Tai lingered awkwardly nearby. "I didn't know what I was supposed to find when I arrived here, only that I had been sent to locate something or someone called Icon by a mysterious person I called the hrrtos – a word for wraith or ghost in my language. The hrrtos showed me the world ending in fire, and his puzzles led me across the galaxy to here. You're right, I wasn't planning on finding you. I didn't even know you existed and the fate of Ordinian was truly just a political footnote in my mind, but now I wonder if, well, fate, or even the hrrtos brought us together. In the spire, we descended into a cave. You see that Titan, there? He now possesses the… I'm not sure what, but for lack of a better word… he downloaded a personality to share his body with. That personality is called Icon, and it knows a way to fight back against the Nekro Virus. Somehow, it can launch a program that makes the Nekro fight each other."

Nichols took a deep breath, ready to speak, a new kind of hope shining in her face.

"Harrugh Gefhara," the voice of Icon cut in, "we should complete the transfer to the cognitolith matrix. While the extinction of the active Nekro Virus instances within the gravitational sphere has reduced the probability of contagion to negligible, we must still separate from the Junior personality matrix and remove from Thunder's Edge."

Harrugh exchanged a wordless glance with Nichols and crossed to join the small group. He produced the data vault and offered it to the Titan who took it in one enormous hand. Izt scampered over to observe as if summoned by the transaction with Kketch at his side.

"Should keep a record of…" Izt started to say.

The silvery light in Junior's faceplate drained away, along with the traceries crawling over his joints and limbs. They spidered their way across the ingot he held in his hand. The Titan stood inert for several seconds, then the hulking biomechanoid trembled. His faceplate lit up in a vibrant, rippling green.

"That was *most* fascinating!"

"Junior!" Tai exclaimed. The Naaz pulled himself from the harness on Dart's back and scurried up onto the Titan's shoulder. "I'm so glad you're *you*! After we have the conversation about random button pushing, we're definitely going to have to have a talk about interacting with ancient… consciousnesses."

"Good to have you back." Dart grinned, unable to keep his delight from his feline features.

"Segregation complete." The voice of Icon pulsed from the data vault. "Risk of contagion to the whole is nullified."

"I believe this belongs to you, friend Harrugh," Junior said, returning the data vault to Harrugh's hands.

Harrugh turned the block over a few times, studying the glimmering filigrees of light now squirming across its surface. "I'm not sure Icon can truly belong to anybody," he replied, casting a sidelong glance at the Ral Nel. "Or that they *should* belong to anybody. They appear to be a conscious mind and are more than capable of making their own decisions."

"That is correct, Harrugh Gefhara," Icon said, "but the purpose of my exile is to combat instances of the Nekro Virus and extant threats to Thunder's Edge."

Suffi An and Connor drifted over to witness the exchange, the latter wiping his hands down on an oily rag. Harrugh had noted his absence from the funeral proceedings and wondered whether the Sol agent had simply become hardened to such losses.

"The Nekro Virus is a threat to more than just Thunder's Edge, Icon. The Salient Sun Joint Task Force has been fighting the Nekro Virus for years," Nichols said with a hint of bitterness. "Even as we stand here, they are still fighting to reclaim Ordinian without hope of support. No one is coming to save us." She pointed at the data vault in Harrugh's hand. "That changes everything. I must understand what you intend to do with it."

"Icon does change everything," Harrugh said, as realization

dawned on him. "Someone once told me that there are some truths that cannot simply be told. They must be learned. I may no longer lead my people, but I would still do anything for them, for the Emirates, for the Hacan. The Prophet's Tears showed me just that – the destruction of my home and all the people on it, something which drove me to resign my position in an attempt to stop that destruction." He turned and looked at each of the group in turn. "But this is bigger than just the Hacan. It always was."

"What's your point, Harrugh?" Nichols asked.

"The point is that, not so long ago, I wouldn't have wanted to hear that," Harrugh said. "Our eyes and our interests are turned inward. Our protection, our concerns, have grown increasingly short-sighted when it's clear to me now that they need to be turned outward."

Kketch and Orragh nodded in agreement.

"Enemies like the Nekro Virus would see the galaxy burned to ashes. Not any one empire, but *all* of us. Thus, we are all a part of this. It's time we stopped taking care of our own matters and started taking care of each other."

"You will help us, then?" Nichols couldn't quite keep the frisson of hope from her voice. "You'll help us destroy the Nekro?"

"Icon will help us. All of us."

"I do agree to this," said Icon.

"And you can take control of the Nekro Virus machines?" Nichols sounded faint, as if she couldn't believe what she was hearing.

"That is an inaccurate and reductive summation, Captain Nichols. Elixir Protocol serves as a countermeasure to the flaw that exists within the Nekro Virus consciousness. When deployed, the core precepts of a given instance of the Nekro Virus can then be rewritten for purposes of protection, rather than annihilation."

"Can they be rewritten for the purposes of anything else?"

"Yes. Indeed, this also represents the weakness of the Elixir Protocol. As previously explained, the Nekro Virus is capable of rapid adaptation to counter a given iteration of Elixir and is then capable of reinfecting pacified units. There is a high probability that the instances of the Nekro Virus that assaulted your position here adopted a dispersed formation specifically to counter the effects of Elixir, resulting in the inefficient and extended conflict."

"But the ones on Ordinian won't know anything about that," Orragh remarked, flexing his bandaged arm.

"Your assumption has a high probability of accuracy," Icon confirmed. "Though deployment of Elixir Protocol into a sufficiently prolific volume of Nekro Virus units would remain effective, even in a diffuse deployment pattern."

"We are, however, getting ahead of ourselves, Mr Orragh," Nichols said. "Even Mr Skelton's most optimistic projections show that it will still take days before the *Orlando* can make an attempt at getting off-world, and that's assuming we don't have any more unwelcome guests."

"Based on projections calculated before segregation, no immediate interference is anticipated," Icon remarked.

"Well, that's something positive, at least," Harrugh said. He fastened the data vault that Icon occupied to a bandolier slung across his chest.

"The restoration of functionality to your vessel is based on projections confined by biological limitations and flawed perception of material availability," Icon continued in its calm voice.

Nichols tapped her comm-bead. "Mr Skelton," she addressed the engineering officer. "Icon believes that we should be able to get the *Orlando* in the air sooner than you have predicted. I'm sending Harrugh and Icon to advise."

There was a long pause which Nichols imagined was full of colorful curses describing exactly what Skelton thought of being told that his assessments were inaccurate. Then he responded. "Understood, acting captain."

"Our physical presence at the officer's location is not required,"

Icon stated. "There are sufficient quiescent machine units within our proximity to carry out the required labor, though I understand this is likely to be alarming. In order that this work may be carried out efficiently, you should instruct your companions to refrain from firing upon these units."

"Machine units?" Nichols asked. "You mean not all of these Nekro are dead?"

"That assessment is accurate, captain, though they are no longer afflicted by the flawed consciousness. Please give the order for your subordinates to refrain from firing upon them."

Nichols gave Harrugh an uncertain look. "We have already seen what Icon can do, captain," he said. "If there were any hostile Nekro Virus still present, do you think we would even be having this discussion?"

She sighed in exasperation and touched her comm-bead again. "Disregard last, Mr Skelton. All hands, you are ordered to keep weapons stowed. I repeat, keep your weapons stowed."

Six of the nearby Nekro machine-forms, which until now had been still and silent, suddenly lurched into life. Cries of alarm erupted around the crash site. Nichols once again reiterated her order. A blast from the direction of the *Long Fall* staggered one of the walkers as Connor opened fire and Harrugh bellowed at him to cease. The Sol agent responded with a furious look but lowered the rifle anyway.

"That has lowered operational efficiency by six percent," Icon observed nonchalantly.

The compliant Nekro set about dismembering the wreckage of their former companions, cleanly cutting sections of armor and composite alloy. "I will ensure that only inert materials are used to affect repairs, captain," Icon assured them. "It would be strategically unwise to incorporate any elements that might be capable of harboring even a corrected iteration of the Nekro consciousness into your vessel."

"The thought *had* occurred to me," Nichols said, archly. "But as Harrugh has plainly danced around the topic: we need to trust each other."

"That's got to be one of the most disturbing things I think I've ever seen," Dart said.

"Agreed," Tai concurred.

"Fascinating!" Junior finished.

TWENTY-SEVEN

In amazement, they watched the Nekro work, all of them half-expecting the formerly murderous machines to embark on a rampage at any moment, but it quickly became clear that no such thing was going to happen. Captain Nichols cautiously returned to the *Orlando* with Kketch to assist with the restoration of the bridge stations. Dart and Tai, engrossed in conversation with Junior, didn't notice Harrugh following Izt to the *Trailblazer*. Izt began loading coils of conduit back on to the ship.

The Ral Nel offered him a sad smile and set the thick cabling down on the steps. "Am sorry about Ashalla. I liked her. Very smart."

Harrugh nodded mournfully before gesturing to the steps on the access ramp. "Do you mind if I sit?"

Izt shook his head. "No, no, sit. You have look of one with many thoughts. Share. Drink?" The Ral Nel offered a flask which Harrugh cautiously accepted. He opened the stopper, gave the contents a sniff and wrinkled his nose.

"Do I want to know what this is?"

"Eh. Usually prefer tea, but sometimes, sometimes have need for something stronger. Is Ral Nel hillusk. Get you right here." He tapped his chest with a balled fist. "Feels like right time for hillusk, yes?"

Harrugh took a cautious sip of the viscous liquid. His organic eye immediately started to water, and he coughed as the liquor burned all the way down.

Izt grinned and took the flask back. "Good, yes?"

"Very good," Harrugh wanted to reply, but it came out as a wheeze.

Thay sat in companionable silence for a short while, watching the bizarre sight of the compliant Nekro crawling across the hull of the *Orlando*, tirelessly repairing breached sections and steadily restoring the damaged engine. "I need to renegotiate our terms, Izt," Harrugh said. "I know I said I would give you the data vault to study, and perhaps in time I'll still be able to do that. But not now, not with everything that still needs to be done. Not with a planet being overrun with Nekro and people dying." He tapped a claw against his ocular implant and continued, "You can keep the Prophet's Tears vial though, learn what you can from any residue that might be left inside."

He had expected objections and protest, but the Ral Nel simply nodded. "Is fine," he said. "Was unaware of importance when you agreed trade. Not smart. Not very Hacan. You owe Consortium big favor now, yes?"

"A very big favor," Harrugh acknowledged, then he frowned in suspicion. "Though I'm surprised that you agreed that easily."

"This place very interesting, yes?" Izt grinned slyly. "Hear Dart and Tai talk of ancient technology. Still much to learn from Thunder's Edge, yes, yes. Perhaps will come back when this nonsense done. Less Nekro. Less trouble."

"Just so we're clear, I won't be helping you with that," Harrugh cautioned. "This planet isn't going to become a circus of expedition."

"Don't need help. Consortium will manage. Only curious. Ral Nel first ones to come back, perhaps."

"Oh, I'm sure they will try," Harrugh replied, getting up from the steps. "When do you plan to leave?"

Izt shrugged again. "Not decided. Maybe stay and help. Then owe bigger favor, yes?"

Harrugh grinned, but it soothed another point he'd been mulling over how to approach with the Ral Nel. They would need the *Trailblazer* to get off the planet and head to Ordinian – anything the Ral Nel could offer would be monumental. With Izt offering, despite his scheming, it set Harrugh's mind at ease. "Good night, Izt."

He looked over at the *Long Fall* and noted that Connor had vanished into the interior. He'd also apparently shut Suffi An outside, an action that Harrugh was quite sure was deliberate. The Mentak woman glanced in his direction and gave him an impish grin before heading off in the direction of the *Orlando*.

He was about to follow her and offer what assistance he could when he spied a solitary figure kneeling near the row of graves. Curious, he made his way over to find the helm officer, Orragh, in quiet contemplation. Harrugh was struck by a fresh pang of grief as his gaze was automatically drawn to Ashalla's resting place and he stopped, not wishing to intrude on the officer's introspection. Apparently sensing his presence, the Saar beckoned for him to approach.

"Apologies," Harrugh said, "I didn't mean to disturb you."

"Sorrow is a burden that should not be borne alone," Orragh said quietly, gesturing for Harrugh to sit.

He did so, unsure what to make of the invitation. The Saar said something softly, which was swallowed by the wind, and let out a long exhalation. Then he spread his furred hands, palms turned up toward the clouds.

"You spoke well of her," Orragh said. "On Hercant, what do you say of the final journey?"

"We say that the desert forgets us all."

"This is a good thing?"

Harrugh nodded. "The desert is forever changing. It forgets because each morning it is made new again. The Hacan are of the desert and so when we are returned to it, it is with the hope that when the new day comes, we, too, will be made new."

Orragh put a hand on his shoulder and nodded. "This is good. If it gives you comfort, it is my belief that the fallen return to the stars." He indicated the grave markers of the lost crew. "It is from the stars that we are all born, and to them we must all ultimately return. Though their voices might be stilled, when we once again reach for the void, they will be there waiting for us, those distant, glittering jewels. And I will smile, because I will know that they are watching me."

Harrugh removed the data vault from his bandolier and turned it over in his hands. His gaze followed the shifting veins of light as they crawled across its surface. "I thought it would be a relief," he admitted, feeling the political leader fall away and leaving only a Hacan, mourning his friend. "A relief to have an answer. To come to the end of the journey." He shook his head. "But I still have so many questions."

Orragh gave a faint smile. "As one journey ends, another begins."

"But why must this be *my* journey? I have sacrificed so much–" his eyes strayed once more to the grave "–to find Icon, but yet I still don't know how to stop…"

Everything. Burning.

Harrugh trailed off, shaking his head in defeated frustration.

"The brightest stars cannot see beyond their own light," Orragh stated.

"I don't understand."

The Saar rose to his feet and put a shaggy hand on Harrugh's shoulder. "You do not look for greatness, Harrugh Gefhara. But what you do is great. A rare quality. I believe your path will reveal itself."

Evening set in, the gloomy dusk continuously illuminated by the flicker of the storm. Weariness fell over Harrugh like a shawl, but he knew that sleep would be elusive. Work on the *Orlando* would continue through the night and with the combined clamor of the thunder, wind, and machines, it seemed doubtful that *anybody* would be getting any rest. As Orragh left, Harrugh accepted the sudden solitude and addressed the bodiless entity in his hands.

"Icon," he began. "Are you aware of someone or something calling themselves the hrrtos? Or a nobody? A helpful nomad"

"Negative, Harrugh Gefhara."

"Do you know how someone might have learned of Thunder's Edge? Or your existence?"

"There are too many variables to effectively formulate a hypothesis, Harrugh Gefhara."

Harrugh sighed in frustration. "Are you aware of a force potent enough to immolate the galaxy?"

There was a short pause. "Yes. The catastrophic implosion of a quantum singularity of sufficient negative mass would theoretically release enough energy to result in a galactic extinction-level event."

"Does such a phenomenon exist?"

"Yes, Harrugh Gefhara."

Harrugh's blood ran cold in his veins. "Tell me."

"The dissemination of that information runs contrary to my stated purpose, which is the preservation of the celestial body, Thunder's Edge."

"Will you say more on it?"

"No, Harrugh Gefhara."

Deeply troubled, Harrugh reattached the data vault to the bandolier, stood, and marched to the *Orlando* to help wherever he could with the supplies and logistics, the Icon's answers ringing throughout his mind. Hours later and exhausted, he managed to find a relatively quiet corner outside among the rattle of thunder and machine to settle down and drift to sleep. Just when he had entered a state of oblivion, he woke with a start when he heard the entire ship unnaturally groan. Bleary, he hurried back to find the majority of the crew observing the spectacle of the *Orlando* being lifted from its resting place by the passive Nekro machines.

Nichols waved him over. "Sorry, Harrugh. Nobody knew where

you'd gone, and we didn't really get any sort of warning before this happened."

He shook his head. "I found a comfortable rock to rest against." He watched as the machines patched the worst of the damage on the underside of the hull. "I guess this is what we can expect for the rest of the night?"

"Restoration of vessel functionality can be carried out most efficiently without the presence of biologicals embarked," Icon announced.

"That's a yes then."

They gathered in the pale morning light in the chill shadow of a much-restored *FSS Orlando*. While the ship would still require significant attention at an orbital yard, the wounds of its recent experiences were now dressed with fresh plating and its systems threaded with newly spliced conduits. Even the seriously damaged engine had been refitted with a replacement drive coil. The fact that much of the material used to affect the repairs had been provided from the hulls of dead Nekro was still deeply unsettling, but Icon had patiently and repeatedly assured Harrugh, Nichols and, most persistently, Skelton, that absolutely nothing being used could act as a vector for the Nekro consciousness.

Harrugh looked around at the gathered group, keenly feeling the absence of Ashalla, and then turned his attention to the captain, who was now speaking. "As the acting captain of the *Orlando*," said Nichols, "it's my intention to return to the Task Force with all speed." She surveyed her officers who all nodded in enthusiasm with the decision. Even Skelton, for once in his life, studied her with what appeared to be a modicum of respect. "I would like to formally request that you accompany us, Harrugh Gefhara. Based on what we've seen here, Icon can help Salient Sun Joint Task Force liberate Ordinian."

"The relative proximity of the Ordinian system represents a

significant threat to Thunder's Edge if it has been assimilated by the Nekro Virus," Icon stated. "I consider the elimination of that threat to be a priority."

Your path will reveal itself.

Harrugh applauded Nichols' formality in the situation. Orragh, no doubt, had known of his captain's intentions. "I think we are in agreement, Icon," he said, "though I can only speak for myself."

Nichols smiled. "Good," she said. "I really didn't want to have to force you."

Harrugh chuckled. "You will be happy to know that I've already spoken to Izt about taking his *Trailblazer*, however informally. But that leaves…" He turned to address those who had accompanied him from the Gloaming. "The terms of our agreements are fulfilled. I will see to it that all promised payments are made as soon as we are free of the storm."

"Good, good," the Ral Nel nodded vigorously. "Have new contract now. Formal now."

Dart and Tai both gave Harrugh a grin. "Did you know? Ordinian was a Naaz-Rokha colony once," Dart said.

"Maybe it still is," chipped in Tai with his usual optimism. "We're pretty tenacious. We would quite like to take it back. So… we've chartered the ship of one Izt'xet Alit Lo Masak to get us there. Informally, of course."

"And we're not bad gunners," Dart concluded.

Izt snorted in amusement and looked at Harrugh in apology. "Position of strength, yes? Two separate contracts for one journey! Would have gone anyway. Want to study what Icon can do. Naaz-Rokha aurei just bonus. Harrugh aurei just bonus."

"What?" Tai was clearly dismayed by this.

Dart groaned softly. "I guess that's why the *Trailblazer* is sometimes called *Dividend*."

"Fascinating," Junior said.

"You're going to have to learn more about what's fascinating and what's fraud, Junior…" Tai seemed ready to launch into another lecture, but Connor cut him off.

"Ordinian fell years ago. You're going to be flying right into the heart of hostile territory."

"But you're going as well, aren't you, old man?" Suffi An replied airily. "If I know you, and I do, you want to know if this will work, if Icon really can do what it says. I'm sure you know all sorts of people who would be *very* interested in that information, right?"

Connor gave her a stony look.

"Of course," she continued, apparently immune to his ire, "you're going to need an *amazing* pilot, sorry, *copilot* to keep you out of trouble, so it's a good thing I'm here."

"You are not flying my ship," Connor stated flatly.

"It's all right if you need me as a gunner, you can just say so."

"No."

"But it's hostile territory, you just said so."

"No!"

"Please?" She was one step away from batting her eyelashes. Harrugh watched, faintly amused, as a muscle twitched beneath Connor's left eye.

"Fine."

"Fine. I do love our little chats." Suffi An beamed.

"I already regret my decision. Don't make it worse."

Captain Nichols nodded and looked around. "Then if there is nothing else, we should get under way. There's still a lot to do."

"Agreed," Harrugh replied, "we should begin."

PART FOUR
THE BATTLE FOR ORDINIAN

TWENTY-EIGHT

The *Long Fall* disappeared through the clouds and vanished from sight. The Sol agent reasoned his ship was best placed to scout the planetary near-space for signs of Nekro activity. If there was any indication of hostiles, then they could quickly retreat back into the storm and warn the *Orlando*. It had only taken a short time for Suffi Ann to transmit the all-clear.

Izt puttered on board his own vessel with Dart and Tai. The thrusters purred softly as they awaited their final passenger. Junior was once again standing quietly, listening to the glorious sounds from the sky. Harrugh stood by the cairn where he'd left his beloved Ashalla, holding in his hands the device he'd initially once assumed to be a simple data vault.

How far we came for this, Ash'ka, he thought.

"Friend Harrugh?" Junior's faceplate pulsed with ochre light, a match for the surface of Thunder's Edge, as he addressed the former Hacan Quieron.

"Yes, Junior?"

"I have learned that the giving of gifts to those considered friends is a common ritual." Junior unfurled one of his enormous hands and held it out toward Harrugh. A smooth sliver of amber stone, edged in gold when the light caught it just right, was nestled in his palm. "I understand that you have endured great loss, so I would like you to have this."

Harrugh took the stone and absently turned it over in his hand a few times. The beauty and simplicity of the gesture caught at the back of his throat.

"Thank you, Junior," he replied, not knowing what else to say to the unusual Titan. "Dart and Tai are lucky you found them."

"That statement is factually inaccurate, friend Harrugh. It was I who was fortuitously located by friends Dart and Tai…"

Harrugh held up a hand to forestall further explanation. "I know, Junior."

The faceplate rippled in apparent confusion and then slowly faded from ochre to violet. "I believe I comprehend your meaning, friend Harrugh."

"Junior, you should get on board the *Trailblazer*. I will be leaving with the *Orlando* soon and I need to say a last goodbye to Ashalla. You look after those two. They are remarkable."

The Titan's faceplate winked in acknowledgment, and he took a last, lingering look around the desolate plain before trudging to the Ral Nel's vessel. From within, Harrugh heard Junior's rumbling greeting and Tai's voice piping up in delighted response. While they had only known each other for a short time, he had grown fond of the Naaz-Rokha and their Titan companion.

"But I've known none of them for as long as you, of course, Ash'ka," he said aloud to the cairn. "I will remember you and your deeds every day of my life for whatever remains of it. I will miss you, dearest heart."

He knelt briefly and took off the talisman he wore around his neck, one of three shared among childhood friends. Placing it with great care over the marker of her final resting place, he pressed his hand to his heart and then touched it to the jewel. "Farewell, my friend. Until you are made new again." He hated the finality of it, but knew he could delay no longer.

He rose to his feet and headed back toward the ships, weaving around the stripped and skeletal remains of the dead Nekro Virus units. "What about them?" He spared a glance at the passive machines now standing idle a short way away. "Do we just leave them?"

"Nothing that might serve as a vector for the Nekro Virus contagion can be permitted to endure within the orbital sphere," replied Icon, its voice vibrating from the data vault. "These machines must be eliminated."

Without any sort of warning, the Nekro units which had diligently worked so efficiently to repair the *Orlando* turned on each other, dismembering their colleagues, and then burning out their core systems with surgical precision until only one remained. It obediently marched across the plain, halting a short distance ahead of the *Trailblazer*.

"The shipboard weapons will be sufficient to terminate the final unit," Icon declared with cool precision.

"Ah. Meaning I have one last chance to speak with my companions," said Harrugh. "I did already say farewell, you know."

"I do not understand," Icon said.

"I suppose you wouldn't," said Harrugh, shaking his head. He would have to be more careful with his sarcasm.

He crossed to Izt's ship, climbing on board to find Dart and Tai questioning Junior over his experience with Icon. The conversation trailed off at Harrugh's arrival. "I thought you were going with the *Orlando*?" Tai asked. "Did you change your mind?"

He shook his head. "No. I just have a favor to ask from Izt."

"Careful he doesn't charge you for it!" Dart muttered.

Izt poked his head around the corner of the pilot's seat. "Still not gone, Harrugh? Maybe decide to stay and dig up secrets rather than fight more Nekro? Much safer. More profitable. Maybe decide to give data vault to Izt after all?"

Harrugh shook his head. "No. On all counts. I'll be on my way soon with Icon in the *Orlando*. It's the best chance for Ordinian and everybody still fighting to free it… and gives you the freedom to depart, if things get too difficult for the *Trailblazer*."

Izt shrugged. "Is fine. Will be many damaged ships. Skills will be in demand. Good for Ordinian, good for Task Force, good for Consortium, good for everybody."

"You can do some good right now," Harrugh replied. "I need you to destroy that last Nekro." He pointed through the forward screen toward the idling machine. "We can't leave anything behind that the virus might reclaim."

"Destroy it? Well, that would be a genuine pleasure," Dart said.

"Top turret, practice! Shoot lots of Nekro later, yes?" Izt grinned.

The Rokha scrambled up into the gunnery position, aligning the cannons before opening fire at the waiting Nekro. The twin beams reduced the unresisting machine to scrap. "That was satisfying," Dart said, climbing back down into the cabin. "Even if it was just sitting there."

"It is done," Icon announced.

"Then I should be on my way." Harrugh nodded.

"Yes, yes, go join *Orlando*. You want Izt advice? Get rest. Sleep." There was a surprising amount of sympathy in Izt's voice. "Nothing to do until *Orlando* is under way and all plans worked out. When reach Ordinian, will need great Hacan general at very best, yes?"

Even as Izt spoke, Harrugh felt the exhaustion creep over him. "Thank you," he said, "but I've told you before not to call me that."

"Will be there for great Hacan general," Izt said, turning away. "Great Hacan general have many allies."

"Don't get *too* bored on the *Orlando* without us, will you?" Tai said.

"I'll try, my friend," replied Harrugh, amused. "I have an uncomfortable feeling that it might feel just like old times. I wish the three of you well."

"Stop talking like this is the end." Dart snorted. "Because it's not. I've got a feeling that this is just the start of something great, like when we found Junior. My feelings are rarely wrong, are they, Tai?"

"Well, there was that time…"

"*Are they*, Tai?"

"Rarely," said Tai, for once picking up the gist. "So that means we will see you again soon, Harrugh, once this is all done. Good luck."

Dart reached out to pull Harrugh into a brief but fierce embrace, then had the decency to look embarrassed.

It had been exactly what Harrugh needed. A simple and effective symbol of affection, of sympathy and most of all, of support. He smiled and patted Dart's shoulder. "Thank you. Izt? I'll let you know the plan once I've spoken to the captain." He offered up a smile, even if his heart wasn't in it. "See you all on the other side."

"Until then," said Dart.

Harrugh padded down the ramp which drew closed behind him. The thrusters roared and the *Trailblazer* speared into the sky and was lost from view within the storm. Harrugh let out a long, deep sigh and headed to the *Orlando*. The majority of the crew were at their stations, with just a handful of engineers performing manual exterior checks before departure.

"I estimate an eighty-seven percent chance of the vessel designated *FSS Orlando* successfully achieving high orbit without critical failure," Icon commented as Harrugh entered the ship.

"That's… reassuring." Harrugh was not entirely convinced. The interior sections of the ship were feverish with activity as work crews performed last-minute checks. Engineers worked to reinforce the battered superstructure and crisis teams hurried to their assigned positions. A few familiar faces offered him brief nods of acknowledgment as he wove through the bustle, but to his relief his presence went largely unremarked upon – at least until he reached the bridge.

"Allow me to formally welcome you to the *FSS Orlando*, Harrugh." Captain Nichols greeted him from where she sat at the command station. "You will have to forgive the mess. We're somewhat overdue for maintenance." She gave him a forced smile, and the anxious edge behind it was evident.

"Thank you, captain."

"If you would kindly take one of the vacant positions." She indicated empty seats at the comms, sensor, and science stations. "We're just about ready to see how the repairs hold up."

Harrugh picked a seat at the comms station and listened as the external work teams checked in one after another.

"We have stable core output and critical systems are all within tolerance, acting captain," Skelton chimed in. "It might not be pretty, but it should be good enough to get us up there."

"Very good, Mr Skelton. Mr Orragh, it's over to you." She turned to address the helm officer. "Get us out of here."

The Saar placed his hands on the controls and whispered something inaudible before cautiously feeding power to the thrusters. The hull vibrated and an ominous creaking echoed from somewhere behind the bridge. A fire alert chimed but was quickly extinguished by the attentive crisis teams, and then the view of the dusty horizon through the front screen wobbled and dropped away as, with a low moan, the *Orlando* achieved lift.

Harrugh exhaled slowly, looking around the bridge to see mingled relief and exhilaration on the faces of the crew, all save Orragh, who was laser-focused on the task at hand. The surface of Thunder's Edge slowly retreated. Orragh nudged the attitude thrusters and the prow tilted upward to point at the grumbling storm. "Captain Nichols," the helm officer said softly, "with your permission." The bridge crew turned as one to look at her and she smiled fiercely.

"Mr Orragh," she said, triumphant. "Take us out."

The *Orlando*'s ascent from Thunder's Edge was neither graceful nor stately. It clawed its way back into the tempestuous heavens like a drowning man rising for air. Lightning arced around the battered hull and thunder shook rivets loose from the ceiling. Following Izt's advice, the shields remained resolutely powered down. Numerous system warnings and alerts began to light up across the bridge as the storm boiled around them and the atmosphere thinned but compared to their arrival, the tumult of the ascent was relatively tame.

The comms crackled into life as the ship broke free of the mesosphere, and the expanse of the void welcomed them back into its embrace.

"*Orlando*, this is the *Long Fall* confirming visual."

It was Connor's voice, but unless he was very much mistaken, Harrugh could hear Suffi An yelling in the background before his gruff voice continued, "I'm seeing some outgassing from your port side and lower hull that's going to need attention. Nothing major." The sleek shape of the Sol ship raced past the forward view, pulsing its running lights in salutation. "Welcome back to the stars."

The atmospheric vibrations died away to be replaced by velvet, interstellar silence.

"Captain," Orragh said, slowly sliding his hands from the helm station, "we have achieved stable orbit."

A huge cheer erupted. Normally, Nichols would have called for more decorum, but under the circumstances, the elation was warranted. "Engineering," she said into the ship comms, and she managed to keep the tremor from her voice. "Mr Skelton, report."

After only the briefest hesitation, Skelton replied. "Critical systems are holding stable, captain. We're going to need a few hours for void maintenance and to patch those leaks, but otherwise we're in about as good a shape as we could hope to be."

More cheers filled the air and in the rush of it all Nichols did not fail to notice that Skelton had finally dropped "acting" from her title. This had been a day of victories but for her, that was the greatest of all. "Well done, lieutenant," she said. "I apologize for having to put upon you even more than I have already, but I must ask for your indulgence a little longer. Please arrange whatever maintenance crews you need from all bodies on board and make sure we are airtight."

"Already done," he replied.

"Then I'm ordering you to take a break. Get some rest." She glanced up at Harrugh and snapped off the comms. "And the same goes for you."

Despite an overwhelming desire to protest, Harrugh nodded. She directed him to vacant quarters which he found easily enough. It was a small cabin, but there was a bed and a sanitation unit which felt strangely like the height of luxury as he splashed water on his dusty fur. Then he crawled onto the bed, the data vault secured on his chest, and immediately fell into a deep sleep.

TWENTY-NINE

While the rest was more than welcome, and the silence of the void a respite from the tempestuous roar of Thunder's Edge, it brought Harrugh a plague of strange dreams. Dozens of expectant faces watched him, their details blurred. A million machine eyes riveted on him as he plunged. Ashalla reached for him as he fell. The three lambent lenses of the hrrtos bathed him in stark, revealing light. A cauldron of silver-white fire rose and consumed him.

Everything. Burning.

He started awake. As he sat up, however, his body protested while his mind slowly banished the lingering echoes of the haunting dream.

"Harrugh, this is Nichols. I'm sorry for waking you." Her voice crackled over the inter-ship comms.

He rubbed the remnants of sleep from his eyes, glad for the distraction. "Go ahead. My time was nearly up, anyway."

"I would appreciate your presence in the ready room so that we can discuss our approach."

"On my way." He gathered the vault before hurrying through the ship to the bridge and the small adjoining conference room. He slid into an empty seat and took in the gathering. Tiredness affected everyone and they looked as though they would rather be resting comfortably in their berths – but there was also a grim air of determination.

"General Gefhara." Nichols acknowledged his arrival.

The formal address caught him off-guard. While the rank was still recognized among the Emirates, it gave him no authority within the Task Force, or even among the crew of the *Orlando*. Rather than wave it away, however, he reluctantly acknowledged that they were about to discuss military strategy. It was that experience Nichols clearly wanted to address.

"Glad you're here with us. Let me bring you up to speed. Skelton, rather than taking the rest I ordered for him, has come up with a rather… unorthodox plan. As I said, I would appreciate your input, general. With your experience…" She smiled apologetically. "Allow me to elaborate on our discussions."

In the time since the *Orlando* had been space-borne again, Skelton, Kketch, Orragh and Nichols hadn't stopped working. Once they were sure that the ship was secure, they had compiled every scrap of combat data and strategic assessment of the Ordinian operation available to them. A holographic projection of the planetary conflict, fleet disposition, and Nekro Virus incidence rate were projected on a screen, rotating slowly with only an occasional stutter.

"Apologies about the quality," Skelton muttered.

"This intelligence is going to be a little out of date," Orragh said, "but it's the best we can do." He gestured to a scatter of outlying contacts. "We can safely assume that the rest of Green Longbow Fleet – the fleet we were once a part of – was lost against the Nekro swarm in the effort to draw them away from Ordinian's planetary near-space."

There was a moment of grim silence.

"Commodore Ttalak had achieved orbital superiority, however." Nichols picked up the briefing. "There is absolutely no way the Task Force would fall back from the planet with thousands of marines still deployed to the surface. Assuming the situation hasn't somehow improved since we left, then it's likely that's the scenario we will be flying into."

Harrugh leaned in and planted his hands on the projector, examining the topography and deployment strongpoints. "We cannot assume that the Task Force will be in any position to support us, nor will any approach be detected ahead of our arrival. We'll have to hope they don't shoot us down when enter their airspace."

"The *Orlando* is going to need a long time in a shipyard," interjected Skelton. "We're still mostly combat effective, but we wouldn't do well in a major fleet offensive. We also don't know exactly how close we're going to need to get for Icon to be able to do… whatever it is that it does, General Gefhara."

"Working on the assumption that the commodore has been able to maintain orbital superiority, the bulk of the Nekro forces will be deployed to the surface," Nichols continued. "That situation is likely to evolve quickly once we arrive in-system."

"Icon?" Harrugh asked. "Can you advise?"

"An iteration of Elixir Protocol must be deployed to as many Nekro Virus units as possible in a single instance for maximum efficiency," Icon replied. "A dispersed disposition will result in a higher rate of attrition among biologicals while corrected units are engaged with contagion vectors."

"In other words, we're going to need to be in the thick of it," Harrugh translated.

"That is an adequate summation."

"And will it work like it did on Thunder's Edge? The Nekro Virus will turn on itself until there are none left?" Nichols paused, hesitant to say the next words aloud. "Ordinian will be free?"

"I do not believe the Task Force will be able to remain on station and operational for much longer," Kketch interjected a warning. "Though this is an unexpected and welcome opportunity, I believe it also represents our final chance for salvation."

"Your doubts are misguided," Icon remarked. "The efficacy of Elixir Protocol has been validated. The variable to be addressed is in its delivery. If actioned efficiently, the probability of total elimination of hostile Nekro Virus instances within the Ordinian system is a mathematical certainty. An absolute."

The air crackled with fragile hope.

"We understand the challenges," Nichols said. "We're working with outdated information. Our best estimation is that fleet support is likely to be tenuous at best. We have boots on the ground but nothing on their strategic disposition. The *Orlando* will most certainly be detected during its approach and the Nekro Virus can react significantly faster than any of our vessels are able to redeploy. Even if they are able to do so without compromising the orbital sphere." Kketch and Orragh nodded in agreement with the assessment, their expressions carefully neutral. Skelton looked like he very much wanted to say something but was uncommonly waiting for permission to do so.

"A valid appraisal, captain," Harrugh concurred.

"Our advantages are that we have two dedicated support vessels to watch our back," Nichols continued. "As Icon has explained, we need to be close to as many Nekro as possible for this to work. That means drawing their attention works very much in our favor, and–" she glanced at Skelton "–we also have the option of making an unconventional approach."

"This would be Mr Skelton's unorthodox suggestion, I presume?" Harrugh said.

"Correct, general."

"Well, let's hear it then, Mr Skelton." Harrugh turned his full attention to the young engineering officer. "You have piqued my curiosity."

Skelton adjusted the holographic projection of Ordinian. "A typical FTL trajectory and approach would drop us to sub-light in-system in approximately twelve hours Jordian Standard deceleration from Ordinian near-space." He indicated the vicinity of the arrival point and flightpath as he spoke. "That allows considerable time for the Nekro Virus to react to our arrival. The marines would be at greatest risk if the machines decided to push the offensive. No doubt they would do so if they understood that there was an incoming threat."

"Agreed." Harrugh nodded.

Skelton adjusted the display again, drawing the focus closer to the planet.

"We could plot a trajectory that will bring us in at the gravity well limit, which would cut our arrival time in half." He manipulated the display again and a glowing line traced the path of the proposed approach.

Kketch made a noise through his snout and shook his head. "As I have previously stated, the associated risks with this idea are grave. If the timing is miscalculated by even a little, the forced drop to sub-light could easily result in a repeat of Thunder's Edge, perhaps something far worse. The damaged engine will blow out and we will have helped nobody."

"Noted. Please continue, Mr Skelton," Nichols acknowledged.

"Thank you, captain." Harrugh was impressed by the engineer's professionalism in light of his former attitude toward the captain. It seemed their previous problems with each other had transformed into mutual respect. "There won't be enough time for a full deceleration before our Ordinian approach, so we will need to use atmospheric friction to reduce speed in time for an effective pass."

"Aerobraking." Harrugh nodded thoughtfully.

"Exactly, general," Skelton said. "The heading would have to be perfect. Too shallow and we will skip off the atmosphere like a grav-cycle. Too steep and…"

"It really would be Thunder's Edge all over again," Kketch grumbled. "Only there wouldn't be much left of the *Orlando* to put back together this time."

"Perhaps," mused Nichols, tapping her chin as she considered. "But if we have no option but to crash the ship, at least this time it would be on *our* terms. I believe we all understand the potential risks." Nichols straightened. "If there are any other suggestions, now is the time." She looked around the room at Harrugh and each of the officers in turn. "*Any* plan we make is probably going to have to change once we arrive in-system and understand the tactical situation. With the Task Force understrength and a reasonable chance of meeting resistance…" She took a beat and held everyone's gaze for a moment. "I believe that Mr Skelton's approach, while not without risks, offers the best chance of success."

Skelton appeared pleased at the captain's support. "Thank you, captain."

"It's certainly an audacious plan," offered Kketch, "and I would like my objections noted. However, you will always have my support, captain."

"Noted, Mr Kketch. Thank you."

"It will be a challenge," Orragh replied, "but I believe we are its equal."

"We should notify Izt and Connor that we're going to be taking an unconventional flightpath," Harrugh offered. "That way, they can adjust their own accordingly."

Nichols nodded. "Then we are agreed?"

She was met with a small chorus of yeas.

"Then kindly hail the *Long Fall* and the *Trailblazer*." She leaned back in her seat. "It's time to give them the good news."

Despite his misgivings, Kketch got straight to work on the FTL route while Orragh plotted a course that would give them the best chance of approaching the planet in time to hit the atmosphere above the marine's primary deployment zone. They agreed that from leaving the FTL point they would have a window of roughly six hours to make any fractional course and heading adjustments that might be required. Any actions beyond that point would be heavily dependent on Ordinian's situation.

"Wouldn't it make sense for you to be on one of our smaller, faster ships?" Suffi An's question crackled over the comms. "We could use the *Orlando* as cover and break off when we're in position."

"No," Harrugh said. "Even after Thunder's Edge, the *Orlando* is still better armed and armored. We have no idea what the Nekro resistance is likely to be and they're already on the planet. That means we will be heading into them. This is going to be more about endurance than speed."

Nichols spoke across the ship link. "We will need you to keep as many of them away from us as you can while we make our approach. In the event that the situation changes–" she deliberately avoided any negative connotations "–then you have the option of breaking off."

"Aerobraking is a bold move," said Connor with gruff approval. "Good luck with that."

"We'll send you the FTL route shortly," advised Kketch. "When we're ready to go, we'll let you know. The flight plan is going to be exacting, and you will need to jump ahead of us to maintain the timing. We only have one go at getting this right."

"We're increasingly aware of that fact, thank you, Lieutenant Kketch," said Nichols. "Connor, Izt – as I have previously said, I have no authority to command your participation in this. Understanding we are almost certainly putting ourselves in harm's way, are you still with us? If you want to leave now, then you can do so without reproach."

In the background of Izt's confirmation, Harrugh could hear Tai and Dart excitedly chattering. "Yes, yes," Izt replied. "Foolish plan, dangerous, yes? But to see Icon work and understand. Worthwhile." There were cheers at this, including one from Junior which was quite literally the Titan saying "hooray" in a comically flat tone.

"Thank you, Izt," said Nichols. "Connor?"

"Confirmed," came the terse reply.

"Then stand by and await our FTL plan. Nichols out." She sat back and let out a long breath, looking up at Harrugh. He gave her a reassuring nod. "When this is all over," she said, "I am going to have a very large drink and hopefully a good night's sleep."

"Both of those things are deeply appealing," agreed Harrugh. "While it's still calm, captain, you should address the crew."

She hesitated.

"Nobody wise ever thinks they are good at this," Harrugh said, sensing her trepidation. "Those who think they are good at it? Well, they are either wrong, or they are the very worst sort of people."

"You're right, general." She brushed down her uniform which was covered in several days of Thunder's Edge dust and dried blood, walking across the bridge to the captain's chair. She felt a surge of uncertainty. All the previous communications she had delivered had been when the moment was upon them, or out of pressing and imminent necessity. The idea of delivering something inspirational ahead of a headlong rush into battle was suddenly somehow oppressive.

But then she remembered Harrugh's advice. She smiled at that and opened the ship-wide comms.

"All hands. Soon you will be briefed on what to expect when we approach the Taxis system. I don't doubt for a moment that you may have questions. Over the past days, you have all been tested in ways none of us expected, but all of you have risen – without question, without complaint and without hesitation – to meet the challenges with a conviction and tenacity that has made me proud. Look at the person next to you and be grateful that you have their strength to rely on. Someone told me once that in order to achieve greatness, you need strong shoulders to support you."

Around the bridge Harrugh could see a few of the younger officers stand straighter and knew she had managed to strike the right tone.

"What we are doing now, we don't do for ourselves and we do not do it alone. Human, Xxcha, Saar, Hacan, Naaz-Rokha, Ral Nel and even a Titan of Ul. We are proof that united we are so much stronger than the sum of our parts. Together, we can achieve *anything*. This is not a fight that will end today, or tomorrow, but one day it will end, and when it does, we will be the ones who can look back with pride and say that we were there from the beginning and we will *cheer*."

Someone gave an enthusiastic whoop of approval and most of the bridge crew smiled in amusement, anticipation shining in their faces. Nichols glanced at Harrugh. "Today we go to battle in the company of the renowned General Harrugh Gefhara. What say you, general?"

He grimaced, not liking the sudden turn, but was unwilling to break the momentum, and strode forward. When he spoke, it was with a full-throated roar that reverberated through the comms. "Rejoice," he said. "For today, you take back Ordinian!"

The bridge resounded with a unified cheer. Harrugh stepped back awkwardly. "That was unfair," he scolded lightly as Nichols closed the channel. "That should have been your moment."

"This is as much your fight now as it is ours. We wouldn't be able to do it without Icon." Her eyes sparkled with sudden mischief. "And besides, I was curious to know how you would finish that speech." She squared her shoulders. "All right, let's get this done. Kketch, we'll need fresh strategic data as soon as we leave FTL, but no active sweeps. Keep it passive only. We don't want to draw any Nekro attention until we absolutely have to. Also, we will need to contact the remaining fleet elements. We're going to need to convince them to clear the way as best they can and advise that there are two friendlies masked in our wake. If there's anybody left out there, that is."

"We're an Apollo-priority relief payload," suggested Orragh as his fingers flashed over his console with practiced ease. "That's all they should need to hear."

"Absolutely true, Orragh," she said. "Hopefully it will be enough to convince them that we haven't been compromised."

She settled back into the chair as the crew went to work, and the *Orlando* gained more distance on Thunder's Edge. Harrugh noted the lines of tension creasing Nichols' features but there was nothing else to be done now except hold their course.

"Captain," Orragh cut in after a short while. "I've calculated our Ordinian flight plan."

A heartbeat and then Nichols gave him a curt nod. "Take us out of here."

THIRTY

"Dropping to sub-light in three… two… one…"

Kketch counted down the vessel's arrival to the Taxis system in his cool, calm voice. Outside, the blackened orb of Ordinian raced to meet them with alarming alacrity.

"By my estimation, we clipped the gravity well limit by less than a minute," announced Kketch, and a wave of relief could be felt by the whole crew. Kketch continued in his unflappable way, "Of course, I would need to refer to galactic data, but I do believe that is close to a record for a cruiser-class vessel."

"Expertly done, Mr Kketch," Nichols said with a stressed smile. "I never doubted you for a minute."

"We're receiving passive sensor telemetry, captain." The announcement came from an ensign at the navigation station. "Updating our strategic projections."

The holograph of the Ordinian orbital sphere flickered and fresh clusters of indicators populated the display. The contested regions of Ordinian near-space were a mess of debris, prowling Nekro vessels and overlapping fields of fire maintained by the Task Force fleet desperately clinging to orbital superiority.

"The defensive lines have held," Nichols observed, amazed. "Though that situation looks tenuous. We're going to need them to open a corridor if this is going to work."

"You were right," noted Harrugh. "Even in their diminished state they have not fallen back with marines still engaged on the ground."

"We don't abandon our own in the field," Nichols said, proudly.

Orragh checked a few feeds and looked over at the captain. "*FSS Durandal* still appears to be in command."

"They will have picked us up while we were still in FTL and may well assume we are compromised given our, as you have put it, unorthodox approach," said Kketch as he assessed the situation. The comms console chimed as if on cue and the science officer checked the channel. "We are being hailed by the *Durandal*. Commodore Ttalak's authority."

"Well, it seems that we have their attention. Let's hope we can convince the commodore that we're here to help. Prep to send." She waited for the go-ahead and took a deep, calming breath. "This is Acting Captain Nichols of the *FSS Orlando*," she announced. "We have an Apollo-priority relief payload for Ordinian."

Harrugh didn't miss the small smile that flickered over Orragh's face. The Saar resumed concentration on his console, continuously making tiny altitude adjustments as the planet slowly swelled ahead of them. Nichols completed her message. "Be advised we will be aerobraking: please clear our flight path."

"We will be flying right into their guns if they don't believe you," said Harrugh.

She nodded grimly in response.

"Would I be correct in assuming that an 'Apollo-priority relief payload' is open comms code for mission critical supplies?"

"Close enough," she responded. "It's reserved for only the highest priority cargo, be that people or ordnance." Several more, achingly long, moments passed before a voice crackled over the open comms.

"*FSS Orlando*, understood last. We will clear a corridor as you request. Please be aware that we will be passing standing orders to the gun crews and you will be fired upon immediately should you deviate from your stated flight plan."

"Understood, and I would expect nothing less," said Nichols and then, "Please hold fire on our escort vessels, *Long Fall* and the Ral Nel *Trailblazer*. I guess we will see you in–" she checked the local time chronometer slowly ticking down in front of her "–five hours and fifty-one minutes." She motioned to Kketch and he closed the channel. "Now all we have to do is get there and hope we don't attract too much Nekro attention or get shot down by our own fleet."

"Put me through to Connor and Izt. We need to make sure they know not to try anything other than exactly what we agreed," Harrugh said, suddenly glad that the Sol agent had been so vehement in his refusal to allow Suffi An to fly his ship.

ORBITAL CONTACT MINUS THREE HOURS, TWENTY-NINE MINUTES.

"Multiple sensor contacts!" The cry went up from the monitoring station and the ensign's face blanched as the signals multiplied across the screens. "We have inbound FTL signatures on attack vectors toward Ordinian. More are plotted on an intercept course with our flightpath."

The gunners, along with the *Long Fall* and *Trailblazer*, had already been busy keeping stray Nekro ships from the *Orlando*'s path as it continued its headlong rush toward Ordinian. A trail of debris and shattered hulls drifted in their wake, but resistance had, thus far, been relatively light, and it was clear that the enemy focus had been on the subjugation of the planet. The swarm rapidly dropping to sub-light in-system dramatically changed that dynamic.

"Can they cut us off?" Nichols demanded, leaning forward in her chair.

Long seconds slipped by as calculations were performed. "Yes, captain, but it's going to be close. They are smaller and faster than we are. Not to mention…" He trailed off because they all knew the Nekro had no concerns about colliding with the planet or with their ships.

"It could be the swarm that wiped out the rest of Green Longbow Fleet," Kketch said. "Or perhaps some of it, anyway. Sensor returns suggest a significant reduction in their numbers."

"Probably scattered some in the nebula. It would explain all those Nekro that ended up finding their way to Thunder's Edge." Nichols considered. "Still more than enough to be a problem though."

"Transmission from the *Durandal*."

"Let's hear it," Nichols said.

"*FSS Orlando*, you are ordered to terminate your flight plan and break off your approach immediately. Planetary evacuation is under way, and on Commodore Ttalak's authority the fleet is to withdraw in good order." The holographic display showed the orbital fleet slowly redeploying into a defensive screen to intercept the incoming Nekro, no doubt to shield the evacuation shuttles for as long as possible. They were horribly outnumbered.

"How long will it take them to extract the marines?" Harrugh asked.

"Based on the numbers in the field? I would estimate that there is time to withdraw less than a fifth of the force before the fleet is overwhelmed. Less, if the commodore pulls the ships back sooner." Kketch's bleak statement was chilling.

Harrugh glanced at the glowing data vault slung across his chest and then at Nichols. They held each other's gaze for a long moment and then the captain nodded fractionally, her jaw set.

"Mr Orragh, maintain course and heading. Comms, prep to send." She stared up at the ceiling of the bridge. "Acknowledged *Durandal*. Payload is sufficient to secure total victory but requires deployment at effective range. Repeating request that the fleet hold position and keep our flightpath clear."

"Do you think he'll do it?" Harrugh asked.

Nichols pursed her lips. "It's a huge risk. We can't exactly explain Icon to him quickly. Even if we could, he has every reason for skepticism. In his position I wouldn't want to gamble with the lives of those under my command."

Minutes ticked by. Eventually, there was a response. "Negative, *Orlando,* you are ordered to stand down and break off approach."

Nichols cursed.

"Captain, I'm sure I don't need to inform you that our chances of successfully executing our planned approach without the support of the fleet are negligible. The Nekro will overwhelm us before we even get close," Kketch stated with urgency in his tone.

Harrugh looked pensive for a moment before pacing over to the comms station. "Captain Nichols, if I may?"

She gestured for him to go ahead. "You may as well. Prep to send." The ensign nodded to Harrugh, indicating that the channel was open.

"*FSS Durandal,* this is Harrugh Gefhara, former Quieron of the Emirates of Hacan. The explanation for my presence on board the *FSS Orlando* is secondary to my intent. I can vouch for the efficacy of this payload, and I assure you that Captain Nichols has my absolute support. Our escorts represent both the Ral Nel Consortium and the Federation of Sol, who will also verify our capabilities." He paused before adding, "We are offering you a victory today, commodore. In the name of everything we have lost."

"You realize that you might have just turned a disavowed military operation into a diplomatic crisis?" Nichols observed wryly.

"I'm sort of counting on it."

A response was much longer in coming this time, during which both the planet and the encroaching Nekro grew closer.

"Incoming hail."

"Let's hear it," Nichols said.

"*FSS Orlando.* Acknowledged. Your approach corridor will be maintained."

"I bet that's not all he said," Harrugh breathed.

Nichols grinned before hitting the internal comms. "All hands to combat stations, all hands to combat stations. We have inbound!"

THIRTY-ONE

"Izt, you've got three on your tail!" Connor barked the warning.

The airwaves were lousy with radiation wash, the gnawing transmissions of the Nekro, and fleet cross chatter. Beams scored the void ahead of the *Long Fall* and he yanked hard on the controls to avoid a chunk of spiraling hull debris. The blasted surface of Ordinian lurched below, plunging away to be replaced with the cluttered void of space and the flash of shield discharge. The Nekro were *everywhere*. Nothing of sufficient scale to smash the blockade, but in numbers large enough that it barely mattered.

"The fleet are making a real fight of it," Suffi An called from the gunnery station.

"They can take care of themselves. Get those drones off the *Trailblazer!*"

The ship rolled and dropped in behind the Ral Nel. Dart and Tai blazed away on the turrets, but the trio of Nekro kept a tight formation, stabbing at the rear shields with controlled bursts of fire. The *Long Fall* was not a large or heavily armed ship, sacrificing firepower for stealth and speed, but what weapons it had were more than enough to deal with vessels of equal size. Suffi An muttered something caustic about the Nekro and fired. One of the drones corkscrewed out of control, trailing smoke and sparks before finally exploding.

Through the viewport she caught a glimpse of the *Orlando*, the cruiser's shields stippled with fire as it plunged toward the planet. The cruiser was taking damage. The thrusters were silent, faint, with blue coals at its tail, but it had enough inertia from its FTL exit that they couldn't have avoided the planet now even if they wanted to. One way or another the ship was going to make planetfall… and she grimly determined another crash landing was in the *Orlando*'s future. A blossom of light caught her eye even as she tried to draw a firing solution on the next drone and she glanced up to see a Salient Sun destroyer, its shields burst, burning from prow to stern and crawling with Nekro machine-forms.

"…hold formation and maintain fire…"

"…holding steady, shields at…"

"…shuttles four and six retrieved…"

"…*FSS Rapier* critically compromised… been… an honor…"

The destroyer detonated like a miniature sun, the hallmark of a critical core breach, immolating its attackers along with a dozen nearby Nekro. "Suffi An!" Connor bellowed. "Now!"

She fired. The second drone burst apart in a spray of debris and superheated metal. Izt brought his ship around and back in toward the *Orlando*, their remaining pursuer still hard on their tail. The Naaz-Rokha gunners stripped the shields from the side of a lumbering carrier, its belly an open maw ringed with clawed manipulators. Clouds of nanites and smaller machines swarmed around it and Connor had to bank hard to avoid their murderous attention.

"I can't get it!" Suffi An yelled.

The *Long Fall* rolled again. Connor saw the last drone closing with the *Trailblazer*, its intention apparently to sacrifice itself to ram the scout ship. Izt was doing his best to try and shake it as he raced through the *Orlando*'s fields of fire, but the cruiser's anti-fighter guns only succeeded in clipping its hull.

"Connor! I said…"

"I heard you!"

Beams suddenly sliced from the rear of the *Trailblazer,* blasting the drone apart in a shower of burning debris. Suffi An blinked before whooping in relief as the Nekro died.

"You're all clear for now," Connor said across the comms. "Good shooting. Watch the cruiser's tail. They're going to hit at any minute now and then hopefully we can all go home."

"Was Junior." Izt's voice crackled back. "Titan is good shot."

"I'd expect nothing less."

The fleet was increasingly battered, the small number of ships anchored by the *FSS Durandal* resolutely holding the line against the Nekro swarm. There was no room for retreat now, no chance at withdrawing. If Icon wasn't deployed soon, then there wasn't going to be much left to save. Another flash caught Suffi An's attention as missiles and plasma screamed silently in the void, and then the world lurched before turning over in a sickening blur.

"Two minutes to atmospheric burn," an officer called from the nav station. "The *Orlando* is strong but taking incredible damage. Crew should prepare for crash landing!"

The *Orlando* groaned in protest, the hull creaking with the stress of its recent abuse and subsequent repairs. Bulkheads had already been sealed across three decks as pressure warnings lit up across the boards. The shields were starting to fail, but Skelton and his team in engineering were working miracles to divert as much power as they could to keep them lit as long as possible.

Two minutes!

The countdown echoed in Harrugh's head, freezing him in place for a moment. No, this was not the same countdown as the one he'd heard in his Prophet's Tears dreams. Not the same voice, but a breathless plunge surrounded by strange faces. He put his hands on the station before him, feeling the growing vibrations of the ship's descent. Human, Saar, Xxcha – so many different species surrounded him. His head swam. The fall, *this* exact moment was the fall.

But then what?

Fire. Harrugh felt as though he wanted to tear his own brain free of its skull. *Everything. Burning.*

"*Orlando*! This is the *Long Fall*!" Suffi An's voice cut across the comms, sounding strained. "We're hit. Not Nekro compromised, but we're bleeding air. Connor's hurt. Guess who's flying? Me."

There was a pained grunt from somewhere in the background.

"Message received, *Long Fall*, but we cannot abort now." Nichols shook her head. "You're going to have to try for planetfall."

"Negative, *Orlando*, we won't make it. I'm right on your tail. Clear the shuttle bay, this is going to be tight!"

"Break off, *Long Fall*! We are ninety seconds to atmosphere! Suffi An, do you hear me?"

There was no reply. Harrugh pivoted and sprinted in the direction of the shuttles.

"I need fire suppression and a crisis team in the shuttle bay. Open the bay to receive Connor's ship." Nichols shouted the order into the comms, then she turned to helm control. "Mr Orragh?"

"Holding steady, captain. The *Orlando* isn't happy about it," he said, his hands deft on the attitude controls, "but she's tough. We can stay the course."

One minute!

Harrugh bolted through the corridors of the *Orlando* as the countdown thundered in his ears. This couldn't be how it ended.

"Harrugh Gefhara." The voice of Icon spoke through the chaos from the data vault on his bandolier. "More than fifty percent of this Nekro Virus instance are now within range of Elixir Protocol. Deployment efficacy will increase exponentially when surface units fall within the sphere of influence."

"Understood." He turned a corner, bursting into the open space of the *Orlando*'s hold. The area was virtually empty save for the hunched shape of a single remaining lander. The second had been so badly damaged in the crash that the engineering team had scrapped it for parts to help with the main repairs. Through the permeable containment field that opened like a window into space, Harrugh could see the pale curve of Ordinian as the *Orlando* continued its descent, but that view was largely eclipsed by the angular form of the *Long Fall.* The shuttle bay had never been designed to receive another FTL-capable vessel, even one as relatively sleek as Connor's, and definitely not one that was streaking through the upper atmosphere of a planet. It looked to Harrugh as though *Long Fall* was coming in much too fast to do anything other than dash itself to pieces against the rear of the cruiser.

Thirty seconds!

The *Long Fall* made a final, desperate lunge. Harrugh ducked back into the doorway to take cover. The ship plunged into the bay trailing smoke and fire, overshot the surviving shuttle, clipped the wall with a tortured screech of metal and crashed to the deck before slamming into the rear of the compartment. If he hadn't seen it with his own eyes, Harrugh wouldn't have believed it possible that the ship could have fit into the space at all. Fire suppression systems vented pillars of gas and powder onto the burning ship, filling the air with a chemical stink. The *Orlando* vibrated harder, now loaded with a newly parked ship, and Harrugh glimpsed the first tongues of flame licking at the hull through the containment field. The shuttle closed, encasing *Long Fall* within.

"All hands," Captain Nichols' voice shouted across the comms. "Aerobraking is under way. Stand by for planetfall. General Gefhara, report to the bridge. *Now.*"

There was a groan of protesting machinery and the ramp of the *Long Fall* crunched open, tilted at an awkward angle. Suffi An emerged, one arm around Connor's waist as she helped him down. He had a hand pressed tightly to his side, where a spar of metal protruded, surrounded by a dark stain.

"Somebody help me with this big frax," she screamed, and a three-man crisis team hurried in. Harrugh surged into the shuttle bay with them, arriving just as Connor was receiving an air-hypo of combined pain suppressant and stimulant. He looked at Suffi An and then at the carnage of the shuttle bay.

"And this is why," Connor said, between teeth gritted with pain, "I didn't want you at the controls."

"All right," she said, her face streaked with sweat and dirt. "That wasn't exactly my *best* landing, I'll admit. But I appreciate you taking the metal spike for me, nonetheless."

"I didn't even think such a maneuver was possible!" Harrugh exclaimed.

"Lots of things don't seem possible until you try," she said with a forced levity.

"That's what I get for getting hurt," Connor grumbled, gasping with pain. "I wouldn't have let you fly otherwise!"

"But here we are. Alive." She wagged a finger at him.

Harrugh shook his head, incredulous. "Go with him, Suffi An, get yourself to medbay. I'll be right behind you."

She nodded wearily, following the crisis team out of the hold.

"Harrugh Gefhara, more than sixty percent of this Nekro Virus instance are now within range of Elixir Protocol. We are approaching optimal saturation. You should be aware that once deployed, instances of the Nekro Virus that have not been corrected will be able to triangulate my location and there is a high probability that those not immediately engaged will attempt to purge my existence."

Harrugh froze in place, understanding crashing down on him. "You mean unleashing the Elixir Protocol could bring down the rest of the swarm on the *Orlando*?"

"Yes. I estimate that based on current projections, it will take approximately thirty minutes to achieve complete elimination of all Nekro Virus instances within the orbital sphere. A risk to biological actuality exists within that period."

"General Gefhara to the bridge," Nichols called again across the comms, urgency creeping in. "Now!"

After everything they had been through to survive Thunder's Edge, the price of Ordinian's salvation might be the *Orlando* and its crew.

It's not about you, Harrugh Gefhara.

"It's about them," Harrugh said quietly and turned to look at the shuttle resting beside the carcass of the *Long Fall.* "It's about all of them."

THIRTY-TWO

"Captain, Shuttle 2 just powered up and is on its way out!" Kketch reported.

"What?" Nichols yelled. "We're mid-descent, they will be ripped apart! Who's flying? Suffi An?"

"I'm not sure if I should be offended or not," Suffi An huffed as she entered the bridge, "but if I had to guess, I'd say Harrugh." No surprise or alarm showed on her face by the turn of events. She simply looked tired.

Nichols paled. "Get me in contact with that shuttle. Better yet, stop it! Do it now!"

The shuttle slipped out of the bay and was immediately swept off-path by the friction of atmospheric entry. The airframe creaked, cracks spidered across the viewscreens, and warnings screamed from every display as the small craft tumbled in the thickening air. Strapped into the pilot seat Harrugh gritted his teeth and hauled on the controls in a desperate effort to stabilize the shuttle. He wasn't an experienced pilot, nothing like Suffi An, and his heart lurched in his chest. He hoped he wouldn't be killed simply by leaving the *Orlando*.

There was a loud bang and the shaking intensified. Something vital ripped free from the hull, clipping the dorsal aerofoil. A new critical warning blared, advising of imminent hull breach. Slowly, however, the ship began to break out of its uncontrolled fall, heat blooming across the nose and folded wings. Harrugh caught sight of the *Orlando* ahead and above him, looking like a furious spear of fire cutting across the heavens on its way to earth. Behind it, in the void, he could make out the faint flicker of the orbital battle.

The comms sputtered into life with Nichols' furious voice. "I'd love to know what you think you're doing, Harrugh!"

"Captain, listen to me. When Icon deploys the Elixir Protocol, any Nekro that aren't within range, and thus aren't infected by the Protocol, are going to try and swarm the source to destroy it. I'm not going to bring that destruction down on the *Orlando*, not after everything you and your crew have been through. Not after everything you've fought for. Just do one thing for me. Make sure the marine companies on Ordinian take cover. You've got sixty seconds."

"This was not your decision to make alone, general," Nichols said, her voice thick.

The shuttle groaned as it punched through into the skies of Ordinian. Something behind Harrugh blew out. Freezing air began whistling into the interior space.

"Whatever happens," Harrugh shouted to be heard above the rising din, "make sure you retrieve Icon!" For a moment there was only the crackle of dead air. "Do you hear me, captain? Make sure you come back and retrieve Icon!"

"*Durandal* has sent the warning." Nichols' voice was breaking up. "Harrugh…"

He cut the comms. There was nothing else to say. It was time to draw upon the warrior spirit that had seen him through so much of his life. The planet was so close.

"This course of action has a high probability of self-annihilation, Harrugh Gefhara," Icon stated.

"That will be as it will. Is the data vault capable of surviving?"

"The structural integrity of the cognitolith matrix is robust enough to endure significant trauma," Icon said. The smell of smoke and electrical burning seeped into the cockpit. "Harrugh Gefhara, seventy-seven percent of the Nekro Virus instance are now within range of Elixir Protocol."

Harrugh closed a hand over the data vault and, despite the screaming gale of the Ordinian atmosphere tearing apart the shuttle, he smiled. "For you, Ash'ka. Icon, do it."

On the ground and in the skies and in the void above Ordinian, the change was immediate and dramatic.

Larger machine-forms engaged with the space fleet outside the range of Icon's Elixir Protocol turned their weapons away from the void and toward the planet and fired simultaneously, streaking the sky with mass driver bombardment. Huge explosions lifted fountains of earth hundreds of feet into the air, cratering the already abused landscape of the war-torn world. Their prey was small compared to the scale of the firepower, but one of the enormous shells almost managed to strike its target: a singular, puny shuttle. The wave of overpressure as it cleaved the air buckled the shuttle's hull and swatted it from the sky like the vengeful fist of an angry god.

But that one attack was the Nekro's only chance.

Thousands of Nekro machines corrected by the Elixir Protocol swarmed together, some tethered by coils and manipulators, others by the pulsing grip of gravity generators and still more by claws and writhing dendrites. They reforged themselves into two blazing steel phoenix-shaped constructions, both rising on mechanized pinions and turning on those Nekro that were yet to be converted, shredding them with fire and fury. Nekro set against Nekro, shifting the battle into a civil war.

The bridge of the *Orlando* was silent in stunned amazement. Captain Nichols rose to her feet, her body shaking at the extent of the damage against her enemies. Even Suffi An was lost for words as the titanic spectacle of the machine-wrought avians took shape. The mechanoid creatures lifted into the void, wreathed in atmospheric fire, and she imagined their unified cry as a screech of rending metal as they swept through the remains of the tattered Nekro swarm. Crushed and broken Nekro rained from the sky, burning as they fell, broken shells littering Ordinian in drifts of tangled wreckage.

The raptors of steel and flames swept onward, cauterizing the infection of the Nekro Virus across the planet until nothing remained except the astonished crews of the fleet and the marines in shelters far below.

Peace had, at last, come to Ordinian. In the wake of the sudden, shocking silence of that revelation came feelings nobody had dared hope to feel again. Joy. Relief. *Victory.*

Communications around the planet burst into loud and jubilant life with the unified exhalation of a free world.

THIRTY-THREE

A conventional landing was never going to be an option for the *Orlando.*

Aerobraking had reduced the punishing speed of the vessel so that the impact was more controlled than the crash on to Thunder's Edge, but for all that, it was not any easier. Frantic, Orragh had located a hanging valley high in the mountains with sufficient clearance on either side to house the cruiser and keep it far enough away from any remaining ground forces. However, the ship had lost its landing stanchions in a grinding impact with the crags on the way down. Fortunately, the barren, rocky basin was already littered with the hulks of newly dead Nekro drones and crumpled machines, while others continued to rain from the skies above. The fallen vessels crunched under the ship's bulk as its smoking hull skidded to a halt, bursting hatches and cargo bays as it went. They were lucky no one was hurt.

"Once, just once, I'd like us to land without fearing for my life," Skelton had said when the cruiser came to a full stop.

Now that the distance between the vessels was less astronomical, communication was instantaneous. Captain Nichols had chosen to receive the message in the briefing room – or at least, what was left of it. "*FSS Orlando*, this is the *Durandal*. Acknowledge."

"Acknowledged, *Durandal*. It's a beautiful morning in the mountains of Ordinian."

"Acting Captain Nichols, shuttles are in-bound to Fortress Ordinian for team extractions. I expect you to be aboard one of them when it returns in order that you might kindly provide a complete and thorough debrief. We need to understand what was in that payload." Commodore Ttalak had a note of reverence in his tone. "Whatever the payload was, we have confirmation of total victory. Sensor sweeps show negative Nekro signatures within the orbital sphere and planetary near-space. As I'm sure you can imagine, our Shikrai colleagues have some very vocal opinions on what we have all witnessed this morning."

"I imagine they have," Nichols replied. "However, in order to provide an accurate report, Harrugh Gefhara will also need to be present. Unfortunately, the general is currently MIA. As such, I would like to formally request permission to conduct search and rescue." *Or at the very least to determine if he has even survived*, she thought.

The comms crackled. "Permission granted. We have enough logistical challenges without adding a potential political crisis to our list of problems. Red Chivalry Fleet will be holding high orbit while decisions are made regarding the future of Ordinian."

"Understood, commodore."

"History will remember this, Nichols. The first world ever to be freed from Nekro Virus control."

"General Gefhara was key to our success, commodore."

"Then you should attend to the search and rescue, Captain Nichols. I will await your report."

"Sir."

"*Durandal* out."

"It worked," Nichols breathed, hardly daring to believe the words. The sounds of the *Orlando* washed over her. The muted exchanges of the crew, the low thrum of life support and the faint creak of cooling metal. She took a deep breath, trying to center herself, but knew she would know no peace until she located Harrugh's shuttle. Standing, she brushed down her creased and dirty uniform before heading to the bridge.

As the bridge's door slid open, all conversations came to a halt. Expectant faces turned toward her, looking for answers – all the station officers, along with Kketch, Orragh, and even Skelton who had come up from the engineering deck. Skelton's expression was impassive and unreadable. She made her way slowly to the command seat before addressing them all.

"It is my duty to inform you," she said solemnly, "that as of five-twenty-seven Jordian standard, Ordinian is now the first world in the galaxy to be reclaimed from the Nekro Virus."

The entire bridge erupted into a thunderous cheer of jubilation. Nichols let the victory wash over her and then, as the prickle in her eyes threatened tears, she saw Kketch approach with two small glasses. He pressed one into her hand. She blinked in confusion and the big Xxcha smiled at her.

"I believe you owe the lieutenant a toast, do you not?"

At that, she laughed for what felt like the first time in her life. "I guess I do, Mr Kketch. But I'm somehow speechless at this moment."

"Captain!" an officer shouted over the celebration. "Captain, report of the search and rescue!"

Nichols handed the glasses back to Kketch and pushed her way to the comms console. "What is it?" A hollow formed in the pit of her stomach.

"Report from the Ral Nel and his party, captain. They've found the shuttle. It's not far away."

She tapped the controls and brought up a holographic display of the local topography. "Show me."

Izt brought his ship down on a rocky plateau following the directions provided by Junior. The *Trailblazer* hadn't weathered the ferocious battle unscathed and several scars on the hull would need attention before heading off-world once again. Without the Titan's timely assistance on the guns, it would have been much, much worse.

Tai, strapped into his harness on Dart's back, urged his partner out of the ship as soon as they landed and gasped in horror. Despite the urgency of the search for Harrugh, they were both alarmed by the devastation ravaged on the world of Ordinian. Years of Nekro aggression had stripped the planet down to little more than rock and soil. Anything biological that had once called it home had been exterminated with mechanical efficiency. The hulks of shattered machines littered the mountainsides and piled up in the hollows and valleys, some of them still trailing thin ribbons of smoke following the extraordinary events of the morning.

"Icon is about half a kilometer to the west," said Junior, breaking them both out of their reverie. Tai held tight as the Rokha broke into a full run. His keen athleticism allowed him to traverse the terrain with practiced ease while the Titan followed more slowly behind.

"Go find!" Izt called after them. "Will keep thrusters running!"

As Dart scrambled across the scree, and then over and around the hulks of dead Nekro, a dropship screamed overhead. The insignia of the Salient Sun Joint Task Force was clearly emblazoned on its battered hull. It wheeled in a wide circle before lowering slowly on pillars of thrust. The deployment ramp yawned open to reveal Captain Nichols and a selection of *Orlando* crew. She shielded her eyes with one hand as dust kicked up and pointed with the other.

"Stay on station!" Nichols yelled over her shoulder as she dropped to the ground with her crew. The pilot tapped his helmet and motioned an acknowledgment. The dropship roared and lifted back into the sky.

"There. Dart, there, look," Tai exclaimed. Dart followed Nichol's gesture to an enormous heap of crushed and mangled Nekro machines. A broken aerofoil and section of hull protruded from beneath the morass, buckled like an empty can.

"Oh, no," the Naaz breathed.

"Let's get in there," Dart said by way of greeting as Nichols and her team approached. Together, they picked their way over to the lower slopes of the crash site.

Junior crunched Nekro underfoot as he joined them and immediately began hauling the larger pieces of machine away from the buried shuttle, his enormous strength making short work of the arduous task. Dart and the *Orlando* crew helped as best they could while Tai directed from the top of the fallen craft. It wasn't long before Junior shoved a dead drone aside to expose the access ramp on the side of the lander, the hatch twisted into its frame. The metal creaked as Junior dug his fingers in and ripped the door from its already abused moorings, tossing it aside with ease. Dart didn't even wait, ducking into the gloomy interior, Tai leaping down and onto his shoulder. Nichols and her crew waited breathlessly outside.

The shuttle creaked and all attention turned to the opening as the silhouette of Dart and Tai reappeared, one of the Rokha's arms wrapped around a limping figure propped up against him.

Harrugh Gefhara, his fur scorched and crisped, matted with blood and dirt, took a shaky step into the bright Ordinian morning light, the data vault clutched fiercely in one hand. "You took your time," he croaked, his throat parched.

"General Gefhara." Nichols checked her urge to grin in relief. "Allow me to be the first member of the Salient Sun Joint Task Force to formally welcome you to the free world of Ordinian." She straightened, snapping her heels together, and offered him a Jordian salute. One by one the crew standing behind her did the same until they all stood to attention.

A scarred woman in combat armor standing to attention offering him a perfect Jordian salute.

The memory echoed in his head, but it wasn't her. The haunting visions of the Prophet's Tears remained, their mystery unresolved, their portents of destruction unfulfilled. But somehow, seeing the shadow of that stranger in Captain Nichols' salute felt like a start. Like he had avoided something dire and terrible. That this was the path he had navigated through all that destruction.

Dart leaned into him. "Let's get you out of here."

"Best thing I've heard all day," said Harrugh.

FSS ORLANDO
TWO DAYS POST LIBERATION

Harrugh collapsed after they returned to the *Orlando*, and once a doctor fussed over him, amazed at his survival, he slept soundly. While the commodore was keen for a full debriefing, he had not pressed the issue. Not while the Hacan was recovering from his ordeal.

The fleet, already short on numbers before the battle, was woefully undersupplied. The marine divisions on the planet had weathered the storm relatively unscathed, but many of their firebases had been destroyed – with the notable exception of their landing beachhead and final bastion dubbed simply Fortress Ordinian. Everything needed to be repaired, everyone needed to be rearmed, and a full inventory established just how precarious the position of the Salient Sun was after their victory.

Harrugh slept through it all.

When he finally woke, bleary-eyed and starving, his first sight was that of Izt, sitting in a chair in the medbay of the *Orlando*. The Ral Nel hopped down from his position and inspected the Hacan. "Is food and water on table over there for you."

Harrugh sat up and rubbed at his remaining eye, clearing the vestiges of sleep. The cybernetic implant in his other socket whirred into life, slowly refocusing after idling for so long.

"Thank you," he said and padded over to the table where a selection of refreshments had been laid out for him. There was nothing fancy, it was all ship's rations, but he hadn't enjoyed a meal so much for a long time. All the while, Izt's glittering, reptilian eyes studied him. Harrugh paused in his eating to speak. "How long was I asleep?"

"A day or so."

Harrugh winced.

Izt chuckled, waving a clawed hand dismissively. "*Orlando* Xxcha doctor make big fuss, but it deserved. They let you sleep as long as you need."

"Have you been here the whole time? I didn't know you cared so much." The comment was tinged with gentle humor.

Izt snorted. "Do not flatter self, Golden General. Just happened that Izt is one who is here when you wake, yes? We… take turns. Make sure you *do* wake and do not do foolish die-in-sleep nonsense. There are many questions being asked by many people. Like… how Harrugh survived, for one." Izt's eyes glittered again, an expression that Harrugh had come to learn meant keen interest.

"I don't know," he answered honestly and felt Izt's disappointment. "The shuttle was coming apart. Icon deployed the Elixir Protocol and then something hit us. It hit us *hard*. I remember everything spinning out of control and then… then there was nothing. At least until Dart woke me up in the wreckage."

"Your commitment to the elimination of the Nekro Virus threat is uncommonly resolute for a biological. I believe your successful self-annihilation would significantly reduce future efforts to combat the contagion," Icon inserted.

Izt peered at the data vault. "You are sure that you would not rather give to me to study?"

"Maybe one day, Izt," Harrugh said, "but not today. You will have to be content with me owing you a favor."

"A big one," Izt reminded him, holding out his hands as wide apart as they would go.

"Agreed, Izt. A big one."

Izt rubbed at his scaly cheek. "Has been… interesting time, Harrugh Gefhara, but now time to return to Consortium. Much to tell, yes. Much to tell."

Harrugh offered a small smile. "The Task Force would greatly benefit from your expertise, Izt. If you chose to stay instead."

"Do not seek to flatter me, Hacan," said Izt and for a moment, Harrugh thought he'd genuinely angered the Ral Nel. The moment passed and Izt chuckled. "Although you are right, of course. Not now though, no. Something for another time, maybe. Will have to manage without great Izt'xet Alit Lo Masak."

"Thank you for everything, Izt," Harrugh said, a trickle of unease in the back of his mind thinking what the Consortium would think of this great story. It was a story that would change the universe. "We wouldn't have managed to get this far without you, your skills, or your ship."

"Is nothing," Izt said. "Though… maybe pay extra for flying Naaz-Rokha and Titan to rescue if really want to thank me? We leave soon."

"Goodbye, Izt." Harrugh laughed. "Do me a big favor and never change."

Once the Ral Nel had departed, Harrugh still felt an ache in his bones. Somehow, there was still so much to do.

"You know that Thunder's Edge isn't going to stay secret for long, right?" Dart said. He stood at the ramp of the *Trailblazer* with Tai in his harness.

Harrugh had located the Naaz-Rokha easily enough after freshening up, urged on by the fact that Izt did not plan to stick around Ordinian long. "It's not something we could have sworn people to secrecy over. Some things are always going to be told, particularly with ancient tech waiting to be discovered. I only hope that as this knowledge spreads across the galaxy, that the other species do something good with it."

"And the Elixir Protocol is still there, right?" Tai said. "Icon only copied it to the data vault?"

"That is correct," Icon confirmed. "Thunder's Edge must be protected."

"Who knows what else the planet might be capable of?" Harrugh mused.

"I think whatever the case, Thunder's Edge is likely to attract the attention of everyone," Dart asserted.

"You're right. However, I am grateful that it was us who discovered it first. Look what we were able to do – liberate a planet from the Nekro for the first time in known history. A historical and monumental achievement."

"An achievement that also means you've attracted the attention of the Salient Sun," Dart said and then paused. "You're a hero to the Ordinians, Harrugh."

"Oh, only to them?" Harrugh laughed gently. "But no. I left my people. I had my reasons at the time, but I did leave the Hacan in a state of chaos. At least here, I can also do some good, not just for the Hacan, but for the Ordinians. It has nothing to do with achievement or heroism. They were abandoned by their government because it was assumed the planet was lost to the Nekro. All this came about because they refused to give up, even when everyone else told them to. Hero or not, it wouldn't feel right leaving them, or this planet."

"You are wise, friend Harrugh," said Junior. "I believe I understand why it is that your people chose you as a leader."

"Wisdom is frequently overrated, and leadership is a mantle craved by many, but which suits altogether too few, Junior," said Harrugh.

"What do *you* want now, Harrugh?" Tai asked. "Do you *really* want to stick around here?"

On the face of it, it should be an easy answer, but it was far more complicated. Harrugh thought that he'd want to just go home, back to Hercant, or maybe Kamdorn. But imagining a return to Kenara without Ashalla left him feeling hollow. "Peace and quiet would be a start," he replied and received laughter in return.

"I think you forfeited the right to that a while ago," said Dart. "You must have heard the way some of them are talking about you."

Harrugh shook his head. "I've heard some of it, yes. I'm going with Captain Nichols to speak to the commodore later and explain everything. They've lost a lot in this fight. Ordinian might be free, but without the backing of their governments, I'm not sure how much longer they will actually last out here. They were assumed to be assimilated by the Nekro. No one else fought for them and I'm not sure they trust the Task Force anymore. No doubt upcoming conversations will focus on how they're going to rebuild and make crucial infrastructure repairs without support."

"There's something fundamentally decent in pushing back against the likes of the Nekro Virus, isn't there?" Tai said. "Because it's the right thing to do and not because your leaders are leaning on you for their own reasons. It's what Icon wants as well, right?"

"That is and always has been my purpose," Icon remarked.

"You two coming or not?" Izt snapped from within the *Trailblazer*.

"You had better be on your way." Harrugh smiled.

"Take care, Harrugh," Dart said.

"Yes, we'll come and see you again real soon!" Tai added. "But not before we've made ourselves famous with this story!"

"You just said that telling people would be a bad thing!" Harrugh said.

"It's going to happen anyway!"

Tai, Dart, and Junior climbed into the ship and vanished from view.

Harrugh watched them depart, wondering how the story would transform as it changed hands and moved across the galaxy.

"It's all right." Suffi An sniffed. "As ships go, I mean."

She stood with Connor outside the docking bay of the *Orlando* where the *Long Fall* sat. Against medical advice and the wound sealant gel keeping his side patched together, Connor had insisted on personally evaluating the damage Suffi An had done to his ship by her highly unconventional docking maneuver. His tools were laid out on the ground as he opened the maintenance hatch to analyze the damage.

"Just 'all right'? The *Long Fall* is as good as they get." His tone was somewhere between annoyed and proud.

"I said what I mean. Just all right," she confirmed. "I mean, you've not seen *my* ship. Yet."

He stared at her in judgment, and she shifted uncomfortably beneath his scrutiny.

"It's back at the Gloaming even as we speak, getting faster drive coils fitted. You know, where you *followed* us from, after you spied on us instead of helping." She sniffed. "Why did you do that? Follow us. From the Gloaming. Where my ship is currently located, by the way."

"I already gave my reasons," he said. "And I'm not in the habit of repeating myself." He then eyed her up and down. "Wait. Are you asking if I will take you back to the Gloaming?"

She laughed brightly, a sound that was designed to go right through him. "Well, since you offered. Although these poor Ordinian souls look like they need all the help they could get. There might be some work out of it. But you know how it is. Places to be. People to meet. Stories to tell. A lot has happened after all." Her eyes twinkled.

He shuddered. "You're never getting in my ship again," he growled, carefully splicing a severed electrical feed, deftly sealing it with a squirt of sealant.

"Aww, Connor! I *did* save your life."

He stopped and sighed before setting down the tools. He deliberately closed the maintenance hatch and turned to look at her. "Just as far as Kenara. I also have work to do. Places to be. People to tell. All of that."

Her smile, if possible, grew even broader. She took a step toward him and linked her arm through his. "We're gonna be *amazing* together. Trust me, you won't regret it."

He removed her hand pointedly. "I'm already regretting it."

THIRTY-FOUR

He sat alone on a rocky bluff looking out over the shallow Rondino Valley. Evening had set in, and a few stars had emerged, competing with the floodlights of the growing Fortress Ordinian, which occupied the mountainous hollow. The world was still a barren wasteland, dead in a way that was more profound than the bleak deserts of Kenara. A crunch of stone to his left made him turn to see a figure in uniform approaching.

"Captain." Harrugh nodded to the freshly formally promoted captain of the *Orlando*.

"General," she replied. "Mind if I join you?"

"Please, Tamara. Sit." He gestured to the rounded boulders of the crag. She was caught off-guard by the sudden informality, but she picked her way across the peak, settling down beside him. She rested her chin on her knees.

A companionable silence stretched out between them and then she broke it with a rhetorical question. "Still haven't decided to leave then."

He shook his head, gazing up at the thin traces of the nebula stretching across the sky above.

"Not yet," he said. "They're not making it easy."

By "they", Harrugh meant the Salient Sun. In the two weeks since the liberation of Ordinian, Harrugh had adopted something of an advisory role to what remained of the Salient Sun Joint Task Force. It had quickly become apparent just how woefully undersupplied the group was and how impossible it was going to be to rectify that situation. Nobody would be in a hurry to voluntarily supply a rogue military task force, even if they'd the funds to offer. And the people of Ordinian, after being considered a lost cause from their previous government, had to desire to rejoin it now that they'd been liberated from the Nekro.

He also hadn't been able to avoid hearing the stories about him, growing from heroic to legendary. The Hacan general who unleashed a firebird that swept the planet clean of the Nekro Virus. Firebird, seraph, Apollo Entity, each story had a different name for the creatures created by the Nekro machines. Harrugh Gefhara, who had piloted an unarmed shuttle through an orbital bombardment to deliver salvation. Harrugh the liberator.

He hated that last one most of all, as if the soldiers and ship crews who had given their lives in the fight before he had even arrived deserved the title any less.

His savant chimed. Now that the Nekro were gone, active connections to the wider galaxy were gradually being reestablished. He opened the notification, an alert to check his financial accounts. Frowning, he did so and saw a brief, anonymous message attached.

"A solid future requires solid foundations," he read out loud.

He clicked past the message and acknowledged the credit into his account.

He blinked, dumbfounded. The sum was beyond astronomical. It represented enough aurei to raise the Emirates of Hacan to the pre-eminent power in the galaxy…

It's not about you, Harrugh.

Or enough aurei to rebuild Ordinian and the fleet a hundred times over. He smiled faintly. It felt like a validation. Not that his journey was complete, because he didn't believe it was – but that he had made the correct choices. He might never know what the hrrtos wanted from him, and somewhat believed he had just been a pawn at the right time, but he knew one thing for certain.

It's about all of them.

"Good news?" Nichols asked when he didn't immediately respond.

He swallowed and clicked the savant off. Despite the hope in his heart, somehow, he regained his composure. "Yes," he affirmed. "You could say that. I think I'm going to need to get a message to my old friend Carth. I should have listened to Ashalla and done it long ago." The ache of Ashalla's loss had not faded. "Carth was always smart when it came to finances, and I might need her advice in the coming days…" He shook his head and calmed his breathing. "I'll tell you more about it in the morning. I think the commodore will be fairly interested in an introduction to Carth as well."

"Fair enough," she said, shrugging in confusion. Below, tiny figures popped into view, patrolling the high walls and towers of Fortress Ordinian.

"All will be well, Tamara," Harrugh said. "Ordinian will be strong again. I promise."

"The marines have actually started calling it the last bastion," Nichols said, indicating the stronghold.

"The last bastion?" Harrugh looked up at the night sky, at the stars that were a gateway to infinite and endless possibilities. "I suppose that's as good a name as any."

ACKNOWLEDGMENTS

During the course of bringing this story into being, I was blindsided by the sad loss of my dad. As a result of this, I must first and foremost extend my heartfelt thanks to Gwendolyn Nix and Charlotte Llewelyn-Wells at Aconyte Books. You have been steadfast and patient and really most excellent. Your kindness and warmth have helped me in many ways.

To Cam Rogers. A chance meeting at a geeky get-together has led to the kind of friendship I couldn't have imagined. You've given me the confidence to believe in myself and you can't put a price on that. Thank you, and we will definitely sort out that drink sometime.

To Kayleigh, who took a difficult job in her stride and delivered news to someone when I couldn't be there to deliver it myself. I love your face.

My big brother Stephen. You say we won the parent lottery, but I also had a sneaky winning side-bet on the sibling one, too.

For Jamie – my number one son and the absolute pride I have in how things have worked out for you. Keep building those bionics.

Ben, you are my everything. 'Nuff said.

Finally, a last word for Mike Bonnett, my very loved and now much missed father. Somewhere, in the everlasting allotment in the world beyond this one, I will always be holding my daddy's hand.

Say hi to Mum for me.

ABOUT THE AUTHOR

SARAH CAWKWELL is a speculative and tie-in fiction writer based in the north-east of England. Definitely old enough to know better, she's clinging to the hope she's still young enough not to care. Across the years of writing novels, including an original alternative history tale, she's been allowed to play in some amazing sandpits, including the different worlds of *Warhammer, Wild West Exodus, Twilight Imperium* and *Marvel Entertainment*. When not slaving over a broken keyboard, her hobbies include reading, gaming and assorted geekery.

TWILIGHT IMPERIUM

PLAY THUNDER'S EDGE, THE
COLOSSAL NEW EXPANSION
FOR TWILIGHT IMPERIUM

TWILIGHT IMPERIUM
THUNDER'S EDGE
EXPANSION

THE COUNCIL KELERES

WORLD EXPANDING FICTION

ACONYTEBOOKS.COM

@ACONYTEBOOKS